SHUTTERED SECRETS

A RILEY THOMAS MYSTERY

MELISSA ERIN JACKSON

Shuttered Secrets

ISBN: 978-1-7361866-0-2 (paperback)
ISBN: 978-1-7351500-8-6 (ebook)
ISBN: 978-1-7361866-5-7 (audiobook)

Front cover design by Maggie Hall
Interior layout and design by Stephanie Anderson, Alt 19 Creative

Published by:

melissajacksonbooks.com

*To Lauren Sprang, Rebecca Jennings,
Cecilie Schulze, and Michelle Brasseur...
see you on Sunday!*

Riley Thomas is a twenty-five-year-old reluctant medium. She's been able to communicate with spirits since she was ten, but the experience has creeped her out more often than not. When Riley was thirteen, her best friend, Rebecca Green, convinced her to use a Ouija board to contact Rebecca's deceased little sister. A malevolent spirit was released, and it tormented Rebecca's family to the point that the Greens move away. Ever since then, Riley has avoided the paranormal at all costs.

Years later, Riley's closest friend, Jade, ropes her into attending a ghost-hunting weekend at the famed Jordanville Ranch, former home of the now-deceased serial killer, Orin Jacobs. The house is nestled in the Gila National Forest, about four hours outside Riley's home base of Albuquerque, New Mexico. Jade doesn't know about Riley's abilities, but along with three other friends, they all discover just how sensitive Riley is when she makes contact with a spirit in the house: a nine-year-old boy named Pete Vonick.

The investigation is being run by a team of ghost hunters from Southwest Paranormal Investigations. Among the group of four is a woman named Nina Galvan, the group's psychic medium. She can immediately sense that there's something notable about Riley.

During the investigation, Riley meets Michael Roberts, who's been dragged along to the ranch by his sister Donna and her wife, Carla. Riley and Michael click right away, and it's that connection that makes her want to tough out the weekend. On the first night of the investigation, however, Michael, Riley, and her friend Pamela are in a breakout session with Nina in the cellar when Orin makes his terrifying presence known. Dying camera batteries, wild temperature fluctuations, looming black shadows, and exploding light bulbs make Riley flee the house. Michael and Pamela leave with her, while the remaining women in their party stay behind.

Once back in Albuquerque, Riley tries to explore her growing relationship with Michael without being interrupted by ghosts. Little Pete Vonick, clad in his beloved Scooby Doo shirt, has other ideas. He'd used his ghostly energy to transfer his beanie into Riley's bag, so that when her bag left the ranch, he did too. Now he's haunting her apartment and wants her to find his body.

Orin Jacobs was known for a string of murders of young girls, making Pete an outlier. Riley's research into the boy and what might have happened to him leads her to Orin Jacobs' sole surviving victim: forty-something Mindy Cho, who had escaped Orin's house of horrors in 1983.

Riley contacts Mindy. She learns that Orin had an accomplice who, when Mindy was a teenager, had gone by the name Hank Gerber. Orin, caught as a result of Mindy's escape, told anyone who would listen that Hank should go down for the crimes too. But no Hank Gerber has ever been found. Orin died in prison still swearing he had help luring young women to the ranch.

With Mindy's assistance, Riley finds Hank Gerber, whose legal name is Francis Hank Carras. Communications between Hank and Riley result in Hank's stalking her as he tries to figure out if she knows the true extent of his past crimes—namely, that in 1983, he raped and murdered a woman named Renee Palmer, who had been hiking in the Gila National Forest during Hank's time at the ranch under Orin's gruesome tutelage.

Through her investigation, Riley gets in contact with Detective Howard, who currently works in Santa Fe. It turns out that Howard had started out in Silver City, where the forest is located. His first case had been the unsolved murder of Renee Palmer.

Riley and Nina Galvan reconnect when Nina invites her to one of her monthly séances. There, Orin gives messages to Riley through Nina, providing clues that suggest there's a hidden "dark room" in the ranch's cellar. With Pete's ghost fading more and more the longer he's away from his body, Riley returns to the ranch with Michael and Mindy in tow, in hopes of both restoring Pete's spirit to full power, and finding the room Orin's spirit insists is there. Detective Howard follows in a separate car.

Though Detective Howard has yet to arrive, Riley, Michael, and Mindy bravely descend the stairs into the cellar. There, behind a rolling bookshelf, Riley finds a hidden passageway that leads to the dark room. They find it filled with preserved human specimens of an additional five victims, including Pete's skeleton. Trophies from each victim lie beside the skeletons; among them is Pete's Scooby Doo shirt.

Shortly after their discovery of the dark room, Hank shows up armed, ready to silence them all so they can't reveal his secrets. Michael springs from behind a door and clobbers Hank with a femur. As Hank regains his senses, Orin, in a fit of ghostly revenge, uses his energy to fling Hank against a wall, knocking him unconscious. Detective Howard arrives, suffering from a gunshot wound. He and Hank had crossed paths on the way to the ranch after Hank stopped to "help" Howard with a blown tire. When Hank realized Howard was a cop heading for the ranch, the two men fought. Hank shot the detective, who then tumbled into a ravine.

Hank is arrested for the rape and murder of Renee Palmer. Orin's four other female victims—previously unknown—are identified by authorities, and the forgotten children are given their identities back. Riley discreetly takes Pete's Scooby Doo shirt with the intention of returning it to Pete's elderly mother, giving her the closure she has so desperately sought for her lost son.

April, 2021

I walked behind her for nearly two blocks before that itchy, lizard-brain instinct told her to turn around. My instincts were stronger, more well-honed than hers, so by the time she glanced back, I had already ducked inside Epicurean Subs.

I stood in the back, hand to chin, as I pretended to examine the menu board. The place billed itself as gourmet, but as far as I was concerned, adding things like arugula, cranberry, and grilled artichoke hearts didn't warrant the average price tag of fourteen dollars. I checked my watch after thirty seconds or so, then offered the sandwich artist behind the sneeze guard an apologetic wave as I slipped back outside.

My charge was farther up the sidewalk now, but I would catch up to her soon enough. Her pace had settled into its usual casual stroll, and her hands were stuffed into the pockets of her black belted trench coat. I didn't know if it was the only one she owned, or if it was just her favorite.

A piece of straight brown hair had escaped from the black-and-white scarf wrapped around her neck. The strand bounced as she walked, like a waving hand. *This way,* it beckoned. *Follow me.*

The predictable ones bound to their routines were the easiest, their well-worn habits and patterns revealed to me after only a few days of observation. It not only cut the needed surveillance time in half, but it allowed me to notice anomalies even sooner.

This one, Kendra, picked up her morning coffee from the same café every morning between 7:45 and 7:55 unless she was running late and left her apartment with a travel mug. She grabbed lunch, usually alone, from one of the three places near the bookstore where she worked.

My client was a rock star-looking wannabe who hadn't taken his breakup with Kendra well. I'd hated the guy instantly, even when our communication had started out as nothing but text in a private chat.

The message had said:

> I hear you're the guy to hire if I need to find someone. I'm desperate. I need my girlfriend back.

I heard the whine immediately, but my opinion of the dipshit didn't matter. His money was just as green as anyone else's—figuratively speaking, anyway. If they had a target and a Bitcoin wallet, I wasn't too picky.

After that first message, I'd given him the number to my current burner. He'd called within minutes. Desperate, indeed.

"What do you need?" I'd asked.

"Hi, uhh … yeah, this is Digby? We were just talking in the chat," he said. "I really need your help. I haven't been able to sleep. I need her back."

I had been right about the whine.

And his name was Digby? For fuck's sake. This was the kind of shit I'd had to deal with over the last decade since my best client had hung up his proverbial hat: whiny bitch boys who couldn't get over their girlfriends—who had likely wisely dumped them.

"What happened with the ex?" I'd asked.

"I can't live without her," Digby whined. "I know everyone says that, but it's true. She's the love of my life. I know she didn't really mean to break up with me."

They always said that. "What was her reason for ending things?"

"Why does that matter?" Digby had snapped. The defensive tone was common, too.

Rolling my eyes, I said, "Devil's in the details, Digs. The more information you give me, the better I'll be at my job."

After some muttering and sniveling, Digby said, "I borrowed money from her once ... well, a couple times. I needed to get my guitar repaired ... and then pay for studio time. When she gave it to me, she'd said it was a gift, not a loan. That guitar is my future, so it's her future, too. An investment for us both. But she got bent out of shape about it. And then out of nowhere she breaks up with me—over the phone. Who does that?"

I suppressed a sigh. "So she just called you up out of the blue and said she was done because you owed her money? This so-called love of your life?"

Digby sniveled some more. "I mean, it wasn't totally out of nowhere, I guess? I was a little wasted and missed one of our dinner dates. I needed to unwind after my gig and fell asleep. I work really hard. She knows that. I woke up because she wouldn't stop calling me. I was hung over after a hard day and she just starts screaming at me that this 'was the last time she got stood up by me' or whatever the fuck. She said it in the heat of the moment, though. I see that now. She didn't mean it."

If I were Kendra, I would have broken up with the dip-shit, too.

"I just need you to find her, all right?" Digby asked. "I got my shit together now and I can pay her back and everything. But she won't answer my calls and blocked me on social media. She moved, too. I can't get her money to her if I don't know where she is. I know I can get her back, but I gotta do it in person. I just need a chance to make her toes curl again and then she'll see she fucked up by letting me go."

Right. "Unlike Kendra, I need payment up front. When I get the standard fee, I'll start. Don't contact me again after this. I'll find her and watch her for a few weeks, then tell you what I learn."

"Yeah, yeah," Digby said. "One sec."

Within a minute, my phone chimed with the familiar sound of a completed transaction. "Got it. Remember: don't call me to check up on my progress. You micromanage me, I'll keep your money, abandon the assignment, and then upload your dirty laundry all over the internet. I'm going to be watching your ass, too."

"You're kind of a dick, yeah?" Digby asked.

I hung up on him.

Currently, it was the third and final week of Kendra's surveillance. I stood outside her house for the umpteenth time in a secluded alley across the street. A bank of mostly vacant office buildings lined this side of the road, so it was always easy to find a dark spot to loiter in. The sun had almost set, making my shadowy alcove feel even chillier on this spring evening.

I gripped my digital camera, a zoom lens affixed to the front. My steady stream of business from bottom feeders like Digby was what funded the purchase of the beautiful Canon EOS R5 in my hands. I brought it to my face now and peered through the viewfinder, giving the lens a few gentle turns until I had a clear shot of Kendra's bedroom through the gap in her curtains. In an artistic sense, I preferred film, but the sheer number of photos I could take with a digital camera was a significant check mark in the "pro" column. I waited, my breath controlled, like a sniper on top of a building, his scope trained on his target.

A flash of movement. Kendra walked by her window, clad in her underwear. I took the shot, snapping a few dozen in quick succession. The curve of a hip here, the swell of a breast there. She was gorgeous, I'd give Digby that much. But I had no good news for him. When Kendra moved farther into her room, I lowered the camera.

I'd found her within twenty-four hours of Digby's initial call. Even if my best client had flown the coop, I'd kept my skills sharp these last ten years. There had been other well-paying clients, but none were ever at the same level as The Client. What we'd had was special. Even still, I made a good living off my ability to go unnoticed, to slip in and out of people's lives without them having the faintest notion I'd ever been there. I was a ghost.

Kendra's routine was so routine, it had become border-line boring during the first two weeks. Then, about five days ago, there was a blip on the smooth surface of her dull life. A big military-looking guy, who probably went by something testosterone-filled like Axel or Gage, started showing up. Three nights in a row, he arrived in a massive black SUV and had whisked Kendra off to dinners, movies, and even a play. Last night, he'd stayed the night. They'd had sex in the living room, or had at least started there, before they wound up in the bedroom Kendra was wandering around in now, half-clothed. Given the guy's sudden appearance, he was probably the result of an online dating app. Digby didn't stand a chance.

I lifted the camera to my face again when I sensed movement in her window. I waited, patient as a wildlife photographer who lay belly to the ground surrounded by camouflaging foliage, waiting for a twitchy-nosed rodent to peek its head out of its hiding place.

I heard the crunch of a footstep one second too late. Something hard slammed into the side of my head and the force of it threw my skull against the brick wall beside me. My vision went black for a moment.

I whirled toward my attacker, making eye contact with Axel/Gage's fist a moment before it collided with my nose, breaking bone and sending a spray of blood onto my shirt and camera. I hit the ground, my camera a second later. Glass shattered, metal pieces bent, delicate plastic pieces snapped off and skittered away.

A booted foot made contact with my stomach and a breath whooshed out of me. Axel/Gage grabbed hold of my bloody shirt in his meaty fist and hoisted me up a few inches off the ground, bringing me nose-to-broken-nose with him. "Stay the fuck away from Kendra, you creepy ass piece of shit."

He dropped me, but the assault kept coming. Hands were stomped, my ribs kicked, and a solid punch to the side of my face slammed my head into the concrete so hard I saw spots.

Wheezing, I tried to beg him to stop, but it felt as if my lungs had been shredded like paper. I was too weak to fight off his grabbing hands as he rifled through my pockets. Wallet, keys, phone—he took them all. The camera he used as an additional weapon, holding onto the strap while he whaled on my back and sides with the clunky thing. Some hard part of the camera met the even harder material of my spine and the pain was so excruciating, I nearly passed out from that blow alone.

He eventually left. I would have heaved a sigh of relief if my lungs had worked. My skin felt hot but the alley's ground was frigid. I felt the chill of it through my clothes. Was the shivering due to warring temperatures, or was I going into shock?

I had a very precarious hold on consciousness when he returned. My already taxed heart skipped a beat, and for a moment I was convinced that had been the last one—that I'd just died in this alley. I managed a weak groan of protest when he took me by one foot and dragged me farther into the alley, covering my broken and bleeding body with discarded, moldy cardboard boxes, wooden pallets, and other trash left by the former tenants of the surrounding abandoned buildings.

I listened to his retreating footsteps and his parting words of "Good riddance, dipshit" as I succumbed to my injuries and let the darkness take me.

CHAPTER 1

R iley grabbed the last two bags of ready-made Caesar salads from behind the chilled door, proud of herself for buying something with vegetables in it rather than purchasing twenty frozen pizzas and calling it a day. If that wasn't the sign of fully being an adult, she didn't know what was.

She was running dangerously low on snacks of every variety, so she pushed her cart down to aisle nine to restock her supply of Cheese Wheelz and pretzels. She'd learned that this particular store had a window of 2 to 2:30 PM where it was largely empty. She'd gotten good about getting in and out of here on her days off in record time, missing the crowds entirely.

When she rounded the side of aisle nine, a man in a black button-up and pants was already there doing an inventory of the shelves. Riley rounded his pallet of crackers and offered him a small smile when he looked up from his clipboard. He glared at her as if she'd insulted his mother. She snagged a family-size bag of pretzels on her way out of the aisle, not wanting to ask him to move from his position in front of the Cheese Wheelz. Perhaps he liked this unique window of dead time in the store, too, and he was upset with her for ruining it. She'd circle back and grab them once she finished her list.

An unbroken, circular thoroughfare ran the outside edge of the store, where most of the cold storage sections were located along the back wall. Here, she picked up eggs, milk, and orange juice. She stopped in the meat section, debating between ground chicken or turkey, when she got the feeling that someone was watching her. Glancing over her shoulder, she spotted the grocery store worker standing in the middle of the thoroughfare a couple of aisles away. "Aggressive" was the word that popped into her head upon seeing his posture—a wide stance, hands balled into fists by his sides, shoulders tense. For about five seconds, they just stared at each other. Then he disappeared back into aisle nine.

"Creep," she muttered, selected the ground chicken, and pushed her cart on.

Turning right into aisle three, she stood before the rows and rows of toothbrushes, trying to decide if she actually needed a new one. Michael had said last week that her toothbrush looked "like a porcupine having a bad hair day." She tried to argue that she didn't want to get a new one when she'd just broken hers in. But perhaps toothbrushes weren't the same as uncomfortable dress shoes.

She felt it again then— the sensation of someone watching her. When she turned this time, the man was a foot behind her. She sucked in a breath and took an involuntary step back. A vein in his temple pulsed, his jaw tight and dark brows smashed together.

Pushing her cart a few feet away, she did her best to ignore him, but this seemed to piss him off even more. Her own emotion mounted, mirroring his note for note. Her chest tightened and her face heated. It started in the pit of her stomach and rose, like the mercury traveling up an old thermometer in a cartoon before the heat got so red-hot, the top exploded.

"Can I help you?" she snapped, whirling toward him when all he'd done for the last minute was stare at the side of her head.

He didn't reply, just kept glaring at her as if she were the cause of all the world's problems.

"Leave me alone or I'm going to get security," she said, forcibly grabbing the handle of her cart and beelining for the other end of the aisle. She startled slightly when she noticed a middle-aged woman standing several feet away. The woman looked from Riley to something over her shoulder and back again.

When Riley reached her, she was about to say, "Watch out for that guy. He's being a total creepshow," but the woman interrupted her with, "Are you okay? Was someone bothering you?"

Riley looked over her shoulder, only to find the guy gone. She sagged in relief; maybe he'd finally given up stalking her around the store.

Turning back to the woman, Riley sucked in a breath. The creepshow was behind *her* now.

The woman spun around, trying to find the source of Riley's alarm, but it was instantly clear the woman couldn't see him. She practically stared right through the guy. When she turned back to Riley, her expression had changed—she still looked concerned, but now, instead of being concerned *for* Riley, she looked concerned about her. Now it was Riley slapped with the unhinged label.

Riley couldn't blame her; she was practically hyperventilating at the reality that a pissed-off ghost had been stalking her, not a person. It wasn't the ghost himself that made Riley freak out, it was the energy coming off him. It was too strong, too out of place in this bright and public space. It made PTSD-level flashbacks of Orin Jacobs's ghost come roaring back.

Was he pissed off at her, or in general? He seemed to get angrier the more she ignored him, but his off-the-charts fury was short-circuiting her brain. Usually she was all flight when she was presented with a scary situation, but currently she was stuck in freeze. She couldn't move. She couldn't slow her heart down.

The shelf next to her suddenly rattled so hard, it sounded like an earthquake. Toothpaste boxes, whitening strips, and bottles of mouthwash abruptly fell off the shelves, hitting the linoleum with a deafening crash. The bank of lights above her flickered. Riley screamed. The woman screamed. The guy disappeared.

Fuck. This.

Riley abandoned her full cart and booked it to the parking lot. The heat of the summer afternoon pressed down on her shoulders and heated her already hot face.

She gave herself a pep talk as she practically sprinted to her car. *You're fine. Breathe. It's not Orin.*

She reached her car, her oasis, and was seconds from un-locking the door when she felt him there. Right behind her. She pulled her shoulders up, anticipating a husky whisper in her ear, a sharp poke of her shoulder, a hand wrapped around her forearm to spin her around. His fury overrode her own panic and almost sent her to her knees. The same sensation from her first time in the cellar of the Jordanville Ranch was back—the feeling of a boulder sitting squarely in the middle of her chest, air shoved out of her lungs in one fell swoop like quickly depressing bellows.

She managed to turn around, her back to her car door. He stood a foot from her, that vein in his temple throbbing, his hand balled by his sides. She fought the urge to cower before him.

What the hell had gotten her out of this feeling last time, when she had been sure she would die on the spot from the tidal wave of pissed-off emotions that weren't hers, but felt capable of drowning her just the same?

Nina.

Nina Galvan had calmed her down. She'd been part of the ghost-hunting investigation team at the Jordanville Ranch. She had taken hold of Riley's hands and had told her to breathe, to remain calm, and not to let Orin's angry spirit force her out of the cellar.

Riley let out a slow breath and tried to assess the situation she was in, clinging to the handle of her car door, back pressed to the glass, while a furious ghost stared her down. She couldn't tell if he was trying to speak to her, and since he couldn't, his frustration had turned to anger. All she knew was that she wanted him to leave her alone.

She imagined channeling her own haywire emotions into a singular location in the middle of her chest, then shouted, "I can't help you! Go away!"

A woman in a parking spot a few cars down cursed and dropped one of the bags she was loading into her trunk. Something crashed and splattered. "What the hell is wrong with you?" she snapped.

Riley still clung to the door, but the ghost was gone. Chest heaving, she scanned the area, then spun, expecting to see that the ghost had just teleported to another part of the parking lot to torture her from a new vantage point.

"Hey!"

Riley's focus swung toward the front of the store.

A security guard came jogging out to see what was going on, likely under the assumption that someone was being accosted in the parking lot. The woman from the toothpaste aisle was by his side. She pointed at Riley.

Riley wrenched open her door, flung herself inside the car, and peeled out of the lot.

Once she was a few blocks away, she pulled over. She cranked up her air conditioning. She was heated externally by the unrelenting summer air, and heated internally by utter embarrassment and fear. Head resting against the steering wheel, she closed her eyes and attempted deep breathing exercises. Even with her eyes closed, she could still see the man's face, his anger etched into his features as if that were his default expression. Perhaps he'd been a curmudgeon as a living thirty-something and now he was a curmudgeonly thirty-something ghost.

Unable to talk herself off the proverbial ledge, she fished her phone out of her purse. With a shaking hand, she scrolled through her contacts, then hit the call button.

"Well, this is a surprise," Nina said after two rings.

"I'm freaking out." Riley held up her free hand, watching it shake. "I was in the grocery store and—"

"An unexpected haunting?" Nina asked.

"Yeah."

"Come on over."

The drive to Nina's house took fifteen minutes, giving the adrenaline time to wear off and the panic to subside—which might have been part of the reason for Nina's suggestion to come over. Her car was an icebox now, her profuse sweating back under control. She turned down the air conditioner, feeling a little foolish now. It wasn't as if she and Nina had become pals after the Jordanville Ranch experience.

The last time Riley had been to Nina's was months ago, back when she and Riley's best friend Jade had attended one of Nina's monthly séances. Riley suppressed a shiver at the memory of the creepy smile that had come over Nina's face at the end of her spirit-induced automatic writing session, when Orin Jacobs's spirit had used Nina as a vessel to relay messages.

When she pulled up outside the white house with its pair of black Adirondack chairs on the porch, Riley recalled sitting here with Jade as they watched Megan and Charlotte, affectionately dubbed the Goth Twins, walk up the steps.

Riley climbed out of the car and cautiously made her way to the door. It opened before Riley had a chance to knock. The woman, in her mid-forties, was short, pale, and had a dyed-black pixie cut.

"Hey, Riley," Nina said, gesturing her inside. The small gold hoop in her right nostril glittered. "Make yourself comfortable. I'll be right back."

Slipping off her purse, Riley placed it on the coffee table in front of the white-and-blue checkered couch and gingerly took a seat. A row of owls on top of a low bookshelf across from the couch stared at her with unblinking eyes. Some of the birds were made of clay or porcelain, while others were made of fabric or pine cones. Eyes had been crafted out of buttons, beads, or painted on by a careful hand.

Riley had never been much of a collector of things, other than a handful of glass figurines. Her mother had gone through a brief sea otter phase a few years back, and now her house was full of them, her friends and family picking up sea otter-themed anything as a go-to gift. When her mother received a sea otter Christmas ornament made out of burlap, feathers, and nightmares from a coworker last year, she confessed to Riley that she was so sick of sea otters but she didn't have the heart to tell anyone. The garage was filled with boxes of the ones too hideous to display in the house. Riley wondered if the same was the case with Nina and owls.

"There was a TV show I watched in secret when I was a kid," Nina said as if she'd heard Riley's musings. Nina approached the owl collection. There had to be at least twenty of them. "I was only about seven when I saw the show for the first time. In it, there was an undercurrent of the supernatural, which appealed to me since I hadn't quite figured out what was going on with me yet. All I knew was that I had an ability that none of my friends did."

Riley knew that feeling well.

"The supernatural creature terrorizing the small town had the ability to shift into an owl and could also use owls to spy on people. From the age of about seven to ten, I was deeply fascinated by owls. Young kids get fixated on stuff all the time, especially animals, so my parents didn't think much of it at first. But one night, my mom found me in the backyard hooting up at the trees. It was two in the morning."

Though Riley had no idea where Nina was going with this, she smiled softly at the image of a little girl in pajamas standing barefoot in wet grass in the middle of the night.

"That's when Mom got freaked out. She tried asking very reasonable questions … you know, trying to be supportive. She asked if I was obsessed with owls because I wanted to be a veterinarian, or if I had heard one outside my window that night and had come out to investigate. I said, 'No, Mom, I'm trying to learn how to talk Owl so I won't be scared when I take my owl form.'"

"Yikes," Riley said.

Nina laughed softly. "My mom said she would like to learn how to become an owl too, and that she'd love to know what it felt like to fly. I told her only I could become an owl because, 'Only supernatural creatures like me can shape-shift. I have until puberty to figure this out.'"

"Oh wow," Riley said. "What did she say to that?"

"She told me to come inside, made us some hot chocolate, and asked me to tell her what was going on with me," Nina said. "For me, my abilities started with my grandma's passing. She died from a quick-spreading liver cancer when I was eight. Even though I hadn't been old enough to really understand death, I knew Grandma was gone and wasn't coming back. Yet, Grandma *did* come back, but only for me.

"It turned out that quite a few family members had taken to using Grandma as a confessional while she was on her deathbed. She got very sick, very fast, and lost her ability to speak, so they told her their secrets, knowing she'd take them to the grave.

"About a week after she died, I had gone with my parents to Grandma's to help clean the place out. Two sets of aunts and uncles and their kids were there too. While we were all in the living room packing and cleaning, I saw one aunt and uncle have a quiet moment together. They joked about something, he kissed her, and even at that young age, I had been struck by how much love was in my aunt's face when she looked at him."

Riley was still deeply puzzled by this conversation, which was made even more puzzling by the fact that Nina said all this with her attention still focused on the owls.

"Confused by what I saw," Nina continued, "I said, 'I don't understand why you'd want to divorce Aunt Jill when she loves you so much, Uncle Rob.'"

Riley winced. "Uh oh."

Nina turned to her then. "All conversation in the room stopped like someone had hit the mute button. Aunt Jill laughed and asked why I would say such a thing. But in the next moment, everyone, even Aunt Jill, saw how pale Uncle Rob had gotten. Aunt Jill said, 'What is she talking about, Rob?' Rob just stared at her for a long time, swallowed hard, and said he hadn't wanted to tell her like this, and that he'd planned to wait until after the dust had settled, and things like cleaning out Grandma's house had been taken care of. Aunt Jill burst into tears and ran out of the room. Their two kids were my age and they started crying too, not understanding why the adults were so angry all of a sudden.

"Uncle Rob got right in my face and told me it was wrong of me to spy on private conversations. His face was bright red and I remember a few drops of spit hit me in the face. He thought I'd overheard him telling Grandma about the planned divorce. Uncle Rob wanted Jill's mom to know that he still loved Jill, but that they weren't a good fit anymore. He was apologizing to Grandma for planning to break her daughter's heart."

"Geez," Riley said. "How did everyone else react?"

"My dad shoved him away from me," Nina said, still standing beside her owl collection, her hands in her pockets. "Mom and Uncle Rob started screaming at each other about respect. I was sobbing. It was a mess. One little sentence and I'd ruined my entire family. My cousins—Jill and Rob's kids—were so mad at me for so long. They blamed me for the divorce. Kids can be mean as hell, and since I already felt awful about what happened, I shouldered that blame for years. I suppose some part of me still does."

"Sounds like this was your grandma's fault," Riley said.

Nina chuckled. "She'd loved drama when she was alive, and that hadn't changed in death. Yet, it was I who had said those things. I was the one who threw the bomb. I was convinced there was something wrong with me. Or something wrong with Grandma. When she told me my seventeen-year-old cousin was pregnant, I kept it to myself. I didn't tell anyone I knew Aunt Sarah had given up her firstborn for adoption."

"Probably a good call," Riley said.

"When that show about the owls came along, something in it resonated with my little seven-year-old brain," Nina said. "I figured that once I mastered becoming an owl, I could fly away and stop causing so many problems for my family."

Riley frowned at that, wishing she could go back in time and give weird little Nina a hug.

"When my mom sat me down with the hot chocolate that night and made me tell her what was going on, she's the one who added 'psychic medium' to my vocabulary. She told me I wasn't a demonic creature, and that Grandma wasn't either. My parents bought me books about psychics, mediums, and the afterlife. We watched every show on the topic we could find. I eventually found a network of other psychics and like-minded people who helped me make sense of my ability."

Riley chewed on her bottom lip, unsure of what to say. She'd been the one to call Nina but now she wasn't sure what she was doing here. Nina had done all the talking. Gesturing to the rows of owls on top of the bookshelf, Riley said, "Are these all owls you got when you were a kid?"

Nina laughed. "My mom gets me an owl every year for my birthday as an inside joke—a reminder of the time I'd convinced myself I was a demonic shape-shifter who could speak to animals." She finally walked over to Riley and sat beside her on the couch. "I'm telling you all this because whether your ability kicks in when you're eight or eighty, there's going to be a learning curve. Your path to living comfortably with it isn't going to be a straight line. It's going to be twisty, messy, and probably weird as hell.

"You can choose to manage it enough so that you can effectively turn it off, or you can swing in the other direction and do anything from paranormal investigations to group readings in packed conference halls."

"Not the last one," Riley said quickly.

Nina just smiled at her. "Some mediums find nothing but peace from communicating with spirits, while others see it as terrifying or a source of stress. Regardless, you get to decide what role you want this to play in your life, and then you can adjust based on that. But you do need to decide, Riley. Your being here right now tells me that what you've been doing isn't working, at least not anymore."

It took Riley a moment to organize her erratic thoughts. "People seem to think that since I've been able to communicate with ghosts since I was ten, I shouldn't be scared anymore. Not all ghosts are the same, though. You don't always know what you're dealing with until you're already in communication. It's not all grandmas just saying hello from the other side."

"No, it's not," Nina said. "And with someone as sensitive as you, you're going to experience the gamut. I won't lie…I was very jealous when Orin reacted to you the way he did in that cellar."

Riley had sensed this immediately, but she was a little surprised Nina admitted to it now. "Getting on the radar of a serial killer ghost is nothing to be jealous about, trust me."

"I wasn't envious of the serial killer part so much as the effortlessness of your gift," Nina said. "But that effortlessness is also at the heart of your fear. Ninety percent of the time for me, if I interact with a spirit, it's because *I've* called on their energy. Even though spirits are around us all the time, I'm often unaware of them. Whether that's because I've learned to put up my defenses enough so that they only contact me when I give them permission, or because my psychic energy isn't as strong as yours, I don't know."

"I sort of think of it like a switchboard," Riley said, and immediately flushed, worried that sounded stupid.

"Oh?"

"Yeah, uhh … like there's a giant board in the Great Beyond with all the psychic mediums' names on it, and when they're open for contact, the light below their name flips from red to green," Riley said, squeezing her hands between her knees. "Lately it feels like mine is always green."

"I think it likely is," Nina said. "You closed yourself off from your ability for a long time, putting up walls to keep the spirits out. Your trip to the ranch tore all those barriers down, and now you're getting a deluge instead of a trickle."

Riley sighed.

After a beat of silence, Nina asked, "Are you ready to tell me what happened earlier?"

Right. The reason why Riley had called Nina in the first place. It took her a few long moments to work up the courage to recount it, but she finally told Nina about the ghost who had stalked her around the grocery store.

"What about this bothers you the most? Other than the ghost sounding downright scary," Nina said.

"I hate that I can't even go shopping anymore without a spirit popping up," Riley said. "I don't know what I want to do with … this … but I agree with you: I need to get enough of a handle on it that going into a store doesn't cause an anxiety attack. And I want to get better at knowing when they're spirits and when they're humans. If I had known about the Poltergeist of Aisle 3, I would have avoided the store entirely."

"Well, you can't be too badly shaken if you still have your sense of humor," Nina said.

Riley managed a small smile.

"There's no formal training manual for something like this," Nina said, "and what works for me won't necessarily work for you. But if you'd like to work with me to help you get a handle on this, I'm happy to try. At the very least, I can get you headed in the right direction."

Riley was just about to tell her that she was game when Nina cut her off.

"First, though, I need you to think about what role you want your ability to play in your life. 'None' is an acceptable answer if that's what you want," Nina said. "Once you figure that out, know that if you want to learn how better to sense spirits, you'll need to be around spirits. Which means venturing into haunted places ... on purpose."

"Hard pass," Riley said.

"Think of it like aversion therapy."

Riley was averse to this all right.

"Think about it," Nina said. "You know where to find me when you make your decision."

CHAPTER 2

Summer gave way to autumn and Riley had yet to contact Nina again. She sent periodic "I'm still thinking!" texts so Nina knew she hadn't given up on the idea entirely, but it was the whole "going into haunted places on purpose" thing that was getting to her. If the childhood bedroom of her best friend Rebecca could be haunted by something decidedly evil, then cemeteries, long-abandoned buildings, and ranch houses in the middle of national forests should be avoided at all costs.

But now mundane places like grocery stores, bars, and miniature golf courses weren't safe either. Miniature golfing should be avoided at all costs anyway, but when a weeping woman had abruptly materialized before the open maw of the clown on the fourth hole, Riley vowed never to go back. Which was too bad for her boyfriend Michael because that man loved himself some miniature golf.

She trusted Nina. She knew the woman truly had a gift, even if it wasn't as strong as her own. Nina was comfortable in her own skin, even when a serial killer ghost had tried to wear that skin during the séance.

Perhaps it wasn't Nina whom Riley didn't trust. It was herself.

"Earth to Riley," Jade said, snapping Riley out of her thoughts. "You with me?" she asked, from the driver's seat, reaching over quickly to pat her light brown hand on top of Riley's much darker one.

"Yeah, I'm here," Riley said, glancing over at her. No one other than Nina and Michael knew about the poltergeist from the grocery store. She'd managed to convince herself that if she avoided talking or thinking about it, then maybe it hadn't happened. It was a Band-Aid on an infected wound and she knew it. "I just didn't sleep very much last night."

"Oooh, do tell," Jade said, her green eyes alight. "Spent too much time letting that squirrel hoard his nuts in your tree hollow?"

Riley snorted. "No!"

Jade grinned at her, then launched—relaunched?—into the latest chapter in her ongoing saga with the owner of her wedding venue. *"The place is a dream,"* Jade had said last week, *"but this woman is horror incarnate."*

If the last few months had taught Riley anything, it was this: being maid of honor should be a paying position. Riley adored Jade. They had been sister-level close for well over seven years. Either one would run into a burning building to save the other. But agreeing to be Jade's maid of honor was perhaps worse than enduring flames.

Jade wasn't a Bridezilla—yet—and she hadn't put any over-the-top demands on Riley's time. But Jade had been engaged for almost six months, and now nearly every week had a task on the agenda that had sent the pair all over town.

Jade had decided from the beginning that she wanted to DIY as much of the wedding as she could. Despite having done well for herself as a financial analyst, and Jonah doing extremely well in the tech industry, Jade would rather get her hands dirty than hire someone to do the work for her. It was one of the things Riley loved about Jade. But after months of this, plus Riley's existential crisis over her ever-evolving psychic abilities, she was exhausted.

She'd seen so many YouTube makeup and hair tutorials that the stars of the videos had started popping up in her dreams. Jade wanted to make her own table decorations and reception gifts, so Riley had seen the inside of more craft stores than she ever had in her twenty-five years on this earth. Jade wanted to figure out seating arrangements for nearly 200 people with only index cards, a white board, and sheer determination, all while keeping family dynamics and shaky friendships in mind.

Though a maid of honor was supposed to help ensure the bride-to-be didn't lose her marbles to stress, Riley wasn't taking on tasks so much as being the voice of reason. Last weekend, they'd tried menus at eight different restaurants and Jade hadn't liked any of them. They were too expensive, or the food was too posh, or Jade simply hadn't liked the attitude of the chef. When Jade had pulled up a video on cooking prime rib for a large group, Riley had to shut her down.

"I will be the first to admit that you're basically Superwoman," Riley had said. "But if you actually try to be the chef at your own damn wedding, I'm going to lock you in a shed until you come to your senses. Jonah will help me."

When Jade had said she wanted to wear multiple wedding preparation hats, Jonah, Jade's fiancé, wisely hadn't fought her on it. If Jade made up her mind about something, the best thing to do was to either get out of her way or hold on—and hope you didn't fall off the back when she hit the gas.

Jonah wasn't a pushover by any stretch, but life's everyday tasks overwhelmed the guy, whose brilliant mind was often too caught up in code to worry about something as pedantic as color swatches. Yet he knew how to put his foot down when his bride-to-be was pushing herself beyond her limits. Riley called Jonah to tell him to nip the chef thing in the bud, which he'd taken care of that same night.

Once Jade accepted that there was a task she couldn't do herself, she allowed Riley to research professionals for her. Her one caveat was that the professional in question had to be an up-and-coming entrepreneur. So, instead of calling up ritzy catering companies, Riley contacted food truck owners, small restaurateurs, and personal chefs offering their services. Each suitable candidate was then put into one of Jade's many color-coded spreadsheets.

Today's mission was a seemingly never-ending one. As part of the reception, Jade wanted attendees to take pictures with cameras she provided. But instead of being a normal person and purchasing disposable cameras in bulk, Jade wanted to track down at least a dozen vintage cameras.

So far, out of the five thrift stores they'd tried over the last couple of months, they'd only found two functioning cameras. Riley was going to give this ridiculous endeavor one more month before she'd intervene and make an online order.

The worst injustice of all was that Riley had yet to find a single plate, mug, or bowl from the barnyard series. A few months ago, Riley and Michael had found a plate in a thrift store featuring tutued horse people. The plate was still on display in Riley's apartment. According to the number on the back, the plate was 4 of 15. It was one of Michael's life missions to find the others. A cake plate adorned with a sexy cow in a tutu would have heightened Riley's mood considerably.

As they pulled up outside Reinholt Consignment now, Riley cast a sidelong glance at Jade. She tried one of her oft-used arguments. "You know we're millennials, right? A lot of your guests are going to be millennials. They've probably never used a vintage camera in their lives. Not to mention that this whole plan will be moot if you can't find a place to develop the film."

"Good news on that front," Jade said, checking her reflection in the flip-down mirror on her visor as she spoke. She gave her ponytail of wild brown curls a tightening tug. "Brie said she'll develop them for me. She had one of her bedrooms turned into a dark room."

Riley involuntarily flinched at the words "dark room." The memory of the deep, gravelly voice of Orin Jacobs speaking to her from the Great Beyond via EVP flitted through her head. Electronic voice phenomena would never cease to creep her out: voices recorded by devices that couldn't be heard by human ears.

Brie's dark room is a room for developing photographs, she told herself. *It's not a room where a madman dismembered the bodies of children.*

"Sorry!" Jade said, catching sight of Riley's face after flipping the mirror closed. "Anyway, she just finished up her … uhh … development studio a couple weeks ago. I didn't want to ask her to do it for me if the room wasn't completed yet, but now it is! She won't let me pay her though. Gonna have to figure out how to thank her. She's very stubborn about that kind of thing."

Riley laughed, resisting the urge to make a comment about black pots and kettles.

Jade wrinkled her freckled nose. "Quiet, you."

They climbed out of the car and headed for the shop, which had a dry cleaner on one side and a dog grooming place on the other. None of the customers in the lot appeared to be interested in the consignment store. Over the last few months, Riley had learned how much the inventory—and clientele—could vary in consignment stores versus the average thrift shop.

The vibe of this one had a more relaxed air about it than the last, which had been run by an uppity woman who wore pearls and a judgy expression. They hadn't stayed long; the store only sold bizarre items, like oversized women's house-coats, giant elaborately decorated vases that looked like they were straight out of the Ming dynasty, and large oil paintings in gaudy frames of dreary landscapes. Here, soft instrumental music heavy on the harp piped in through the speakers, and the place smelled like lavender incense instead of mothballs. The Caucasian lady behind the counter on the right side of the room had a wild mop of curly gray hair that hung halfway down her back. A huge pair of glasses rested on her nose, magnifying her eyes to borderline-comical size.

The only other person in the store was a twenty-something Black lady perusing something in a glass case on the left side of the rectangular building.

"Hello, ladies!" the older woman said from behind the tiny C-shaped glass-fronted counter. "Anything in particular you're looking for today?"

Jade, ever the extrovert, strolled up to the counter. "Hi," she said. "My research says this is one of the best places in Albuquerque to find film cameras?"

The woman grinned. "Indeed. Follow me."

The shop had two long racks that ran down the middle of the store. One side was full of vintage card and board games,

and the other had all manner of small appliances and electronics. There were old gaming consoles, games, and DVDs,
but also random items like small steam irons that looked like
they'd had their heyday in the 1950s.

Part of the left wall was lined with vintage signs and
framed advertisements for things like Coca-Cola, lye soap,
and headache pills. A glass case displayed old-fashioned dentistry equipment—which was what the other patron was most
interested in. Toward the back corner, where they were headed
now in a single-file line, stood a few carousels of old postcards.
The back walls were lined with several racks of old magazines,
records, and vintage posters. And taking up most of the space
was a wide table covered in photography equipment—camera
bags, lenses of various sizes, tripods, and mounts. There were
several Polaroid cameras and boxes of film and, to Jade's delight,
three film cameras.

Jade pumped a fist in the air. "Do they work?"

"I had them appraised by someone and I've been assured
they're functional," the woman said.

Odd way to say yes.

"Can you tell me anything about them?" Jade asked.

"I don't know much about where they came from, honestly,"
she said, lightly wringing her hands. "I get a lot of my inventory
from estate and yard sales, and a few storage unit auctions when
we get lucky. That's where I got these cameras. Well, my friend
did. It's like those reality shows where you bid on a unit and get
whatever's inside. I don't like going to the auctions anymore,
but my friend is a bit obsessed with them. We split the cost and
she brings me the games, electronics…you know, entertainment stuff, and she gets all the clothes and accessories." She
punctuated that with an awkward laugh.

If Riley hadn't known any better, she would have said the woman was nervous. It would explain the mild case of verbal diarrhea, at least. Maybe the woman *hadn't* had them appraised at all. Perhaps "assured they're functional" meant the knobs and dials on the cameras worked as long as you didn't try to use them.

"What do you think, Ry?" Jade asked, breaking Riley's focus on the fidgety woman. "Should I get all three?" She tapped a pointer finger to her lips as if she were in a museum studying an ancient piece of art.

"Do you have a return policy?" Riley asked the woman, already knowing the answer.

"All sales are final."

Addressing Jade, Riley said, "If you ran into any problems with the functionality of the cameras, do you think Brie could fix them?"

Jade chewed on her bottom lip. "I think so. And she's got a few photography nerd friends. They could probably help."

Riley shrugged. "Seems like a good haul. This is the first time we've found more than one in a single trip."

"You're right," Jade said, standing to full height. "I'll take 'em."

"Wonderful!" the woman said, her voice jumping an octave. She cleared her throat. "They come with camera bags as well. I'll grab those for you and meet you up front, hmm?"

Riley grabbed one camera and Jade grabbed two, and then they made their way back to the front of the store. The dentistry cabinet had been abandoned by the young woman who had been studying it earlier. With a collection as eclectic as this, Riley wondered how the place stayed open.

"Did you see something over there you liked, dear?" came a voice from behind her and Riley jumped, almost losing her hold on the camera. She glanced over her shoulder and found the store owner behind her, carrying a black camera bag.

"Oh, no…" Riley said, facing forward again. "I'm not here to shop. I'm the moral support."

As the woman rang up the cameras, Jade happily told her about her upcoming wedding. Now that they were at the front of the shop, the woman's demeanor was relaxed again. Riley eyed the handwritten **"ABSOLUTELY <u>NO</u> REFUNDS!"** sign that had been taped to the glass top of the counter. Hopefully the woman hadn't just sold Jade three lemons.

"Have a lovely day, ladies," the woman said, gently sliding a camera bag across the counter's surface once the payment had been made. "There are two smaller ones inside."

The bag was bulky, awkwardly shaped, and made of a dull blue-gray fabric. Riley was sure it was perfectly functional as a camera bag; it just wasn't very cute. She draped it over her shoulder, offered the woman a small smile, and followed Jade outside.

After packing the cameras into a cardboard box in Jade's trunk, Riley took the camera bag off her shoulder.

Jade gingerly took it from her. "It's so hideous. And it smells musty. I might be able to repurpose it, though. With a little love and care, maybe I could turn into a picnic basket or something." She placed it on the floorboards behind the passenger seat.

They had just climbed into the car when Jade's phone rang, dispelling the last of Riley's idle worries about the shop owner and her odd behavior. Especially since Jade hadn't seemed to notice anything out of the ordinary.

Brie's face popped up on Jade's screen. Attaching the phone to her dash, Jade answered the call, putting it on speaker.

"Hey, Brie," Jade said, strapping herself in. "Riley and I just picked up more cameras."

"Hi, Brie," Riley said, strapping in, too.

"Oh my god," Brie said in her flat monotone. "I am having the worst day … hi, by the way. So I am at the mall with the kids and I managed to lock my keys inside my car. I am driving the stone-age minivan because the fancy SUV is in the shop again. Greg is stuck at the office for a few more hours."

A screech rose in the background, followed by a child's wail.

"Both of you need to stop right now. I am very upset with both of you," Brie said with all the passion of a sleepy sloth. "I am trying to talk to Jade."

"Hi, Jade!" a small voice called out.

"Sorry you had to hear that," Brie said. "I try not to yell at the children in front of people. I really do hate to ask, Jade, but could you please pick me up so I can get the spare keys from home? I will owe you for the rest of time."

When Brie was stressed out, she talked even slower and abandoned all contractions. She sounded like a mildly irritated butler from a period piece.

Jade laughed. "Of course! I'll be there in a jiff. I just need to drop Ry off first."

"Totally fine," Brie said. "You are a gem. Sorry to steal her from you, Riley, but I am desperate."

"Are you kidding?" Riley asked. "This is perfect. She's been running me all over town. Now I get to put my feet up and watch Netflix, which is the only way to spend a Friday, if you ask me."

"Despite her surliness, she actually loves me," Jade said. "She can't express deep feelings. Unless it's about Michael. Then she can't stop gushing."

Riley's face flamed. "I hate you."

"See?" Jade said, laughing.

Brie was laughing, too. "See you soon."

Even after Jade disconnected the call, she didn't start the car. Slowly, she turned toward Riley and said, "Speaking of Michael…"

Riley braced herself for a friendly interrogation. There hadn't been one of those in a couple of months. They were overdue.

"Have you heard anything more about this family vacation?"

"Just that the way they're making their decision on where to go involves one of their food challenges," Riley said.

"Now that you've had a chance to think about it more," Jade said with all the caution of approaching a scared kitten, "how are you feeling about getting an invite?"

"Still a little nervous." That was all Riley was going to say, just like the last time Jade asked. Yep. Nothing more to say. Jade waited her out. All of a sudden, Riley was spewing all her insecurities at Jade as if a dam had broken. "We haven't even been dating a year yet and they already want me to come on their *annual family vacation*? We haven't even said we love each other yet! I've almost said it like three hundred times but I keep chickening out. Michael is the hugest cornball in the world. If he hasn't said it, he probably never will, right? What if he's over it and his parents are forcing him to prolong it?"

Jade rolled her eyes. "I knew you were wigging out about this, but good lord, girl. Get a grip. He adores you. And it's a family vacation that's still months away. They clearly think you'll still be in his life then. Have you considered the possibility that maybe he keeps chickening out, too?"

Riley's face was still on fire. She wasn't really the type to fall fast, but she'd fallen into a relationship with Michael within a month or so of knowing him and they'd been going strong ever since. "It's all so fast. But it's also so … easy? Effortless, really. Being with Casey wasn't easy. We were hot and cold. I think I convinced myself that meant we were passionate?"

Jade wrinkled her nose. "Easy isn't a bad thing. Easy, as far as I'm concerned, means it's working. Being with someone shouldn't be a chore or stressful or any of that. You two click. Effortless is how it should be. I mean, don't get me wrong, you'll still want to strangle each other. Jonah drives me bonkers. But he's my person, you know? I want him around all the time even *when* I want to strangle him."

Riley nodded.

"I know it can be hard to trust a good thing," Jade said. "But I hope you give it a full chance even if it scares the shit out of you."

"I already agreed to the food challenge," Riley said reluctantly. "His parents won't give any of us any details, but they promised that it will be delightfully awful. Even Michael and Donna are scared. I'm convinced whatever their parents have planned is going to involve a lot of mustard."

Jade cackled.

Last month, a huge group of Riley's friends had gone to a new gourmet hot dog place that had opened in town recently. Michael had an abhorrence for mustard on a level that was unbridled. He'd requested his dog come without mustard nearly ten times, and yet, when he bit into his, mustard had been hiding below the healthy layer of grilled onions. He'd managed to swallow the bite down, but had practically wept while doing so.

"Jonah is like that about capers," Jade said, grinning. "That man will eat just about anything, but capers are 'little salty nuggets of despair.'" She started up the car. "I'm going to need a video of this food challenge, just so you know."

"Absolutely not."

When they got back to Riley's apartment, Jade pulled into a guest parking spot. "So in addition to ditching you, I need a favor."

Riley had called at least ten craft stores yesterday to ask which ones had faux beech wood. If Jade wanted her to make more phone calls, Riley was going to lose it. The new season of *Tiana's Circle* was dropping tonight and she and her friend Rochelle had a viewing party scheduled. Instead of replying, Riley squinted menacingly at her.

"Chill," Jade said. "I'm not going to make you miss your precious show. Can you keep the cameras with you tonight? Jonah is low-key obsessed with vintage tech." Nose wrinkled, she braced herself as she added in a rush, "Last night he might have dismantled one of the ones we bought."

"Can he *remantle* it?" Riley asked, inwardly groaning at the fact that this likely meant even more thrift shops would be added to their search.

"So far, no," Jade said. "Thankfully I got the other one away from him before he ruined that one too. I was so mad. I almost wish we were already married so I could divorce him."

Riley laughed.

"So, can you keep them with you?" Jade asked. "I want them far away from him until the wedding. He can take them apart like the weirdo he is *after* we're married."

"I can do that."

Once upstairs, Riley set the box in the corner of her living room along with a couple of boxes of other wedding supplies

Jade had yet to pick up. She flopped onto the couch. Since it was nearly 4 PM, she put on the local news for a few minutes, just as she had every evening for the last six months. She knew if something big had happened in the Francis Hank Carras case, Walter Palmer or Detective Howard would keep her in the loop. Yet, she still checked daily—both on TV and online. She supposed she didn't want to be caught off guard if the slippery bastard somehow got released. The fact that Hank had stalked her long enough to find her apartment and had left a vase of flowers on her doorstep had never stopped unsettling her. Any time she heard a strange noise outside, her brain screamed *He's out there!* even if logically she knew that was impossible.

This afternoon, just like every other afternoon, there was no news about Hank. He presumably was still in his prison orange, awaiting trial for his assault and murder of Walter's daughter, Renee Palmer, in 1983.

Rochelle got to Riley's apartment around seven. The tiny curvaceous brunette flipped a lock of her shampoo-commercial hair out of her face when Riley opened the door. Holding out a tote bag as an offering, she said, "I have wine, popcorn, and a jumbo bag of M&Ms."

"You may enter," Riley said, ushering her in.

Riley didn't have to start her shift at The Laughing Tiger, a dim sum restaurant where she waitressed five to six nights a week, until 5 PM tomorrow night. She and Rochelle planned to get through as many episodes of the new season as they could handle in one sitting. They made it through four before Rochelle started to fade on her, exhausted from a day at work.

"What if I pass out on the couch for a few hours and then we finish up in the morning?" Rochelle asked.

Riley got her a pillow and blanket, but by the time she returned to the living room, Rochelle was fast asleep with one leg thrown over the armrest and her mouth hung open. She issued a clipped snore in greeting. After draping the blanket over her friend, she left the pillow on the coffee table.

As Riley took a shower, her mind was awhirl with theories about what Rose's new ability to wield lightning meant, considering that her mother was a werewolf. Crawling into bed, Riley sincerely hoped Rochelle didn't sleep the morning away. Otherwise Riley would be forced to watch the next episode on her phone without her. Howie's recent confession couldn't be real, could it? The waiting would drive her mad.

After half an hour of lying there wide awake, she re-downloaded last season's episodes of her favorite *Tiana's Circle* recap podcast. Fans even nerdier than herself dissected the show, tossing around their theories about what was to come in the season Rochelle and Riley had just started.

Riley startled awake after what felt like a moment, yet her room and the world beyond her windows was still dark. Had a sound woken her? Groping around her comforter, she found her phone and earbuds, placing them both on her nightstand table.

She waited a moment, wondering if some piece of a dream would come floating back. As her eyes adjusted to the dark, a shape at the foot of her bed didn't melt back into the shadows.

An unmistakably human-shaped shadow.

Riley scooted away like a startled crab, her back to the headboard. Her sleep-addled mind ran through a panic checklist of *nots*. This was *not* Hank. This was *not* a man at all.

It was a woman.

The person was too tall to be Rochelle and the body type was all wrong.

Riley's heart slammed against her rib cage. How had someone gotten in here without Rochelle noticing?

But that was logic trying to explain away the obvious illogical reality. A reality she'd known immediately but had rejected just as quickly because she couldn't deal with this shit right now.

And the reality was this: there was a ghost in her bedroom. Again.

It had been six months since a ghost had woken her up, and at the moment, she would have much preferred to see the familiar form of nine-year-old Pete, not a twenty-something woman.

As Riley's eyes adjusted further, recognition kicked in. It was the same young Black lady she'd seen in the thrift shop earlier. Riley pursed her lips. "Hi?" she asked, her voice cracking. "Are you—"

The woman abruptly vanished.

Dramatically throwing herself onto her side, Riley let out a groan. Cycling through what few "rules" she knew about hauntings, she quickly assessed the situation. Ghosts had a tendency to latch onto objects of importance. If that item were moved, the ghost went with it—like Pete riding back to Riley's apartment after he'd snuck his beanie into her duffel bag. Ghosts sometimes latched onto people, too, but Riley hadn't been anywhere notably haunted recently. Except that grocery store.

Which meant two things. First, at least one of those cameras that sat in a box in her living room was haunted.

Dammit.

And second? She had to call Nina.

Double dammit.

CHAPTER 3

She peered into the mirror, scrutinizing her face, then squeezed another dollop of hair cream into her hand and scrunched the ends of her curly hair still damp from the shower. She stared down at the tube of unused red lipstick on her counter. Tentatively, she picked it up, turning it this way and that. Lipstick intimidated her anyway, but red? It was such a bold statement. She knew this bout of insecurity was silly. People had told her all her life how pretty she'd be if she stopped hiding behind baggy clothes and drab colors. But she didn't really like attention.

So it was a mystery even to herself why things had changed for her, why she felt like crawling out of her shell for one of the first times in her life. She'd had help, of course, but it was a significant shift and she knew it.

She stared at the lipstick tube still held between her fingers. "Do it," she told herself. "He said you're a natural beauty. It's time for you to start believing it."

She leaned forward and swiped on the lipstick.

Standing back to admire herself, she gave a little nod. Not bad. Gently tugging on the cap sleeves of her sunshine-yellow sundress, even she had to admit that the color looked great against her dark skin. The color last time had been a mistake. Hell, everything about that had been a mistake.

Her phone chimed from the counter and she picked it up to see Bruce had texted her again.

BRUCE: What color are you wearing?

ME: Yellow, just like you requested.

BRUCE: I bet you look amazing. You doing okay on time?

ME: Yep! I was able to get home from work in time to freshen up. Should I meet you in the parking lot?

BRUCE: That would be perfect.

ME: Great. I'm excited!

BRUCE: Me too.

With one last look at herself in the mirror, she headed for the door, stumbling slightly over the clothes heaped on the ground. Gray slacks, black button-up, gray suit jacket. She stepped over the pile, her bright yellow dress swishing around her legs as she did so. She grabbed her purse off the back of a chair in the dining room and stuffed her phone inside.

She let herself out of the apartment.

As the door closed, Riley's eyes sprang open.

Blinking rapidly, she shook her head as she tried to untangle her own reality from the one in the dream. A dream about the same woman who had been at the foot of her bed earlier, and in the thrift shop before that.

She waited a few moments as her eyes adjusted, searching every corner, half-expecting the woman to be lurking, ready to discuss what Riley had seen. Her bedroom remained empty.

Creeping out into the living room, Riley checked on Rochelle, who was still passed out on the couch. She was curled up under the blanket in a more comfortable position than she had been a few hours ago, at least, and the pillow was under her head now. A quick glance at the clock told Riley it was just after seven in the morning.

She shot a death glare at the box of cameras in the corner of her living room and considered dumping them out a window. If she told Jade it had been an accident, would she believe her? The problem with Jade was that she was obsessed with ghosts. The whole reason the spirits of serial killer Orin Jacobs and little Pete Vonick had entered Riley's life in the first place had been because Jade forced Riley to attend a ghost-hunting investigation weekend at Orin's former home. And now another ghost was in her life, thanks to Jade.

Maybe she needed a new best friend.

A voice in the back of her head told her she couldn't blame the Poltergeist of Aisle 3 on Jade. Or the weeping woman from miniature golf. She told the voice to shut up.

Heading back into her bedroom, she grabbed her cell phone off her nightstand, put on some house slippers, and eased out her front door. She dialed Michael as she carefully headed down the steps.

He answered immediately. "You're calling me before noon. What's wrong?"

"Rude," she hissed.

"Did you and Rochelle stay up all night watching your show?" he asked. "Is that it … you haven't slept yet?"

"I think my apartment is haunted."

Michael sputtered. "What? Is Pete back?"

"I wish. Actually, no I don't. Pete being gone and staying gone means he's in a better place now. Wherever that place might be."

"It's not the poltergeist, is it?" he asked. "Ghosts can hitch a ride on people, right? Do we have to burn your whole apartment complex down to get rid of him? I'll start siphoning gas out of my neighbor's cars if you need me to. Just say the word."

"It's very sweet of you to offer arson as a solution to my problems."

"Anything for you, babe," he said in an over-the-top tone she knew *he* knew would make her roll her eyes.

"Cheeseball," she said, then told him about the thrift shop, the cameras, and her dream. "Arson isn't the key. But maybe getting rid of Jade is."

"If you get rid of Jade, you know she'll haunt your ass for the rest of your days," he said.

Riley wrinkled her nose. "I didn't mean *murder*. Geez. But also you're right." She walked out into the quiet parking lot and started chewing on a cuticle as she paced near her carport.

"Do you think it's time to call Nina?" he asked.

"Probably," she said.

"I think she's right: you're going to need to figure out how to live with being a ghost whisperer. You've been driving out of your way to a different grocery store to avoid the poltergeist, which is working well enough, but you can't avoid your apartment forever. You're always welcome here, but if you start bringing ghosts home with you, we're going to have to get a therapist for Baxter. Mine doesn't see cats."

Riley laughed, picturing Michael's orange cat stretched out on his back on a therapist's couch, yowling his complaints.

"Did this ghost seem angry or anything? Demonic?" Michael asked when Riley hadn't said anything for several long seconds.

"Not at all," Riley said. "She's … sad. Miserable might be a better word."

"I'm going to be devil's advocate here because you've probably automatically jumped to her death being the result of foul play. But remember Nick Button from your old place? His death was tragic, but it wasn't murder. That could be the case here, too. Maybe this lady was a photographer and you have one of her favorite cameras. Her unfinished business could be totally benign, like she just wants to make sure the camera finds a good home," he said. "Maybe Nina could help you figure that out."

As a car headed her way through the parking lot, Riley stepped up onto a curb that surrounded a row of small shrubs. Once it was out of her vicinity, she resumed pacing. "That's true. I'm just assuming the worst. Should I give the cameras back to Jade and pretend this never happened?"

"I'm not sure you're going to be able to *not* tell her the things are haunted," he said. "You're a horrendous liar."

"You are *very* rude this morning."

The smile was evident in his voice. "You can tell her you can't keep them with you because you don't want ghosts in your apartment."

Riley nodded. "Yeah. Yes, you're right. I'm worrying over nothing."

"You're also doing a very good job of not committing to calling Nina."

"I'm working up to it," Riley said. "I'm standing on the edge of the deep end. I just haven't jumped in yet."

"Fair enough," he said. "Try to get some more sleep. We still on for tonight?"

Since they still lived an hour apart—he in Los Lunas, and she in Albuquerque—they alternated sleepover weekends, this weekend being an exception for *Tiana's Circle*. As much as she adored Michael, a lady had her priorities. They'd only get late Saturday evening and Sunday this weekend.

"Yes," she said.

"Good. Baxter and I were very lonely here last night."

She smiled. "Poor Baxter."

After ending her call, she crept back up the stairs, hoping the rattly outdoor staircase wouldn't wake Rochelle. But as Riley eased her way through the front door, she found her friend already awake, her phone in hand.

"Oh, hi," Rochelle said, waving her cell. "I was just about to text you. Where'd you go?"

Opening her door caused a brief flash of memory to flit through her head of the woman in the yellow dress leaving her own apartment. She had been leaving for . . . what? A date? The woman and Bruce were planning to meet in a parking lot—but an endless number of places had parking lots.

Nope, she said, shaking her head. *Don't think about it.*

"I was just talking to Michael," Riley said, and plopped onto the couch with Rochelle. She stared straight ahead at the black TV screen and willed her gaze not to travel down to the right and land on the box of cameras. "Ready to start episode five?"

Rochelle propped her elbow on the back of the couch and her head on her fist. "Something's up."

Riley chewed on her bottom lip. When she'd been forced on the trip to the Jordanville Ranch, Riley had kept her psychic medium abilities a secret—even from Jade. When she finally told her group of friends, including Rochelle, that she could communicate with spirits, they hadn't looked at her like she'd lost her mind. She knew Rochelle wouldn't bolt out of the apartment if she told her what had happened last night, but she was reluctant nonetheless. It was less about the fear of being judged, and more about how much more real it became when she talked about it. And the more likely it was that the lady in the yellow dress would reappear.

"A ghost showed up here last night," she said to her lap.

Rochelle lightly smacked her shoulder three times. "Tell. Me. Everything."

Turning to glance at her friend, she found her expression open and curious, not suspicious and dubious. So she told her.

"Oh wow," Rochelle said, staring at the box as if the young woman would be standing beside it. "And you don't know anything about who owned the cameras, since they came from a storage auction?"

"Yeah," Riley said. "And what Michael said is true: it could be something benign. The woman could have died of natural causes and the storage unit went up for sale because no one in her life kept up the payments."

"Maybe if you give Jade the cameras, the ghost will go with them," Rochelle said.

Nodding, Riley vowed to do that later. "Fine. *Now* can we watch episode five?"

Rochelle grinned and reached for the remote.

Later that afternoon, Riley drove the cameras to Jade's house. Rochelle had placed the box in the back of Riley's car for her so she wouldn't have to touch anything, thereby avoiding triggering any potential snapshots of the past.

As she drove, her gaze kept flicking to her rear-view mirror, convinced the lady would materialize in the back seat. Or, worse, the passenger seat, and freak Riley out so badly that she swerved into a tree. But the ride to Jade's picturesque storybook house was uneventful.

Jade hurried outside just as Riley was getting out of the car, casting quick looks over her shoulder as she approached, no doubt hoping Jonah wouldn't come wandering out and spot the "vintage tech." Perhaps he could sniff the stuff out like a bloodhound.

They stood side by side at the now-open trunk, peering in at the box of cameras.

"What if the ghost is a poltergeist or something and starts throwing crap around the garage?" Jade asked.

Riley tried not to react to the word "poltergeist," knowing Jade would ask her countless questions if she opened *that* can of worms. "She doesn't strike me as a ghost with a lot of juice," she said instead. "She doesn't manifest for very long, and when she does, she doesn't communicate with me."

Jade nodded at this as if it made perfect sense. "I think I'm obligated as the best friend to present the other possibility. Maybe the owner of the camera is the one who caused this woman harm and she's reaching out to you for help figuring out who knocked her off."

Riley tossed her head back and groaned, staring at the wispy white clouds scudding across an otherwise clear blue autumn sky. It was the kind of story she loved, but only if she were reading about it, not living it. "I can't get sucked into another murder mystery, Jade. I'm not emotionally ready."

"First off, you absolutely are."

Riley groaned again, keeping her focus upward.

"Secondly . . . " Jade said, and Riley rolled her head toward her. "If you don't want to, you don't have to. But you also know it's my dream for you to become Albuquerque's celebrity medium."

Riley couldn't think of anything she wanted less.

Jade grabbed the box out of the trunk and hugged it to her chest. "They're here if you change your mind."

As Riley backed out of the driveway a few minutes later, she tamped down her guilt about this ghost woman possibly being stuck in Jade's three-car garage, rather than in the thrift shop. At least there, the woman had a variety of clientele to observe.

When Riley reached the street, she glanced down the length of the driveway through her rear-view mirror to wave goodbye to Jade, as she always did. Jade stood in the doorway of the garage, a hand in the air, and there beside her was a young Black woman in a yellow sundress, her lips painted a bright red.

Pit in her stomach, Riley drove away.

A week passed with no more visitations from the ghost woman and Jade hadn't reported any strange sights or sounds. Riley still hadn't called Nina. With each day that passed without a reappearance from the woman in the yellow dress, Riley felt better about not making a decision.

It was Michael's turn to stay with her that weekend, and he and Baxter were already inside her apartment when she got home from her shift just after ten Friday night. She had a takeout bag of shao mai, stuffed eggplant, and baked pork buns. It had taken everything in her power not to eat it all on the drive home.

She took a scalding hot shower to get the scent of food out of her hair. Since Michael had already eaten, she scarfed the food straight out of the bag because she was starving and had no shame, then settled onto the couch with the guys. It was a perfectly normal evening, just like the perfectly normal evenings she'd been having for months on end now. After a week of no activity, she'd almost started to believe that things would stay that way.

That night, her sleep was interrupted by a new dream. In this one, a young woman sat at a table with a newspaper in front of her. A large photo of a Caucasian girl smiled up at Riley. Tears splashed onto the words, the ink running in places, but Riley saw enough to learn that the woman had been twenty years old, and after being missing a week, her body had been found on the shore of the Rio Grande River in a recreation area near Taos. Her name had been Brynn Bodwell.

Riley woke with a start. At first, she thought it had been because of the dream, but then she heard an odd sound. When she'd originally drifted off to sleep, Baxter had been stretched out between her and Michael, his head on Riley's arm. Now the orange cat faced the other direction, his ears pinned against his head, and a low, steady growl rumbled out of his throat.

Swallowing, Riley looked to the foot of her bed. There stood the woman in the yellow dress. Her sudden presence was what Riley found terrifying, more so than the apparition herself. The woman's energy was calm, though still heartbreakingly sad. Riley's chest and throat tightened, like she was on the verge of sobbing. Pete's ghost had spoken to Riley. This woman was unnervingly quiet.

Like Orin and the grocery store poltergeist, this woman was projecting emotions to get her own feelings across. Miserable was definitely the word for this. Abject misery. Yet, Riley didn't think the woman was necessarily projecting this emotion on purpose—it was more that this misery oozed out of her like a cloying fog.

Riley couldn't shake the sense that this woman was waiting for her to do something. She was expectant, yet not demanding.

"You need my help, don't you?" Riley whispered, her voice shaky. Baxter had yet to stop growling low in his throat. Michael was still fast asleep.

The quiet, sad woman nodded her head up and down, up and down, then vanished.

CHAPTER 4

Riley paced in front of her kitchen's open doorway as Michael tried his hand at the waffle maker Riley's mother had given her two Christmases ago. It wasn't going well, but Riley was too worked up to worry about the state of her messy counters. Baxter groomed one of his front paws while perched on the back of Riley's couch, his orange tail swishing periodically.

"The cameras haven't been here for a week," Riley said before turning around to head back the other way down her hallway.

"You've said that at least six times," Michael said. "Dammit! Is the batter supposed to be this … watery? These things look like floppy disks, not waffles."

Riley stopped abruptly in the kitchen doorway. *"Floppy* disks? You're thirty, not ninety!"

Michael ignored that, too focused on prying the sickly-looking waffle out of the maker. It also appeared that he'd forgotten to grease the thing—again—so most of it was holding fast to the machine. "Would you be mad if I just threw the whole thing in the trash? I can buy you a new one."

"What if we buy already-made waffles. You know, cooked by professionals?"

He whirled and pointed a fork in her direction. A blob of half-cooked batter landed on the floor between them. "How dare you."

Rolling her eyes, she resumed her pacing. "There aren't a lot of ghost rules, but I was banking on the fact that an object significant to the person had to be around in order for the ghost to manifest."

"Need I remind you that the toothpaste poltergeist broke all the rules?"

No, Michael did not.

"Who the heck is Brynn?" she asked. "That would make two dead women. *Two*, Michael. That's one short of a serial killer. Serial killers are fascinating in large part because they're *rare*."

"To be devil's advocate once again," Michael said. "Psychic mediums are pretty rare, too."

Since he couldn't see her, as she was halfway into the living room again, she took the opportunity to silently mock him with all the maturity of a teenager. She was mostly upset with him for being right and levelheaded all the time.

She stalked into the kitchen, wiped off a sliver of counter space, and hopped onto it. After a minute of trying to scrape the waffle maker clean, Michael cursed, unplugged the machine, and moved to stand in front of her. He wedged himself between her knees and placed his hands on her hips.

"Have you worn yourself out yet? What's bothering you most?" he asked.

Nina had asked her something similar after the incident at the store.

She lightly draped her dark arms around his fair-skinned neck, playing idly with the tag at the collar of his shirt. She studied his face for a moment, liking the beard he'd started shaving less and less. It wasn't growing nearly as fast as the hair on his head, which was inching dangerously close to being a too-long brown mop. As much as she found him wildly attractive, she might have to have a serious conversation with him if he was planning to go the man-bun route.

"I'm worried I'm losing control of this," she said. "Going to the ranch messed everything up."

"Hey…" he said, mock-offended, gently squeezing her hips.

"Okay, not everything," she said. "But I thought I'd figured out how to avoid all this—ghosts in stores and bars and *my apartment*. The rules being broken means maybe there weren't actually any rules to begin with and I'm even more out of my depth than I thought."

"All of that is valid," he said. "Like Nina said, there's a steep learning curve."

She sighed, still playing with the tag of his shirt.

His phone on the counter next to her buzzed and she looked down to see a text had popped up on his screen from a "Reggie Reg." The message read, "My pot got here today! You get yours yet?"

Riley unhanded him so she could pick up his phone. She stared at the screen, incredulous. Then she angled a pointed glare at him. "Did you buy that really expensive diamond-encrusted pot off that infomercial? I thought you agreed it was too expensive."

Michael made a half-hearted grab for his phone, but Riley held it up and behind her, just out of his reach. Lowering his arm, he winced slightly when he said, "I might have bought the whole six pot-and-pan set."

"Michael Roberts!" she admonished.

"It's only eight easy payments of $39.99!" he said. "Your dad swears by them!"

"My dad also owns more cooking appliances than any human needs. Their garage is full of even more boxes of cooking crap than my mom's sea otter collection," Riley said, bringing the phone toward her so she could look at the screen again. "Second, did you honestly program my father into your phone as Reggie Reg?"

He easily reclaimed his cell, stuffing it into his back pocket. "What's wrong with Reggie Reg? He likes it. Are you shocked to learn you're dating such a cool cat?"

"Oh my god," she said, laughing.

Grinning, he pulled her a little closer to him. "You can't get out of this conversation. What else is bothering you about the woman in the yellow dress?"

It took a long few seconds, but she finally asked, "What if she and Brynn aren't the only ones?"

"They might not be," he said. "But I think it's safe to say there are countless victims out there. More than all the police and psychic mediums combined could ever find."

It wasn't comforting, but she knew what he meant: she couldn't worry about every "what if" under the sun if she wanted to maintain any semblance of sanity.

"I'm also scared of running into another Hank. And that if I ignore the woman in the yellow dress, then I'm allowing the person who hurt her to hurt someone else."

"Sounds like you're getting close to making a decision," he said.

She wrinkled her nose, not looking at him.

"You always seem to forget that you *stopped* Hank," he said, lightly squeezing her hips again, forcing her to look him in the eye. "He may never have done anything else that was as awful as what he did to Renee, but I saw the way that guy looked at you. He was a predator. He's locked up and that's a good thing."

Riley nodded absently at that. "I guess it just feels like a lot of responsibility."

"You don't *have* to look into any of it," he said. "It *isn't* your responsibility. But I still think things happen for a reason. Maybe you're obsessed with true crime as a way to deal with your ability. Or maybe you have this ability because you were already destined to be interested in it. This all suits you, even if it scares you."

It wasn't anything she hadn't heard before.

Michael grabbed her more tightly by the hips so he could slide her toward him until their chests were flush. He nipped at her ear. "I have an idea of what we can do to keep you distracted while you think about it."

Her eyes had slipped closed. "Oh yeah?"

"Mm-hmm," he murmured, his breath hot on her neck. "I can slide you off this counter…"

"Uh huh…" she said, breathless.

"Then take you somewhere with professional waffle chefs."

She groaned. "That's the hottest thing you've ever said to me."

Riley was in a waffle-induced food coma—that was why it took her longer than usual to realize Michael wasn't driving them back to her apartment. "Where are we going?"

"You can't be mad," he said, not looking at her.

A minute later, she figured it out. Ten minutes after that, Michael pulled into a spot outside Reinholt Consignment. A woman and her delicate dark brown poodle mix came sauntering out of the groomer's next door. The dog had small pink bows affixed to the top of either ear.

Riley crossed her arms and glared at the shop's front door.

"You *are* mad," he said, shutting off the car and turning to face her.

"Of course I'm mad," she said. "You've basically kidnapped me. I am under extreme duress."

"Well, we've reached the melodramatic portion of our show…"

Riley angled her glare at him now, instead of at the front door.

Michael winced and held his hands up in innocence. "Are you actually mad about the kidnapping, or are you mad at yourself that you want to go in there?"

It took her a moment, her glare refocused on the consignment shop. "To be honest, I'm mostly mad at *you* now for knowing it's the second one."

"Do you want me to come in with you or…"

"Ugh," she said, unfastening her seat belt and opening her door. "Come on. There's a bunch of vintage games and stuff in here I'm sure your old ass will love. I think I saw a couple Game Boys last time."

He gasped dramatically and scrambled out of the car. "Why wouldn't you lead with that?"

When Riley reached the door she paused, hoping the door would be locked and they could leave and never come back. But the door pushed open with ease, and the faint scent of lavender whooshed out to greet her.

The same older woman from before was behind the counter, her attention on a magazine laid open on the glass top. Her head snapped up when they walked in, a bright smile on her face that faltered just slightly when her magnified eyes behind her thick glasses landed on Riley.

Michael had only been slightly exaggerating his excitement over the Game Boys. "Oh, man. You weren't kidding. Do you need the moral support—"

"Go crazy."

Michael offered the woman behind the counter a polite "Good afternoon, ma'am," before heading down the middle aisle, gaping at the games. He held up a Game Boy and mouthed, "There's a box, too!"

What the eff was it with guys and "the original box"?

Shaking her head, she shot him a thumbs-up, then steeled herself as she walked to the counter.

"Hello again," the woman said as Riley approached. Her name tag said Carol. "You were here the other day to purchase the cameras, weren't you?"

Riley wondered if Carol had so few customers that she easily remembered them. But then she recalled the woman's odd behavior and she wondered again if the cameras weren't actually in working order. "Yep, that's me."

"What … uhh … can I help you with today?" Carol asked, hands folded on the magazine. A quick glance revealed that it was a tabloid. She unfolded her hands, laying them flat on the glass surface of the counter. After a moment, she scratched the side of her nose.

Riley cocked her head. "I was wondering if you knew any-thing about the person who owned the storage unit where the cameras came from."

"I'm afraid I don't," Carol said. "The units usually go up for auction due to the owner not paying their fees. The details of why the customer stopped paying—assuming the storage unit facility even knows—aren't disclosed to the buyers. I didn't attend the auction. It's not really my bag. But my friend has a good eye for these kinds of things, so I trust her judgement. Plus, I believe this one was way out in Clovis."

Clovis was on the eastern edge of New Mexico, near the border with Texas. Brynn Bodwell, according to the article Riley had seen a snippet of last night, had lived in and been found in Taos, which was in the north end of the state. Information was supposed to help her sort out her jumbled thoughts, not confuse her further. Was there no connection between Brynn and the woman in the yellow dress? Maybe her psychic wires had gotten crossed.

"Is there something wrong with the cameras?" Carol asked, derailing Riley's train of thought. "All sales are final," she said, tapping the small, handwritten "Absolutely <u>No</u> Refunds!" sign taped to the corner of the glass countertop.

"I'm not looking to return them," Riley said. "The cameras just have a … quirk, and I have very specific questions about that quirk." Chewing her bottom lip, she shot a glance over her shoulder. Michael was halfway down the shop now, still perusing the shelves. Her gaze jumped past him and landed on the glass case of dental equipment that the ghost woman had been standing in front of the last time Riley had been here. Turning back to Carol, Riley asked, "Has the owner of a storage unit ever come in trying to track down their items?"

The crease between Carol's brows smoothed out. "You've seen her, haven't you? The woman in the yellow dress, I mean."

Riley's brows shot toward her hairline. She stared at Carol dumbly for what felt like an hour before she finally asked, "*You've seen her?*"

Eyeing Michael for a moment, Carol lowered her voice. "I had a feeling you saw her when you were here. I saw her that day, too. Since those cameras left the store, I haven't seen her. When you deal with this many old items, it's sort of inevitable you'll pick up a few ghosts along the way," she said. "Most of my friends in the business have said they've dealt with a haunting at least once. One friend gives every new item she gets a good sage before she brings it into her store. She had a nasty malevolent spirit once. Gives 'bull in a china shop' a whole new meaning. That ghost was hopping mad."

Riley stared at her. "How'd she get rid of it?"

"Oh, it was a big to-do," Carol said. "She hired a demon-ologist and everything."

"And that worked?"

"Nope! Ticked the thing off even more. She culled half her inventory and moved," Carol said. "I heard the old location is still haunted. Every business that sets up shop there ends up shutting down in a year or less."

Riley winced. For the sake of both Riley's sanity and Jade's three-car garage, Riley was glad her ghost wasn't "hopping mad." Just a very sad woman who wanted Riley's help. "You didn't feel the need to disclose the fact that they were haunted?"

Carol flushed. "I'm sorry. As harmless as that poor girl is, I have to say I was a bit relieved that she left with the cameras. She's just so … miserable. The mood of the whole shop changed when she appeared. And I did try to be honest with customers before, but it scared them off. You're the first customer who saw the woman in the yellow dress, far as I can tell, so I guess I thought she'd be in better hands with you."

Riley wanted to be angry with her but couldn't muster up the emotion. After all, Riley herself had foisted the cameras off on Jade after a few visitations from the sad spirit. "Do you see ghosts often?"

"Oh, goodness no," Carol said. "I only ever see them here and it's very rare." After a thoughtful moment she added, "But I get the feeling you see them all the time. What are you special ones called again … the indigo children? Are you one of those?"

Riley hadn't known her maternal grandmother for very long; she had passed away when Riley was eight. But Grandma Nat had "the gift of sight" too, able to see and communicate with ghosts the way Riley could. She'd talked to Riley about the indigo children a few times; Grandma Nat had been a bit of a new agey hippie. The indigo children were said to be on a different plane of existence, here to shake up the status quo. Riley didn't think that description fit her, but Grandma Nat liked to tell Riley and her mother how special they were. Riley's mom had only inherited the psychic part of psychic medium.

"Something like that," Riley said.

Carol nodded. "You might have more luck talking to my friend who went to the auction. Would you like her contact info?"

"Sure," Riley said. "Thanks."

Carol rummaged around on the shelf below the cash register, then produced a small pad of paper and a pen.

Just because Riley got the woman's phone number, it didn't mean she had to do anything with it, she assured herself. She could palm the piece of paper Carol was writing on now, then discreetly drop the wadded ball in the trash outside the groomer's without Michael seeing her do it, and that would be that.

Until the sad woman in the yellow dress materialized at the foot of Riley's bed, that is. Or another dream about Brynn pulled her from sleep.

Carol tore the note off the pad and handed it to Riley. "That's her cell, the number to her shop, and the address. Her name's Martha but she goes by Marty. I'll let her know to expect a call or visit."

Riley offered a tight-lipped smile to the note, then to Carol. "Thanks."

Michael came up behind her then. "Do you have any games for the Game Boy?"

"Everything I've got is on the shelf," Carol said. "But I've seen quite a few pop up on eBay."

"Ugh, don't give him any ideas," Riley said.

After Michael paid for the ancient console, they thanked Carol and headed for the door.

"If you ever find out what makes the poor girl so sad, do let me know, will you?" Carol called after them.

Riley offered her an awkward wave goodbye in response, then followed Michael outside.

That night, Riley couldn't sleep. She lay awake, staring at her ceiling, listening to Baxter squeaking periodically in his sleep, and Michael lightly snoring in his. She knew she had likely already stepped over the "I'm not getting involved" line.

Her mind buzzed with questions.

She gave it another few minutes, screaming *Sleep, dammit!* at herself, which she quickly learned wasn't conducive to maintaining a calm and relaxed mind. Eventually she muttered a mental *fuck it*, and crept out of bed. She grabbed her pajama pants off the floor and her cell phone off the bedside table, then tiptoed into the living room without waking anyone up.

Once she'd pulled on her pants, sat cross-legged on the couch, and settled under the blanket Michael had left pooled on one of the cushions, she opened a browser on her phone. She squinted as the bright white of the search page nearly blinded her in the dark. After adjusting her screen settings to low brightness, she typed in "Brynn Bodwell."

A photo popped up immediately of a beautiful blonde woman with blue eyes and an infectious smile. After some searching, Riley found the same article that the woman in her dream had been crying over. It had been in a 2003 article from the *Taos Sun Times*.

Young Woman Found Slain

According to a press release from the Taos Police Department, the body of Brynn Bodwell, 20, was found at the base of a boat ramp in the Orilla Verde Recreation Area early this morning, near the Taos Junction Bridge. Her nude body had been washed prior to being dumped at the site. Bodwell had been reported missing by her family a week ago. They had known immediately that something was wrong when she hadn't been in communication with any of her friends or relatives for several hours.

Bodwell's boyfriend, Liam Sotheby, 22, had a date scheduled with Bodwell that evening to celebrate their two-year anniversary. "She said she had a surprise for me and was going to show me after she went to the gym," Sotheby said. "I hate that I'll never know what the surprise was."

Bodwell left her parents' house around 7:45 PM that evening with her gym bag and a change of clothes. "She liked going to the local gym up the road in the evening because there were fewer people there," her mother said. "She said if she got there close to 8, the after-work crowd would be gone and she could be on the treadmill as long as she wanted. We'd signed up for a 10K this summer."

The security footage from the parking lot of the gym provided little insight into what happened to the 20-year-old the night of her disappearance. The angle of the camera only shows part of the parking lot. It captured enough to show that Bodwell arrived at the gym a little before 8, as planned, but she didn't immediately get out of her car. Within a few minutes, a second car arrived and pulled in behind her, perpendicular with her trunk. The angle of the camera provided only a partial view of this second darker car—possibly blue or black.

Bodwell got out of her vehicle without her bag and rounded the car that had pulled in behind her. Shortly after that, the car drove away with Bodwell presumably inside. The security camera didn't pick up the license plate. All of Bodwell's belongings except for her phone were left in the vehicle. Robbery has been ruled out as a motive.

A week later, Bodwell's nude body was discovered in the recreation center. She had been strangled and sexually assaulted.

The Taos Police Department encourages anyone with any information about what might have happened *to Brynn Bodwell to contact them or Crime Stoppers. A $100,000 reward is being offered to anyone who can provide information that leads to an arrest.*

Despite living in New Mexico all her life, Riley had only been to Taos a handful of times, most of which had been when she'd been a kid taking in-state road trips with her parents.

A bit more searching revealed that Brynn's case had made national news. Riley had been eight or nine when it had happened; she had no memory of it. She wondered if her parents did. The story had been covered by *Unsolved Mysteries, Disappeared, 20/20,* and *Dateline.*

Riley climbed off the couch long enough to pluck her earbuds out of her purse on the table by her front door. A quick search for videos about Brynn Bodwell turned up a clip of her *Unsolved Mysteries* episode. In it, they discussed the list of suspects. They ran the gamut—her boyfriend, an employee at the gym, someone from the veterinary program she had been in. It appeared as if she'd known the person who had pulled up behind her, as no struggle had been evident in the grainy black-and-white footage from the security camera. But, Riley supposed, if the person in the car had a gun, perhaps Brynn merely hadn't struggled because of self-preservation.

Though friends and family had been adamant that Brynn and Liam were devoted to each other, there still had been a search of Brynn's computer in hopes of finding plans for a clandestine meeting with someone she had been seeing on the sly. A ping from her missing phone had led police on a wild goose chase, ending in the discovery of the phone in the brush on the side of a road across the border in Texas. It was speculated that the phone had been thrown out a window as a way to throw police off the scent.

After years of tracking down every lead and tip, the case grew steadily colder.

The only two breadcrumbs Riley's psychic medium abilities had given her so far were Brynn's name and the sightings of the woman in the yellow dress that had been triggered after acquiring the cameras. Carol had said that the auction had taken place in Clovis, though, not Taos.

Riley typed "missing women New Mexico 2003" into her search bar. There was a Facebook page devoted solely to women and girls who had gone missing in the state, or who were believed to have last been seen here. When she narrowed it down to Black women, nearly a dozen popped up. The term "human trafficking" came up with alarming frequency.

The longer she looked, the more disturbing the statistics became. According to the National Center for Missing & Exploited Children—a site she'd gotten familiar with when tracking down both Pete Vonick and Francis Hank Carras—more than 600,000 people went missing every year, and two-thirds of them were people of color. Black, brown, and Indigenous women especially went missing at higher numbers than other demographics. Though Black women made up less than ten percent of the United States population, they comprised upward of twelve percent of those missing. There were often as many as 75,000 missing Black women across the country at any given time, and yet their cases were often both grossly underreported and discounted as runaways, especially with younger women.

Riley scanned the faces of the women who were listed as missing in the state around the same time Brynn had gone missing, but the woman in the yellow dress wasn't among them. She thought about Brynn's phone pinging in Texas, and suddenly the map of the United States opened up in her head. With so little information about the woman in the yellow dress, it was impossible to know where she'd come from. Had she been snatched from Taos and taken across state lines? In human trafficking cases, stolen girls and women were moved constantly, both to keep them removed from anything familiar, and to help keep their kidnappers from being caught. The woman in the yellow dress being a native of New Mexico was just as likely as her being snatched from elsewhere and later dying here.

The possibilities, each one more awful than the next thanks to her wild imagination, ratcheted her anxiety. It still felt like too much responsibility.

Heaving out a sigh, Riley pulled up Netflix on her phone and settled in to watch one of her favorite early episodes of *Tiana's Circle*. There was an unexplainable comfort in watching something so familiar, in knowing what would come next. The real world was too much of an unpredictable mess.

Sometime in the middle of the night, Michael must have realized she wasn't in bed with him, because when she woke in the morning, he was on the couch with her in an awkward semi-upright position, Baxter draped across them both.

When she finally drifted back to sleep, it was blissfully dreamless.

2007

The feeling in my gut was unbearable. I'd woken up with it, as if some ten-ton animal had crawled onto my stomach in the night and the pressure had forced me awake. It wasn't hunger or thirst, because even after breakfast and coffee, it was still there. In fact, it had shifted from gut to chest, and the sickening pressure had turned to a soul-deep yearning.

None of my usual tricks were working.

Desperate, I went for a run in the apartment complex gym. A line of five treadmills were lined up along a wall-length mirror. Though my back faced the door, the mirrors would let me see if anyone came in. It was one of the amenities that rarely got used here, though, so I was confident I would be able to sweat this out in peace.

It was just my luck that when I was only two miles in, Apartment 16 pushed her way into the gym with her tight little pants, swaying ponytail, and a towel draped over her shoulder. For two years, I'd been coveting her. I'd learned her patterns over the years, allowing me to steer clear. And now, when I was practically crawling out of my skin, she was here. Why was she *here*?

The music roaring in my ears helped drown out the mental roar I unleashed when she sauntered in. It only got worse when, after she offered me a friendly wave in the mirrors, she got on one of the elliptical machines facing the other wall. And, because the universe fucking hated me this morning, she chose a machine that would give me a perfect view of that perfect bouncing ass.

I told myself not to look, to focus straight ahead. I was being tested again and I would fight it. I had to. I had plans in place and Apartment 16 was not among them. I paid The Collector too much to ruin everything now over an idle temptation.

I cranked up the music. I ran harder.

By the time I cleared another mile, I was practically sprinting. The yearning in my chest had been replaced by a burning in my lungs that had everything to do with my level of exertion and nothing to do with Apartment 16's tempting assets. My gaze shifted, just for a second, and it locked on Apartment 16—on that ponytail, on the line of sweat that had started to soak through the bottom half of her tight, tight tank top.

Fuck.

I pulled out the emergency brake card on the treadmill, and when the belt had gone from nine-and-a-half miles per hour to two, I yanked my towel out of the cupholder, then stalked out of the gym. I slammed the door open with enough force that Apartment 16 gave a little yelp. A sharp intake of breath.

Fuck.

The yearning was back and was in my throat now, trying to choke me. I tried to get The Collector on board with this one, but he wisely assured me she was too risky. This complex's walls were too thin, the neighbors too nosy. I'd learned my lesson about risky targets. Four years had passed since Brynn and I still looked over my shoulder, convinced my day had come.

After a freezing cold shower, I dressed quickly. I grabbed my camera bag, wallet, and keys, and headed out the door. I didn't have a gig booked today, so I didn't need the camera, but I rarely left home without it. It was my constant companion. After locking up, I stuffed my earbuds in. Apartment 5, the old lady next door, poked her head out.

"How many times I gotta tell you not to slam your door!" she barked. "You knocked my picture off the wall again."

I stalked past her, not hazarding her a glance. I cranked up the music on my iPod just as she called me a few choice words. It was a game we played that neither enjoyed.

Once in my car under a dilapidated awning, I turned off my music and took out the earbuds.

"Pay attention to the signs," I said out loud. "Apartment 16 is your first sign. *She's* the one who made you leave today. This isn't your fault. You had a plan and she disrupted it. She's never been in the gym at the same time as you. She was there for a reason. Maybe today is the day after all. You have all the information you need." I took in a deep pull of air, then slowly let it out of my nose. "Stay open to the signs. They'll tell you what to do."

The yearning in my throat eased a little—a pebble in my esophagus rather than a small boulder. As I eased through the lot and out onto the street, the yearning told me where it most wanted to go. If the signs led me there, I would know it was time to approach her. I clicked on the radio.

The DJ said, "And now for a brand-new one by Sean Kingston. This is 'Beautiful Girls.'"

I grinned. My first official sign. She was one of my beautiful girls. I belonged with her, of that there was no doubt.

Where I needed to go was only ten minutes away. I hit green light after green light. Sign after sign that I was headed in the right direction. Her beautiful face was so clear in my mind, I was sure I could have drawn it from memory.

The light ahead, the last one on my direct path to the mall, turned yellow. The driver ahead of me slowed, rather than flooring the gas as I would have done. This stranger had effectively shut me down. I grimaced as I came to a stop, the yearning knot in my throat growing in size.

I cast a glance at my passenger seat, where my camera bag sat. It was my ticket to getting closer to her, but the signs had just told me today was not the day. I knew what happened when the signs and my desires didn't line up. It made me act prematurely. It got me closer to being found out. And this one already toed the line of too risky, since she was from my hometown, but my god, she would be worth it.

Alas, my camera would have to wait, as would I.

A siren sounded behind me, and my heart lurched into my throat alongside my manifested yearning. Had the police heard my thoughts? But it was an ambulance barreling up behind me on the two-lane road. The light turned green and the car in front of me quickly rounded the corner. I followed suit and pulled to a stop at the curb to get out of the ambulance's way. It tore through the intersection. Several other emergency vehicles arrived shortly afterward, including a police car that parked horizontally halfway up the street, cutting off oncoming traffic. There had been an accident—a bad one if all the commotion was to be believed.

After a minute, the car in front of me pulled back out onto the street, heading east now instead of north.

The knot in my throat eased.

Another sign. Another chance. I gave my camera bag a pat. "We're back in business, my trusted friend."

Within two more lights, I was granted access to the parking lot. My beautiful rose was just inside, waiting for me.

I parked farther back in the lot, where I knew the cameras lining the building couldn't see me. With a baseball cap wedged tightly on my head, I climbed from my car and retrieved a shopping bag from the trunk. It was a shirt I'd shoplifted last week for this very occasion. The tags had been removed, so my lovely rose at customer service would have a doozy of a time trying to help me sort out my problem. As I walked, I kept my head down and moved casually yet confidently to the department store entrance.

The cool air of the store washed over me like a second cold shower. I shivered a little, not from the temperature drop, but from anticipation.

My rose was working with a customer when I got into line. I waited patiently for her. I'd already been waiting for months, what was a few more minutes? She was calm and professional, even when the woman ahead of me got testy. My rose was able to joke and laugh with the woman, and the customer was all smiles by the time she left.

"Hi. I can help who's next," my rose said, smiling brightly. A smile just for me. The yearning in my throat shot down past my belt. Yes, the signs had been right.

I explained that I had received the shirt as a gift and that my friend had accidentally removed the price tags. The shirt, unfortunately, was a size too small. No, I didn't have a receipt, but I knew this was the store he'd purchased it from.

My rose smiled more, her white teeth a sharp contrast to her dark skin. While she typed things into her computer, trying to track down the date of my fictional friend's purchase, we made small talk. With her attention focused on the screen, she asked how my day had been going. Just fine, I told her, then asked about hers.

As the solution to my quandary proved ever elusive, she asked what I did for a living, trying to maintain conversation to keep me, the customer, in good spirits. Little did she know that her presence was what comforted me.

She had asked the perfect question.

"I'm a photographer," I said. "I work for newspapers and magazines, but I also photograph events like graduations and weddings, as well as taking headshots for actresses and models. A friend of mine—the one who bought me this shirt, actually—works for a local magazine. Since he's always on the lookout for more models, I often send many of my clients his way, and vice versa. We have a great working relationship and we're thinking about going into business together. It's an exciting time. I really feel we're on the brink of something amazing."

The typing had stopped after the second sentence, and her big brown eyes were focused on me, as I knew they would be. The Collector had found her Myspace page a few weeks ago, which I'd studied with great interest. On it, my rose shared borderline risqué pictures, her dreams about becoming a model, and even a few videos of her singing soulfully to the camera. She wouldn't be winning a Grammy anytime soon, but my god, that face.

She wrote beautifully about feeling alone. She'd grown up here and had left briefly to attend college, only to be dragged back to care for her ailing aunt, her guardian. Her aunt had died months before, and now my rose was alone, trying to make ends meet enough to care for a house that was too big for her. On the side, she worked on her modeling career, hoping for a big break.

"I don't want to be presumptuous," I said, "but have you ever considered modeling?"

She stood straighter, opening up to me like a flower—which was fitting, given her name—exposed to the first rays of sunrise. "I have, yes. I've booked a few jobs, too. My portfolio isn't that impressive yet, but I'm working on it."

"That doesn't surprise me. That you've had modeling jobs already, I mean. Your bone structure is exquisite."

From the way she ducked her head, I knew she was blushing, even if her dark skin masked it. "Thank you."

"I'll give you my card," I said, pulling a small container of business cards out of my pocket. I had built a rudimentary website to use for this very purpose and had a separate prepaid cell phone I maintained specifically for women such as my rose. I slid the crisp white card across the counter. "If you're interested in making another modeling connection, please consider me. I would also be happy to offer you a discount on headshots. It's rare that I come across someone with beauty as natural as yours. It would be a treat to photograph you. Just give my site a look over and contact me if you're interested."

She took the card and peered down at it as if it were a precious gem. "Thank you," she said again, glancing up.

After a few more minutes, she admitted that she'd been unable to find the purchase in the system. When she asked if I would like her manager to come over and help them, I declined and took my stolen shirt back, returning it to the bag. She apologized profusely.

"No problem," I said, waving away her concerns. "To be honest, the pleasure of meeting you has taken the sting out of it all."

She beamed again.

"I hope to hear from you soon," I said as I departed.

The yearning had settled in my gut again, but it was no longer unpleasant. Seeing my rose had quieted my desperation. The Collector had proven to be invaluable once again. Perhaps he was due for a raise.

I would make the proper arrangements in preparation for my rose contacting me. I was confident she would.

Within a week, she proved me right.

CHAPTER 5

"I'm ready to call Nina," Riley said, noting the conviction in her own tone. She and Michael were seated at her coffee table and had just finished breakfast. Michael stared at her, eyes wide, over the rim of his orange juice glass. "But I'm still freaked out, so can we go on a walk or something while I talk to her?"

"Sure," he said. "I'm guessing this is tied to why you were asleep on the couch?"

"I'll tell you about that, too," she said. "I just feel really antsy."

Ten minutes later, they walked through her apartment complex, out the pedestrian gate, and made a right down the sidewalk, heading for the park a few blocks away. As they walked, she told him about Brynn and that even if the few details she currently had didn't fit into a neat puzzle yet, her gut told her Brynn and the woman in the yellow dress had to be connected somehow.

When she was done, she called Nina.

"Hi, Riley," she answered almost immediately. "I was starting to worry I wouldn't hear from you again."

"I'm ready to learn whatever you have time to teach me," Riley said. "I think I'm getting sucked into another mystery and I want to be better prepared than I was with the last one."

"Great," Nina said, smile evident in her voice.

"How do we start?"

"I believe the best way to learn is with hands-on training," Nina said. "The more spirits you come in contact with, the more you'll learn what to expect. The majority of the ones I come across in my work are not malevolent. There are rare instances where I'm called into places like the Jordanville Ranch, or places known to have high paranormal activity, but for the most part, my clients are seeking closure with a loved one who passed unexpectedly. They are emotionally charged situations, but aren't scary, as was the case with the cellar at the ranch."

Riley was slightly mollified by that.

"From what you've told me, you've had only a handful of interactions with spirits, and the majority of them have been traumatic—it's no wonder you're so reluctant to open yourself up," Nina said. "And, as I've told you, I don't know what it's like to have an ability as strong as yours. Apparitions are rare for me. Messages usually come to me in voices or thoughts that I then interpret for my clients. While I *have* run into a few nasty spirits, most have been quite tame. I would be happy to expose you to more of these kinds of hauntings. If you see how rare spirits like Orin are, as well as the Poltergeist of Aisle 3, it may start to lessen your fear."

Riley recalled Nick Button from her old apartment. He had been persistent, but she'd never felt threatened by him. He'd hung around because he needed to get a message to his little sister. If most ghosts were like him, maybe she could find a way to handle this. "Okay," she said, crossing the street with Michael toward the park.

"Excellent," Nina said. "Actually, if you have time this afternoon, I have a consult with a new client."

Riley swallowed.

"You're guided by precognition more than you likely realize," Nina said. "It's the psychic part of your psychic medium abilities. This particular client and I have been playing phone tag for a week trying to set up a meeting. She called me ten minutes before you did to let me know she was available today."

Blowing out a slow breath, Riley said, "Works for me."

"I'll text you the address," Nina said. "See you at two."

Riley hung up and shoved her phone into her back pocket. It buzzed a minute later, presumably with Nina's text.

Michael slipped his hand into hers as they stepped onto the walking path, the grainy dirt crunching under their feet as they walked. "How you feeling about all this?"

It took her a minute to reply. "I was riding high for a week after we took Pete's shirt to his mom."

Michael squeezed her hand. "I know. It was pretty cool."

"I know that finding Hank and helping get him arrested didn't magically hcal Mindy of all the trauma she went through," Riley said. "But even being a tiny blip on her path to getting better felt good." She chewed on the inside of her cheek. "If the woman in the yellow dress is one of the thousands of women who has gone missing and no one knows about it … if I could help find her, that would be amazing."

"I agree."

"So I guess what I'm trying to say is I'm still scared, and I probably always will be on some level," she said, "but I think the good that could come out of it overrides everything else.

The woman in the yellow dress had her whole future stolen. I want to help her."

As they walked for a while longer, hand in hand, Riley wondered what on earth Nina had in store for her.

Even though Nina had said that most of her clientele contacted her about tame hauntings, it didn't stop Riley from considering the possibility that Nina had lied. What if Riley had just inadvertently agreed to meet at a terrifyingly haunted location? She imagined something in the vein of an old textile mill that had burned down with hundreds of people trapped inside—and had also been built on top of a sacred Native American burial ground. Instead, her GPS led her to a suburban house in a quiet, pretty neighborhood on Gimar Court. The street was a cul-de-sac, and the house in question sat on the last stretch of straight sidewalk before it curved.

It was one of those planned neighborhoods where the same four or five designs were repeated on a loop. The exteriors were mostly beige, with tan, dark red, or brown roofs and accents. Some had stones lining the bases of the pillared arches before their front doors—others had brick. The personalities of the families inside were expressed with things like potted flowers on the porch, welcome flags wedged into the grass, or bird feeders hanging from the eaves. Otherwise, "cookie cutter" was an apt description. It wasn't the sameness that surprised Riley so much as the newness. These houses seemed too young to have ghosts.

As she sat in her car across the street from the house, a pair of kids went by on their bicycles, laughing. A woman walked by with her dog. The picture of normalcy.

Nina arrived shortly afterward. It wasn't until Nina was standing on the sidewalk in front of the house, arms crossed as she stared at her, that Riley got out of the car. Thankfully Nina didn't seem annoyed by Riley's reluctance. If anything, she was amused. Nina wore black jeans, a dark blue polo shirt with "Galvan Investigations" stitched in white on her right breast pocket, and had a messenger bag strapped on. Sunlight winked off the gold hoop in her nose.

"Hi," Riley said, stopping in front of her. She'd left everything but her keys and phone in the car, both of which were stuffed into her pockets. She wiped her hands on the sides of her jeans. "Have, uh … you been here before?"

"Nope," Nina said. "This is an initial consultation. The owner, Julie, contacted me to help find out what's going on in the home. They've lived here for a year and have experienced a handful of strange incidents. She says the spirit is starting to frighten the children because its persistence has increased over time—especially at night."

Riley swallowed, nodding.

"She knows I'm bringing an assistant with me," she said. "I don't expect you to do anything other than observe, feel, and then we can debrief after the consult is over. If I determine that the house indeed has a spirit, I will schedule an investigation where the owners clear out for the evening and I try to make contact during the witching hour. Sometimes it takes several investigations to make contact, sometimes it happens on the first, and sometimes not at all."

"Do the guys from Southwest Ghost Investigators join you?" Riley asked, thinking of the team who led the investigation at the Jordanville Ranch.

"It depends," Nina said. "The level of the haunting and the guys' schedules all factor in. We keep fairly busy individually, but we help each other out as much as possible. I also have several people in my network I can ask to join me, depending on what the job requires."

Riley nodded again.

Nina smiled and squeezed Riley's shoulder. "You'll be fine. Just keep me in the loop about how, what, and who you're feeling."

Riley didn't like the "who" part of that one bit but followed Nina up the front walk anyway.

This house was beige with muted gray accents and a brown garage door. A small garden sat out front lined by a semicircle of bricks. There was an identical garden outside the house Riley had parked in front of. A three-tiered fountain burbled softly on the corner of the small porch, a box of sidewalk chalk sitting beside it. Nina had just reached the porch when the door swung open and a pair of giggling girls came running out. The older one grabbed the handle of the chalk bucket, called a hello, and kept moving down the front sidewalk without breaking stride. Riley had jumped out of the way just in time to avoid a collision. The smaller girl laughed sheepishly, her front teeth missing. She waved a small chalk-stained hand at Nina and Riley before darting after her sister.

"Sorry about that," came a woman's voice.

Riley refocused on the front door where an exhausted-looking woman stood. Her hair was in a messy ponytail, and she swiped a wayward brown curl out of her face.

"They're seven and five and never stop moving," the woman said, laughing softly. "Thanks so much for coming by. I sent the girls over to their grandparents' house. They're two doors over." She stepped aside to let them in.

"I'm happy we found a time that worked," Nina said. "Sounds like the girls have a busy schedule."

"We keep hoping that if we put them in enough activities, it'll wear them out," she said, smiling at Riley as she stepped into the small hallway after Nina. "I think it's wearing out my husband and me more than the kids. I'm Julie, by the way," she said to Riley, her hand out.

Riley shook it. "Riley. Nice to meet you."

The short tile-lined hallway was littered with discarded dolls, shoes, and a pair of roller skates. Nina navigated the maze with ease, making her way into the living room. Riley followed her. A black leather sectional couch at the back of the space was piled with laundry. Given the small folded stack on the ottoman, Julie had only just started.

Julie closed the front door and joined them, looking around her living room in dismay as if suddenly realizing there was no comfortable place for anyone to sit. Something thumped upstairs and she jumped, a hand to her chest. Her eyes immediately welled with tears.

Nina closed the space between them and placed her hands on Julie's elbows. Nina had done the same for Riley in the cellar at the ranch when she'd been sure Riley was in the throes of a panic attack. In her usual calm, soothing voice, Nina said, "Julie, it's okay. You're fine. Don't worry about the state of the house. Don't worry about who's upstairs. Shall we have a seat in the kitchen?"

"Um . . ." Julie said, a hand still to her chest. "The, uh . . . dining room." When another thump sounded from upstairs, Julie tipped her head back to scowl at the ceiling, then broke away from Nina's light hold. "This way."

The dining room table was positioned near back patio doors that revealed a pool and a yard in desperate need of landscaping. On the opposite end of the space was the kitchen.

Once they were seated at the long oval-shaped dining table, Julie said, "You said in your email that this just is an evaluation, right? How exactly do you figure out if a haunting is real or not?" She flinched when another thump sounded. "Do you use some kind of equipment like they do on those shows on TV?"

"I'm just going to ask a few questions," Nina said, her calm tone a sharp contrast to Julie's increasingly anxious one.

"Okay," Julie said, pulling the sleeves of her sweater over her hands, and then sitting back in her chair. She crossed her arms. Chewed on her bottom lip.

"What have you personally experienced?" Nina asked.

"For me, it's usually the thumping," Julie said. "When we first moved in, it only happened occasionally, but starting about six months ago, we started hearing them at all hours of the day. We hear footsteps going down the upstairs hall at night. Doors open and close at night, too—sometimes the actual doors open and close, and sometimes it's just the sound." She sighed. "Last night … it sounded like someone threw ten bowling balls down the stairs. It was a horrible, horrible sound. All of us heard it. The kids woke screaming. My husband flew out of bed and grabbed a baseball bat, sure someone had just broken in."

"Had something fallen over?" Nina asked.

Julie shrugged helplessly. "Nothing we could find. The doors and windows were all still locked. The alarm was set. It's hard to discount something like that when four people hear it. It seems like every night something happens now. We're all exhausted. The girls are fine during the day, but they get really anxious around bedtime."

"I understand how stressful this must all be," Nina said. "Especially when you've only been here a year."

"And we're not really in the financial position to just pack up and leave … but you saw how fast the girls ran out of here," Julie said, tears welling in her eyes again. "I hate the idea that they're growing scared of the house."

Nina nodded. "Has most of the activity happened upstairs?"

"Yes, almost exclusively," Julie said.

"Do you know anything about the previous tenants?" Nina asked.

"We didn't when we moved in," Julie said. "A neighbor across the street just told me last week that the woman who used to live here overdosed. The assumption is suicide. I'm wondering now if that's who's haunting the place. I know it's not a state law that sellers have to disclose deaths that happened in the house. We didn't even think to ask." Another thump. "I guess we should have asked."

"I will do my best to figure out what's happening here," Nina said. "Would it be okay if Riley and I explored upstairs alone?"

"Sure. Take all the time you need. I'll be in the living room … that laundry isn't going to fold itself. If the ghost did *that* instead of making so much noise, she could stay as long as she wanted," Julie said, covering up her awkward laugh with an even more awkward cough. "Anyway, my husband won't be home for a few hours, so it's all yours."

Riley smiled just as awkwardly at Julie and stood, following after Nina. The stairs were in a small recessed alcove. Riley followed Nina up.

There were three bedrooms and a communal bathroom upstairs. The doors to all the rooms stood open. The master bedroom was to the left of the landing. A short hallway snaked off to the right, leading to the remaining rooms.

They stood on the landing facing the stairs, with the master bedroom to Riley's right, and the open doorway of an office to Nina's left.

"All I want you to do today is let yourself feel the energy of this space," Nina said. "I know that sounds like fluffy nonsense, but humor me. Think of your ability as an additional sense. Cutting off sensory input to one sense will help heighten the others. So I want you to hang out in this hallway with your eyes closed and see what your other senses pick up. That's all I expect of you." She pulled a handheld tape recorder out of her messenger bag. "I'm going to attempt to get a few basic EVPs."

Riley nodded. She walked to the middle of the hallway, pressed her back against the wall, and then slid to the floor, sitting cross-legged. Having something solid behind her would help convince her brain that nothing could sneak up behind her. Granted, that argument wouldn't work when the threat was an incorporeal being…

"Good," Nina said. "Now, close your eyes and try your best to relax."

Riley did so, placing her hands on her bent knees. She blew out a slow breath. She could feel Nina a few feet away, and she could hear the faint sound of Julie moving downstairs, working her way through the massive pile of laundry. A clock ticked somewhere nearby. Other than that, the space was quiet.

"My name is Nina Galvan," Nina said, and Riley flinched at the sudden sound of her voice in the near-silence. "We're here to talk to you. Are you here with us?" A long pause followed. "Can you tell me your name?"

Riley tracked the sound of Nina slowly moving around. Her voice grew distant as she moved into the master bedroom, where she asked the spirit how long she'd lived in this house, followed by a question about how she'd died. Footsteps shuffled closer to Riley, then disappeared into the office to Riley's right. Nina asked why the spirit was still here.

As Nina passed in front of Riley, she asked, "Was the overdose an accident?"

A thump sounded so loudly to Riley's left, she jumped, her eyes flying open.

"Are you okay up there?" Julie called from downstairs.

"All good," Nina said, her tone as calm as ever.

Riley had a hand pressed to her chest, where her heart galloped at the speed of a herd of wild horses.

At the end of the hallway, where the bathroom was, stood a small credenza. The top was lined with framed photos of Julie and her family, along with a small potted fern on one side, and a decorative vase on the other. Stuffed into the credenza's four cubbies were board games and random toys. Nearly all the framed photos had been knocked over, and the fern in its wicker pot lay on its side, soil spilled across the floor.

The thump, Riley realized, had come from the credenza lifting off the floor and then crashing back to the ground—like a mini, localized earthquake.

A familiar sensation, like she was being watched, washed over her and Riley's attention whipped toward the top of the stairs. She sucked in a breath at the sight of the haggard woman stumbling from the master bedroom. Her black hair was pulled back in a short ponytail, but wisps of it had come loose. She wore a T-shirt, jeans, and an open bathrobe, the ties hanging by her sides. The bags under her eyes were dark.

There were a few scrapes on her face and arms, like road rash. Her bottom lip was split and swollen. Had she been in a car accident? Though the woman stared toward Riley, her focus wasn't fixed on one spot. Her gaze darted here and there, and she placed a hand on the wall near the top of the stairs, as if to steady herself.

Riley was so startled by the sight, she couldn't speak, couldn't alert Nina.

The woman doubled over then, groaning with her arms wrapped around her stomach. With a hand pressed to her mouth, she attempted to make a quick turn back to the bedroom, presumably where there was a master bathroom, but the abrupt movement seemed to cause a wave of vertigo. She stumbled back a step, tripped over her own feet, and flailed wildly for purchase on the wall or the stair's railing.

Riley instinctively reached out a hand. "Hey, watch it—"

The woman's eyes grew wide, as if she'd heard Riley, and then lost her balance, foot slipping off the edge of the top stair. Riley ran to the top of the staircase as if she could keep the woman from tumbling down, but all she could do was watch in horror as the woman bounced hard down the steps, hitting the wall, the sharp edges of the stairs, the railing, thudding her way down until she sprawled on the hardwood floor below, her arms and legs twisted at awkward angles.

Riley pressed one hand to her mouth and the other to her stomach. She wanted to run down the stairs and check her pulse, to call for help. But she knew the woman was already dead and had been for at least a year. The sound of her flesh slamming against hard unforgiving surfaces replayed in Riley's mind on an awful surround sound loop. Somehow the fall had lasted hours and mere moments at the same time.

The woman vanished abruptly, causing Riley to expel a shaky breath.

Julie was there at the bottom of the staircase a moment later, eyes wide. "That was the sound we heard last night!" she said, hands pressed to her temples. "Please tell me you heard it, too. Tell me I'm not losing my mind!"

Riley slowly shook her head, lowering her hand from her mouth. "You're not losing your mind. We heard it, too."

Nina, keeping her voice low so only Riley could hear, said, "Looks like we have enough reason to come back."

Once back downstairs, Nina told Julie that she'd be in contact soon to schedule a more thorough investigation of the house.

"She's not malevolent," Riley told Julie, feeling compelled to reassure her even if she was equally compelled to shield her from the specific details of what she'd seen.

Julie, near tears, had only nodded in reply.

Nina walked Riley to her car across the street. "So, what did you see?"

The horrible sound of the woman tumbling down the steps echoed in her head and Riley's stomach roiled. "I don't know about the overdose part of the story, but the woman who lived here fell down those stairs. That horrible sound is her falling to her death."

Nina nodded. "She felt sick in her stomach before she fell. Confusion, too. Did you get that sense?"

Riley nodded. "So did the overdose kill her, or the fall?"

"Good question," Nina said. "Her energy spiked when I asked if her overdose was an accident. She's definitely trying to tell us something, but I agree with your assessment—she's not a danger to the family."

Riley looked back at the house, scanning the exterior and the windows for any sign of what had happened here.

"How do you feel? Seeing her fall couldn't have been easy," Nina said.

"It's burned into my head—the sight *and* the sound," Riley said. "But I think I'm okay. I just hate that I had to watch her fall and couldn't do anything to stop it."

"The visual component of your ability is always going to add an extra layer of intensity for you. Are you comfortable returning here?"

"Yes," Riley said with little hesitation. "Before she fell, it looked like she was already banged up pretty good. I think something happened to her even before the supposed overdose."

"Interesting. Good to know for the investigation. I'll be in touch later in the week to coordinate coming back, okay? I have a friend who may be a good fit for this case. Between the two of you, we may be able to figure out what happened."

Riley watched Nina walk toward her own car. She'd called Nina today because of Brynn and the woman in the yellow dress. In the events of this afternoon, Riley had managed to forget that for a few hours. "Nina?"

She turned back, brows raised.

"When I called earlier, I mentioned I'd been sucked into another mystery…" Nina closed the distance, and Riley told her the gist of what she knew so far. "I don't know where to go from here. It seems like there's a connection between the mystery woman and Brynn—I mean I don't know for sure, but—"

Nina held up a hand. "Does your gut say they're connected?"

"Yes."

"Then trust that. You have to learn to trust your own instincts. Beyond that, I have another séance coming up next week. It's my usual monthly group. If you want to join and bring the camera in question, just let me know."

Nope! It wasn't a fear of attending another séance. It was just a visceral gut reaction to the suggestion.

Nina had told her moments ago to trust her instincts. The séance was out. Still, she thanked Nina for the offer.

On Riley's drive home, she marveled at the fact that the number of mysteries she needed to solve had doubled in less than an hour.

CHAPTER 6

Three days later, she had no new insights into Brynn Bodwell or the woman in the yellow dress, and Nina had yet to confirm a return date for the investigation at Julie's. Riley did her damnedest to slip back into her usual routine, but she was so tired. She'd woken with a start twice last night, heart racing, unable to shake the sense that someone had just been leaning over her bed.

Which was why she was sitting on her kitchen counter at seven in the morning, eating cereal out of a widemouthed mug. She hadn't done dishes in a week. Shortly after chugging a full cup of coffee and feeling both manic and jittery, she'd called Detective Howard at half past dark thirty and left him a message asking if he'd ever heard of a Brynn Bodwell. The detective was based out of Santa Fe, only two hours from Taos, where Brynn's body had been found. The case had not only gone national but wasn't far from his neck of the woods.

Riley's sleuthing had originally led her to the detective because he'd been one of the officers on the scene when Renee Palmer's body had been found bludgeoned in the Gila National Forest back in 1983. The case had been cold for decades before Riley's trip to the forest had both heightened her abilities and revealed secrets of Renee's past.

Riley's relationship with the detective had smoothed out since their first series of interactions. She'd called several times a week to check his progress on reopening the cold case—though the detective might have used the word "pester." The final showdown with Hank had resulted in the detective getting shot in the arm, but he had also been able to apprehend Hank, a man who had eluded capture for the majority of the detective's career. Once Hank had been handcuffed and stuffed into the back of a cruiser, Detective Howard had said, "I might have to seriously reconsider how often I use psychics" before one of his fellow officers had escorted the "stubborn old man" to the hospital.

When her phone rang, she nearly toppled off the counter. The jolt of surprise caused her to slosh milk onto her pajama pants. Cursing under her breath, she swiped away the milk and a corn flake, then put down her mug and picked up her phone.

"Hi!" she said, with more pep than this early hour ever required.

"Hi, Riley," the detective answered slowly.

Despite proving that her skills could be an asset to him, and that he was returning *her* call, he still spoke to her with an air of trepidation. Riley hadn't convinced him yet that "psychic medium" wasn't synonymous with "mind reader."

"I would have called you back sooner but I needed to do a little digging to refresh my memory on the Brynn Bodwell case," he said. "Hearing that name threw me for a loop … it's been years since I've heard it."

Riley forgot all about the small puddle of milk on her pants. She hoped the detective would have some insider information that had been left out of the true crime shows. "What can you tell me about her?"

"I suppose you were too young to have lived through the media hoopla," he said. "What were you … six?"

Riley laughed. "I think I was nine."

"You're even younger than my daughter!" the detective said, chuckling. "Anyway, her body had been dumped in the Orilla Verde Recreation Area after she'd been missing for about a week. Taos really went to bat trying to find her when she first went missing. There was media coverage every night for weeks. Her name and picture were plastered all over newspapers. Every few years it seems like a new documentary comes out about her, adding more suspects to the ever-growing list."

Suppressing a sigh, she said, "Yeah, I found most of that on an episode of *Unsolved Mysteries*."

"You sound disappointed in my intel," he said, the smile evident in his voice. "Did your research turn up the name Shawna Mack?"

Riley cocked her head. "No. Who's Shawna?"

"About six months *before* Brynn was found, the body of another woman was found in that same recreation area at one of the campgrounds."

Sitting up straighter, Riley said, *"Really?"*

"There were striking similarities between Shawna Mack's disappearance and later murder—as well as the disposal of her body—and what happened to Brynn. Both had been strangled and nude. It's believed she was also washed prior to being left there, but because of the location—a fine layer of dirt and plant debris had coated her body—that part of it has been hotly debated," he said. "Yet Shawna barely made the news. There's still no consensus among law enforcement about whether the two cases are even connected."

"Seems like you think they are," Riley said, then hopped off the counter and hurried into the living room where her laptop lay on the coffee table. While Detective Howard talked, Riley powered on her computer, sat on the floor using the couch as a backrest, and pulled up a search engine.

"I do. There are too many similarities for it to be a coincidence, if you ask me. We heard about it in Santa Fe, since Taos is relatively close and several of the officers here have family out there and vice versa. A buddy of mine worked the case," the detective said. "Both cases went cold, but Shawna's went colder a lot faster than Brynn's. Maybe it was because Brynn's family had more resources to keep the search going. But my guess is that Brynn got all the coverage because she was blonde and blue-eyed and was well on her way to becoming a veterinarian, while Shawna was a Black single mother working three jobs and had had a few run-ins with the law."

Riley lightly shook her head. As an avid consumer of true crime, she'd read about dozens of similar stories, yet somehow each instance managed to disturb her all over again. She typed "Shawna Mack, Taos NM" into her search bar, then hit the images tab. The pictures that popped up were of a very pretty Black woman in her early twenties. Riley wasn't sure how she felt about the fact that Shawna wasn't the woman in the yellow dress. "So the suspects in Brynn's murder didn't overlap with the suspects for Shawna's?"

"They had tunnel vision when they went searching for Shawna's killer," the detective said just as Riley's internet search pulled up an article about the arrest of a Black man named Rodney Elgin in connection with Shawna's death. She didn't immediately see anything about a murder conviction.

"Rodney Elgin?" she asked.

"Yep. There was a rumor that someone in the department had an informant who pinned it on Rodney, but the name of the informant was never revealed. Rodney had been Shawna's on-again, off-again boyfriend for years. They'd gotten together young and had a son, but there had been a lot of problems in the relationship. Police knew of Shawna and Rodney because of how many times neighbors had called the cops on them for domestic disturbances. Shawna eventually got a restraining order against him.

"It was well-known among Shawna's neighbors that she loved taking her son to the recreation area to go hiking. It's about half an hour outside of Taos. Rodney and Shawna had taken the kid out there dozens of times, too. It was a cheap place to take kids and spend the weekend—most campsites are five to seven dollars a night—so it wasn't uncommon for neighbors to run into each other out there. The police figured Rodney had been there without the kid one day and killed her. Her body was found by the campsite host early one morning."

"Did Shawna or Rodney have a campsite booked for that night?"

"Nope," the detective said. "The theory is that they were out there for some kind of tryst that went sideways."

Riley's brow furrowed. "Wouldn't other campers have heard it? Or heard him leave?"

"It never sounded plausible to me either," he said. "When you compare that to what happened to Brynn, it was clear that they'd both been killed somewhere else and then dumped in the recreation area. Wildlife is very active up there—the killer left the bodies in locations where tourists, campers, or nature guides were sure to find them before the animals did."

A click of the images tab pulled up Rodney's mugshot. She knew appearances didn't account for much—the gorgeous Francis Hank Carras, who was capable of terrible things, was proof enough of that—but Riley didn't see a dead-eyed killer when she looked at Rodney. She saw a man who had made a lot of bad decisions early on, and then life had chewed him up and spat him back out. She switched to the news tab.

Murder suspect arrested for role in drug trafficking ring, read a headline. He was only twenty-five when he had been arrested. The same age Riley was now.

"So he was suspected of the murder but convicted for something else?" Riley asked.

"Yep," the detective said. "The day Shawna's body was found, they opted not to announce it to the media right away. They must have paid off that poor campsite host and the campers to keep their mouths shut about the whole thing for a while. Police picked up Rodney after they pulled him over for running through a stop sign. He had a flimsy alibi for the week during Shawna's disappearance, and his story changed so often during his interrogation, they were convinced he was lying. Truth was, he'd been pretty heavily involved in a drug trafficking ring that sold crack cocaine, which was why he was cagey about giving up his whereabouts. But when they broke the news to him that Shawna was dead, he told them everything, unwilling to go down for the murder. His confession about the drugs eventually got him thrown in prison for twenty years."

"Damn," Riley breathed.

"According to my buddy, there was enough chest pumping going on after Rodney's arrest that it was clear they all thought they'd gotten Shawna's murderer. They didn't have the evidence to nail him for it, though. Everything they had on him was circumstantial at best. I think Rodney's arrest got a couple of media spotlights, but it was more about getting a 'lowlife' like Rodney off the street rather than focusing on the fact that a young mother had been murdered and carelessly discarded. Those campers finally got their fifteen minutes too. But even that turned into commentary about the increase in crime rates and the idea that people can't even go camping anymore without stumbling over a body."

"Ugh," Riley said. "And then Brynn disappeared six months later and was killed in the same way, but left in a different part of the recreation area?"

"Correct. But Shawna's case was considered solved at that point. Shawna's had been labeled as a domestic abuse case gone awry, while Brynn's was treated as something else entirely." After a beat of silence, with the faintest hint of hope in voice, he asked, "What's your interest in this?"

"I had a dream about Brynn. Well, sort of. It was about a friend of hers reading the newspaper about Brynn's death," Riley said. Then Riley told him about the box of film cameras Jade had recently purchased. "Ever since the cameras were here, I've been visited by a Black woman in a yellow dress. She's twenty-something, too. The storage unit where the cameras came from was in Clovis, though, not Taos. And I just looked up Shawna Mack—it's not the same woman. I have a bunch of pieces and I don't know how any of them fit together."

The detective let out a sigh, but Riley couldn't tell if it was one of relief or not. "There weren't any other homicides that matched the M.O. after the discovery of Brynn's body, which lent credence to the Taos police department's conviction that the cases hadn't been connected. Both were one-off homicides where the killers happened to use the same dumping grounds. But if your woman in the yellow dress is connected to Brynn and Shawna, it could mean that the killer didn't stop after Brynn, just changed tactics."

"Unless the woman in the yellow dress came before Shawna," Riley said.

"True," he said. "It's too bad your ghosts don't come with time stamps."

Riley managed a faint laugh.

"Well, if you get any insights on the Shawna Mack case, let me know, yeah? It's one of those cases I think about a lot. When Shawna was killed, my daughter was around the same age. She looked a bit like Shawna, too. It rattled my daughter so badly, I think it's a big part of why she became a prosecutor."

"I will," Riley said.

She hung up and dropped her phone onto the couch. Shawna Mack's smiling face was displayed in several small boxes on her screen. One of the pictures was of Shawna holding her son on her hip. He looked about six years old in the picture. If Shawna had been killed eighteen years ago, Riley supposed her son was about the same age as Riley now, maybe a few years younger.

Sitting cross-legged on her couch, she grabbed the computer and settled it in her lap. She scoured the internet for Shawna first, finding most of the same information the detective had just told her, as well as Shawna's son Malcolm. He was twenty-four and was married with kids of his own—newborn twin girls from the few public posts of pictures she could find on his social media. It didn't look like Malcolm had done any interviews about what had happened to his mother. Riley wondered if that was because Malcolm had refused to give interviews, as the privacy settings on most of his pages might suggest—or if no one had asked.

She only found one article that made the connection between Shawna Mack and Brynn Bodwell. The article had been published in the *Taos Daily Journal*.

Reddit had a thread for each individual woman's death, as well as one that speculated that the two were not only connected, but that there were more bodies the police hadn't found yet. There were theories about the investigations being botched—whether on purpose or not. Some speculated that since the small town of Taos hadn't ever had a case like this before, they hadn't known how to deal with not only one homicide, but two.

Forensic science had made leaps and bounds by the early 2000s, and more was known about the psychology of the small percentage of murderers who killed strangers. But Taos hadn't had a formal homicide unit then; they still didn't. Had the police force in Taos not connected the Brynn and Shawna dots because they hadn't had the experience to know what they'd been looking at? Of course, maybe there had been no connection to find. Maybe Rodney Elgin really had murdered Shawna, high on the same drugs he'd been convicted for distributing. Perhaps Brynn had been murdered by an ex who had been jealous of her relationship with Liam. Could her disappearance on the night of her two-year anniversary hold any significance?

But, as Detective Howard had said, if the cases *were* connected, and confirmation bias had snuck in, it was possible the connection hadn't been made due to reasons that had little to do with experience or availability of evidence.

Riley leaned back against the couch and crossed her arms, staring at the Reddit thread for so long, her eyes ached.

As she rubbed them, Michael's voice echoed in her head. *"You don't* have *to look into any of it. It* isn't *your responsibility."*

She tried to let that thought carry her off to sleep that night, but the dead women she'd learned about in the past few weeks got jumbled up in her dreams. Riley relived the horrible tumble down the stairs, yet the woman who was splayed at the bottom was Brynn Bodwell. Julie sat at a table weeping over an article that featured Shawna's name, but with a picture of the woman in the yellow dress.

Riley woke in the middle of the night, sweaty and with a head full of ghosts. The sound of the woman falling down the stairs replayed in her mind, the thud and crash of flesh losing its battle with gravity. Riley recalled the woman's scraped skin and unfocused eyes. Riley's gut told her something had happened to the woman *before* her overdose. Did she continue to haunt Julie's house because she regretted what she'd done, or because of something else? Did she have family who mourned her loss now?

As Riley lay in the dark staring at the ceiling, she found herself thinking not about the deceased women, but the people they'd left behind. The friend weeping over Brynn's death. Malcolm forever without his mother, and his newborn children without a paternal grandmother. The unknown loved ones of the woman in the yellow dress who had no doubt gone years without answers.

When Riley and Michael had returned Pete Vonick's Scooby Doo shirt to his mother, Riley and his mother Janet had held each other and cried for what felt like hours. They wept for the little boy they both missed, even though Riley had only known him in death. Even Michael had gotten choked up. As much as unraveling a mystery could thrill her, what kept sucking her back in was the living people who made up the tapestry of the story.

They were who she did this for.

This time when she fell asleep, the ghosts let her be.

CHAPTER 7

The next day, Riley's phone rang as soon as she got out of her car behind The Laughing Tiger, ready to start her one-to-nine shift. She expected it to be Michael calling to say hi at the end of his lunch break as he often did, but it was Jade's smiling face that filled her screen.

"Hey," Riley said. "You all right?"

Jade laughed. "You can't assume the worst every time someone calls you."

"Try and stop me," Riley said, pausing a few feet from the back entrance of the restaurant and leaning against the brick wall. Nosey-ass Roberto was loitering in the lot having a smoke, and though he was navigating his phone with his thumb, she knew he was doing his best to listen in.

"Anyway," Jade said, "something you said the other day clicked with me. We're millennials! None of my friends know how to use film cameras!"

Well, at least she'd come to her senses before she dragged Riley on another thrift shop run.

"So, thanks to your astute observation …" Jade began. Riley narrowed her eyes suspiciously even though Jade couldn't see it. "I booked an appointment with one of the photographers you researched for me a couple of months back. His name is

Ian Chambers and not only is he a full-time photographer, he also gives classes at the adult school a few times a year on film cameras."

Riley had no idea where Jade was going with this. Did she want her to help interview photographers now? At least when they interviewed chefs, Riley got to sample so much food, she hadn't needed to eat dinner that night. According to the color-coded spreadsheet, Jade still hadn't chosen a chef, though. The idea of meeting half a dozen photographers wasn't terribly appealing. Maybe she needed to call Jonah and ask him to split some of this wedding prep stuff with her.

"I was thinking," Jade singsonged, "that I could kill two birds with one stone. I can interview him to see if he'll be a good fit for the wedding, but we could also bring the cameras to him and see if he knows anything about them? Maybe one of them is really rare and was only made in 1975 or something and it'll help you narrow down who might have bought the things."

"I'm in."

"Whoa, that was easy," Jade said.

"I'm not *always* disagreeable, you know."

Jade laughed long and loud. "Good one. Thursday is still your day off, yeah? Ian said we can come by his classroom at the adult school Thursday evening around 5 PM before his class at 5:30."

Jade hadn't yet been filled in on the added wrinkles to Riley's current mystery, mostly because Riley only had bits and pieces. But at this point, she didn't know what to try next. She still felt resistant about the séance idea, but it was also the only one she had.

Just before 5 on Thursday evening, Riley pulled into the parking lot of the school. Apparently the place was mostly geared to adults working toward their GEDs, but it also offered several art classes. It was a plain, unassuming place. She'd actually driven by here zillions of times and never registered what it was. Several blue doors lined the length of the beige façade, and a mowed, patchy lawn ran along the front of the building, bisected by a sidewalk periodically dotted by benches.

Jade arrived within a few minutes and headed for one of the benches. After placing the cardboard box of cameras on it, she pulled her phone out of her denim jacket and tapped at her screen. Riley's phone chimed a moment later.

Stop loitering in your car like a weirdo.

Riley rolled her eyes, snatched her phone off her dash, and joined her.

"So … did you do your obsessive internet wormhole thing and stalk Ian Chambers?" Jade asked.

"Nah," Riley said. "Why?"

"Oh, nothing," Jade said nonchalantly. "But if you'd looked at his social media, you would have seen that he'd just finished an engagement photo gig for Victor Warren and Rachel Isaacson."

Riley gasped and gave Jade's arm a light slap. "Shut up. Victor Warren as in Howie from *Tiana's Circle?*"

"Sounds like it," Jade said, smiling smugly at her, and clearly enjoying how Riley could come unglued at the mere mention of that show.

"If I hug him," Riley said, "would it mean that I hugged Howie through osmosis or something?"

Jade just stared at her.

Riley scoffed. "Rochelle would understand. Howie is the most attractive fictional man that has ever been created. How have you still not watched it? You'd get it if you watched it."

"I tried! It's so—"

"Choose your words carefully, woman."

Jade laughed, shaking her head. "How are you into both hardcore true crime and also the fluffiest, most dramatic TV show in recent memory?"

"I contain multitudes. Also, how dare you," Riley said. "I can't be held responsible for any fan-girling that may happen when I meet Ian, by the way." She pulled out her phone to text Rochelle about this very intriguing development.

Jade's retort was cut off when, on the other side of the patchy lawn, one of the blue doors swung open in Riley's peripheral vision. Looking up from her phone, she craned her neck and spotted a forty-something man standing in the doorway of a well-lit classroom.

"Ms. Higgins?" the man called out.

Jade grinned at Riley, then turned around, arm in the air. "That's me!" She grabbed the box of cameras off the bench. Riley followed after her, her text only half written, and stuck her phone into her back pocket.

"Welcome, ladies," he said as they stepped into the room. "Thanks for meeting me here. I would have met you somewhere closer to you. I—"

Jade shook her head, cutting off his apology. "It's no trouble." She beelined for the long table in the front of the room where Ian had already laid out several film cameras, presumably for the class starting in a half hour, and set down the box. The only other furniture in the room was the large chalkboard on the wall behind the table, and on the other side of the room, three rows of blue plastic chairs.

Riley studied Ian. He had a hipster vibe—dark jeans; plaid shirt; full, well-trimmed beard and mustache; dark hair styled with just enough gel that it looked like it took some time, but not hours; and chunky Timberland boots. She guessed he was around forty-five. He joined Jade at the table, standing on the opposite side of it.

"And what do we have here?" he asked, gesturing to the box.

Jade said, "I bought these from a consignment store and I was wondering a) if they work, and b) if you can tell me anything about them. This isn't part of the interview or anything. I just saw that you teach classes on how to use film cameras and thought you could give me some information on them."

"The woman who ran the consignment store was a little squirrely when we bought them," Riley added. "I was worried she had sold us defective merchandise."

Ian peered into the box, his eyes alight, like a kid getting a birthday present six months early. "Well, let's have a look. May I?" he asked, reaching toward the box, and then pulling his hand back a fraction.

"Please," Jade said.

He grabbed one and popped open the film door, brought the viewfinder to his eye, tested dials and knobs. "This is a great piece. Definitely not defective. It's extremely well-maintained. Whoever owned it first took great care of it. It's a Canon AE-1. This was an extremely popular camera in the '80s."

"Extremely popular" meant Jade's hope of finding a rare camera had just grown more unlikely.

The next camera was given a similar assessment to the first. "This is a Minolta SRT-101. It's Japanese made, and I believe they first went into production in the late sixties. This is in exceptional shape, too. You really lucked out on this buy. I'm half tempted to make you an offer on these."

The guy was practically salivating. It made Riley wonder even more who had owned these cameras and what their circumstances had been that resulted in their losing that unit.

Shortly after Ian picked up the last camera, he let out a little, "Oh!"

"What?" Jade asked, getting on her tiptoes to peer across the table.

Ian turned the camera around so the film door faced them. He pointed to a vertical oval-shaped window on the back, something green showing through. "See this? That's a sliver of a film cartridge. There's still film in this thing! Sorry for geeking out, but this collection plus a roll of mystery film? I'm very jealous right now."

Riley and Jade shared a wide-eyed look. There was *film* still in it? They were so unversed about film cameras that they hadn't even considered checking if film was in them. Had Carol, a supposed connoisseur of vintage games and entertainment, not noticed the film either?

"Can I check to see if the film is spent or not?" Ian asked, a giddy trill to his tone.

"Yeah, sure," Jade said, and Riley knew Jade didn't have the first clue what that meant.

"This knob up here," Ian said, pointing to a circular piece on top of the camera, "is what you use to rewind the film. If I lift this and turn…" He turned the knob. "There's no resistance, so that means the film has been fully used." As he gingerly placed the camera back in the cardboard box, he said, "If you decide to get that developed, you'll have to let me know what you find."

Riley could sense how desperately Ian wanted to take all three cameras, the roll of film, and sprint from the room without looking back.

"I will for sure," Jade said. "I know you're limited on time, and that this isn't the most conventional of interviews, but could we discuss my wedding plans for the next fifteen minutes so I can determine if our visions align?"

Ian snapped out of drooling over the cameras and nodded. "Yes, of course."

As maid of honor, Riley wasn't sure if she should have been paying better attention to their conversation. Her thoughts kept drifting back to the cameras. She'd been thinking about them all week. Detective Howard had speculated that the woman in the yellow dress could have been the victim after Brynn, and that the killer's M.O. had changed. But it was just as possible that she had been killed before Shawna.

What had truly been bothering Riley since her conversation with him, though, was his conviction that Shawna Mack hadn't received the same media treatment as Brynn solely because Brynn was the type of victim people generally had the most sympathy for. The pretty blonde-haired blue-eyed girl-next-door was the epitome of innocence, and when innocence was violated, people were horrified. It made for a good story. But if the victim were less perfect, whether it was appearance, criminal history, life choices, or profession, that story somehow wasn't as compelling.

The end result was tragic in either case, no matter what either woman had looked like, or what kind of life she'd led. Neither one deserved what happened to her, and worst still, the person who had done it had never been caught.

But even more upsetting—the thought that had kept Riley awake more nights this week than the ghost had—was that if all three of these women were connected, it meant that the woman in the yellow dress had gotten even less attention than Shawna.

The woman was a ghost both literally and figuratively—and there could be others who had slipped even Riley's notice.

Something poked her side and Riley flinched.

Jade jerked her head toward the door where a few people had started to wander in. The class was starting soon. Riley's gaze shifted to the box of cameras still on the table.

If only Riley knew when the woman in the yellow dress had died. Was she victim one, three, or some number further down a chain of unknown length? Detective Howard's words returned. *"It's too bad your ghosts don't come with time stamps."*

"Would prints from any of these cameras come with dates on them?" Riley suddenly asked.

Ian nodded. "A lot of older models had a feature that could print the date directly on the negative, and you could turn it on or off." He picked up the camera that still had film inside. "Ah, here. You see these dials? These are used to set the date."

The key to figuring out the identity of the woman in the yellow dress might be inside that camera, and there might be a time stamp to boot.

Once Ian had placed the camera back in the box, Jade picked the whole thing up and smiled warmly at him. "I really appreciate you taking the time to talk to us. I'll be in touch really soon, okay? I think you'd be a great fit."

"Excellent," he said. "And thanks for letting me see those. That was a real treat."

Riley offered him an awkward wave, then followed after Jade. She was halfway to the door when she remembered something vitally important.

She hurried back to the table with such speed, Ian took a step back as if he feared she was going to punch him. "Did you *really* photograph Victor Warren and Rachel Isaacson's engagement?"

His eyes were alight again. "Yes!" he said and quickly fumbled in his back pocket to pull out his phone. He tapped the screen a few times, swiped a few others, and then turned the phone around to show Riley. Ian was standing right next to Victor.

"You took … a selfie … with Howie," Riley managed.

"I know I'm a forty-seven-year-old man," Ian said, pocketing his phone again. "But *Tiana's Circle* is hands down the best show on television right now."

"Thank. You!" Riley held out her hands to him in deep appreciation. "If Jade doesn't hire you, she is a fool."

Ian laughed.

Riley couldn't wait to share this with Rochelle. She'd lose her mind with the appropriate level of excitement that was severely lacking in her best friend. When Riley emerged from the classroom, she found Jade standing beside the same bench they'd loitered in front of earlier.

It was still light out at this hour, but a few of the lampposts lining the parking lot had turned on. A swarm of gnats flew wildly around the lit bulb of the post nearby.

"We have to get this film developed, right?" Jade asked.

"Definitely," Riley said. "Is that something Brie could do?"

"As much as I love that girl, I think we should get a professional to do it," Jade said. "Yes, I know, I know, I want her to develop the film from the wedding, but those are memories and this could be, like, smoking-gun evidence in a murder case."

Riley chewed on her bottom lip, staring at the box Jade still held.

"Don't worry. I'll take them home with me. We can both research where to get film developed and then we can touch base in the morning, okay?"

They chatted about random things for a few more minutes, then parted ways, each heading for their own cars. Riley sat in hers without moving for long enough that the cabin lights dimmed to black again. Her mind was awhirl with all the possibilities of what could be on that film.

Her passenger door flew open.

"Shit!" she yelped, hand to her chest, as Jade settled into the passenger seat and closed the door.

"All right," Jade said, arms crossed. "What's going on with you?"

"What's going on with me is that I almost just suffered cardiac arrest," Riley said.

Jade turned in her seat and arched a single eyebrow.

Ugh. The look.

Riley groaned.

"You've been weirdly distracted this whole time. What's going on in that head of yours?"

Reluctantly, Riley grumbled, "I've officially been sucked into another mystery."

Jade squeaked and clapped. Then she narrowed her eyes and lightly slugged Riley in the arm.

"Ow! Shit! What the hell?"

Jade lips were pursed. "Didn't we have this discussion six months ago? You don't get to leave me out of your paranormal sleuthing anymore. Now, explain. Spare no detail."

So Riley told her about Brynn, Shawna, and the mystery ghost woman, including her own musings from just minutes before.

Jade was quiet for a moment, frowning. "Is that poor woman trapped in my garage? Or, I guess, in my trunk right now?"

"I don't think so," Riley said, though she didn't really know for sure. There was no way to know if traumatic events bound the woman's energy to that camera, or if she was just able to use that energy as a way to move between planes. Hell, there could be an option C Riley hadn't even thought of. "But the curiosity of what happened to her is really starting to eat away at me. I wish you could see her … she's so damn … sad."

"Anything I can do to help? Any ideas beyond getting the film developed?" Jade asked.

"Nina said I could bring the cameras to one of her séances to see if we can get the woman to talk to us," Riley said. "I'm totally willing to accept that I'm invested now. I mean, I even agreed to go on another ghost-hunting investigation. But … god, this is going to sound stupid, but I want to give the woman a chance to communicate with me on her own. A séance to pull the woman *to* me feels invasive. She's not only sad, but she's … shy? She doesn't talk. She just waits. A séance feels like making an introvert go to a party she doesn't want to go to and then forcing her to make a speech to a bunch of strangers or something. I can't explain it."

"It makes sense," Jade said. "You have a very strong intuition. You always have. If your intuition is telling you a séance is wrong for her, then don't do it. Do you have any ideas of what *would* work?"

Riley mulled that over. "Well … I've never actually touched the haunted camera. Touching Pete's beanie, and touching the doorjamb in the Hyssop Room at the ranch both showed me windows into the past. Maybe touching the camera could do that, too?"

"You know I'm totally down for this plan," Jade said. "Want to head to my place? Jonah should be at the office for another hour or two, so we don't have to worry about him creeping in with his screwdriver."

Riley laughed. "Okay. Let's try it."

"Yes! My plans for your future are slowly clicking into place." She let herself out of the car before Riley could say anything else, and then got into her own. Though Riley's stomach was in knots, she followed Jade back to her house and down her long driveway.

One of the doors on Jade's garage gave a lurch, and then began to roll up, bright yellow light spilling out onto the pavement. Jade slowly pulled her car inside.

When Riley got out of her car, the burbling fountain in the middle of the yard was the only sound save for the occasional chirp of a bird making its final rounds before settling in for the night. Little solar-powered lanterns on stakes were wedged into the ground at intervals along the short, curved stone path that wove around Jade's front garden. The lights glowed dully in the early evening darkness, reminiscent of will-o'-the-wisps in a fantasy painting.

Riley jumped when Jade said, "Get in here. We're on borrowed time."

She followed Jade to her garage. It was a spacious area which easily fit three cars. To the back of the room was a pool table neither Jade nor Jonah had used in ages, given that several boxes of Jade's various wedding craft materials were piled on top of it. The entire right side of the garage was lined with floor-to-ceiling shelving. Half of it was filled with Jade's gardening supplies, gallons of paint, and various tools, while the other half was lined with neatly labeled plastic tubs—Christmas decorations, cleaning supplies, holiday-themed linens. Jade took the box of cameras out of her trunk and set them at Riley's feet.

As Riley stood in the open space of the garage—the spot that would be filled with Jonah's car in the next hour or so—she held her breath, sure the woman in the yellow dress would appear at any moment. Riley could swear she felt her here and resisted the urge to look over her shoulder. The woman wasn't a lurker like Orin, hovering somewhere behind her, trying to unnerve her. Orin had been a creepy-as-hell ghost because he'd been creepy-as-hell as a person. What had the woman in the yellow dress been like when she was alive?

Jade told her that her intuition was strong, and Nina had told her to trust her instincts. The more Riley thought about it, the more she was sure she'd been right in her earlier assessment: the woman in the yellow dress was shy. Perhaps the woman's introvert-leaning personality had latched onto Riley's, like calling to like.

Jade and Riley stood on either side of the box, both staring down at the cameras lying innocently in their cardboard home.

"Do you usually get messages in words or in images?" Jade asked, voice hushed.

"Both? It depends. Gladys, Walter Palmer's wife, spoke to me. But the woman haunting Julie's house showed me what happened to her, rather than speaking," Riley said. "It's weird because I really couldn't tell you if they use speech the way you and I do, or if whatever is happening between me and the spirit gets translated into words so I can understand the message that's coming through. Does that make any sense?"

"Yeah, it totally does. This is *very* cool. It's like my own private episode of *Paranormal Playground*."

Riley sat cross-legged before the box and quickly scanned the cameras. Jade followed suit. She assumed the woman in the yellow dress was bound to the one that still housed the film, but she touched a different one instead. She had to work herself up to this.

Jade involuntarily tensed and squeezed one eye shut.

Nothing.

Riley touched the one with the film. The woman in the yellow dress instantly materialized behind Jade. Riley sucked in a breath.

Jade's green eyes doubled in diameter. "Oh, hell, there's a ghost behind me, isn't there?"

Riley nodded, not breaking eye contact with the woman. "Hi," she croaked out.

The woman nodded once in acknowledgement. So she could hear and understand Riley, at least.

"Can you tell me your name?" Riley asked.

The woman's forehead creased. The two fluorescent shop lights at the back of the garage flickered twice.

Jade shivered. "Did it just get colder?"

"Yeah. I think she's trying to pull energy into herself." Riley grabbed the camera out of the box, then glanced up at the sad woman in the yellow dress. "Are you on this roll of film?"

The temperature in the garage still steadily dropped, and the woman's face was even more pinched now.

Yes, someone said directly into her ear, causing goosebumps to skitter down Riley's arms.

The woman vanished, taking the cold air with her.

Jade shuddered. "Is she gone?"

"Yeah," said Riley, looking down at the camera. "I don't think this belonged to her. She clearly has a connection to it, but it's a weak connection. I might be able to communicate with her better if I have something of hers."

Jutting her chin at the camera, Jade said, "Like a picture?"

A little flutter of hope took flight in Riley's chest. "Yeah, like a picture."

They were silent for a few beats.

"Since Michael isn't here, I guess I'll be devil's advocate," Jade said. "What I said earlier … that what's on that film could be the smoking gun in a murder case … it's kind of eating away at my brain now. Do you think you should take the camera to the police?"

Riley had started shaking her head before the question fully left Jade's mouth. "The problem is, there's currently nothing about this camera that connects it to Brynn or Shawna. What would I say? 'Here's a camera that was owned by an unknown person who may have murdered three people'? If they ask what evidence I have and I say I had a sort-of dream about Brynn, what are they supposed to do with that?"

Jade chewed on the inside of her cheek.

"And who do I turn it over to? The Taos police department, since that's the town where Brynn and Shawna were found? Or to the Clovis police, since that's where the unit was? What if the woman appearing to me now wasn't killed in Taos *or* Clovis … what if she wasn't from New Mexico at all?"

"True," Jade said slowly, brows furrowed. "Maybe you can find the officer or officers who worked on the Brynn or Shawna cases and give the camera to them, like you did with Renee? That worked with Detective Howard."

"Yes, but I also had indirectly witnessed Renee's murder by then," Riley said. "He was skeptical from jump, but when I told him what details I had been shown from the crime scene, that's what helped sway him. I knew things someone my age with no connection to the crime shouldn't have known. And even then, I got a lot of 'We're working on it' when I called to check up on his progress. He had been swayed, but not so swayed that he made researching the case his top priority or anything." She lightly shook her head. "All I have is a dream about a friend of Brynn's crying over the article about Brynn's death. I don't know the friend's name. I don't know anything about the crime scene. I know even less about Shawna and the woman in the yellow dress."

Jade sighed, her shoulders slumping a little. "And I guess just because Howard was open to the idea of psychic mediums, it doesn't mean the next cop will be."

"Right," Riley said. "And even if the next cop *is* open to it, he or she can't know who is legitimately a psychic and who is making things up, or is mentally unstable, or whatever else. Who knows how many psychics have called them about this case already, giving them countless leads that don't pan out? If I go in with nothing to back up my psychic claims, they'll be twice as likely to discount me immediately.

"Plus, if Detective Howard is right, and the Taos police department messed up in connecting these cases, they might not *want* to investigate what's on the film. At best, they say they'll look into it and the camera gets stuck in an evidence box to collect dust for years, and at worst, the camera and/or the film goes missing. It wouldn't be the first time evidence disappeared to control the outcome of a case, or to protect the culprit or the department. Not to mention there might be nothing on this film other than flowers and landscapes."

Jade sighed. "Okay. So, same plan: we get these pictures developed on our own. We'll keep the cameras here until then since I'm assuming you don't want them in your apartment overnight."

"That would be a solid hell no." Then she winced slightly and eyed the spot over Jade's shoulder where the woman had stood not that long ago. "No offense." Riley gently placed the camera back in the box, wondering not only what secrets were hidden behind the closed film door, but who had taken the pictures in the first place.

CHAPTER 8

Jade assured Riley that both she and Jonah would be out of the house by eight the next morning, so Riley headed there at a quarter after. It would have been more logical for Riley to have taken the camera or film cartridge with her last night. She knew that. It wasn't as if not having the camera in her possession hindered the woman in the yellow dress's ability to pop in unannounced. But the woman had managed to communicate with Riley for the first time. It had only been a single word—*Yes*—but it was more than she'd been able to do so far. Either Riley's proximity to the camera had given the woman an extra ghostly jolt, or the spirit was getting stronger. Nina told Riley that she could get better at dealing with ghosts if she practiced. Did the same go the other way, with ghosts learning to communicate with the living the more they tried? Sleep was already hard to come by. If the camera had been in her apartment, she wouldn't have slept at all—it felt like having guests over and being compelled to keep them entertained.

Riley called Michael on the way.

"You there yet?" he asked, the sounds of the road audible in the background, meaning he was in his car, too, on his way to work.

"Just left," she said, then stifled a yawn. She and Jade had been up late into the night, texting each other links for places scattered all over the country that offered film development services.

Michael had been caught up on her latest theory: that the woman in the yellow dress, Brynn, and Shawna were all victims of the same killer—and that there could be more.

Then she yawned so deeply again, her eyes watered. This was not a safe condition for driving.

"How late did you two stay up anyway?" Michael asked.

It was her sleep deprivation that made her say, "Not that long. I just haven't slept."

"*Riley,*" he said softly. "Why didn't you say anything?"

"Kinda comes with the territory. Once I start letting the spirits in, they can get persistent. Which is why I usually haul ass in the opposite direction."

"Now I feel bad for encouraging any of this. Maybe it's too soon for you to be looking into another serial killer," he said. "Wow, that's really a sentence I just said to my girlfriend."

Riley smiled ruefully. "Eh. It's too late. I'm curious as hell about what happened to her."

Sighing, he said, "Me too. I'm just worried about you. At least you'll be here tonight. I'll make sure you sleep. It's just too bad the days of one-hour photo places are long gone. We could have looked at these pictures together tonight."

"Yeah, agree. The place we're going to send the film to said it'll take at least a week to get them back. But they'll send a CD of the pictures, prints, and return the negatives. I don't know if we'll even need the negatives, but it sounds like most drug stores don't return them anymore."

"Now we just have to cross our fingers that what's on this film isn't some Freddy Krueger-level shit that makes the film tech get the vapors and pass out," Michael said. "Or send the FBI to your house to ask what in the hell you've been up to."

Ugh. "Do you think there are support groups for psychic mediums? This is stressful."

"I'll do some research," he said. "I just got to the office so I have to head in. Call my desk phone if you need me."

She almost—almost—said, "Okay, love you!" as a sign-off, but chickened out and said, "All righty!" instead, like the weirdo she was.

Pulling into Jade's driveway, she hit the button on the garage clicker Jade had given her last night. She climbed out and then crept into the garage, as if she were sneaking into the woman-in-the-yellow-dress's house. The woman didn't materialize. Jade had hidden the cameras behind an old red toolbox last night. Riley beelined for it. She slid the box toward her on the wooden shelf, grabbed the camera in question, and then pushed the remaining two back into their hiding place.

Mission complete, Riley got back in the car, placed the camera on her passenger seat, and hit the button for Jade's garage door.

She eyed the camera. "Please don't appear in my car while I'm driving."

She got no response, which suited her just fine.

Before she headed out, something suddenly occurred to her. If this camera truly had been owned by the person who had killed the woman in the yellow dress, was it possible that his fingerprints were still on the film cartridge? Finding fingerprints on the camera was already a moot point. Between the camera being sold at auction, its arrival at Reinholt Consignment, and eventually being purchased by Jade, countless people had touched the body of the camera. But maybe the film itself, since it was still inside, hadn't been handled much aside from the person who had put the film in the camera to begin with.

She fished her cell phone out of her purse sitting on the passenger seat floorboard, did a quick search, and then called Reinholt Consignment.

"Thank you for calling Reinholt Consignment," a woman said. "This is Carol. How may I help you?"

"Hi, Carol," Riley said. "This is Riley Thomas. The … uhh … indigo child."

"Oh, yes! Hi, dear. Have you solved the mystery of why our friend is so sad?"

"I'm working on it," Riley said. "I had a question, though. Did you notice that one of the cameras had film in it?"

Carol was quiet for a moment. "Yes. The whole lot of cameras felt so haunted, I was worried that if I altered them in any way, it could cause problems. My friend, the one who dealt with the poltergeist? That's what happened to her. She bought a locked jewelry box from an estate sale. The woman running the sale was the previous owner's granddaughter. She had no idea where the key was. Well, that ghost was already ticked off about being taken from his home after the sale, and then my friend jimmied that lock open and broke the mechanism while trying to open the box. Hoo-boy! That's when the grumpy ghost went poltergeist on her. When I told her I'd picked up a ghost in addition to the cameras, and that there was film in one of them, she told me to sell it all as is, and not to fuss with anything."

Which explained Carol's squirrelly behavior.

"So no one has opened that camera?" Riley asked.

"Not that I know of," Carol said. "I got them appraised to make sure they were in working order, but I told the man to leave the film cartridge alone."

"Got it. Thanks. If I figure out who she was, I'll let you know."

"All right, hon," she said. "Good luck."

Riley dropped her phone back into her purse and headed for the post office, unsure of what to do with this information. Even if Carol and the appraiser hadn't touched the cartridge, someone else might have. When she reached her destination, she pulled into a parking space and killed the engine, but didn't immediately get out. If the killer's prints *were* on the cartridge, they would get rubbed away by the techs at the company in California when they opened the package. Not to mention that part of the instructions for shipping the film was to label the cartridge with a Sharpie—that alone could ruin any potential prints.

She grabbed her cell again, this time calling Detective Howard.

It rang four times before he picked up, chatter muted and persistent in the background. "Hi, Riley. Is this urgent?"

"I just had a quick question. It's about the Brynn and Shawna cases. I may have found something."

She bit down on her lip during the silence, wondering if he was going to humor her. He issued a little sigh. "Mark, I'll be right back. I want pictures of every inch of this place, okay?" The sound of chatter dwindled in the background, and she heard the sound of a door open and close. "Okay, Riley, what did you find?"

Was he at a crime scene? She had to tell her true-crime-loving self to chill the eff out and not ask a million questions.

But it also reminded her that detectives like Howard were constantly busy with current cases; making time for cold ones wasn't always possible, especially if the department was small, like the one in Taos.

Not wanting to keep him for too long, she told him the latest—about the camera, the woman communicating that she was on this roll of film, and Riley's concern that prints might be on the cartridge.

"Interesting…" Detective Howard said. "I cannot advise you on what to do here, mostly because I don't want this to bite me in the ass later. There are resources online that will help you lift prints if you're so inclined to try, but it's also not something I would necessarily recommend, because if you don't know what you're doing, you risk damaging the cartridge. All I can say is that if you do this, document everything. I can't say that even if you find a print that it would stand up as viable evidence in court, but if there's documentation, it might help lend it some credibility."

"Howard!" someone called out in the background. "I think we got another one."

"Shit," Howard muttered. "Sorry. I gotta go, Riley. Let me know if you find anything out."

He hung up before she could say goodbye.

Resources online to help her lift prints, huh? She pulled up a search engine on her phone and Googled "DIY fingerprint powder." Though she shouldn't have been surprised, finding what she needed took a matter of seconds. Once she had her list—latex gloves, graphite powder, clear plastic tape, microscope slides, and a delicate makeup brush—she backed out of the lot.

She got everything she needed in two trips; one to a hardware store, and the other to a craft supply one. She'd known that the craft shop by her apartment sold microscope slides, thanks to all her maid of honor shopping for Jade.

She supposed being maid of honor for her best friend wasn't all bad.

Within an hour, she had returned to her apartment with her supplies. It was just after ten now; she still had a couple of hours before her shift. She placed her purchases and the camera on her coffee table, then grabbed a small bowl out of the kitchen.

"May I also request that you don't pop up in the apartment right now?" Riley said as she returned to the living room, addressing the camera as she situated herself in front of the table, her back resting against the couch. "Detective Howard already has me freaked out that I'm going to destroy this thing, and if you materialize in the middle of this, graphite powder is going to go everywhere—and my vacuum is broken."

She didn't actually own a vacuum, but she didn't need the woman in the yellow dress to know that. She watched a quick video on how to get the film out of the camera. Then she stared down at her supplies in dismay.

Document everything, he'd said.

Grabbing her phone, she pulled up the video function and flipped the camera view to selfie mode. She hit record, then addressed the camera. She stated her name, the date, where she had gotten the camera, and when. "I'm going to open the film door, take out the cartridge, and attempt to lift a print. I will document the process."

Wincing slightly and shrugging, she propped the phone against a small stack of books. She fiddled with the angle until she had a good view of the table and her supplies. Once she had a small amount of the graphite powder poured out into the dish, she strapped on her gloves. The button on the side of the film door didn't give right away and she had to jiggle it to get the latch to pop free. She cautiously lifted the door, peeking inside, relieved to see that the film was fully inside the green-and-black cartridge. She did her best to give a verbal play-by-play to her phone's camera.

Once the cartridge was free, she held it up between her purple-latex-covered forefinger and thumb, unsure if latent fingerprints were usually visible to the naked eye. Shrugging, she gently sat the cartridge upright. It was cylindrical, with a short, upraised tube at the top, like a small straw.

Pulling the makeup brush from its packaging, she swept it across the back of her gloved hand a few times—more of a nervous tic than anything—and then pulled the small dish of graphite powder toward her. She had visions of being struck by a surprise sneeze attack and sending powder across the table.

With the cartridge once again held between forefinger and thumb, she picked up a small amount of powder on the brush and then very gently swept it along the cylindrical cartridge. She tried to channel all the forensic scientists she'd seen doing this on TV, yet was fairly certain real forensic scientists would be horrified she was trying this at all.

"Note to self," she muttered, "befriend a forensic scientist." Then she blushed furiously when she realized that would be on the video now, should anyone ever watch it.

Back and forth, back and forth she went with her brush, hoping some sign of a fingerprint would reveal itself. She had just turned the cartridge for the third time, preparing to brush the last section, when what looked like half a print emerged, outlined in black powder. Riley almost dropped the cartridge in her excitement. Willing her hands to remain steady, she brushed on a bit more of the powder. Definitely a partial print.

She wanted to pump a fist in the air, but her hands were full. She gently blew on the cartridge and sent a fine spray of graphite powder onto her coffee table.

She carefully set the cartridge down and removed her gloves, knowing that handling tape with them on would be a chore in itself. Getting a piece of tape onto the cartridge without screwing this all up was going to be a miracle, but she would try it anyway. Pulling free a stretch of clear plastic packing tape, she hovered the piece over the cartridge to get an approximation of size, then trimmed the tape so it was the same width as the cartridge. In doing all this, she noted that the tape was now covered in her own prints. So she tore off another piece and started again, trying to be more mindful.

Once she had the piece lined up properly, she hovered it in place again, her fingerprints only littering the ends of the strip. Letting out a long, slow breath, she lowered the tape onto the partial print, and gently smoothed it onto the spot with a gentle rub of a pointer finger. Would too much pressure smear the print?

Pulling on another pair of gloves, she grabbed hold of the cartridge between two fingers, and with her other hand, gently pulled the tape away from the cylinder. Holding the tape up to the light, it looked like her little experiment had worked. She held it up to her phone's camera, turning it this way and that, hoping the image wasn't too blurry. Carefully, she transferred the tape onto one of the microscope slides, then placed another slide on top of it. She labeled the end of the slide with the date and time, and showed that to her fictional audience as well.

She pulled off her gloves, tossed them on the table, and then crossed her arms. The only police connection she had was Detective Howard, and he was currently busy. She didn't have time today to drive the slide over to Santa Fe anyway, assuming he would even accept it from her.

"Here's a random fingerprint from a person who might have killed three or more women eighteen years ago in a city you don't work in. You're welcome. Bye!" probably wouldn't go over well.

It would go even less well if she dropped it off at the Taos police station. She hit the stop button on the video.

After getting the slide into a plastic zippered bag, Riley placed it in her nightstand drawer. It occurred to her then that the killer she was after could be dead himself. *That bastard better not show up.*

Thankfully, she would be at Michael's over the weekend. She just hoped that she didn't come back to her apartment Sunday night to a grumpy ghost situation.

She wrote her name, as well as the request of "prints and negatives" on the cartridge, put it in a zippered bag, and then headed back to the post office. Once the cartridge was inside its padded, neatly labeled shipping bag, she walked it over to the drop box. She just stood there a moment with her hand on the handle, staring down at the missive and the address of the film development studio in California.

Pulling the handle down to reveal a shelf, she reluctantly slipped the package onto it, as if it were the woman in the yellow dress herself Riley were sending away. She released the handle and the shelf disappeared back inside the box, taking the cartridge with it.

All she could do now was wait.

July–September, 2021

I awoke in a hospital bed. A monitor beside the bed displayed my vitals—a series of colors, numbers, and pulsing lines. My head ached, my mouth was parched, my mind fuzzy. How the hell had I ended up here?

As I tried to push myself up, I groaned. My limbs—all of me, really—felt like lead.

A door to my left swung open and a woman in a white coat walked in.

"Well, I'll be damned," she said, walking to my bedside, a wide smile on her face. "You woke up."

"What … " I coughed, clearing my throat. "What happened?"

"You were found in an alley. It appears you were badly beaten." She shone a pen light in my eyes and checked the vitals on the monitor and on my chart. "You have been in a medically induced coma for almost four months."

Nothing made any sense.

"You're a very lucky man," she said. "Do you remember your name?"

I blinked, searching my memory. There was a black hole in my head. A few of the lines on the monitor by the bed jumped. The doctor placed a hand on my shoulder.

"It's quite all right. Try not to tax yourself," she said. "Because you suffered blows to the head—and there had been quite a bit of swelling—you'll likely experience some memory problems for a while. Brain injuries aren't all the same, so I cannot tell you for certain what your journey to recovery will be like. For some, memories return in days, and for others it could take decades. My guess is retrograde amnesia."

I tried to repeat the phrase, but I got lost halfway through the words.

"It's not uncommon to suffer from confusion, to forget what you were doing, and to have problems focusing." The doctor folded her hands in front of her lap. "Essentially, you'll have a hard time remembering the event itself, at least for a while, and find it difficult to recall past memories. The lost time might encompass only the traumatic event itself, it could be a handful of years, or it could be a much longer chunk of time."

At the moment, I found it hard to remember anything at all.

"Would you like something to drink?" she asked.

"Yes, please," I croaked out.

Over the course of a week in the hospital, I remembered bits and pieces of my life. I remembered my name and address, but I couldn't recall a conversation I'd had an hour ago. Dr. Singh had to tell me about "retrograde amnesia" many more times over the week before it started to stick in my scrambled brain. A few other things she'd told me over the course of the week started to stick, too.

It had been early April when I'd been brought into the hospital, barely holding onto life, and now it was the middle of July. The hospital I was in was a teaching hospital, which had been responsible for saving my life as much as those teenagers dicking around in the alley who had found my body. The hospital had seen my battered body as a learning experience for medical students, and many discussions had been had beside my body over the last few months.

"Amnesia isn't like it is in the movies or on soap operas. Total memory loss is exceedingly rare," Dr. Singh said one morning during the start of week two. We slowly walked together down the hallway. Most of my wounds had healed up quite nicely after four months, but my muscles had gone soft. I tired easily. "Often what's affected the most are facts—names, dates, events—but you'll retain skills. You remembered how to walk, for example."

"Are there any medications for this? Surely there's something given to Alzheimer's or dementia patients." I could remember words like "Alzheimer's," yet couldn't remember what truly mattered. The event that put me here was still a mystery.

"Unfortunately not," Dr. Singh said. "Memory issues such as yours often resolve themselves on their own with time. There are a few things you can try. Foods such as whole grain cereals, nuts, beans, lentils, and lean pork could help. The brain is a muscle, just like the ones in your legs that you must strengthen again. Activities such as crossword puzzles are a way to build that muscle back up."

Crossword puzzles and lentils? What was I, eighty?

"Memories sometimes come back all at once," she added, as if she too could feel my dark mood hovering above us like a cloud. "Sometimes bits of things can be triggered. Smells, music, and photographs are often quite helpful."

I stopped in my tracks. Photographs. There was an itch at the back of my brain, but I couldn't scratch it. What was it about photographs that called to me?

Two weeks after I first awoke in the hospital, some of my physical strength returning, Dr. Singh discharged me. This wasn't because I was suddenly cured of my amnesia, but because I had overstayed my welcome. Now that I was no longer a medical marvel, I was seen as a drain on the hospital's coffers. The chunk of time missing spanned at least half a decade as far as my taxed mind had been able to discern. Dr. Singh believed I could benefit greatly from psychotherapy, but when it became clear that I was sure I didn't have medical insurance, my potential contributions to science no longer seemed to matter. Dr. Singh had the decency to be worried about me.

"Is there anyone you can call to pick you up?" she asked as I stood in the hospital lobby, back in my old clothes—which they'd laundered for me, at least—and she in her pristine white coat. A little line of worry pulled her dark brows together.

I didn't need a fully intact memory to know the answer to that. "No. I'll be fine. I remember where I live. The walk will do me some good. I'll call a cab if need be."

The worry line grew deeper. "Take care of yourself, hmm? Avoid stressful situations as much as you can. Be mindful of your diet, try to exercise—both your body and your mind. If your memory loss gets worse, or if you develop bad headaches, come back and see me."

Autopilot, instinct, the earth's magnetism—something led me back to The Water's Edge apartment complex. I wandered down the streets of uptown Albuquerque in the oppressive summer heat for what felt like hours before I arrived at the familiar complex, as if it had been luring me there like the northern star guiding home a lost sailor. The place was small—maybe ten units total—and was somehow both well-maintained and shabby.

I didn't have keys, so I stumbled into the tiny office of the complex. My skin felt slick and hot. The guy behind the counter quickly lowered his feet off his desk and stood abruptly, his mouth hanging open. My fuzzy memory told me this was the landlord, but I didn't have a clue what his name was. I clenched my jaw in frustration. He was a lanky guy with long hair pulled back in a low, greasy ponytail and he wore a dingy white shirt and dark green khakis. His brown beard was lightly sprinkled with gray and was patchy in places.

"Jesus, Anderson," he said, rounding the desk. "You look fucking terrible."

"I *feel* terrible."

"I … uhh … haven't seen you around much lately."

The silence that followed was long and strained, partly because my legs hurt so damn much, I thought my knees would give out. My head throbbed. Sweat soaked the back of my shirt.

"Look, Anderson, it's none of my business what you get into, but do you need a ride to the hospital or something?"

A laugh unexpectedly bubbled out of me, which quickly devolved into a coughing fit. I braced myself on the back of a chair with one hand, the other pressed to the stitch in my side. "Fuck. I just came from the hospital. I've been in a coma for almost four months because someone kicked the shit out of me."

"Jesus H," the guy said, arms crossed. "Ain't that some shit. The fuck you do to get beat that bad? Not gonna lie, you're a weird dude, but I wouldn't have thought you'd be weird enough for someone to do this to you. Was it a robbery or something?"

"Your guess is as good as mine," I said, wincing. "Do I … do I even still have a place to live anymore after being gone for this long?"

The landlord stared at me, his wide gaze roaming my face. "Man, they really did a number on you. Yeah, you got a place to live. You pay for this place in cash every six months."

"How long have I lived here?"

After some thought, he said, "Going on five years now."

Which confirmed that my black hole was at least half a decade wide.

"You're the best tenant I've got. You pay up front, don't ask for anything, never complain. I honestly didn't even notice you were gone. You're still paid up for the next two months. I hope you don't have a cat or something you needed someone to check on, 'cause that thing is dead for sure. No one has been around looking for you or anything. I thought it was business as usual."

I didn't know how I felt about any of this. "Could I get a set of keys? I lost everything."

"Yeah, of course." He walked across the room to what looked like a supply closet. He disappeared inside.

While I waited for him, I continued to breathe deep. I longed for the comfort of a bed I currently didn't remember.

Once the landlord had returned with a set of keys for apartment 8, I took them, thanked him, and made the trek across the small complex and up an excruciating flight of stairs. My legs knew the way even if my head didn't. The smell of the apartment, as musty and stuffy as it was, was so familiar, my head spun. I stumbled into my bedroom, peeled off my pants and shirt, collapsed face first on my unmade bed, and slept.

I slept on and off for a few days after I got home. Once I started to feel human again, I took stock of my apartment. It was a tiny one-bedroom, and my living room-slash-dining-room-slash-kitchen was littered with photography equipment. Photographs in sleek black frames covered one wall. As I stared at them, I knew instantly which ones had been mine and which had been my father's. He'd been a photographer too.

In his twenties, before he'd gotten married, he'd been a fisherman in Alaska. Half the photos on my wall were gorgeous shots of towering snow-capped mountains, massive chunks of ice floating in a vast expanse of sea, sweeping landscapes of green grass dotted with bright wildflowers of pink and purple. My father had been his best self when on a fishing boat, in the wild with a lungful of fresh, frigid air and with his trusty camera by his side.

He met my mother, they had me, and life had been good for a while. But then he'd gotten severely injured during a freak storm and had to give up his prized life. They moved away to the mainland, taking the doctor's orders that a warmer climate might do him some good. He wasn't the same after his accident, my mother said. Bitterness and resentment turned him into a raging alcoholic. In his rare sober moments, he taught me about photography. They were the best—only—good memories I had of him.

I reached up now and gently brushed my fingertips along the glass of a framed photograph of a moose, its wide fanned-out antlers backlit by the setting sun.

My photographs were never good enough for him, though. I dropped my hand as the memories of his insults slapped me across the face. He said I lacked discipline to go from a good photographer to a great one like him. I was worthless. A waste of space. I needed to make money to support the family and being a professional photographer clearly wasn't in the cards for me. I didn't have his talent. His drive.

He didn't know that I practiced all the time. I read everything I could about photography, determined to make a career of this art form I loved so much. *I* was a waste of space? I was the one out in the world practicing my craft while he was in a drunken stupor on the couch, exhausted from smacking my mother around for the hundredth time.

In high school, I flourished in my photography class. I was the photographer for the school newspaper. I had always been shy, but behind a camera, I could watch the girls on campus I was too scared to talk to without them thinking anything of it. Hardly anyone noticed me anyway. I don't know when I started snapping pictures of more private things—of students making out under bleachers, of staff member trysts behind buildings, of classmates in their bedrooms—but the thrill of not getting caught doing it was intoxicating.

Online, in some of the darkest corners of the internet, I found other photographers who liked what I liked—voyeur photography. After a while, I shared my work, too. They didn't insult me the way my father did. They praised my skill. Soon, people started to contact me to make specific requests, like catching a wife in the act of cheating on her husband. Private investigators did it, so why shouldn't I? When money had started filling my old ePassporte wallet, I knew how wrong my father had been.

I walked away from my wall of photographs, away from the memories of my father, and toward my desk. Business cards stacked on the surface told me I'd been a photographer in the more traditional sense, too. When I started that endeavor, I had no idea. It was lost in the black hole in my memory where facts apparently had gone to die. I'd photographed things like graduations, engagements, weddings, newborn babies. I thanked my past self when I spotted a Post-it note with a couple of passwords written on it beside my laptop. I logged into my email where messages had piled up in my inbox from people irate that I'd missed appointments and hadn't returned calls. Refunds were requested. Negative reviews were threatened.

When my heart rate spiked and a headache started low in the base of my skull, I walked away from my computer, too.

For several days, I split my time between getting items of importance back—a burner phone, a bank card, a driver's license. And I took the doc's advice—I stocked up on legumes, nuts, and lean pork. I did crossword puzzles, played music stored on my computer, and I willed the black curtain blocking me from the event of my beating and the years before it to drop and reveal my own past to me.

But after almost a month of being awake, I was no closer to remembering what my life had been before the assault in the alley. On a lazy afternoon while feeling sorry for myself, I scoured social media for old high school classmates since I couldn't remember if I had any friends currently. Matt Summers had worked for the school newspaper, too. Seeing his face reminded me of the photography forums where my online friends had resided. Those sites were ancient now, but surely I had found new ones, hadn't I?

It took an hour of poking around before muscle memory and three password attempts eventually guided me where I needed to go. The site's layout was so familiar, it was as if someone had wrapped a warm blanket around my shoulders. I recognized a handful of the usernames on recent posts. I had been here during the black hole years, I was sure of it.

After drafting a post about my ordeal, I hemmed and hawed, second-guessing myself—my old insecurities from high school returning. Of course it would be *those* memories that had been left untouched.

I submitted the post and immediately popped out of my chair, pacing in the small space. What if no one replied? What if someone only asked, "Who the hell are you?" I would be back at square one.

But I did get replies.

> Glad you're alive!
> I was worried about you.
> Thank god that asshole didn't snuff out the best in the biz!
> This place hasn't been the same.

I'd found my people.

Elated, I scanned the forum for hours, scrolling back as far as I could go, finding posts as old as five years ago. Memories didn't necessarily come flooding back, but the black curtain in my mind was full of holes now, pieces of my old life shining through. The work I'd done back in high school was work I still did now: I followed, tracked, and photographed people for a fee. And, most recently, a post from a little over four months ago had been from a guy with the handle "stratodigster" who said:

> I hear you're the guy to hire if I need to find someone. I'm des-
> perate. I need my girlfriend back.

It was *this* job that had resulted in my hospitalization. I just couldn't remember who the hell he was or who he'd had me follow. I added to our short thread, *I need to talk to you.*

As I waited for a reply, I made a second post, letting everyone know I was open to jobs again. I played the sympathy card and told them I was drowning in medical bills. I hadn't actually received a bill yet and hoped I never would. A few replies trickled in, but they were all along the lines of "That sucks, man. Good luck!"

Days went by with no new jobs, and no response from stratodigster.

My frustration mounted every day. I needed money. I needed my life and my memory back, but it was all just out of reach. I felt as if I were slowly going insane.

On the first of September, a month and a half after emerging from the coma, a bill from the hospital arrived in my mailbox. Unless my nonexistent health insurance company got involved, I owed the hospital over a hundred grand. My bank account wouldn't even cover two percent of that. How long could I go without paying it? Would I have to declare bankruptcy? A headache walloped me like a sledgehammer to the face.

I staggered back to my apartment and I lay on the floor for a while with a cold rag over my eyes, but my head wouldn't stop throbbing. My brain was on the verge of exploding in my skull. The doc told me to avoid stress, but she was the reason I was under stress in the first place! How could she have allowed me to be billed such a laughably high fee when I'd *told* her I didn't have insurance?

"If your memory loss gets worse, or if you develop bad headaches, come back and see me," she'd said, as if she cared.

My brain pulsed again.

I only had enough money to get me through the next two months. Bills and rent had been taken care of, but nothing else was.

By that evening, once the sun had set and my apartment was dark, my headache had faded back to a dull hum. There was still no response from the useless stratodigster.

However, there was a message from Anon9876: *You ever do more than take pictures?*

I told him to call me.

Minutes later, the screen of my burner lit up and a private number scrolled across it.

"Yeah," I said.

"If you need cash, the real money is in the girls, not pictures," a deep male voice said. "Ever snatch one before?"

I honestly had no idea if I had. "Sure."

"Well, I'm always in the market for ones that are in the eighteen-to-twenty-five range. I'm okay with a little younger, but no older," he said. "White girls. Brown or black hair. Small breasts."

"How much?"

"Eighteen grand for your first one."

My head started to throb again, but it wasn't as painful this time. That much money would give me time to breathe. To heal.

"I know you're hard up for cash, so if you send me proof of capture, I'll send you an advance," he said. "The Client monopolized you for years. If you're as good as you were back then, we can make a fuckload of money together."

The Client. Another hole tore open in the black curtain.

"I'm better."

"Proof is in the picture," he said. "Hit me up in the private chat when you have it." The call ended.

Who the hell was The Client?

My brain pulsed.

I'd figure that out later. For now, I had work to do. Finally. I'd start in Nob Hill. It was nearby and was full of college students. I was sure to find a young brunette there.

I donned all black, then grabbed a small notebook, my keys and phone, and headed for the door. I doubled back into my bedroom and rummaged around in a drawer until I found what I needed—a black bandana.

CHAPTER 9

Riley's stomach was in knots as Michael pulled up in front of his parents' house. It wasn't because she was nervous about meeting them—that had happened months ago. It had been awkward at first, but Michael's father, Jake, was somehow even goofier than Michael, which made it impossible to stay uncomfortable for very long. Riley had decided that day that it was a Roberts family trait to have the ability to make anyone on the planet feel welcome solely by being charmingly ridiculous.

She was nervous because the evening of the food challenge had arrived. It had been five days since she'd sent the film off to California, and last night her account page had been updated with a "Congratulations! Your prints are on their way!" Normally something like that would have occupied all of her available brain space. But today, she'd been too worried about the food challenge to think about anything else.

A few times a year, and on most major holidays, the Roberts siblings partook in a food challenge. The winner got to choose an activity the other sibling had to participate in. When Michael had lost the Ghost Pepper Challenge, the result was that he had to go on a ghost-hunting investigation weekend—where he and Riley had met.

This challenge, however, had been chosen and organized by the Roberts parents. Now, Riley and Carla, Michael's sister's wife, were also playing. Riley's participation had been presented by Michael as a mere suggestion, but she got the impression that saying no was akin to slapping Michael's parents across the face with a pair of dueling gloves.

"I don't understand how it's fair that your parents are torturing us and yet *they* get to decide who wins," Riley said, staring out at the house from where they were parked at the curb. "Shouldn't they have to eat whatever this horror is, too?"

"My dad said that since they're footing the bill for the vacation, they should be able to inflict pain," Michael said. "When I was talking to my mom last night, we were in the middle of a conversation when she started giggling out of nowhere and said, 'Oh, I just thought of another one, Jake! Get the keys!' and then she hung up on me."

Riley frowned at him. "And we don't know what the nature of this challenge is?"

"Don't have the foggiest clue. Donna tried to sneak into my dad's office the other day to see if she could find a list or something since Dad writes everything down. The door was locked. He never locks his office."

"If I had known when I started dating you that participation in this madness came with the territory, I—"

He leaned over the center console and cut her sentence off with a kiss that made her head spin. "You what?" he asked, face still only an inch from hers.

She smiled, her eyes still closed. "Yeah, yeah."

"Don't worry, babe," he said, opening his car door. "I packed barf bags."

Ugh.

Riley followed Michael up the front walk to the tidy one-story house. There was a tall stone goose that sat on the porch. Michael's mom, Nancy, dressed the goose up based on the holiday. When Riley had first come to the house, the goose had been wearing a red, white, and blue top hat for the fourth of July. Today he wore a bib with a smiling taco on it, its stick arms raised in mid-cheer. "Let's Taco 'Bout It!" was written below it.

The door swung open just before Michael reached it and Donna appeared there, wide-eyed. "I'm a nervous wreck."

Riley poked her head around Michael's back. "Do you have intel?"

"None!" Donna quickly hugged Michael, and then Riley, ushering them in.

Riley and Michael deposited their things on a bench seat by the front door. Riley grabbed her phone out of her jacket pocket and slipped it into the back of her jeans, just in case she needed to call an ambulance. Jade had requested—begged, really—that Riley record every second of this challenge. Riley had downright refused, but when she followed the Roberts siblings into the dining room, she saw that a camcorder on a tripod had already been set up at the far end of the table. Riley would do everything in her power to make sure that footage never left this house nor ended up on the internet.

The kitchen was connected to the dining room by an open doorway directly behind the strategically placed camera. Carla came hurrying out at the sound of voices, glancing over her shoulder every few seconds as if she were being pursued by a wild animal.

"Oh, thank god," Carla said, pulling Riley into a hug. Holding her by the shoulders she said, "Since neither one of us is a Roberts by blood, I don't understand why we're being subjected to this."

"That's what I said!" Riley hissed back. "If we say we'll pay for our own tickets, can we get out of it?"

Carla unhanded her and crossed her arms, shaking her head. "Nope. I tried that."

"Dammit. Did *you* get any information while you were in there?"

"Negative," Carla said. "There are a bunch of small metal containers in the fridge with foil lids so you can't see into them. Jake was in the bathroom and Nancy and Donna were outside talking, so I tried to get a sneak peek. Jake appeared out of nowhere and said, 'Out of there, you!' right behind me and I screamed so loud, Donna and Nancy came running in here, sure I was being attacked."

"Serves you right!"

Riley and Carla yelped, and spun around to find Jake Roberts standing behind them. His office was on the other side of the small foyer, so Riley guessed he'd come from there. He had his fists on his hips, doing his best to look menacing. He was as ferocious as a puppy that had just gotten caught in a rainstorm. He had two small envelopes in one hand.

"Hi, Jake," Riley managed when her heart rate slowed.

"Hey, Ry," he said, pulling her into one of his too-tight hugs. "I'm really glad you could join us," he said in her ear with such sincerity, she knew it would be impossible to back out of this now. This was a tradition and the Roberts family wanted her to be a part of it, despite the newness of Riley and Michael's relationship.

"We got this, babe," Michael said, grabbing Riley's hand and giving it a squeeze.

Nancy joined them, and after another round of greetings, the Roberts parents told the four of them to take a seat. Michael guided Riley to the table.

"For this challenge," Nancy said, "Riley and Donna are on a team, and Michael and Carla are on the other."

Michael immediately dropped Riley's hand, took several steps back and said, "You're going down."

"How quickly your alliance changes!" Riley said.

"He's the literal worst," Donna said, laughing. "I got you, girl. We're going to destroy them."

Carla and Michael were seated across from Riley and Donna. It struck Riley in that moment how deeply unfair it was that the woman in the yellow dress would never get to experience things like this. How Brynn and Shawna's ability to spend time with family and friends, to participate in something fun and silly, had been taken from them.

"Ry?"

Riley looked across the table at Michael, his brows pulled together.

"Are you okay?" he asked.

Nancy, who had been standing beside her, bent forward, hands on her knees so she could examine Riley's face. "We haven't overwhelmed you, have we? We can get a little carried away."

Riley shook her head. While she was here, she would try to live in the moment, and not in the past. "I'm okay. Honest. I'm ready."

"Okay then," Jake said from the head of the table beside the camera. He clapped once and rubbed his hands together. "Nancy has an envelope for both teams."

Once Riley and Donna got their envelope, Donna tore it open and the two of them huddled together to see what they were dealing with. Inside was a card about the size of two standard business cards. The top had the words TEAM NANCY written on it, and below that were two columns with four boxes each. The boxes were numbered 1 through 8.

"As much as this is a competition between the two teams, it's also a competition between me and Nancy," Jake said. "Whichever team guesses the most mystery foods wins, and then that team also gets to weigh in on the family vacation. Nancy and I will ultimately choose the destination, but the food challengers will get to choose one out-of-the-box excursion. I personally am terrified of heights, but if we end up in Costa Rica and Nancy's team wins, I could be forced to go zip-lining, for example."

"Ooh," Michael said from across the table. "If we're going somewhere tropical, sister dear, your ass will be going swimming with dolphins."

Donna shuddered violently beside Riley.

"She was bitten by a dolphin at SeaWorld when she was a kid," Carla told Riley.

"Demon fish," Donna whispered softly to herself.

Riley suppressed a laugh.

"Four of the foods were chosen by yours truly," Jake said, "while the others were chosen by Nancy. They're all awful either in taste, smell, texture, or, if you're lucky, all three. There are no palate cleansers between rounds, so each subsequent horrible food will get harder and harder to identify, as it will be mixing with the terrible food before it."

Carla and Riley shared a look of horror across the table, while Donna and Michael had resorted to playful name calling.

"I hope they *all* have mustard in them," Donna said to Michael.

Michael narrowed his eyes. "Maybe you'll get something with a nice big dollop of tapenade on it."

Donna pressed a hand to her mouth.

Theatrically, Jake said, "Nancy, my love! Bring out the blindfolds!"

The blindfolds turned out to be four puffy sleep masks, each with half-moons stitched onto the black fabric with white thread, along with a wide fan of pink curly lashes to resemble closed eyes. Nancy affixed Donna's first, then moved behind Riley. Riley shot a death glare at Michael, who merely laughed and blew her a kiss.

"We will bring out the foods one at a time," Jake said. "You will be given thirty seconds to taste the selected food. Once it has been removed, you may take off your blindfold and consult with your team member so you can write down your guess. Once a guess is made, you cannot change it."

Something was slid onto the table on the other end, closer to Jake. Perhaps the foil trays Carla had seen in the fridge earlier.

"Ready?" Jake asked.

"No!" Riley and Carla said in unison.

"Bring it," said Donna.

"Your defeat will be swift and merciless, Team Nancy," Michael said.

Jake said, "I love you to the moon and back, Nance, but I hope your team is running for a toilet by round two."

"Likewise," Nancy said.

Riley listened to the crinkle of what was most assuredly foil. Nancy walked across the dining room and placed something in front of her and Donna, and then in front of Michael and Carla.

Standing at the head of the table to Riley's right, Nancy said, "When I say go, grab the cup in front of you and do what you must to figure out what it is. You have thirty seconds. Your time starts … now. Go!"

Riley fumbled for her little plastic cup. She brought it to her nose to give it a sniff. She cocked her head, though, when whatever was inside rattled. Sticking a finger inside the cup, she found several small hard objects, quickly determining they were jelly beans. She loved jelly beans! She popped two in her mouth, assuming it would be hard to guess the difference between, say, strawberry or cherry, but maybe her heightened senses from having her eyes covered would allow her to—

"Oh my god …" she groaned, and in a very ladylike fashion, quickly spit the chewed-up jelly beans back into the cup. She gagged.

Over the sound of Nancy and Jake's laughter, she could hear Carla cursing the Roberts family name, while Michael said something along the lines of "Who would do this to candy?"

Knowing time was limited, Riley worked her tongue around her teeth, trying to find little bits of the horrible "candy." She got definite notes of something seafood-like. She gagged again. She jumped when an egg timer went off.

"That's time. Leave your blindfolds on while I collect the cups." A minute later, Nancy said, "You may remove the blindfold and consult with your teammate."

Riley pulled up the sleep mask, resting it on her forehead. A pen had materialized beside their card, and she picked up both. Using the card to shield her mouth, she sat back in her chair. Donna did the same. Michael and Carla across the table had turned their chairs slightly to help better discuss the food's identity without being overheard.

"I was thinking something like oyster or sardine," Donna whispered.

"Me too," said Riley. "I'm leaning toward sardine. There's something fishy about it."

"I already hate jelly beans. Now I hate them even more," Donna said. "That one was probably from my dad. He's a despicable man."

"Ten seconds left to write down your answers," Nancy called out.

"So 'sardine jelly bean' is our answer?" Riley asked.

"Yep."

While Riley did her best to write down their answer without the other team seeing, Donna distracted them with more of her creative insults. Michael lobbed them back with ease.

Riley flipped over the card when she was done, then offered Michael a smug little smile.

"Don't try to seduce me here in my parents' house, Ms. Thomas," Michael said. "That's tacky and won't work."

She laughed and rolled her eyes. The jelly bean was gross, but if that's what the Roberts parents thought was a challenge, Riley was confident Team Nancy had this thing in the bag.

"Masks back over your eyes!" Nancy demanded.

Riley had been very wrong.

The next offerings, to the best of Riley's and Donna's guesses, were caviar; quinoa and dill relish; a peanut butter and onion sandwich; a hot dog topped with raspberry jelly; hummus, though the flavor of it was a mystery neither one could settle on other than "disgusting"; and popcorn coated with ketchup as well as something that tasted like sour cream.

"One more," Carla said from across the table, letting out a slow breath as if she'd just run several miles before flinging herself into her chair. Riley's stomach had started churning after the peanut butter and onion sandwich. When Jake had first said that they wouldn't be allowed palate cleansers like water or crackers, Riley hadn't thought much of it. Now, each offering was compounded by whatever last awful thing they'd consumed. By the fourth one, they'd all started laughing, mildly delirious, the moment they tried a new concoction.

"I don't know how much more of this I can take," Donna said.

"You giving up? The dolphins will be happy to see you," Michael said.

"Don't try your reverse psychology on me, Mikey," Donna said. "You know Ry and I are going to smoke you and you'll be forced to take a Segway tour."

Michael grunted.

"All right, everyone. If you're done bellyaching—ha ha—here is the last one," Nancy said.

One whiff of this one told her it was going to be a doozy. She dipped a finger into the cup and found it both spongy and squishy. She hooked a finger into the mess and popped it into her mouth, trying to pretend it was a delightful scoop of perfectly normal frosting. Her stomach almost instantly lurched as a series of flavors that had no business being together exploded in her mouth. The spongy texture of a cupcake or a Twinkie. The sickly sweet softness of cream. Definitely a Twinkie. And then the unmistakable pungent taste of mustard. The tastes all collided at once then and nearly took her to her knees. And to make matters even worse, it was Dijon mustard, which always had a very distinct tinge of sweaty feet.

A moment later, she realized Michael's worst nightmare had come true. Both his parents clearly knew Michael's abhorrence of mustard. Riley wondered which one had come up with this horror. Saving it for last was particularly cruel. They'd lured him into a false sense of security. The Twinkie covered in Dijon mustard would have been a war her taste buds would have lost anyway, but with the residue of seven other devilish concoctions still residing in her mouth, this last one was especially heinous. Riley's stomach lurched again. It was such a shockingly horrible experience that she threw her head back and cackled, and then was caught in a vicious cycle of laughing, gagging, and trying to wipe at her eyes while they were still covered with the sleep mask.

"I feel like this one is my fault!" Donna said, coughing. "I jinxed us. Oh hell, this is … so … "

"Noooooo!" Michael said. "Oh my god … why … oh no … " This was followed by gagging so dramatic, it sounded as if a cat were trying to dislodge a hairball. "Why … ohh sweet Jesus. If I weren't already an adult, I would file for emancipation!" Another dramatic heave.

Now Donna was cackling too, doing so with such intensity that the vibration of it shook Riley's chair.

"The combination … it's so … " Carla coughed hard, then sneezed. She let out an involuntarily little scream. "Oh my god."

Riley had her forehead on the table and was laughing so hard she was practically crying. She needed to spit the foul thing out, but she couldn't stop laughing long enough to do it.

"I can't!" Michael shouted, followed by a chair being pushed back along the hardwood floor.

Riley lifted her head enough to pull up her mask, and watched as Michael, hand to his mouth, went sprinting into the kitchen. Jake was bent over at the waist, laughing so hard he could hardly stand up. Nancy rested against a wall, hand to her chest as she cackled and wiped at her eyes.

Donna and Carla pulled off their blindfolds, too, and the three of them spit the food into their cups, no longer caring about things like decency. All five of them had just started to get themselves under control when another wave of dying-cat gagging sounded from the kitchen.

"I can feel it in my eyes!" Michael called out, which sent everyone into hysterics again.

Riley got up to hurry past Michael's sister and parents to find him at the counter, his arms resting on the lip of the sink and his forehead on his arms. He dry-heaved every few seconds. She tried to tamp down her laugh, and placed a hand on his very sweaty back. "You okay?"

He groaned in response. "I threw up a little."

After letting out a very undignified snort, she poked around in the cabinets until she found a glass, then filled it with water from the dispenser in the fridge door. After downing half of it herself, she refilled it and returned to him.

"Here, drink this," she said.

Pushing himself to a standing position, he turned around and rested his backside against the counter and took the water. He chugged down half of it, then stopped and pressed his free hand to his mouth. "That unmoored some of the Dijon mustard seeds hiding behind my teeth and now…" He coughed. "Oh, it's truly awful."

Riley's stomach rumbled a little. "You had to know one of them was going to use mustard against you."

"I didn't think they'd actually do it." Michael swigged some water, sloshed it around, and then spit into the sink. He shuddered. "I thought I was their favorite. Clearly, I was wrong."

Riley stood in front of him and wrapped her arms around his waist. "Vacation decisions are serious business. You'll appreciate the mustard once you're lounging on a beach somewhere."

The sound of tinny voices floated in from the living room, followed by a soft "Noooooo!" Another wave of laughter went up and Riley figured Jake was playing a recording of Michael's mustard-induced meltdown for Donna and Carla. A small smile graced Michael's face at the sound of it, even if she could hear his stomach grumbling in protest.

After a moment, he said, "Thanks for doing this. My dad was really happy you agreed to play. They both love you," he said softly. He stared at her for a beat, then brushed an errant curl out of her face before cupping her cheek and gently rubbing a thumb back and forth across her skin. "So do I. Love you, I mean."

Riley eyebrows hiked up. "Yeah?"

"Yeah."

She flushed. "Me too. Love you, I mean."

He grinned, then bent down to kiss her. It was sweet and tender—and ended *very* quickly. "I know we just said 'I love you' for the first time, and not to kill the mood or anything, but babe, your mouth tastes like a sewer."

She gave a shudder. "So does yours."

Carla poked her head into the kitchen. "C'mon, lovebirds. We gotta tally up the scores."

Riley let him go and took several steps back. "This defeat will be so horrific, it'll haunt your nightmares. Which is saying a lot, coming from me."

"Harsh!" he said, following her with a goofy smile on his face. "I'm a lucky guy."

CHAPTER 10

Just as Riley was heading into work the next day, her stomach still a little off from yesterday's food challenge of doom, Nina texted her that the investigation at Julie's was a go for the following evening at 11 PM. Her waitress hours meant she could finish a shift at The Laughing Tiger at 10, hurry home to shower, and still make it to Julie's in time.

The night of the investigation, Riley arrived first, so she parked in front of the house across the street and waited. She knew one other person was attending tonight, but Nina hadn't disclosed who. Riley wouldn't have minded seeing one of the guys from the Southwest Ghost Investigators again, and she was in the middle of trying to remember the names of the two younger guys who worked with Xavier and Nina when a woman pulled up in front of Julie's house. Nina arrived shortly after.

Riley only loitered in her car like a creeper for a few seconds this time, rather than minutes, and then joined the pair standing on the sidewalk.

While Nina was in her mid-forties, the new member of their trio was closer to early thirties. She reminded Riley of a pinup girl, with short curly brown hair, high-waisted black slacks, and a white shirt tucked into them. When she wasn't on ghost-hunting expeditions, Riley guessed, she was a fan of vintage dresses, red lipstick, and couture shoes.

"Hi, Riley," Nina said. "Riley, this is Olivia. Olivia, this is the clairvoyant I was telling you about."

Olivia smiled warmly at Riley and held out a hand to her. "Nice to meet you."

Riley shook it. "Nice to meet you, too."

"So, what kind of information do we have?" Olivia asked. "Do we know the spirit's name?"

Nina said, "I asked Julie about her tonight when I was confirming times with her. She never met the previous owners when she was going through the process of buying the house, and the realtor never disclosed any information. All Julie has are a couple of possible names based on the mail she sometimes gets here. She said she left a few of the letters on the kitchen counter. Iris Velasco and Amy Velasco. Mother and daughter, sisters … we don't know."

Olivia nodded.

"So, as usual," Nina said, addressing Olivia, "I would rather not give you too much information about the haunting itself before you go in. Riley, if you can keep what you saw last time to yourself until later, that would be appreciated."

"No problem," Riley said.

"Olivia, I would like for you to go in first and do your usual sweep of the place. See what you pick up on, then Riley and I will join you afterward with the equipment."

"Cool," Olivia said. "See you in there."

Riley watched her walk up the front path and then let herself in through the unlocked door. There was only one light on inside downstairs. Riley watched the shadow of Olivia move to the left and out of sight. Hopefully none of Julie's neighbors thought Riley and company were a trio of house burglars.

Though the silence that descended on Nina and Riley hadn't lasted long, Riley felt compelled to break it. "How do you know Olivia?"

"We met at a psychic expo a few years ago. It was in Ohio and we clicked in part because we're both from Albuquerque."

Riley nodded absently at that, wondering what in the world a "psychic expo" was like.

"She's seen quite a few apparitions in her day, but she's primarily clairaudient and a clairsentient. She hears voices and senses feelings," Nina said, answering a question Riley hadn't asked. "Picking up on emotions is at the heart of her ability."

Riley always thought of mediums as being able to *see* ghosts, but Nina was proof enough that one could be highly sensitive and hardly ever set eyes on a spirit. "Which clair are you?"

"Clairaudient and claircognizant. For you, spirits appear visually with little warning. For me, it's almost always thoughts that pop in my head. I don't need a doorbell because before someone even pulls up in front of my house, a voice will say 'Someone is here.' I might not know which someone it is, but I usually have a warning. Many psychics have some combination of the four clairs, but often one or two clairs are more dominant than others, like your predominant one being clairvoyance. But after what happened at the séance, when you sensed Megan's pregnancy, and the anger you say you felt from the ghost at the grocery store, you clearly are clairsentient, too. Strong intuition. Hopefully coming with me on assignments like this will help hone your intuition even more and get you to trust it."

She could practically hear Jade cheering in her head.

"Let's start getting ready," Nina said.

From Nina's trunk, they unloaded a lot of the same equipment Riley had used on the investigation at the ranch: tape recorders for EVPs, four camcorders and tripods, as well as electromagnetic field readers. What was new was a box of blue plastic cylinders. There were nine in the box Riley took out of the trunk. They looked like rows of neatly arranged Russian dolls.

"What are these?" she asked.

"Motion sensor lights," Nina said. "I keep trying things out. If a spirit passes by one of these, sometimes it'll trigger the light to come on. It all depends on the spirit and how strong their energy is. I figured since this one showed herself to you, there was a good chance she'd do it again."

They had just walked up to the porch with all of their materials when the door opened and Olivia poked her head out.

"I just finished up. This should be interesting. This one is … feisty."

Riley had a brief flashback to the Poltergeist of Aisle 3 and hoped the woman inside hadn't grown increasingly pissed since the last time she'd been here.

"Oh, don't worry, Riley," Olivia said. "She's not malevolent. She's desperate to tell us *something*, though."

She cocked a brow at Olivia. Maybe this was what Detective Howard felt around her, always worried she was reading his mind. Riley reminded herself that Nina had said Olivia was a clairsentient and could pick up on feelings—which clearly applied to the living as well as the dead.

"Can you grab the tripods? There are still two more propped up by the car," Nina said.

"Sure thing." Olivia made her way across the front walk while Nina and Riley headed into the house.

The inside was dark save for a couple of nightlights plugged into sockets near the baseboards in the living room. Riley wondered if Julie's whole family was at the grandparents' house two doors down, or if they'd sprung for a hotel for the night.

Riley followed Nina into the dining room, where they placed the equipment on the table. Olivia joined them with the tripods. Without a word, she grabbed several of the motion sensor lights out of the box and wandered off to place them in strategic locations around the house.

"Even though the owners say the majority of the activity happens upstairs," Nina said, focused on checking the battery packs on the camcorders, "we'll set up two cameras down here. One to record the kitchen, and the other facing the base of the stairs."

Once the cameras were primed and recording downstairs, they took the rest of the equipment to the second floor. Riley held her breath during the ascent, half-expecting the woman to do another demonstration of her fall down the staircase while Nina and Riley were on it. But the house remained still, the only sound on the top floor coming from Olivia in the master bedroom, and the faint shuffling of her movements as she laid out a few more motion sensor lights.

Another camera was set up in the middle of the hallway where Riley had been sitting last time, recording both the top of the stairs and the doorway of the master bedroom. The last camera was set up between the master bedroom and the office, so that if the woman decided to lift and drop the credenza directly opposite the camera, they might catch it on film.

They reconvened at the top of the stairs when they were done. Nina gave each of them tape recorders, while she pocketed an EMF recorder. "For the first hour or so, I just want to get a feel for the place. Move around if you want to. Follow any sensations you have. Investigations are often frankly boring, Riley. It's also common for nothing to happen the first time we show up with equipment, or even the first dozen times."

Olivia laughed softly. "Remember Thatcher's place?"

Nina groaned good-naturedly. "The client was convinced his house was 'teeming' with ghosts. Our initial evaluation told us the place wasn't remotely haunted, but Thatcher didn't believe us. Over the course of a month, we spent I think sixteen nights there, usually in five-to-six-hour blocks. Found absolutely nothing."

"We made bank on that one, though," Olivia said. "Not our fault he didn't believe us."

"True enough. Thatcher helped me pay off my car."

For the next hour, they rotated who hung out in which rooms. Riley spent a good chunk of time in the hallway in the same location she'd been before, sitting beside one of the tripods, waiting to see if the woman made a repeat performance. She asked questions while standing near the credenza, the tape recorder held out and recording the ambient noise of the house.

By hour three, Riley was bored out of her skull, which she supposed was better than being terrified. She lay flat on her back on the floor of the master bedroom, near the end of the four-poster bed. The doorway to the bathroom was a few feet away, and her tape recorder lay on her chest but wasn't on. Riley saw it rise and fall in her peripheral vision, her head turned toward the window on the right side of the room. All she could see outside was the top of a leafy tree, and a too-bright street light behind it doing its best to shine through the spaces in the branches.

Her mind wandered to the package on its way back to her from California. It was bizarre to think that not long before she was born, dropping a film cartridge off at a one-hour kiosk in a big box store would have been the norm. Someone could drop the film off, go about their shopping, and pick up their pictures on the way out the door.

Though it was even stranger to think that the cell phone—a pocket-sized camera—hadn't been a reality back then. Now, dozens of pictures could be taken instantly; needing to wait an hour to see them seemed like an eternity.

Much like the time spent in this boring house.

She rolled her head back to the neutral position so she could stare at the ceiling. It felt like she'd spent *three* eternities in this house. How in the world had Nina and Olivia done this for sixteen nights, especially when they'd known it wasn't haunted? Maybe they'd played a lot of card games. How she longed for a game of solitaire! She didn't even like solitaire.

A bright light flashed on in the bathroom and Riley sat bolt upright.

Something had triggered the motion sensor light.

She turned toward the open doorway of the master bedroom, thinking one of the other ladies had wandered in, but the space was deserted. The faint hush of a voice told Riley that the ladies were either talking to each other, or one of them was attempting to get more EVPs.

The light in the bathroom turned off and her gaze swiveled back to the bathroom's doorway. She couldn't see anyone. In the midst of convincing herself that a towel or flap of toilet paper had triggered the sensor, she heard a soft scrabbling sound. Remembering what Nina had told her about shutting down one sense to enhance another, she closed her eyes and listened.

The scrabbling shifted to the gentle rustle of paper, then the crinkle of plastic. A drawer slid on its runner and then slammed closed. Riley's eyes popped open and she quickly got to her feet. Swallowing, she cast another quick glance at the open doorway of the master bedroom, saw neither of the other women, and then inched toward the en suite bathroom.

Just as she reached it, the motion sensor was triggered again, by her this time, filling the space with light. It revealed that the bathroom was empty; no one was crouched low in the tub or standing in the glass-walled shower. All the drawers were closed. Nothing was out of order. The motion sensor on the bathroom counter had nothing immediate in its path that could have set it off earlier. She was bent over the sink, checking the area around the sensor's sides and base when the sense that someone was behind her made her whirl around.

The woman from the stairs stood in the bathroom with her now, but she didn't seem to notice Riley. She held her tape recorder out, ready to ask, *Are you Iris or Amy?* Riley lightly cleared her throat, so as to not startle the woman. No reaction. Heart hammering, Riley waved a hand near her as if she too were a motion sensor she could trigger to react to her presence. The woman only had eyes for the medicine cabinet above one of the two bowl sinks. Riley slipped the recorder into her pocket; it wouldn't be of much use if the ghost wasn't a talker.

Riley took a few steps back, moving farther into the bathroom to give the woman some room. Instead of screaming bloody murder and bolting for the safety of the living with Nina and Olivia, Riley forced her shoulders to relax and her breathing to slow.

Trust your instincts.

As the ghost woman hobbled for the medicine cabinet, Riley studied her. She wore the same outfit she'd been wearing before taking that tumble down the stairs—a T-shirt, jeans, and bathrobe. Her black hair was up in that same messy ponytail, and scrapes marred her arms in a few places, as well as her cheek. The woman stopped at the counter, and though she reached for the medicine cabinet, she was caught off guard by her own reflection. She touched her cheek gently with two fingers, then her swollen lip. Pulling her lips back from her teeth, she was taken even more off guard when she noted that one of her front teeth was cracked. She whimpered and tenderly touched a pointer finger to the jagged edge.

"I gotta go, lady!" a male voice suddenly called out.

The ghost woman turned and walked unsteadily toward the doorway of the master bedroom, a bit like a newborn deer. Riley followed her but froze when a young man appeared there. She reminded herself that he wasn't actually here; Nina and Olivia would have reacted if someone else had entered the house at two in the morning. Riley made herself study this person, too. The guy was eighteen or so, but had one of those youthful faces, where he could have just as easily been fifteen on one end of the spectrum, or twenty-five on the other.

"My ride is here." The young man's dark brows bunched as he took in the woman's appearance. Frowning, he said, "Are you sure you're okay?"

"Yes, thank you. I really appreciate your help."

"No problem," he said, but his words lacked conviction. He wore a backpack and held a skateboard by his side. "I think if you get really dizzy or something, you should go to the hospital. Aren't you not supposed to sleep if you have a concussion?" He shifted, holding the skateboard in front of him now with both hands, the rows of wheels flush with his forearms.

She lightly waved him away. "I don't think I have a concussion. I'll be okay."

"Seems like you fell pretty hard," he said, weight switching from foot to foot. "Is the headache still bad? I could get you some more pills—"

Another dismissive wave of her hand. "Three did the trick. I'm feeling much better."

His mouth bunched up on one side. "Well, okay. Promise you'll go to the doctor if it gets worse, yeah?"

"I will. Thank you," she said. "You're a good kid."

He ducked his head. "Thanks. Take care."

"You too."

The thud of his footsteps down the stairs was quickly followed by the slam of a door. Riley and the woman both jumped at the sound. The woman turned toward the bathroom but must have moved too quickly, because she listed to the side and collided with one of the posters of her bed. She grabbed and held on, her arms wrapped around it as if it were a mast of a ship that was capsizing beneath her. Once the wave of vertigo seemed to have passed, she moved into the bathroom again. Riley watched from the doorway as the woman went about washing her face, touching up the cuts on her cheek and arms, and putting an ointment on her split lip. The longer she watched the woman, the more spacey the woman became, as if she'd forgotten what she'd been doing in the middle of the act. She walked out into the bedroom twice, stopped halfway toward the master bedroom door, and then returned to the bathroom to repeat things she'd already done. She brushed her teeth three separate times in what must have spanned fifteen minutes.

After the third brushing, the woman's behavior grew even more erratic, her breathing became shallow, and she scratched absently at her arm. Small red welts had sprung up on her arms.

"Oh god," she muttered, hand to her temple. "Oh god. He gave me the wrong ones. Oh … *shit.*"

She stumbled for the bedroom, staggered across the space, and accidentally bumped her shoulder into the doorway that led out into the hall. The jolt gave her the spins, and she grabbed hold of her head as she waited for the world to right itself. Another stumble. She groped at the wall.

Riley recognized the scene now and called out, "She's heading for the stairs!" Though she was startled to hear her own voice after all this time in silence, the sound didn't affect the stumbling woman.

By the time Nina and Olivia had joined her, the spirit was swaying atop the staircase. When her foot slipped out from underneath her, Riley turned her back to the scene, not needing to witness it again. Hearing the horrible crash of her body tumbling downstairs, colliding with the wall, railing, and the hard, unforgiving edges of the steps was bad enough.

"Oh, damn," Olivia muttered behind her. "God, she felt so … sick when she fell. Her arms and face itched. Her stomach was a mess. She was so … confused. Even before she fell."

Riley turned then, relieved that the body at the bottom of the steps had vanished. The haunting was residual in a lot of ways, where the spirit appeared unaware that she was reliving her death on a loop, while also unaware that Riley, Nina, and Olivia witnessed it. Yet, she had looked toward Riley the last time she was here, and she'd lifted and dropped that credenza to get her attention before the fall. She'd wanted Riley to see it, and now she wanted Riley to see what had led up to it.

Olivia leaned against the banister, a hand pressed to her stomach.

Nina approached her, hand out. "You okay?"

Olivia waved her away, much like the woman had dismissed the young man, preventing Nina from touching her. "Just…give me a minute. I feel like I'm going to throw up."

When Olivia had righted herself, hands on hips and taking in large pulls of air that she slowly let out through her mouth, Riley asked, "Did either of you see her?"

"Nope," Olivia said.

"Tell us what you saw," Nina said.

Riley recounted the scene she'd been shown. "I can't be sure, but—"

"Trust your instincts," Nina said.

"Okay…so the young kid who was here…he mentioned a fall, which obviously happened *before* this one." Riley pointed at the stairs. "I think she fell—outside, I'm guessing—and this kid saw it. He helped her inside and got her some pills for her headache. Based on what Olivia said about how she was feeling, I'm wondering if she had an allergic reaction to the meds the kid brought her?"

"That would make sense," Olivia said. "I know you said she had scrapes on her arms and face, but the itchiness I felt was…everywhere. Like *all* of my skin itched. It reminded me of the time I fell in poison ivy as a kid. That feeling I got from her definitely jibes with an allergic reaction."

Nina said, "But we still don't know why she's haunting this house every night. Why keep showing us her fall down the stairs? This is clearly an intelligent haunting even if it has elements of a residual one."

Riley had no idea. "Do we know yet if she's Iris or Amy?"

"No," Nina said. "We might have gotten a name confirmation on the tapes."

After another half hour of EVP sessions, they called it a night. The woman made no further appearances no matter what was asked or who asked the questions, even though they were now armed with new information. Julie had agreed not to return to the house until late morning, so Nina would leave the cameras running overnight to see if anything further was caught once the house was empty of living occupants.

The motion sensor lights were left where they were; Nina would box them up in the morning. Riley and Olivia handed over their tape recorders. Nina's task tomorrow was to sift through the hours of recordings in search of ghostly replies from one of the Velasco women.

After they locked up the house, Olivia wished them a good night and headed for her own car.

"I know you have a tendency to go into internet wormholes when you have a piece of information," Nina told Riley as they stood beside her car. "If you want to try searching for Iris and Amy online, I'm fine with that. I wanted your first session here to be as organic as possible, uninfluenced by outside information. But now that you've been here, go for it. Research can be a big part of this job, too."

Riley had to admit that part of it did appeal to her. "Thanks for letting me tag along," she said as she headed across the street.

"Of course. Have a good night … what's left of it."

Riley sat in her car, staring up at Julie's house for a long time even after Olivia and Nina had driven away. Nothing shifted the curtains on the upstairs windows, no lights flickered on inside. The house was still.

She grabbed her phone, swiping away text messages from her friends, parents, and Michael, all asking how the ghost hunt went, and instead pulled up a search engine. Twenty minutes of searches eventually revealed what she'd been looking for: a social media page for Amy Velasco. Dozens of people had posted their condolences on her wall about the death of her mother on the 15th of March last year. It had been almost exactly a year and a half since the day of Iris's death.

One of the posts was an article about dealing with the death of a parent due to suicide. It was the only post Amy had replied to. *I know you mean well*, the message said, *but my mom didn't kill herself.*

Riley glanced back up at the house, squinting as her eyes adjusted to darkness after staring at the bright screen of her phone for so long. It seemed bizarre that a fall down the stairs had been labeled a suicide, as that seemed like such a hard thing to prove. Lethal accidents happened in people's own houses—what had made the medical examiner determine suicide?

"*She's desperate to tell us* something, *though*," Olivia had said.

Of all the things Iris could have shown them, she repeatedly shared her fall down the stairs. From what Iris had shown Riley, she'd suffered from a concussion somehow, the young man had helped her inside, and had then fetched pills for her to lessen the pain of her headache. In her confusion, Iris possibly hadn't warned him which meds she was allergic to, or he hadn't understood Iris's instructions—either way, he'd given her "the wrong ones." The allergic reaction caused even more confusion, which led to a second fall down the stairs, which was what had killed her.

Clearly, from the posts on Amy's wall, the reported cause of death was suicide. Rumor had even reached Julie by way of a neighbor. Iris wanted them to know it wasn't true.

Putting her phone back in her purse, Riley finally started the drive home. She had cold-called someone with information from the other side before, but it had been nerve-wracking. Grief was a sticky landscape to wade through anyway, but when adding a psychic medium element to it, things got even stickier. She was glad in that moment that this was ultimately Nina's job; Riley was just along for the ride. She'd share her findings with Nina in the morning.

Riley crawled into bed that night, comforted that a spirit had conveyed a message and she'd understood it. Maybe she'd find a way to get a handle on this after all.

CHAPTER 11

O n Thursday, her day off, she awoke close to 10 AM. When she checked her phone for messages, she had a few from Jade stating that she'd officially hired Ian Chambers as her photographer. There was a good morning text from Michael, and a link from Rochelle to an article about *Tiana's Circle* being renewed for another two seasons, followed by a row of celebratory emojis. She was in the middle of typing a reply to Rochelle when another message popped up, this one from Nina.

> **NINA:** I have some EVPs and video ready. I usually bring the relevant clips for the client to check out, and then I tell them my findings. Would you be willing to go to Julie's tomorrow to see what a post-investigation looks like, as well as share your discoveries with her?

Riley supposed breaking the news to Julie, someone with no familial ties to Iris Velasco, that Iris had died by way of an accidental allergic reaction and not a suicide would be easier than contacting Iris' daughter out of the blue. Julie would be the test run.

RILEY: Sure. I have to work from 12 to 7, but I can come by any
time before or after.

NINA: Perfect. She was hoping for something around 10 AM.
Let's meet at my place around 9 so we can discuss things before
the consult, and then we can head to Julie's together.

RILEY: See you then!

She had just switched back to her message to Rochelle
when she heard a gentle rumble outside that made her sit bolt
upright. The mail truck! She flung back her comforter and
scurried into her living room, peering out the window with
the side of her face smashed against the glass to give her the
best view of the bank of mailboxes below. When she saw the
boxy white vehicle round the corner out of sight, she let out a
squeal, quickly changed her clothes, and ran down the steps
like a kid on Christmas morning who was sure she had a new
bicycle waiting for her under the tree. The mailman today,
however, was the older guy who moved at the pace of a mor-
tally wounded snail. The wait forced her to clean out her car.
She spent an inordinate length of time prying a melted hard
candy off her floor mat.

When the ancient mailman finally got back in his truck
and made the short trek to the next bank of mailboxes, she'd
speed-walked across the parking lot to open her box. A brown
package lay inside.

Her little-kid-excitement made a veering turn into
grown-adult-panic once the package was in her hands. The
fact that the package arrived without an FBI escort was likely
a good sign, but what if the pictures were something weird,
like someone's doll collection?

Deciding she would need company when she opened the package, she hurried back inside to send a group text to Jade and Michael.

RILEY: The pictures have arrived. I'm too scared to look.

JADE: Holy crap! I can come by after work.

MICHAEL: I'm debating about whether I want pictures of the pictures, or if I should just wait until Ry is here tomorrow night.

JADE: You should wait. Seeing them live and in person will be so much better.

MICHAEL: Easy for you to say! I'm stuck over an hour away and have to wait a full day.

JADE: I would say I'm sorry, but that's a lie.

MICHAEL: I would say I'm offended, but if this situation were reversed, I would have no sympathy for your plight.

JADE: Fair.

This would be the longest day off in her life.

Dramatically throwing herself onto her couch, she turned on the TV. As usual, it was set to a local news station. The 11:00 hour of news was coming to a close, and nothing about Francis Hank Carras had come up, nor was anything about him scrolling along the bottom of the screen.

Just before she switched to Netflix, her true-crime-loving brain was tickled when a female news anchor said, "And now for a disturbing story that we first reported on last night. Several women from uptown Albuquerque, namely in Nob Hill, have contacted our station about a man, seen here, that has been prowling the streets late at night, peeping in women's windows."

Goosebumps sprang up on Riley's arms.

The picture shown wasn't of Hank, of course, but the memories of being stalked by him came slinking back. On screen was a grainy photo of a person wearing all black—dark pants, dark boots, gloves, and a black bandana tied over half his face. He had light hair, likely blond or sandy brown, but since the picture was in black and white and taken from a low-quality security camera, it was hard to tell. Age-wise, it was only clear that he wasn't a teen, and likely wasn't older than forty-five. Height was hard to discern from the picture.

"The police have been informed of the situation and are investigating," the news anchor said. "Concerned young women in the area are speaking out because they're hoping someone in the community can help them identify the man, who is causing a widespread sense of fear among the female population in Nob Hill."

The screen switched to a pair of twenty-something Caucasian women standing beside a chain link fence with a field of dying grass wafting beyond it. Riley supposed the women didn't want to be interviewed in a spot that would give away their location. They were both girl-next-door brunettes, and either college students or young professionals.

"This has been going on for a full week," one of the young women said. "Yesterday, I had been sleeping in after a long night of studying and woke up when I heard someone whispering. I woke up totally freaked out because I thought someone was *in* my bedroom, but it was this guy outside my window. He had a black bandana over his face, and the hood of his sweatshirt was up so I couldn't really see any features other than blue eyes. He said he'd been partying too hard last night to drive home, so he'd slept in his car, but hadn't turned it off and had run his battery down. He said his cell phone was dead, and that he just needed an Uber. He asked me if I could call one for him."

"Did you?" the reporter asked.

"No," said her friend. "I was in the other room getting ready for work and I went to check on her since she'd only gone to bed a few hours before. And then I see this man outside her window. I screamed at him to get the hell away and he took off."

"The freaky thing," the first woman said, "is that I'm pretty sure I saw him a couple days ago. I was eating lunch at the park near campus, and I could have sworn I saw a guy with a camera standing behind a tree."

"You think he was photographing you?" the reporter asked.

"Maybe? Both guys had the same general build and light hair, but he also could have been birdwatching," the woman said, color rising in her cheeks. "There's a popular rose garden there too, so maybe he was photographing something else but just came off as really creepy. I feel so paranoid now."

Riley shivered.

The news anchor was back on screen—a blonde woman in a pink blouse and black slacks—standing on a sidewalk talking to the camera. "Another woman told me that last night, she'd been doing laundry in her apartment complex laundromat. As she came and went from her apartment and the laundry room, she didn't lock her door. When she came back from one such trip, she found her front door ajar. Too scared to go back inside on her own, since she'd been hearing rumors about the Nob Hill Prowler, she went across the hall to her neighbor's apartment. The young man went in to check that the coast was clear, and found the young woman's bedroom window wide open, and the screen slashed. The prowler had also rifled through the woman's drawers before fleeing the scene."

The grainy picture of the man was back on screen now.

"If you have any information about this quickly evolving situation, please contact the Albuquerque police department," the woman said.

The memory of that small vase of roses on Riley's porch popped up in her mind. *Hurry up, my little medium*, the note had said. *I'm going crazy waiting* ...

Hank had put a tracker on Riley's car. He'd taken pictures of her as she walked to her car after her shift at The Laughing Tiger. He'd traveled to her work, to her parents' house, to Jade's house—and had taken pictures of all those places, too. Then he'd emailed the pictures to her to make sure she *knew* he had been watching.

She could only imagine how much more terrified she'd have been if Hank had gotten inside her apartment. Or if he'd ever gone through her belongings.

Peeping, Riley knew, was like a gateway crime. For a small percentage of peeping toms, voyeurism was where they started. The longer they went without getting caught, the more apt they were to escalate to more dangerous, invasive crimes—breaking and entering, assault, murder. She had to hope that the media coverage would scare the guy off, and that this was as far as he'd go.

Grabbing the remote off the couch, she powered the TV off. So much for lounging all day until she could look at the pictures with Jade.

Full of nervous energy, Riley went grocery shopping half an hour away. Before she loaded her new purchases into her fridge, she scrubbed every inch of it. Then she scrubbed her cabinets, the bathroom, and mopped the small swatch of tile floor in the kitchen. The woman in the yellow dress never materialized during Riley's cleaning binge, but Riley was almost positive she was loitering in the apartment, watching Riley slowly grow delirious from cleaning-product fumes.

A little after 4:30, her phone chimed from where it had been lying on the coffee table next to the package of photos that were practically burning a hole in the surface.

> **JADE:** Girl! I'm having a D A Y. I'm stuck at work longer than planned, but I can get there by like 6:30?
>
> **RILEY:** I can go to you if that's easier. Traffic will be a nightmare for you.
>
> **JADE:** Yes! You're my favorite person! I'll be home by 6!

Exhausted from all the cleaning, Riley made herself a snack, then arranged everything in her closet by color.

When 5:45 finally—*finally!*—rolled around, Riley snatched up the pictures, threw them in her purse, and practically sprinted to her car. While flooring it on her way to Jade's house, she swerved slightly when she thought she saw the woman in the yellow dress walking down the sidewalk. It was a miracle she arrived in one piece.

Riley had just pulled into the driveway when the front door of Jade's house flew open and Jade came rushing out onto the porch. She was already in pajamas, and somehow she made even those look chic. Her curly hair was pulled back into a messy bun, and she wore house slippers.

"Get your butt in here!" Jade whisper-shouted as Riley stepped out of her car. "I'm losing my mind."

Riley grabbed just the package of photos and her keys out of her purse and left the rest on her passenger seat. "Me too!"

she said as she hurried across the cement pathway to the front
door. "My apartment has never been this clean!"

She followed Jade inside and across the wooden floors
toward the kitchen. The house smelled amazing, and Riley
soon found the source: a crockpot on the counter, the glass
lid dimpled with beads of steam. They each pulled up a stool
positioned along one side of the kitchen counter. Riley dropped
the package of photos on the faux-stone surface.

Jade visibly swallowed. "So that's them, huh?"

"Yep…"

After a long beat of silence, Jade said, "Now I'm scared, too!"

The front door opened then. "Jade?"

"Oh crap…" Jade said.

"Is someone here?" he asked.

Riley turned on her stool. "Hey, Jonah."

Jonah was best described as a Black Clark Kent—boy-next-
door good looks, glasses, and wholesome charm. He smiled,
revealing bright white teeth. "Hey, Riley."

Hopping off the stool long enough to give him a quick hug,
she said, "I just came by to…uhh…ask Jade something," she
managed, realizing halfway through her sentence that she wasn't
sure if it was safe for Jonah to know the reason for her visit, as
the reason could be tied back to his kryptonite—vintage tech.

He'd been informed of Riley's ghost-seeing abilities a couple
of months ago. Despite being a man firmly rooted in science
and technology, he had accepted her ability without much of
a fuss. Years of friendship dating back to college surely had
played the biggest role in that acceptance, though. He wasn't
any more of a fan of *Paranormal Playground* than Riley was,
but that had more to do with his healthy distaste for "reality"
TV than his belief in the supernatural.

He shrugged out of his jacket, which he draped on the back of a dining room chair. He deposited his keys and wallet on the table, then continued into the kitchen and grabbed a bottle of water from the fridge.

"There's stew in the crockpot if you're hungry," Jade said, trying to discreetly pull the package of pictures off the counter before he saw it. She wasn't quick enough.

"What's that?" Jonah asked.

Riley shot Jade a side-eye as she slid back onto her stool.

"Nothing?" Jade ventured.

Jonah rounded the center island and stopped on the other side of the counter. He rested his folded arms on the surface and looked at Riley and his fiancée in turn. "Jade, honey, you are an awful liar. So is Riley."

"Hey," Riley said, mock-offended, but she'd heard the same from Michael countless times.

Jade groaned and dropped the unopened package on the counter again. "You have to promise not to go snooping! I need them for the wedding."

He stared at her for a beat. "I have no idea what you're talking about."

After Jade had explained everything to him—from acquiring three more vintage cameras, finding a roll of film, and sending it off to get developed—Jonah looked hurt more than anything. "Sorry I ruined that other camera," he said softly. "I'm bummed you felt like you had to hide this, though. Finding old footage is low-key a dream for me."

Jade reached across the counter to place a hand on his arm. Sweetly, she said, "You know I love you, but if you had destroyed another camera, I would have had to murder you and we've already spent so much money on this wedding…"

Jonah laughed, dispelling the tension. "And then I would have been forced to haunt Riley and we both know she would have hated that."

"So much." Even though Riley had been desperate to look at the pictures all day, she asked, "Will you forgive us if I let you open the package?"

Jade offered her a thankful smile.

"Yep!" Jonah said, standing up to full height and quickly opening and closing his outstretched hand in a "gimme, gimme, gimme" gesture.

Jade slid the brown envelope over to him.

Grabbing hold of the red pull tab with two fingers, he bit down on his bottom lip. "I'm sort of nervous. I feel like I need a drum roll or something."

Jade rolled her eyes. Riley, however, slapped her palms on the counter in her best attempt at a drum solo.

"Thank you, Riley," he said, offering Jade an exaggerated look of disappointment, then tore the package open.

As he pulled the envelope of pictures free, Riley and Jade leaned forward. Jonah carefully pulled the prints out. He studied the first photo, then placed it face up in front of Riley and Jade.

Riley gasped, immediately recognizing the woman in the yellow dress, except here, she wore a T-shirt and jeans and was just about to get into her car. The next was of her walking down the sidewalk while she talked on her phone. In the next, she was caught mid-stride as she crossed the street. Photo after photo of the woman in the yellow dress doing various everyday tasks.

"I wonder who she is," Jonah said, still slowly placing the photos on the counter as he made his way through the stack. "This is kind of creepy, right? Like someone was watching her? Do you think the previous owner of the camera was a PI or something?"

"The woman in the picture ..." Riley said. "Her ghost appeared in my apartment the same day Jade bought the cameras."

"Oh ..." Jonah said. "Well ... shit."

Riley sighed. "Yeah. I still don't know who she is, though."

"There are time stamps on these," Jade said suddenly. "I just noticed. I was too caught up in the creepy surveillance part of it. These were all taken in 2005. So that's two years *after* Brynn and Shawna, right?"

"Wait. This last one is of someone else," Jonah said.

Riley took the offered picture and whooshed out a breath. The time stamp on this one was 2003. "Holy shit."

"What?" Jade asked, leaning over. "Who is it?"

"Shawna Mack."

"No way ..."

"Can someone fill me in?" Jonah asked.

Riley mulled over the implications while Jade explained this next part of the mystery to Jonah. Did the owner of the camera stalk women before he killed them? Would another roll have Brynn on it? Had this roll been left in the camera as an oversight? Riley wished she knew who had owned the storage unit this film had come from. Someone, until three months before the sale of the unit, had been paying rent. Had the person suddenly died?

"Damn," Jonah said softly.

Riley, elbows on the counter and fists propped under her chin, scanned the rows of pictures of her ghost. "I don't know what to do."

"You know ..." Jonah said, his folded arms on the counter. "I bet I could scan these and run a face-recognition search. My company is working on perfecting the technology for a project we're working on. Could I keep a few of the ones that have a clear shot of her face?"

"Yeah, that would be awesome," Riley said. "Thanks."

As Jonah studied the pictures to pick out the best candidates, Jade turned on her stool to face Riley, an arm resting on the lip of the counter. "You have crazy-face. What's going on in that head of yours?"

Riley chewed the inside of her cheek for a moment. "I still don't know why the police would actively investigate any of this if I brought it to them. *I* know the woman is dead, but as far as anyone else knows, she could just be a missing person. I don't have any proof she's dead other than the fact that she pops up in my apartment and has—on at least one occasion—scared the crap out of Michael's cat." She paused. "Are these cameras the property of a serial killer?"

Jonah was clearly on a train of thought of his own. "You said the connection between this woman and the one from your dream … Brittany?" he asked, looking up from his perusal of the twenty-four photos.

"Brynn," Riley corrected.

"Right. Brynn," Jonah said. "There's a connection between the ghost lady and Brynn, partly because your dream happened after the ghost showed up. There's a clear connection to Shawna now too, since she's on the same roll of film as the other lady …"

"Where are you going with this, babe?" Jade asked.

"What *exactly* do you see in that dream of Brynn?" Jonah asked. "Maybe there's something else in it that's a clue you haven't been paying the right amount of attention to. Or maybe you're looking at small details when you should be looking at the bigger picture somehow."

Riley couldn't recall much from memory other than the profile of the crying woman with her arms wrapped around her bent knee, the date of the crime, and Brynn's name. She sighed.

Jade patted her shoulder. "You've had the dream a few times now. If you have it again, try to take notes when you wake up next time, okay?"

Riley nodded.

Jade's stomach grumbled loudly.

"All right, you two need to eat dinner," Riley said.

"Want some?" Jonah asked. "There's plenty."

"Nah, I'm okay." The adrenaline rush was waning, and Riley suddenly felt deflated. The daylong rollercoaster of emotions had completely wrung her out.

They collected the rest of the photos. Jonah's selected three were in a small stack off to the side. Once she had the pictures secured, she hugged Jonah goodbye and thanked him for the help.

Jade walked her to the door and gave her arm a squeeze. "You okay? You can crash here if you're too tired to drive home."

Of course Jade would be able to take one look at Riley and know how she was feeling. "I'm all right."

Jade frowned slightly, but changed the subject. "You have your first post-ghost-hunt client consult tomorrow, right? Are you going to talk to the daughter too?"

"Not sure. Nina hasn't even brought up the possibility of tracking down Amy yet but I assume that's on the agenda at some point. The message Iris has been trying to send is that her death wasn't a suicide. I'm sure Julie is interested to learn who's haunting her house, but I don't know if our discovery will be enough for Iris. It's possible the haunting won't stop until Amy knows it, too."

"I have the coolest best friend," Jade said, sighing happily.

Riley rolled her eyes. Jade hugged her anyway.

At home, she took a long hot shower, leaving the package of pictures on her bed for safekeeping. She had just emerged from the bathroom, clad in pajamas and drying her hair, when a chill slid down her spine. She spun to find the woman in the yellow dress standing in the corner of her room.

Riley wished she could hug her the way she'd hugged Jade and Jonah earlier. She needed the woman to know how invested she was now. "I'll figure this out, okay? I'll keep searching until I have enough to share with the police."

The woman didn't speak. Instead, she placed a hand over her chest and bowed her head slightly. *Thank you*, the gesture said. Then she was gone.

Riley hoped like hell she didn't let her down.

CHAPTER 12

The front door to Nina's house swung open just as Riley reached the top step of her porch the following morning at 9 AM.

"I made coffee," Nina said in greeting.

"You're an angel."

"I've got everything set up in the dining room," Nina said after she closed the front door and led the way across the creaky living room floor, past the low bookshelf covered in owls, and into the circular dining area surrounded by windows on three sides. The blinds were open, one of the windows cracked and letting in both warm morning sunlight and a breeze of slightly chilly autumn air. Four chairs ringed the table, and the two opposite the windows had been pushed close together before an open laptop. "Have a seat and I'll grab the coffee."

Riley dropped her purse onto one of the open chairs and sat, staring at Nina's computer screen. It appeared to be a movie-making program, the background dark, with two small boxes making up the top half, and one long rectangular box taking up the bottom. The left box was cluttered with files and folders labeled in white text, while the right had a black box with blue lines of varying heights. The rectangular area at the bottom appeared to be an enlarged version of the right-hand box. A ruler ran along the top, time stamps marked at intervals.

Nina set a mug adorned with a yawning cat by Riley's elbow, placing small containers of sugar and creamer nearby, along with a spoon. Riley dumped a generous serving of each into her coffee and gave it a stir while Nina got situated beside her.

"Okay, so I have four EVPs that are significant enough to share with Julie, as well as one video," Nina said, taking hold of her mouse and guiding the cursor to a file in the upper left box on the screen.

"Did the cameras pick up anything after we left?" Riley asked.

"Not a thing," Nina said. "It was a very boring five hours—multiplied by four."

"Yikes. You watched all twenty hours by yourself?"

"Yep. And close to twelve hours of EVPs to listen for," Nina said. "It's a very glamorous job, ghost hunting. At least I can do other things while listening to recordings—a lot of housework gets done then. But watching the video?" She wrinkled her nose. "That's the real slog."

Somehow the mundane nature of this part of it centered Riley. Information had always been the thing that soothed her. This—these snippets of audio and visuals—were a way of taking something unknown and rooting them in the concrete land of data. It was a form of proof that could be used to prove people like Riley and Nina weren't making things up.

"All right," Nina said, getting the first clip cued up. "First you'll hear Olivia asking a question, followed by a reply." She hit play.

Riley tightly grasped her coffee mug with both hands, letting the warmth seep into her palms.

"Is your name Amy Velasco?" came Olivia's voice, the sliding red line of the time marker moving to the right over the blue lines indicating the peaks and valleys of Olivia's voice.

Several seconds passed by as Olivia allowed her potential ghost to reply.

"*Daughter.*"

"Whoa," Riley said.

"Right? It's a slog, but when you find EVPs like this, it's like discovering gold."

The next two were harder to parse out, the replies a bit garbled and staticky. To Riley, the reply to Nina's "Why are you still here?" sounded like "painted" while it sounded like "placement" to Nina.

When Riley asked, "What happened to you?" the ghostly reply sounded like "down the hall" to her, but sounded like "I had it all" to Nina.

"This last one is the clearest," Nina said, navigating to the last audio clip.

Riley's own voice rang out as she asked, "Are you here intentionally?" to which the immediate reply was "*Help Amy.*"

The warmth from Riley's mug wasn't enough to stave off the chills that forced goosebumps to spring up on her arms. "Are you planning to contact her daughter?" she finally asked, unable to keep her curiosity in check any longer.

"It seems we might have to. I believe Iris won't move on until Amy is informed about what happened to her mother. Your research showed the conventional wisdom is that she died by suicide. She wants her daughter to know she didn't leave her on purpose."

"Do you have to make cold calls about messages from the other side often?" Riley asked.

"It's rare. I'm going to ask Julie how she feels about getting in contact with her realtor. If she explains the situation to them, we might be able to get in contact with Amy that way. If the message comes from a source of authority to start off with, sometimes the message is better received."

Riley nodded. "And there's a video clip, too?"

Nina directed her cursor back to the file section and pulled up the short twenty-second clip. "It happens quickly, so I can play it a couple times if you miss it."

The shot was from the kitchen, where the camera had been set up in the corner by the patio doors and aimed toward the dining room table, kitchen sink, and the window facing the front of the house. Riley worried at her bottom lip as she watched, gaze darting wildly around the image. Something dark and possibly shiny whooshed past the window beyond the kitchen sink. Riley jumped.

"What was that?" she whispered.

"I'll play it again. Tell me when to hit pause."

When the video restarted, Riley focused on the window alone, waiting. "There."

With the image frozen, Riley leaned forward even more, head cocked. "That looks like a ladder, doesn't it? Like it tipped sideways? If she fell in the front yard, she could have easily hit her head on the cement walkway or any of those bricks that line that little front garden."

"Right. It could explain the cracked front tooth too," Nina said.

Riley nodded, recalling Iris's little whimper at seeing the state of her own face. A cracked front tooth must have hurt like hell, yet she was so disoriented, she hadn't noticed until later.

"For the consult, only jump in to offer information if you're comfortable doing so," Nina said. "We'll be explaining to Julie what the nature of the haunting is, show her the evidence, and then let her decide how she wants to proceed. I'm hoping she'll happily contact the realtor on our behalf if it means getting the ghost out of her house. Usually if you give the client a little bit of agency, they'll step up to help."

After they finished their coffee, Riley followed Nina to Julie's house. Her daughters were outside on the lawn when Riley and Nina arrived. They were sprawled out on their stomachs on the lawn on top of a towel, each busily working crayons across their coloring books. The older girl was filling in the tiny details of a mermaid's scaly tail, while the younger one was coloring the sky a blood red with furious strokes of her crayon. They hardly looked up when Nina and Riley walked past them.

Nina made her way up the steps, where Julie already had the door open, but Riley stopped a few feet from the porch. Eyeing the bricks that lined the small garden of bushy flowers, Riley tried to imagine Iris falling here and chipping a tooth on one of the sharp edges. She rubbed her tongue back and forth against her own front teeth as she walked across the grass and squatted before the garden. She had just reached out a hand to touch the brick when a little voice sounded beside her.

"You're here 'cause of the ghost lady, right?"

Riley glanced over to find the youngest little girl squatted there, mirroring her own posture. "Yeah. Have you seen her?"

"Only one time," the little girl said. "I heard a scream at night. It woke me up and I came outside 'cause I thought it was my mom. But it was the ghost lady. I saw her lying in the grass right here and I thought maybe she'd fallen off the roof, but then she went poof."

"That sounds scary," Riley said, a pang filling her chest. This little girl reminded her so much of Pete in that moment for some reason. She knew he was in a better place, wherever that was, because he was no longer trapped on that ranch, but she still sometimes wished she could see him again.

"Yeah, I ran back inside and jumped in bed and pulled the covers over my head," she said, pulling at a long piece of grass between her bare feet. "I told my sister I sawed the ghost lady but she said I was lying." She looked up at Riley then, her blue eyes wide. "But I really sawed her. And she really did go poof."

"I believe you. I've seen ghost people since I was about your sister's age. They go poof a lot."

The little girl nodded sagely at that. "I want the ghost lady to go away. Mommy and Daddy don't like her and they fight sometimes."

"That's why my friend Nina and I are here. We're trying to figure out why the ghost lady is here, and if we can help her, she'll go away."

The little girl thought about that for a moment, then successfully pulled the piece of grass from the earth. She tossed it into the garden and got to her feet. "Cool. Bye!" She ran off to rejoin her sister.

Riley, smiling softly to herself, reached out and touched one of the bricks. No snapshots of the past were triggered by the contact. Giving the brick a parting tap, she stood and went to join Nina and Julie inside, following their voices toward the dining room.

"I hope Lucy wasn't talking your ear off," Julie said as Riley rounded the kitchen counter and stepped into the dining area.

Riley shook her head. "She's a cute kid."

Nina and Julie were seated side by side in front of Nina's computer, so Riley took a seat across from them, listening quietly while Nina gave a brief explanation of what EVPs were. She then played them in succession. Riley was amused to hear that Julie's guesses for the middle two were different from Riley's and Nina's.

Julie had her fingers pressed to her mouth as she listened to the last EVP, tears in her eyes. Finally, she lowered her hands. "How does she want you to help her daughter?"

"We're not sure yet. We believe Iris's death was an accident," Nina said. "Not suicide."

Julie asked, "Do they really think she committed suicide by throwing herself off the steps?"

"We haven't figured that part out yet either," Nina said, "but I had a favor to ask of you. Are you still in contact with your realtor? We'd like to talk to Amy, but we hoped either you or your realtor could be a buffer for us so we don't have to contact Iris's grieving daughter out of the blue with news about her mother's ghost."

"Oh, goodness, I hadn't even thought of how complicated this all could get for you. I can call him. I'll let you know if he can give me any information."

"That would be great," Nina said.

After a few more minutes of talking, the consult was over, and while there weren't any guarantees in place that the horrible crash of Iris falling down the stairs wouldn't wake the family again, Julie stood a little straighter as she walked them toward the door. She didn't yet have a solution for the problem plaguing her home, but she had more answers than she'd had two weeks ago.

Riley came up short in the front hallway, gazing up the stairs at where Iris stood. The spirit was more lucid now, even if she was still in her disheveled state.

Help Amy, she said.

"We will," said Riley.

Iris nodded once, then turned back toward her old bedroom. Riley heaved out a relieved breath, then turned toward Julie, who had her head cocked in Riley's direction.

"She's still here, but I think the activity will decrease for a while," Riley told her. "She was making all that racket because she needed to share a message. Now that she knows we have it, she doesn't feel compelled to disrupt you."

Julie gazed up the stairs now too, as if she herself could see Iris. Her wide-eyed expression swung back to Riley. "Thank you. You know, as a mom, I imagine I'd haunt this house if I was taken from my girls too soon. It makes me feel better to know that's why she's here—because she's reaching out to her daughter after death. Hopefully we can track down Amy."

"I hope so, too," said Riley.

2005

My skin tingled in anticipation. It had been two years since my last companion, and the yearning had reached a fever pitch. I knew I had to bide my time—that playing it safe was better for all involved. But this was so hard. She was so close, nearly within reach. I had paid too much and waited too long to blow this opportunity now. I would be patient as I sat here watching, even as my body, as my very soul, called out to her.

I don't think even The Collector understood the difficulty of waiting, and he understood me better than most.

When I got like this, I often returned to the message The Collector sent almost two years ago to the day. It grounded me as much as it pissed me off. I pulled it up on my phone.

> I don't care what you do with the information I give you, but Brynn was a mistake. Choose the ones who don't have parents with fat checkbooks and you'll succeed for a lot longer. And the longer you succeed, the longer I get paid. Win-win. Be smarter.

I paid the little weasel for his services, not his opinions. But he was right. Brynn had been a pie-in-the-sky dream. I'd watched her for weeks before I'd hired The Collector to put in the due diligence to get the information I needed. I thought, after Shawna, I could do it on my own. I'd tried to grab one once—a young girl by herself. But she'd been feisty and fought back. I'd been outmatched by a mere child.

Foolish. Mother always said hubris would be my downfall.

I wasn't a ghost like The Collector. When I walked by, heads turned. When he walked by, people hardly blinked. It was a wonder he even had a reflection to look back at him in the mirror.

I'd seen Brynn for the first time when she was out for a run. I'd been on a walk along a nature trail, scoping out the site as a possible photoshoot location for a client who had booked me for engagement photos. I truly had been minding my own business when the blonde-haired goddess ran past me, the white wires snaking out of her earbuds swaying. She'd been accompanied by a tongue-lolling brown-and-white puppy that had snarled at me as they ran past.

The sight of Brynn had taken my breath away, and I'd forgotten why I'd been on the trail in the first place. It was as if I'd been turned by the force of a magnet, and I'd spun to watch her go. She wore such tiny shorts; my gaze glued to those shapely calves. I refused to be ashamed of how attracted I was to her. If she didn't want people to look, to covet, she would cover herself up.

But it was more than how beautiful she was. Something in me was drawn to her in a way I've been drawn to few others. The ones I'm drawn to are the ones I assign to The Collector, and his job had run past me in minuscule pink running shorts and matching shoes.

I needed Brynn in a way I hadn't experienced since Shawna. I let Brynn get farther down the trail before I headed in her direction, knowing she would reach the parking lot in a few minutes. The fear that I would miss her, that she would be gone before I got back to the parking lot, sent a jolt of pain to my chest that was so acute, I almost collapsed. If Brynn was meant to be mine, the signs would show me the way. But perhaps the sign had been her arrival on that trail, running down the path. She had smiled at me when she went by, hadn't she?

Hi, the smile said. *Fancy meeting you here.*

I ran.

By the time I reached the lot, my chest ached not from exertion, but in relief that my goddess was still there. She stretched by her car, earbuds still in. The puppy was too busy lapping up water from a bowl to notice me. I clocked her license plate number as I walked by, committing it to memory, knowing The Collector would need it. I didn't know what her name was, but when I learned it a week later, I was pleased that my goddess had a name as pretty as her face.

Alas, that was all in the past now. Brynn was gone, as was Shawna. Though I cherished the time I'd spent with Brynn, she had caused so many problems for me. I had considered quitting altogether after the media storm. I watched the news with great interest, wondering if they were closing in on me. But authorities hadn't connected Shawna and Brynn—hadn't even come close. The idiots had been looking the wrong way. They still were.

After six months, the yearning could no longer be ignored, so I kept my eyes peeled for a new companion while out on the road. The publicity surrounding Brynn had made me nervous about straying too far from home, so when the gorgeous woman in Apartment 16 moved into the complex, I'd flown The Collector out to make an assessment. He shut me down. He shut down my next three as well. I trusted his judgement implicitly even while my frustration, my yearning, mounted. Apartment 16 wasn't for me. Sometimes life wasn't fair; you couldn't always get what you wanted.

I had chosen more wisely this time, though. She was Collector approved. Another wannabe model, though her pursuits were a tad different than Brynn's. Still, she was a beauty in her own right. I had spotted her just last month while out of town on one of my longer jobs. I was lucky both my careers allowed for so much travel, giving me the opportunity to experience all the nooks and crannies the country had to offer.

Months passed before I received the information I needed for this companion. The Collector's extensive research allowed me to be in the right spot at the right time today.

My new beauty was in the midst of a photoshoot with a wet-behind-the-ears photographer who had no idea what he was doing. The lighting, the staging, even the colors the beauty wore were all wrong. The Collector had told me this guy was a joke, but I hadn't thought it was *this* bad. The guy was sweating under his collar, likely because he knew he was out of his depth and the woman in front of him deserved better.

I watched from afar, perched on a bench pretending to read my book. To reach this spot, one had to walk up a tree-lined incline. The hiking trail either continued forward, or it veered off to the right to this flattened park area. The circular oasis boasted several park benches, well-tended grass, and a small play area for children. On the other side, surrounded on three sides by trees, was a massive gray boulder ringed in wildflowers.

The imbecile had the beauty atop the boulder like a mountain goat, encouraging her to do this with her hair, that with her arm, and to pout a little more dramatically. He was making her look like a buffoon, and the shadows cast by the wall of pine trees behind her were doing nothing for her. Not to mention she wore dark green, like the trees behind her—with skin as dark as hers, the amount of editing he would have to do to make these pictures salvageable was enough to make me pull my own hair out.

At some point, he realized he'd brought the wrong equipment bag with him. That was after he'd switched position to capture her from a better angle and had tripped over his own feet, face-planted, and been halfway swallowed up by the wildflowers surrounding the boulder.

He apologized profusely, told her he'd be right back, and then sprinted back down the incline at the speed of a frightened jack rabbit. That was my cue, my first sign. I abandoned my book on the bench and approached her. The poor beauty looked so dejected up on that rock, but as I stood at the base of it and looked up, I couldn't help but feel like I was a peasant at the feet of a queen.

"I'm sorry if this is an overstep," I said, and she glanced toward me, momentarily shaken from the thoughts that plagued her. The frown lines marring her smooth skin deepened. "I couldn't help but overhear everything. Can I guess … you're an actress?"

The beauty smiled sadly. "A model. Well, I'm trying to be. This guy was the cheapest I could afford right now, and, well …"

"You get what you pay for?"

She groaned and pressed a hand to her face. "Did it look that bad?"

"Dreadful," I said, but smiled as I said it, pulling a smile from her as well. My heart fluttered at the sight.

"Ugh, I'm such an idiot," she said. "I can't believe I agreed to this. And now he's got basically all of next month's rent in his pocket and I'm going to have unusable pictures because this guy tricked me into thinking his credentials were legit. I'm just trying to get started and if this is already such a mess, clearly this was a mistake. A sign from the universe that I was fooling myself." She whimpered. "And now I'm spilling my guts to a stranger! Sorry, I need to get out of here."

I stared at her, dumbstruck. She also lived according to signs. This was a sign in itself.

She glanced around, trying to find the best path off the boulder. She was a good five feet off the ground and wore a clingy dress and flimsy sandals—certainly not climbing attire.

"Here, let me help you," I said.

I was a complete gentleman as I helped her, only briefly glancing down the front of her dress and catching sight of the beige-colored bra lying flush to that supple dark skin.

"Thanks." Once back on her feet, she brushed off the back of her dress, and readjusted her top. "Have a good rest of your day."

But I was already reaching into my pocket for my case of business cards. "I agree that this was all a sign from the universe, yet possibly not the way you think." She turned to me, a dark brow cocked. I held out the crisp white card between two fingers. "I work for newspapers and magazines, but I also photograph events like graduations and weddings, as well as headshots for actresses and models. A friend of mine works for a local magazine. Since he's always on the lookout for more models, I often send many of my clients his way, and vice versa. We have a great working relationship and we're thinking about going into business together. It's an exciting time; I really feel we're on the brink of something amazing."

She delicately took the card from me.

"If you'd be interested in making another—dare I say, a *better*—modeling connection, please consider me. I would also be happy to offer you a discount on headshots. It's rare that I come across someone with beauty as natural as yours. It would be a treat to photograph you. Just give my site a look over and contact me if you're interested."

"Wow, this sounds great," she said, sounding as dumbstruck as I'd felt earlier. "Thank you."

"No problem," I said, walking backward toward the bench and my discarded book. "Oh, and if we *do* end up working together, might I suggest you wear yellow?"

CHAPTER 13

On Saturday morning, Riley sat cross-legged on Michael's couch with her computer on her lap, and Baxter curled up and purring by her side. Michael was busy making breakfast with one of his new "only $39.99 a month!" pans. Riley and Michael had early lunch plans with her parents tomorrow, and she planned to ask "Reggie Reg" to refrain from suggesting any more cooking accessories for a while. The spare bedroom in Michael's duplex had boxes for a new juicer, an air fryer, and two crockpots—all unopened—that hadn't been there two weeks before.

The photos of the mystery woman lay in their envelope on his coffee table. Last night, after discussing the consult at Julie's house, Riley and Michael had laid out the pictures in neat rows before going over the same theories Riley had discussed with Jade and Jonah. The Brynn dream hadn't reoccurred, which, strangely, had disappointed Riley.

Jonah's suggestion that Riley possibly hadn't been looking at the dream from the right angle had struck a chord with her. So while the scents of coffee and bacon drifted through Michael's duplex, Riley searched for every article she could find about Brynn and Shawna. She'd already done this, but she'd been treating them as separate cases, just as the police had.

Instead, she scoured the internet for any articles written about the possible connections between the two cases. There were plenty of forums where she could find sub-threads and conspiracy theories, but she wanted something written by someone with a more official byline than "monster_m@$h_69."

Eventually she found the same article in the *Taos Daily Journal* that she'd seen during her last search. It was the only one she'd been able to track down. The year on the article was 2004, and in it, Carter Quincy speculated exactly as Detective Howard had: that the two murders were related, and that the police department hadn't made the connection. He point-blank made the claim that the police in Taos saw a down-on-her-luck Black woman and automatically assumed her death had to be at the hands of her abusive ex, even when his alibi put him out of the area during the time of Shawna's murder, and when the residents of the neighborhood were all adamant Rodney hadn't done it.

A quick search of Carter Quincy revealed that he still worked at the *Taos Daily Journal*. Riley didn't know if reporters were any more predisposed to believing in the abilities of psychic mediums than cops were, but she figured it wouldn't hurt to at least contact Carter to see if he'd be willing to talk to her.

She wrote him a quick email.

Hello Mr. Quincy,

My name is Riley Thomas and I'm from Albuquerque. I wanted to find out if you would be willing to talk to me about the Brynn Bodwell and Shawna Mack cases. I may have information on an additional victim.

Riley stared at the unsent message for a while, then placed her computer on Baxter's other side on the couch and got up slowly enough to not disturb the dozing cat. He yawned and stretched, paws splayed wide for a moment, then settled back into a ball. Riley padded to one of the two open doorways into the kitchen and rested her shoulder against the doorjamb.

Michael had finished cooking the bacon and had moved onto scrambling eggs. "Hey," he said, glancing over when he realized she stood there. "Almost done."

"I found a reporter who thinks Brynn and Shawna were killed by the same person," Riley said without preamble.

Michael cast her a side-eyed look. "Did you email him already?"

"Started to. Do you think I should drop the ghost-seeing thing before or after I meet him? Assuming he even replies."

"After," Michael said. "Feel the guy out first. Never know what a journalist is going to do with information like that."

Riley cocked her head. "Do you not trust the media, Mr. Roberts?"

He smiled, but his attention was focused on the eggs. "I don't think all media sources are created equal. If you meet him and he's cool, then go for it. You're a good judge of character."

She stepped into the kitchen long enough to kiss him on his scruffy cheek, then returned to her computer. After rereading the short email, she added her contact information and hit send.

Late Sunday morning, Riley and Michael went to her parents' house for brunch. They had met Michael for the first time a few months ago, just after Riley and Michael had returned from their trip to Arizona to take the Scooby Doo shirt to Pete's mother. Michael had charmed the pants off her parents in a matter of minutes, as Riley suspected he would. Her father, the Thomas Family Self-Proclaimed Top Chef, had been cooking that night and he and Michael had gotten into a deep discussion about food. Michael was a horrendous cook, but he was experimenting more and more lately, determined to advance beyond the basics. By the time they left, Michael had a long list of suggested appliances typed up in his phone, as well as her father's number, apparently.

While the men had been in the kitchen, Riley and her mom had sat at the dining room table, drinking wine and playing cards. It was then that Riley had gotten into the details of what had been going on months before—the ghost of Pete Vonick taking up residence in her apartment; Orin Jacobs and the remains of five additional victims Riley, Mindy, and Michael had found in the dark room; and her run-ins with Francis Hank Carras. Her mother had drunk twice as much as Riley that night.

Currently, Riley helped Michael out of his coat in the foyer of her parents' house so he could still hold onto his prized potato casserole dish.

"Ah, you brought it!" Riley's father said.

"It was a very challenging recipe, Reggie Reg," Michael said.

Riley and her mother groaned in unison.

Her father launched into an animated tale about his latest nemesis: a homemade cheese sauce recipe. Michael slipped out of his jacket without breaking conversation with her father, and then the two men, in mid-ramble, wandered through the dining room and into the kitchen.

"Better Michael than me," her mother said. "That man won't shut up about his damn cheese sauce. He burned the flour the first time and I swear he took it as a personal offense."

Shaking her head to herself, Riley busied herself in the foyer with hanging up both her coat and Michael's while her mother followed the chattering men toward the kitchen.

A wooden block with hooks for jackets and keys hung on the wall just inside the door, the wood painted with expressive faces of sea otters. Each hook was fashioned to look like an otter's curved tail.

Riley had every intention of keeping her latest ghost-hunting mystery to herself this afternoon, recalling how ashen her mother had gotten the last time Riley had told her about her time spent with serial killer ghosts and living predators. When she walked into the dining room, she came up short.

Her mother stood in the middle of the room facing Riley, her arms crossed and brow cocked. It was a Jade look. Riley mirrored the expression, defiant.

"Are you all right?" her mother asked.

"Yeah, fine. Need any help with lunch?"

Her mother took a step to the side, not allowing Riley past her. "Sit down." It wasn't an aggressive command, but one that brooked no argument.

"Mom…"

The cocked brow somehow went up farther.

Grumbling, Riley pulled out a chair and flopped into it. Mothers already had a sixth sense when it came to their children. But having a mother with a literal sixth sense could be a pain in the ass.

"Spill," her mom said, taking a seat as well.

A pair of sea otter salt-and-pepper shakers stared at her from the middle of the table.

Riley started talking. When she got to the Shawna Mack part of the story, her mom's eyes widened.

"Oh, I remember that. We were actually just talking about this at book club last week," she said, sitting up a little straighter. "Do you remember Norma Kling? She used to work at the elementary school?"

"I think so. She worked in the office, didn't she?"

"Yep," her mom said. "Well, she's got family in Taos. Her grandmother lived in the same neighborhood as Shawna, so the whole area was on high alert when she disappeared. It wasn't the best neighborhood, so shady stuff went down there on occasion, but everyone knew how much Shawna loved that boy of hers. No one believed she would have abandoned him, so everyone was sure something horrible had happened to her when she went missing. When they found her body, people lost their minds. The cops were sure it was her ex; the locals all knew it wasn't him. But that meant a killer was roaming the streets and the police weren't looking in the right place.

"Anyway, so Norma's younger cousin, who was about sixteen at the time, was almost kidnapped a month after Shawna was found."

"Whoa, really?" Riley asked.

"Mm-hmm," her mom said. "She'd cut school early and was walking home using one of the longer routes through a rural area, and a blue car pulled up next to her. It didn't have any license plates. I don't know why that detail sticks with me. Anyway, there was a white guy behind the wheel with light blond hair in a buzz cut. Gigi said the weirdest part about his hair was that it looked white, like an old man's hair, but the guy was in his forties at the youngest. He apparently was asking for directions because he was lost. He kept asking her to approach the car because he couldn't hear her very well."

Riley winced.

"Mm-hmm. She said the guy had an almost military look to him, like he could have been a cop. All she knew was that the guy made her hair stand on end. As a young Black girl on the back roads when she should have been in school…" Her mom shrugged. "She didn't know what to do. One decision could piss the guy off, and another could put her in even more danger."

Riley nodded. "So what did she do? You said *almost* kidnapped?"

"She approached the car, and when she did, the guy grabbed her by the arm through the open window. Once he had her, he started to get out. Little did that guy know, Gigi had four brothers who had taught her how to defend herself, so she slammed her elbow into the bridge of the guy's nose. He let her go and she took off running. She ran to a friend's house in the opposite direction of her own so the guy couldn't follow her home. She never walked through the back roads again."

"Did she report it to the police?" Riley asked.

"The family tried, but it took Gigi over two weeks to work up the nerve to do it. Gigi's parents knew Shawna's family, so tensions were already high in that neighborhood. Her family thought they could possibly track the guy down based on white men who had recently gone into the hospital to treat a broken nose. Her family was worried about Gigi being followed again, for one, but there was also a growing fear in the area that someone was targeting Black women. The cops were so convinced

Rodney had been the one who killed Shawna, they didn't even entertain the idea that the person who took Shawna had tried to take Gigi, too."

Riley frowned.

"Plus, where Shawna lived was a predominantly Black neighborhood back then. The cops found it very hard to believe that a military-looking white man would have been able to creep around a Black neighborhood and not stand out like a sore thumb. The cops more or less suggested Gigi had made the story up to get attention."

"Ugh," Riley said. "And then Brynn disappeared and I'm sure it was even harder to get them to listen to Gigi, since they thought the cases were unrelated."

Her mother cocked her head. "Brynn?"

Riley launched into the rest of the story, and how Brynn, Shawna, and the woman in the yellow dress all were the victims of the same killer. Riley wondered if young Gigi had been grabbed by the same man, or if there had been another one prowling the back streets of Taos looking for young women to pluck off the street for his dark purposes.

"I remember that, now that you mention it. I think it was happening right around the time your grandma passed … I was a bit distracted."

Riley reached across the table, her hands out. Her mom placed her hands in them.

After a beat, Riley said, "I don't know how to find out the identity of the ghost."

"I'll give Norma a call," her mom said, giving her hands a squeeze. "She still has family in that area even though her grandma is long passed by now. Maybe some people from back then are around. Any idea if Rodney is still in prison?"

"I don't know. It didn't come up in any of my searches," Riley said. "I guess it's possible that he was just quietly released and no one wrote about it. If he died in there, an obituary likely would have come up."

"True. I'll call her this week and let you know if I get any good info."

Michael emerged from the kitchen holding a large salad bowl. "Your husband can't find the tongs and would like assistance, Mrs. Thomas."

Riley rolled her eyes at his over-the-top formality. He did it solely because Riley's mother thought it was funny.

Her mom laughed. "One of these days you'll call me Sabine."

"One day, yes, Mrs. Thomas," he said, setting the bowl on the table.

Riley's mom gave her hands another squeeze, then excused herself to help Riley's dad.

Michael rounded the table and planted a kiss on Riley's temple, then sat in the chair her mother had just left. "How's it going in here?"

"Oh, you know, just talking about murder, kidnapping, and ghosts with my mom," she said.

"You say that like it's not normal," he said.

Her father poked his head out of the kitchen. "Did your mother give you your gift?"

"What gift? What occasion?" Riley asked.

"Oh, I can't believe I almost forgot," her mother said, hurrying out of the kitchen, through the foyer, and around the corner toward the guest bedroom.

When her mother returned, she placed a small unmarked box on the table in front of Riley. It had a flap that was tucked into the box, somewhat like a cupcake box. Michael got up to sit beside Riley, and her mother sat across from them. Her dad rested his hands on the back of her mom's chair.

"The occasion is that this find was too great not to share," her dad said.

Riley glanced over at Michael and shrugged, then pried the flap free and lifted it up. Inside the box was a nest of tissue paper, and on top of that was a cake plate.

"Sabine! You are my hero," Michael said.

"My god, it's hideous," Riley murmured, then looked up at her parents in awe. "It's perfect."

Carefully, she picked up the plate to examine it more closely. This one featured chickens. One was dressed in a wedding gown, the other in a tux. The chicken in the dress sat on a chair, one skinny leg stuck out toward her tuxedo-clad partner, who was blindfolded. In either one of the tuxedoed chicken's feather-hands were the sides of a garter belt. It was unclear whether the belt was being slipped on or off. The chicken in a dress had an expression that implied she was in the throes of intense pleasure.

Flipping the plate over, Riley noted that this one was number 10 of 15 in the barnyard series.

"I realize this is going to be a very heteronormative question, but shouldn't the one in the tux be a rooster? Are these lesbian chickens?" Riley asked.

"*That's* your question?" Michael asked.

Riley glanced up at her parents. "How did you find it?"

"It was actually your father who found it on eBay," her mom said. "There was a very spirited auction battle last week."

Michael said, "Well, thank you. This is the best gift I've ever gotten—which is saying a lot since you gave me Riley and I think she's pretty great. But this hideous plate is next level."

Riley jerked a thumb at Michael as she said to her parents, "Can you believe I'm in love with this weirdo?"

Smiling, her mother sweetly said, "To be fair, you're weird as hell too, child."

Laughing, Riley's father ducked back into the kitchen long enough to grab a platter of sliced prime rib. "Lunch is served!" As he placed it on the table, he looked at Riley and said, "His potato casserole is passable."

Riley and Michael shared cartoon-like open-mouthed expressions.

"Passable!" Riley said, putting the plate back in its nest of tissue paper. "It's a step up from abysmal."

"I can't even be offended because abysmal was generous," Michael said, taking the box and moving it farther down the table so it wouldn't be in the way while they ate.

Riley got up to grab plates and silverware while her mom grabbed the casserole.

"As much as we adore you, Michael," her mother said once they were all seated again, "that last casserole was so bad we couldn't even get the feral cats next door to eat it."

"And the abysmal one was like try number five," Riley said, spearing a slice of prime rib to add to her plate. "We taste tested one of them and there was so much salt in it, we both immediately spat it out."

Michael shuddered. "I somehow used a cup of salt instead of a tablespoon. It was supposed to be a cup of *flour*. Baxter came running over to sniff a blob of it that had hit the floor, and I swear to you he hissed at it and then fled the scene."

Her parents laughed.

"What's most important is that you keep trying," her dad said, adding a tong-full of salad to his plate. "Do you remember that time when we were dating, Sabine, and I tried to make pepper chicken?"

"God, that was easily the worst meal I've ever had." Her mother dramatically gagged. "Luckily he's better in the bedroom than he is in the kitchen."

Riley literally did a spit take, Michael nearly choked on a piece of prime rib, and her father threw his head back and laughed heartily.

It was a good day.

# CHAPTER 14

Riley had just finished one of the dreaded 11 AM to 3 PM Monday shifts. The Laughing Tiger had a weekly lunch special that was always extremely popular. Riley worked the evening shifts more often than not, so she usually avoided Monday Madness, as the waitresses called it, but she'd gotten roped into this one because one of the ladies, Fran, was dealing with a sick kid at home. In Riley's usual fashion, she picked up the shift for her.

Her feet were killing her and she desperately wanted a nap, or at least a long bath and a glass of wine. She settled into her car, marveling at the early hour, and grabbed her phone out of the purse she'd tossed onto the passenger seat. In addition to a few texts from Michael, and her dad asking if she had any ideas for birthday presents for her mom, she also had a voicemail from an unknown number.

She dialed her inbox.

"Hi, Riley. This is Carter Quincy. I would be happy to meet with you. It's currently 2:45 in the afternoon on Monday. I'm free until about 4 today if you happen to have any time. I'm in Albuquerque until then. Otherwise, we can arrange a phone conversation later in the week, as I'll be heading back to Taos this evening."

Riley quickly fumbled to call him back, hoping an hour was enough time for them to meet and chat. Suddenly she wasn't nearly as tired and her feet didn't ache quite as badly.

"This is Carter," a man answered.

Riley's cheeks inexplicably heated. "Uh. Hi. This is Riley Thomas returning your call."

"Ah, hello, Ms. Thomas," he said. "Are you able to meet today?"

"Yep. I just got off work."

"Perfect. Are you familiar with The Roast?"

It would take her at least twenty minutes to get uptown, so she quickly put her phone on speaker, attached her phone to her dash, and backed out of her parking space before she and Carter had even ended the call. "I'll head there right now."

There was a prolonged pause before he said, "Sounds good. I'll be there in a few minutes. I'm wearing a dark blue polo shirt and jeans."

Maybe he was just as unsure about what to expect from this meeting as she was.

When she arrived outside The Roast, she sent a text to the group chat with Michael and Jade.

> **RILEY:** I just got to The Roast. The guy's name is Carter Quincy.
>
> I just wanted you both to know the details in case I go missing.
>
> **JADE:** Your sense of humor is terrible.
>
> **MICHAEL:** Agreed.
>
> **RILEY:** I'm hilarious and you know it.

The smell of very strong coffee seeped out of the place before she even grabbed hold of the handle of one of the heavy glass-fronted doors and cautiously pushed it open. The coffee shop wasn't very big, and sat at the corner of a busy street, giving the building a triangular shape. Two of the sides of the triangle faced the street, each wall made mostly of glass. A long counter ran along the rightmost window, with attached bar stools, all of which were occupied by people working diligently on their laptops and wearing earbuds or chunky headphones. The other window had two bench seats in front of it, tables and chairs positioned before them. One long table was set a few feet from the bench seats and was filled with more laptop-working individuals. Given how many open books, notepads, highlighters, empty mugs, and crumb-covered plates littered the surface, Riley guessed it was a study group.

The right side of the café had a couch and a few plush chairs taking up most of the space, as well as a low, round coffee table. A Black man in a dark blue polo shirt sat on the couch, a computer on his lap and a half-consumed, widemouthed green mug of something frothy and brown on a coaster before him. A small notebook sat beside the mug.

The man must have sensed her staring at him because he looked up. A moment later, he raised an eyebrow in question. "Riley?"

Swallowing, she made her way over. He was in his late thirties, maybe early forties. She plastered on her best waitress smile and stuck out her hand. He stood when she reached him and shook her offered palm. He wore a gold wedding band.

"Did you want to get anything to eat or drink?" he asked, motioning to the large V-shaped counter that took up most of the base of the triangle. A chalkboard menu displayed the various types of coffees available, as well as pastries and a few lunch items. She was always ravenous after a shift, but suddenly her appetite deserted her.

"I'm good," she said.

He nodded, then gestured for her to have a seat. Instead of taking the spot next to him on the two-seater couch, she slunk into one of the nearby single chairs, clutching her purse in her lap.

When he sat back on the couch, he chose the cushion closer to her, elbow propped up on the armrest. "So what is it you wanted to talk about, Riley? You said you're interested in the Brynn Bodwell and Shawna Mack case? It's over eighteen years old at this point. No offense, but you can't be much older than that yourself."

"I'm twenty-five," Riley said. "But yeah, I was only eight or so when their bodies were discovered. I know Brynn's discovery made national news, but I don't personally remember it unfolding."

"Okay … so what's the interest in the case now? You said you might know something about another victim?"

Riley heaved out a breath. "I'm really into true crime, and—"

Carter barely—just barely—avoided rolling his eyes. "If you're looking for an internship or something, there are better avenues to go about it than this."

"No, no," Riley said, shaking her head. "It's not that. I'm not looking for a job or anything. I stumbled on the Brynn case by accident. It was during one of my late-night true crime marathon binges that I heard about Brynn's case for the first time. I started researching it, like I do, and I came across your article. If there were other articles published at the same time connecting the two murders, I couldn't find them. I was wondering why you were so sure there was a connection when no one else did."

Carter stared at her for a long beat. "In your research, did you pick up on how they were killed?"

"Both were strangled. The ligature marks were consistent with nylon rope. Both had burst blood vessels in their eyes, and they were both found nude and had been sexually assaulted. The killer had washed both bodies before dumping them in two different locations in the Orilla Verde Recreation Area six months apart."

He nodded, his shoulders relaxing a fraction. It was clear she'd actually done the research, at least.

"Right," he said. "Shawna was found first, and since her ex was a real piece of work, they searched for evidence high and low to prove he'd killed her. Police dug into his family's lives, his friends' lives. The case got a lot of media coverage in Taos, but it was focused more on what a garbage human her ex was. Shawna was almost an afterthought, even though she was the one who had been brutally murdered."

Riley softly shook her head, frowning.

"They brought the guy in for questioning after they pulled him over for blowing through a stop sign," Carter said. "They interrogated the guy for something like twelve hours straight about Shawna's disappearance. Did all the bullshit you hear about when it comes to pushing a perp to confess. He was so exhausted and hungry that they got a confession out of him for his involvement in a drug trafficking ring. When they finally dropped the bomb that they'd found Shawna's dead body, the poor guy was so wrung out that he started snitching on fellow members of the ring, all in an effort to make sure he didn't go down for murder. They put him away for twenty years for the drug charges, but they treated it like they'd gotten the killer off the street. His alibi for the week Shawna was missing could never be fully corroborated, since getting the timeline confirmed relied too heavily on unreliable sources.

"I've talked to a few people off the record, and at least among some of the department, they realize their tunnel vision meant they'd screwed up. But it was worse than tunnel vision, honestly. The community there was adamant that Rodney wasn't the killer. Regardless of his history, those people knew him better than the cops did. A killer was on the loose, and while they had their thumbs up their asses, refusing to listen to and give validity to the voices of the people in Shawna's neighborhood, the killer got to Brynn."

"So you think they didn't publicly admit to a connection so the department could save face?" Riley asked.

"That's exactly what I think happened. Plus they didn't want an internal review to reveal shady interrogation techniques that could end up affecting Rodney's conviction somehow. The way they treated Rodney and his family was abhorrent, frankly. People connected to him were getting pulled over and arrested for nearly every possible offense. There was a rumor about a secret informant who named Rodney as the killer, but if that person existed, the identity was never revealed—so it very easily could have been bullshit.

"None of what the cops were doing had anything to do with avenging Shawna, though. It was about wanting people like Rodney off the street. In the months after Rodney was arrested, crime in the area markedly dropped for a while. Mostly because they'd cracked down on Rodney so hard, other criminal types in the area got spooked and either left the town or laid low till things cooled off. The department was lauded for their hard work. Shawna's name hardly ever came up. The sheriff at the time was a real jackass. He was trying to get reelected and there are rumors that he was paying people off left and right to keep any media stink out of the news. When Brynn's murder went national, the chief was at every press conference, got interviewed on all those national shows, and outright denied a connection between the two cases. He said it was a coincidence, and that anyone claiming otherwise was undermining the investigation."

"Pretty gutsy of you to write that article then," Riley said.

"Or stupid, I don't know. My editor green-lit the story, but she was also days away from retirement. No one outwardly threatened me or the staff of the paper after it was published, but the newest editor-in-chief told me to drop it. I was really young at the time, in my early twenties, and just getting started. After Brynn was found, the killing stopped. As more and more years went by with nothing to indicate this killer had struck again, it got easier to think that maybe it *had* been two separate killers." He shrugged. "I've never forgotten that one, though. The disparity in terms of which victim supposedly mattered the most was too great—and it's not even a case of, 'all cops are terrible people.' It was a case of the cops deciding that a Black woman like Shawna and a white woman like Brynn were too fundamentally different for a killer to choose them both. They swept Shawna under the rug, and plastered Brynn's face everywhere. It's not like this is the first time it's happened. But when I wrote that article, I was young and … not naïve, because I'm a Black man living in the United States so being naïve to this shit isn't an option, but I really thought if I put my best work forward, if I presented the case that there was a murderer of multiple women out there, that someone would notice or care. But no one did."

"Did you try to get more articles written about it?"

"Yeah, I tried, but I got pulled aside a lot—constantly told that I needed to make a name for myself before I rocked the boat too hard. So I stopped."

"And it's not like there's ever a shortage of awful things to report on."

He laughed humorlessly. "For real. And the part that really gets me is that even though Brynn got all the media coverage, she's been done a terrible disservice, too. If they were looking at the case as a dual murder, there might have been something in that investigation that led them to the killer. That asshole could still be out there to this day. Who knows what else he's gotten away with, all because his victims were treated based on media worthiness before they were treated like women … like human beings who were robbed of justice."

Riley decided in that moment that he'd won her over. "I'm fairly certain he killed at least one other person. Another Black woman."

Carter cocked an eyebrow. "Care to explain?"

Letting out a calming breath, her hands a bit clammy, she said, "I'm a psychic medium."

Carter stared at her for a beat. "*Dammit.*" He shook his head, lips pursed, and reached forward to close his laptop. "I should have known this would be a waste of my time. Why would a kid know anything about this? I'm clearly still a hopeful idiot." He slapped his legal pad on top of his laptop, grabbed both, and started to stand.

In the same moment, Riley pulled the package of prints out of her bag and tossed them onto the coffee table where they landed with a muted plop.

Carter stilled, his focus on the envelope. "What's this?"

"Open it."

He clenched his jaw, then slowly lowered himself back onto the couch cushion. He unhanded his laptop. "If this is—"

"Open it," she repeated. "If you still don't want to hear me out after you look at them, I'll leave and never bother you again."

He picked up the envelope, then pulled out the stack. Silently, he leafed through the pictures, one by one, his dark brows pulled together. When he got to the last one, he froze. She knew he'd reached the heartbreaking one of Shawna. She stood on a sidewalk, part of a porch behind her, reaching for her young son Malcolm who ran toward her, arms outstretched and a grin etched across his young, innocent face. While it was a picture of a woman who had been taken from this world too soon, it was also a picture of a young boy who had no idea that the person behind the unseen camera was putting actions into play that would change his life forever.

Carter's gaze snapped up to hers. "This is Shawna."

"Yep. That's the only one of her on the roll."

"What roll?"

Riley held out a hand and he passed the pictures back. Once they were in her purse, she stood and walked around the coffee table so she could sit on the other side of the couch. No one was currently in direct earshot of them, as the row of nearby patrons were all busily working. The guy on the end of the row closest to them was bopping along to whatever was piping out of his headphones. Beyond that, the coffee grinder or milk frother whirled to life every few minutes.

"Just hear me out, okay?" Riley asked.

He eyed the purse in her lap for a minute, as if he could see through the black faux leather. When his eyes met hers again, he said, "I'm listening."

She went through the whole story for the umpteenth time. Carter did his part to listen intently, only interrupting her a couple of times, but otherwise was at least pretending to take her seriously. When she was finished talking, he appeared a little shell-shocked, so she excused herself to order a to-go iced coffee while he mulled over everything she'd told him.

As she sat down with her drink a few minutes later, Carter said, "Okay, so your working theory is, since Shawna is on the film along with this mystery woman, that the owner of the camera must be the person who killed them both?"

Riley shrugged helplessly. "Maybe? But then why is the mystery woman from 2005 on the same roll as Shawna from 2003, when Brynn presumably was the victim in between? I don't know. What I know is, it looks like this woman, whoever she is, was being followed for a while. I personally know she's dead, and that she died when she was the same age as she is in these pictures. That picture of Shawna looks like a surveillance picture, too. So it would stand to reason that the owner of the camera at the very least was following two women who later ended up dead."

"Shit," he said, elbows on his knees and head in his hands.

"Are you having a harder time with the fact that three women are likely dead at the hands of the same person," she said slowly, after he hadn't changed position for a full minute, "or the psychic medium thing?"

He sat up then and studied her. "Honestly? The second one. Because you seem very normal. But … talking to ghosts? Really?"

Riley shrugged. "You either believe me or you don't."

He sighed. "I guess my other question is … what did you expect to accomplish in talking to me? Did you hope I'd recognize her?"

"Or that you might have resources to find her identity or insights into who could have murdered her, since you're one of the few people who believe Brynn and Shawna had the same killer."

"Unfortunately, I'm all out of insights," he said.

"Is there any chance your current editor would let you print one of the pictures and ask if anyone knows who she is?" Riley asked.

"I don't know … that's a big ask. Especially since I'm not going to be able to give him too many details without him thinking I'm out of my damn mind." He winced. "Sorry."

Riley's gut told her Carter was a reasonable, logical guy, and even if he didn't fully believe in someone's ability to speak to ghosts, she knew he believed *her*. It was up to him to decide what to do with that. "I'll give you a picture of the mystery woman just in case."

"Okay," Carter said, though he sounded deeply unsure again.

Riley pulled the pictures back out of her purse and selected one for him to keep. "You have my contact info now, so if you want to talk again, you know how to find me."

She left the coffee shop, leaving Carter in the same place she'd originally found him, but now with his perspective of the world knocked a little out of whack.

CHAPTER 15

W hen Riley got home that evening, she curled up on the couch and turned on a local news station. There hadn't been any news about the Nob Hill Prowler in a while, so Riley hoped the guy had gotten spooked by the media coverage, stopping his creepy behavior before it escalated to something more violent. Twenty minutes into the news, neither Francis Hank Carras nor the Nob Hill Prowler had been mentioned.

As she picked up the remote to switch the channel, a breaking news bulletin flashed across the screen.

"Early this morning, a young woman, Brooke Winters, was on a run near The University of New Mexico, not far from her home in Nob Hill, when a man ambushed her," the female news anchor said. "Brooke survived the encounter, and escaped relatively unscathed, but she wanted to share her story today to encourage other women to be vigilant."

The screen cut to a pretty brunette standing on a sidewalk in what looked like a park. She had a long-distance runner's body—thin and toned. She had a scrape on her cheek, and a haunted look in her brown eyes, but otherwise looked okay. A male reporter stood on the sidewalk with her. Riley sat forward, her elbows on her knees.

"I've been on that run so many times, I never thought about it being unsafe," Brooke said. "I run really early in the morning, between 4 and 5, so the only people who are out are usually other runners. I've seen the same people every week for months. Anyway, I'd just rounded a corner when someone came flying out of nowhere and tackled me. It knocked the wind out of me, so I couldn't scream or anything. But after we wrestled a bit, I got a look at his face and realized he was wearing a ski mask. It was honestly the scariest thing I'd ever seen. That's when I started screaming."

"And someone heard you then?" the reporter asked.

"Yeah," Brooke said, heaving out a relieved breath, nodding. "This guy, Richard, who is usually out there running at the same time as me, heard me screaming and pulled the guy off me. The two of them were whaling on each other, but Richard was so winded from running that it gave the other guy a chance to wriggle away. But not before Richard yanked the ski mask off his head. He had sandy blond hair, blue eyes, and is in his thirties. We both saw that much before the guy punched Richard in the face, took his ski mask back, and ran off."

"What a harrowing ordeal," the reporter said. "I'm glad you're okay and that Richard was able to come to your aid."

"Me too. Ladies, take pepper spray with you when you're out alone. Carry a whistle. Run in areas with other people around. I love that run but now I'm too scared to ever do it again. Keep your eyes peeled. You never know who's out there watching you."

Riley shuddered.

When the news anchor in the studio returned, on the screen beside her was a composite sketch. "This is a rendering of Brooke's attacker. If you've seen this man, please contact Albuquerque police."

Though the reporter hadn't outright made a connection between this man and the Nob Hill Prowler, Riley's gut told her the voyeur had escalated after all.

When two days went by without a follow-up from Carter, Riley got antsy. Even if, deep down, she believed Carter would come around on accepting she was a psychic, it didn't mean he'd do anything with that acceptance.

She told herself that the frustration of being back at square one was what made her decide to drive across town to Marty's Thrift N Save, the store owned by Carol's friend. Riley hadn't called Marty first to warn her she'd be stopping by with questions.

According to Carol, Marty had been the one who attended the auction in Clovis, where the cameras had come from. When Riley hadn't been able to sleep last night, she'd done a little research on how these auctions worked. She'd woken up with her phone on her chest, the battery nearly drained. Riveting stuff, storage unit auctions.

Riley had been disappointed, but not surprised, to learn that what was on TV—*Storage Wars*, *Auction Kings*, and the like—wasn't totally accurate. Rare, expensive items were almost never left in storage units, as the units were more often than not purchased by people down on their luck who needed a safe place to store their belongings when they could no longer afford rent on their residence. If their luck kept proving to be elusive, paying rent on the unit became impossible, too. She'd read a few heartbreaking stories of families losing their units, and then attending the auction, standing outside the fence as they watched all their worldly possessions getting packed onto someone else's truck bed.

In other cases, units were abandoned on purpose because they held illegal items—guns and drugs, mostly. When the lock was cut on those units after 90 days of missed payments, unsurprisingly no auction happened, as everything had to be turned over to the police.

And in rare cases—treated as the norm on the reality shows—units held items of value, like the one Marty and Carol had bought. So it begged the question once again: who had owned that unit and what had caused said person to fall behind on payments? Was he or she out of the country, broke, in prison … dead?

It was that last one that made Riley get out of the car and cross the parking lot to the glass doors of Marty's Thrift N Save. If the unit owner was now dead, Riley could potentially make contact if Marty had any items from the unit in her shop. She pushed open the door and cautiously stepped inside. Like Carol's store, this one was fairly small, but the layout was more open than her friend's.

A few feet from the door stood the cashier counter. It was made of glass, and had small glass figurines of fantasy creatures— unicorns, fairies, dragons—lining its two shelves. Bookshelves stacked with leather-bound books stood to either side of the counter. The rest of the space had free-standing shelves and stands scattered haphazardly, stuffed with accessories like handbags, shoes, and scarfs. The back wall was covered in framed black-and-white photos, all of which were of iconic Hollywood women—Marilyn Monroe, Audrey Hepburn, Elizabeth Taylor.

She walked a little further inside the shop, not seeing other patrons or employees. "Hello?" she called out.

No response.

Riley stopped in front of a coat rack hung with purses of all colors and sizes. The smiling face of a gaudy sequined cat stared back at her from the side of a leather messenger bag.

"Oh, hello," someone said behind her, and Riley whirled to find a five-foot-nothing woman standing there. "Can I help you find something?"

Riley noted a faint Spanish accent.

"I hope so," Riley said. "I'm not sure if your friend Carol mentioned that I might come by to ask about a storage unit auction you attended where you bought three cameras?"

She smiled, laugh lines prominent at the corners of her brown eyes. "Riley, yes? The one who can communicate with spirits?"

Riley flushed. "Guilty."

"Well, this is exciting!" Marty said. "I've never met a real live psychic before." She cast a wide look around her store, then hunched into her shoulders a little. "Are there any spirits in here now? I've always loved the idea of a shop ghost!"

"Sorry," Riley said, laughing. "It's pretty quiet in here from what I can tell."

"Drat! One of these days I'll get me a shop ghost. Anyway… I'm glad you came by. Finally someone who will appreciate the weirdness of that auction. I've already talked to my husband about it, but none of my friends care a lick about auctions and I can't tell Carol."

"I am intrigued," Riley said, brow cocked.

Marty laughed. "Oh, it's nothing scandalous. It's just that the inside of the unit struck me as so odd. There wasn't much in it, which was odd if only because these things are usually loaded with people's whole lives. Some of these things are just wall-to-wall boxes thrown in all willy-nilly. It's a wonder everything doesn't come falling out when some of these doors are opened. But in this one … here, let me show you."

As Marty pulled her phone out of her back pocket, Riley walked over to stand beside her. Marty scrolled through a few pictures—most of them of happy, round-cheeked kids; grandchildren, Riley guessed—before she went, "Ah, here it is," and tapped one of the thumbnails.

In the room was nothing but an industrial desk and a desk chair. The desk looked heavy, likely made of metal. The only items on the surface were a lantern that Riley figured ran on batteries, and a mug. The desk sat in the center of the space. Perhaps it had been used as a very isolated office.

"Isn't that so bizarre? It kind of gives me the creeps if I look at it for too long," Marty said.

"You're not allowed to go *in* a storage unit during an auction, right?"

"Nope," Marty said. "And with this one, no one needed to."

"What made you bid on it? It doesn't look like the kind of thing you or Carol sell."

"Partly curiosity. The mug on the table had what looked like coffee in it, but it clearly hadn't been touched in at least three months, seeing as the unit wouldn't have been on sale otherwise. I was thinking maybe it was a writer's shed, and that the next great American novel could be in one of those drawers. Maybe the author had recently dropped dead or something. That, and my husband is very handy and he's been looking for a desk like this for a long time as a workbench."

"Was there a lot of competition for it?" Riley asked, still staring at the nearly empty unit.

"Hardly any. I got into a bidding war with an auction veteran I see at a lot of events, but once it got over $700, he dropped out."

Riley whistled. "$700 for a desk?"

"That's the part you can't tell Carol," Marty said, wrinkling her nose. "I told her it was only $300, and we split the difference. Kenneth outbid me on a rare unit a year ago and I've been sore about it ever since. There were two tubs in the back of the unit that had ended up being stuffed to the gills with Disney memorabilia. Kenneth apparently sold the lot of it for close to ten thousand dollars. That jerk! So when Kenneth showed interest in *this* one, I kept bidding higher out of spite. Oh, the look on his face when he found out there were cameras in those drawers! Worth every penny."

"I love a person who can hold a good grudge," Riley said.

Marty laughed again, then pocketed her phone.

"How long ago was the auction?"

"Hmm … about two months ago?"

"Was there anything else in the drawers? Just the cameras?"

"Yep, just the cameras," Marty said. "Oh, and there was a jacket. You can't see it in the picture because it was on the ground behind the chair. I took that for myself. There's a clothes-selling app I post items on exclusively for a few weeks before I make it available for purchase here. The app lets me sell the item to anyone in the country, so if there's interest, it usually sells there first. It's a brown leather bomber jacket. A relic of the '80s, for sure. I've already got a couple nibbles."

Riley really didn't love the idea of communicating with another serial killer ghost, but she'd promised the woman in the yellow dress that she'd do everything in her power to figure out what had happened to her. "Could I see it?"

Marty cocked her head. "I suppose so. I'll be right back."

Riley told herself that if this *did* make a ghost appear in Marty's shop and he went poltergeist on them, Riley would do what she could to cover the damages. She was mentally cataloguing what she could sell in her apartment for quick cash when Marty returned with the jacket draped over her arm. It was a warm dark brown, the leather a bit distressed, and had fabric cuffs and a fabric hem.

Marty unzipped the jacket, took hold of it by the shoulders, and held it out for Riley.

"Oh, I didn't want to try it on," Riley said, face heating.

Marty took it in stride, though. "You just want to feel its energy, then? That's cool. Don't worry. Carol told me all about the indigo child thing."

Riley gently took the jacket from Marty, bracing herself for something to happen, but other than the sensation of the supple leather under her fingertips, Riley didn't feel anything.

"Was she murdered?" Marty asked suddenly. "The woman you and Carol have both seen. Is that why she's so sad? Someone killed her?"

"I think so," Riley said softly.

Marty had a hand to her throat as she stared at the jacket. "So does that mean that the person who owned this unit…" She frowned, clearly already second-guessing her desire for a shop ghost.

"That's what I'm trying to find out," Riley said as she unzipped pockets and rooted around in their shallow corners. She assumed Marty had done this already, but since handling the item hadn't triggered anything, Riley was already out of ideas.

The lack of materializing ghosts could mean he'd already moved on—or it could mean that it hadn't been death that had kept him from paying his storage fees. The jacket was in very good condition if it was truly from the '80s, and had been well cared for, which was what Ian had also said about the cameras. Between that, and the unfinished mug of coffee on the table, something unexpected and traumatic must have happened to the owner to make him abandon items he'd loved.

When the pockets offered no secrets, Riley checked in the inside lining, hoping a name was written on a tag or near the collar. Her dad had an old jacket like this, and he'd written R. THOMAS on the tag in Sharpie. No such luck here.

The fabric cuffs were surprisingly not dingy. Perhaps the owner got the item dry cleaned regularly. She did find a small, dark stain on one of the cuffs, though, and idly rubbed a thumb across it.

An odd, low buzz filled her head.

A moment later, she got kicked in the stomach so hard, it knocked her breath from her body. She gasped and stumbled back, crashing into the coat rack hung with purses. The rack toppled over easily, taking Riley with it. The rack hit something—an end table, maybe—and split in half underneath her. She fell in a tangle of broken wood, purse straps, and jacket sleeves. The buzzing in her head persisted.

Something as hard as rock clocked her on the side of the face and spots swam before her eyes. The buzzing grew louder. The crunch of bone sounded close to her head, where her hand had just been smashed by an object as heavy as a bowling ball. Another crack to her face, and her head whipped to the side from the impact. It was a wonder her mouth wasn't full of loose teeth. Nausea roiled in her stomach. Had her jaw just shattered like the coat rack? Panic rose up in her chest like a tide, unable to see her assailant in part because she was wrapped up in the jacket and fallen purses, like she was caught in seaweed that had grabbed hold of her limbs, trying to pull her into the depths. One of the curved pieces of wood from the rack's base jabbed her painfully in the back.

"Riley!" Marty cried out. "What on earth is going on?"

Another slam to her side, and she was sure then that a rib had snapped in half, shards of which were tearing into her lungs. She groaned, doubled over in the fetal position. "Get the jacket off me!" she choked out.

Marty grabbed hold of the jacket and hurled it behind her where it fell with a muted thud.

The buzzing in her head instantly quieted and Riley sagged. The purse with the sequined cat stared at her again, this time from only half an inch away. The straps of another purse were around one arm and it felt like several others were draped across her legs. Riley pulled the cat purse free and stared up at the ceiling. A significant water stain marred a section near the right-hand corner.

Marty's face swam into view. "Good heavens! Are you okay? That was the freakiest thing I've ever seen."

Reaching up to rub her jaw, Riley was surprised to find it didn't hurt. "Is my face bruised?"

Marty cocked a brow. "Not that I can see," she said slowly, then held out a hand. "Let me help you up."

Riley grabbed onto it and used her free hand to push herself to sitting. The only spots on her body that actually hurt were on her back and tailbone, where she'd made contact with the coat rack. Her stomach, jaw, and sides, where she'd been hit so forcibly, felt fine.

Once out of the debris, Riley turned back to look at the destruction caused not by a poltergeist, but by some weird psychic reaction to that jacket. Riley glared at it, where it lay pooled on the ground. It took her a moment to piece together what had happened, much like how she had to figure out what Iris Velasco had tried to tell her based on a series of images and impressions.

Her gut told her the spot on the jacket had been blood, and it had been his blood that triggered the psychic reaction.

"The owner of the storage unit got beaten up really badly," Riley said. "I think that's tied to why he abandoned it." He couldn't have been wearing the jacket when he'd been attacked since the unit was lost because of the attack. The blood that was on it now had been from something else. Maybe the guy got smacked around a lot.

"Oh my. I'm not sure I want something with mojo this bad in here. I surely don't think I should sell it."

All Riley knew was that she didn't want it anywhere near her. They both glanced over at it.

"What do I think I should do with it?" Marty asked.

If it did belong to the man who killed Brynn, Shawna, and the woman in the yellow dress, the blood on that cuff could prove useful, just like the fingerprint slide in her nightstand drawer. But she didn't have an identity for this man, which meant a trip to the police station was still on the back burner.

"Would it be too much to ask you to hang onto it for now?" Riley asked.

"Not at all. I'll take it down from the app right away. If it ends up being necessary in figuring out what happened to that young lady, I'll turn it over to whoever needs it."

As the adrenaline started to wear off, a pit formed in Riley's stomach. "I'm really sorry. Just let me know how much it'll cost to fix all this and—"

Marty waved her off.

Frowning, Riley worked through the possibility of sending Marty a check in a week or so.

Marty craned her neck to force Riley to focus on her instead of mental math. "Now you listen here," she said, turning to face Riley head-on now, partially blocking her view of the destruction. She put her hands on her slender hips. "Carol said that the young woman showed up the day I brought her the cameras. She saw that woman nearly every day, and every time she said the same thing: 'I wish I knew what made her so sad.' She felt guilty when she sold the cameras to your friend and the ghost went with them. Carol couldn't shake the feeling that the woman needed help, that she was lost, you know?"

Riley nodded.

"When she called me to tell me you might come by, she was so relieved. She said she thought a lot about the chain of events ... how you wouldn't have come into her store looking for those cameras if I hadn't gone out to Clovis to that auction. If Kenneth hadn't outbid me a year ago, I wouldn't have been so determined to get that unit in the first place. Carol and I are both big believers in things happening for a reason. So if that dumb ol' coat rack getting smashed to bits means that young lady will eventually be put to rest, that's A-OK with me."

Riley wanted to hug her. "Thank you."

"Of course," Marty said, then took out her phone, tapped a few things and then handed it over. "Put your contact info in there for me. You have my number, right?" Riley nodded as she keyed in her name and number. "Keep me updated on this as payment, and I'll be in touch if I happen to think of anything else. Or if that new workbench of my husband's has a secret compartment in it stuffed with incriminating evidence."

Riley managed a laugh, handing the phone back. "Sounds good."

As she left the shop, limping slightly as she did, she thought about how the ghosts who had started demanding her attention lately had all met some horrible end at the hands of terrible people. It was easy to grow even more cynical than she already was in light of that. But she had to remind herself that while she'd searched for Pete's and Renee's killers, she'd met people like Michael, Mindy, and Detective Howard. And now the woman in the yellow dress was leading her down a path that had intersected with Carter Quincy, Carol, and Marty. The good people far outweighed the bad.

She winced as she climbed back into her car, her lower back aching so much already that she knew a scalding bath was in her near future, but despite all that, a small smile still managed to break free.

CHAPTER 16

Riley might have been getting better at trusting her instincts and dealing with ghosts when they materialized, but it still didn't mean that she wanted to run the risk of another altercation with the Poltergeist of Aisle 3. Which was why she had driven half an hour out of her way—again—to go grocery shopping. She'd only been here for a whopping five minutes and was already regretting her decision; she picked a hoity-toity Whole Foods knock-off by accident. As she dubiously eyed the wide variety of kombucha, her phone chimed with a text message. It was from Carter Quincy.

A photo of your mystery woman is going to run in tomorrow's paper. Send me your email address and I'll send you a link to the article.

"Oh shit," she whispered at her phone's screen.

The woman next to her turned up her nose and pushed her cart a bit farther down the aisle.

Riley ignored her and sent Carter her address.

Her phone immediately rang.

"Hi, Carter," she said, a little breathless.

"Is this a good time? It's the middle of the day so I assumed you were working . . ."

"I have the day off."

"Oh." The awkward silence that slammed down on them told her he still hadn't fully embraced the whole psychic medium thing. "So…uh…the article is more focused on Shawna Mack than anything else. It would have been her 45th birthday tomorrow."

"Oh wow…"

"Your mystery woman will be added to the end of the article. A 'this woman may be connected to the case; do you know who she is?' kind of deal," he said. "Not mentioning you or your…gift."

"What did you tell your editor to get him to agree to include the picture?" Riley asked.

"I told him I have a very reliable source whom I couldn't reveal yet," Carter said. "He trusts me, so he's running with it. Let's hope for both our sakes, and the sake of the mystery woman, that this pans out."

Riley didn't know what to say.

"I'll be in touch."

After putting away her groceries—minus kombucha—Riley called Jade. The sound of wind answered the call before she did.

"Crap," she said in greeting. "Hang on."

The wind quieted.

"Sorry, I'm on my way home. You still coming over tonight?" Jade asked.

"Yep. Need me to bring anything?"

"I don't think so. The card stock showed up yesterday. It all looks amazing."

Tonight's maid of honor task was wedding invitations. Jade wanted to handcraft all one hundred and fifty, of course. They had raided quite a few scrapbooking sections of craft stores over the last few months, leaving Jade with piles of wedding-themed stickers, decals, and other paper decorations. She'd also apparently taken a few online calligraphy classes. Riley had no idea when she found the time to do it all.

Jade had thankfully allowed Riley to put in an order for card stock and hadn't tried to make her own stationery, at least. The stock had been printed with the location, date, and time, and Jade would handwrite people's names on the cards and envelopes.

"Also … Jonah said he's got something to show us," Jade said. "I think he got a hit on the face recognition thing. I didn't get too many details. He called just before I had to go into a meeting and now *he's* in a meeting."

"You people and your fancy meetings."

Jade laughed. "See you tonight."

Riley arrived a little after five. Jonah wouldn't be home for at least another hour, so they got to work while they waited, covering Jade's giant dining room table in supplies. It didn't take long for Riley's fingers to ache from affixing tiny puffy champagne stickers and gluing black bow ties to the corners of the printed cards. When she finished attaching the decorations, she added the cards to the growing pile for Jade to add her handwritten flourishes.

By six o'clock, they were two-thirds through a second bottle of wine—most of it consumed by Jade—and were so deep in conversation, neither one had noticed Jonah had entered the room until he cleared his throat. Jade jumped so abruptly that a splatter of red wine landed on the corner of one of the cards.

Riley gasped as if Jonah had just walked into the royal palace and slapped the queen across the face.

"Jonah Henderson, I will strangle you!" Jade said, hopping to her feet, but swayed a little, and Jonah had to grab her by the elbow to keep her from pitching over the side of her chair.

Jonah merely smiled at his wife-to-be. "Making any headway on this very large undertaking, my love?" he asked in a dramatic tone that elicited a giggle out of Riley.

Jade pointed a finger at her. "Don't encourage him. I'm not above firing you."

Riley grinned. "Don't threaten me with a good time."

Jade, clearly having forgotten that she was upset with him only a moment ago, threw her arms around Jonah's neck and kissed him. "Are you here to help us, almost-husband?"

"Absolutely not," he said, hands on her hips. When she just stood there gazing at him with a goofy smile on her face, he asked, "Do you remember what I told you earlier?"

It took Jade a second and then she dramatically let him go. "You have done some nerdy tech sleuthing!"

"Indeed I have," he said chuckling, then picked up his laptop lying on the table. Riley wondered when he'd set it there.

Jade cleared a small section of table for him, and then she and Riley huddled on either side while he pulled up his findings.

"Okay, so this program we're using pulls all images from the internet it can find. It deems a photo a match with the face you're searching for based on a certain set of criteria," Jonah said. "It's still very buggy. Issues come up constantly because at the end of the day, a computer isn't as good at recognizing faces as a human is, so there's a lot of sifting through findings. It's still way more efficient than a human would be if they were scouring the internet on their own for something like this. Plus, it's just looking for images—I had to search the images' metadata to track down where the pictures had come from."

Jade was waving a hand in a circular "less talk, more pictures" motion.

Jonah either didn't see it, or he chose to ignore it. He clicked a link in an email he'd sent himself. "So I flagged two things that I think fit our mystery woman. One is a Myspace profile."

"Oh geez!" Jade said. "Isn't that super old? When was Myspace around? 1990s or something?"

"It launched in 2003," Jonah said.

A quick scan of the page with its dark blue background revealed that it had belonged to an Emery Dawson. The profile picture sent a chill racing down Riley's spine. It was absolutely the woman in the yellow dress.

Now she had a name.

"She's beautiful," Jade said softly. "But … I thought Myspace went the way of the dodo. How are you able to still see her profile?"

"It never really went away. Nothing on the internet ever truly dies. Someone is keeping the platform live, therefore you can still find profiles if you know where to look."

There wasn't much on the profile, just her name and a few pictures. The sections where she could have put descriptions or posts were all empty. Either there hadn't ever been much on the profile to begin with, or the page had largely been scrubbed since Emery's disappearance.

"The next one is an article," Jonah said. "You'll see why you've been having a hard time figuring out who she is. I haven't read the full article yet. I just bookmarked it."

The article was from the *Socorro Gazette*, based out of Texas, in 2005. The picture accompanying the article was the same one from Emery's Myspace profile. Jade and Riley hunched forward even more to read the article, Jonah's head between theirs. Hopefully the poor guy didn't pass out from the wine fumes wafting off them both.

Young Woman Goes Missing

Emery Dawson, 22, was last seen a week ago. Dawson moved to Socorro only six months ago for a job opportunity in nearby El Paso. She lived with a roommate, Abbigail McKinley, who worked the graveyard shift at a hospital, so the two rarely saw each other. McKinley said, "Emery was a really nice girl. I talked to her briefly a few days ago when she was leaving for work and I was coming home. We were like two ships passing in the night most of the time, so I don't know much about her even though we lived together. If she ever had friends or guys over, I didn't know about it."

Dawson's parents live in Odessa and hadn't heard from their daughter for a few days, but that wasn't unusual, according to her father.

"Emery was always a quiet girl. Introverted, I guess you'd call it," he said. "She liked her books and video games. It's always bothered me that her laptop went missing. There could be clues there. She spent a lot of time online, like kids do these days. We didn't bug her too much about what she was doing on there, but we didn't think we needed to. She's a good girl. Now I wish we'd paid more attention. She thrived online since she was so shy till she got to know someone. Who knows who she befriended on the internet?"

One coworker recalls how, the day before her disappearance, Dawson had asked her if she thought red lipstick would look good on her. "I was a little surprised she asked me that. She and I weren't really close—she wasn't close with anyone at the office. She was very nice and great at her job and everything, but she kept to herself, you know? She never wore makeup, didn't do much with her hair . . . had a really neutral-colored wardrobe. It was like she was in a shell. She had this natural beauty to her but she seemed too shy to flaunt it. When she asked about the lipstick, I thought maybe she had a date or something. But then she didn't come into work the next day. I regret not trying to get to know her better, not asking her more questions."

When Dawson didn't call in sick for work, her co-workers tried to get a hold of her. When that didn't pan out, her manager contacted her parents.

"Nothing in the apartment looked out of the or-dinary," her mother said. "When her manager called us, we expected to find the worst. But there's no sign of her. It's like she disappeared into thin air."

The only things missing from her apartment, according to her roommate, were her laptop, purse, and phone. It appears as if she'd left for a normal outing. Her car was found in a parking lot at the Rio Bosque Wetland Park in El Paso. The car was locked, the windows intact. None of the items her roommate mentioned were found in the vehicle. It's speculated that she drove herself into the Rio Bosque Wetland Park, but never came back out. It's possible she crossed into Mexico, as her phone pinged towers there in the few days after her disappearance. The phone hasn't been found.

An extensive search of the area was conducted, but the park is largely flat and the bodies of water calm. There has even been speculation that someone attempting to cross the border illegally abducted her with the hope of monetary gain in the form of ransom. But no such demands have been made on her family.

Anyone with any information on Dawson's whereabouts is encouraged to contact Crime Stoppers or the Socorro police department.

Riley stood to full height, suddenly feeling sober. She crossed her arms, glaring down at Jonah's screen. "I guess this explains why her energy feels so weak. Even if the camera brought her to New Mexico, she's not from here. And possibly wasn't killed here."

Jade rubbed her hands up and down her arms. "Ugh, this is awful."

Sighing, Riley said, "Did you find anything else?"

"Just a few other articles that had been written about her disappearance. She hasn't been mentioned anywhere I could find since 2005," Jonah said.

The mood in the room had changed from carefree wedding prep to something much more somber. Even though "the woman in the yellow dress" had a name now, it didn't make Riley feel any closer to figuring out what had happened to her. Not even her parents had any real guesses. Professional search teams working in one of the last areas she'd been had turned up nothing. What did Riley expect to find?

"We can work on the invitations later," Jade said, who had come around the other side of Jonah's chair to stand beside her. She placed a gentle hand on Riley's elbow.

Jade didn't need claircognizance or strong intuition to know Riley would be consumed by this information now, lost in her own thoughts, and that she'd need to work through it in her own way.

"Sorry," Riley said, collecting her purse and jacket.

"Don't be sorry," Jade said.

"If anyone should be sorry," Jonah said, turning in his chair to face her, "it's me. I killed the party. I should have read the article first so I could warn you."

Offering him a small smile, Riley said, "You did great. I'm very impressed with your nerdy tech skills." But even she could hear that her heart wasn't in the banter. "I'll talk to you later," she said, giving them both a hug before she let herself out.

On her drive home, she called Michael, a knot of tension unfurling in her chest when he said, "Hey! How was your day off?"

"The woman in the yellow dress has a name," she said. "Her name was Emery Dawson." It felt strange to say it out loud.

He was silent for a long moment, followed by the faint jangle of keys. "Are you driving?"

"Yeah. Headed home from Jade's."

"Crack open a bottle of wine and start a bath." A door creaked shut. "I'll be there in an hour or so with a pizza. You can tell me about Emery."

October, 2021

My financial situation was not improving. I'd snagged a couple of surveillance jobs over the past week. Standard "I need proof my girlfriend is cheating on me" stuff. Five hundred dollars here, three hundred dollars there. Between that and what little I already had in my account, I was able to pay October's rent, but what the hell was I going to do next month?

My snatch-and-grab had been a bust. I would have to try for another one. My contact hadn't given me a due date, just that he wanted proof of capture once I had her. Something he'd said last month had been eating away at my mind, though. An earworm chewing another hole in that black curtain blocking my view of the last five years—if not more.

"The Client monopolized you for years. If you're as good as you were back then, we can make a fuckload of money together."

The Client.

Ever since, I'd been trying to find evidence of who this had been. I couldn't explain it, but I was sure his identity was the key to unlocking my own. Who had I been five years ago?

I couldn't find him on the main forum I frequented. Anon9876 had also mentioned a private chat. I had no clue what or where that was either. I tore my apartment asunder looking for anything I had missed. Curiously, I found a footlocker under my bed. What the hell was in it, I didn't know. Perhaps the key to the lock had been on the same ring of keys that my apartment keys had been on when I was attacked. If my current search turned up nothing, I'd track down a pair of bolt cutters.

In the back of my closet, I found a suitcase. There were several other bags stuffed inside it—a couple of empty duffel bags and a smaller gym bag. In the very bottom of the suitcase was an attached zippered garment bag, and inside that lay a small black notebook. It fit easily in the palm of one hand, and the cover was made of a sturdy material. Familiarity hit me in the chest and I ran idle fingers over the cover a moment before opening it.

I sat on the ground and leafed through the book, the sight of my small, neat handwriting pulling up brief memories of me scribbling things down. I had pages and pages of notes about a woman named Shawna Mack, while others were about Brynn Bodwell. Neither name registered with me, but that annoying tickle was at the back of my brain for a moment before fading. Like the annoying tingle in your nose when you need to sneeze, and just before you do, your eyes watering, the sensation goes away, robbing you of satisfaction.

For reasons unknown, I flipped to the back of the note-book. It was muscle memory more than a hunch; a repeated action wired into my marrow. Notes were written on the inside back cover.

The Collector Private Chat

The Client Exclusive Chat

Websites and passwords were listed for both, as well as an email address and password I had no memory of. My heart thudded in my chest but there was no stress-induced headache. Hope swelled like an inflated balloon. I scrambled to my feet and darted for my computer.

Hours of poring over the wealth of information in these newly revealed locations didn't just poke holes in that black curtain—it tore great swaths of fabric loose.

Years ago, I had ventured into the world of photography forums. I sought other "shutterbugs" who loved the craft. People I could talk to when I'd no longer been able to talk to my father—losing him first to his alcoholism, and later to death caused by his addiction. In the forums, I'd found a new family. A family who understood me.

Over time, a few revealed they were voyeurists, as we called ourselves. There were more of us than I ever imagined, so I created a safe haven for us. Nudists have colonies. We had the private chat. A place where we wouldn't be shamed for our interests. It was in this chat that I first met The Client. We didn't use names for years to help protect our privacy.

The voyeurists issued each other challenges. They started out juvenile—snapping a picture under a woman's skirt without her knowing, for example. But the challenges evolved over time. They got more complicated, more difficult, more dangerous. I excelled, though. I captured images and tracked down information better than anyone else.

It was through these challenges that I caught The Client's eye. He started offering to pay me handsomely for challenges exclusive to me. His first challenge had been to watch a woman named Shawna Mack in Taos, New Mexico. I'd been living in Central California at the time, and my father's health had gotten so bad he was on hospice care, being tended to by my doormat of a mother.

I had originally planned to visit New Mexico just for a few weeks, but I'd loved it there. So I moved to the state permanently, settling in Albuquerque after the Taos jobs were done. I happily left my parents behind. Before I fled the state, I took three of my father's most prized film cameras. He'd made me clean the things once a month like clockwork for years. I knew those machines better than he did. He couldn't even use them anymore, and my mother was too much of a mess to notice they were gone. They belonged with me.

From then on, for ten glorious years, The Client would contact me when he had a new woman for me to surveil. He footed the bill for my travel and extended stays in whatever place he wanted me to go next.

But that all stopped in 2011, when The Client suffered an accident on a construction job. After a long hospital stay, several surgeries, and physical therapy, he wasn't the same man. Just like my father. And just like with my father, I'd been cast aside, though The Client had done his best to sound upset about it.

"We had a good run, but the signs tell me it's time for a change. If you keep my secrets, I'll keep yours."

That was it. Ten years of working together and I was dropped.

I made the best of it. The skills I gathered while working for him allowed me to create a lucrative business for myself. But it had never been the same. No one ever paid me as well, no one ever appreciated my skills as much. A pang that was some part grief, some part longing wracked my soul as I read old messages between us. The black curtain was in tatters now.

He was who I needed. He could get me out of the horrible financial mess I was in.

Alas, life was unfair.

Closing my laptop, I gathered my belongings, got dressed, and went out into the night again, searching for a woman who could solve my problems.

CHAPTER 17

Riley awoke the next morning a little after 10. Michael had left hours ago. They'd stayed up for several hours talking about Emery Dawson and doing another search for her online, now that there was a name to put in the search bar. But not much more came up than what Jonah had already shown them.

The lack of a "Body of Missing Woman Found" article about Emery suggested she was still considered a missing person. Were her parents still holding out hope that their introverted daughter was out there somewhere, maybe living a secret life across the border? Since Emery was from an entirely different state, Riley could understand why her disappearance hadn't been connected to Shawna's and Brynn's—especially if her body had never been found. But it begged the question: Why was a photographer with a storage unit in Clovis, who had presumably been in Texas—over five hours away—taking surveillance pictures of Emery, in addition to two women from Taos? How had he even found Emery, and what had he done with her afterward?

After a quick breakfast of oatmeal and toast, she took a shower, and then settled in front of her laptop. She knew she needed to let Carter know that she'd figured out the identity of her "mystery woman," as he called her, but doing so through text messages felt a little too informal. She was halfway through an email to him when her phone chimed.

NINE: Made contact with Amy Velasco. Available for a meeting this afternoon? She can meet during her lunch break today at 12:15.

Riley checked the time. It was 11:45.

RILEY: Yep. Text me the address of where we're going. I'll leave here in a few.

She closed her laptop on the half-written message, vowing that she'd let him know about Emery later. After changing her outfit four times, she went back to the first thing she'd put on, pulled on some flats and hurried out the door.

Epicurean Subs was a gourmet place Riley had only been to once. It was a bit overpriced, but the turkey, cranberry, cream cheese, and arugula sandwich she'd gotten had been surprisingly good. Riley had arrived at the shop first, so she put in her order and was waiting at a table with a numbered card when Nina strolled in. Amy cautiously walked in a minute later.

Amy had the same dark hair as her mother, Riley noted. She felt a pang at seeing both how anxious Amy was, and how young. She guessed Amy was even younger than she was.

Once food orders for everyone had been placed and received, they settled at a table near the back of the small space. There were only half a dozen tables here, and they were currently the only ones dining in. The handful of people who'd come in since Riley had arrived had only placed to-go orders.

"Thank you for meeting with us," Nina said, guiding the conversation. If it had been left up to Riley, she'd still be in the awkward silence stage.

"Sure," Amy said, her tone tentative as her gaze shifted from Nina to Riley and back again. "Curiosity got me here more than anything."

"Who was it who contacted you first?" Nina asked.

"The realtor who sold the house to Julie Young. He told me there had been a ghost hunt at the house and that someone had …" She swallowed. "Someone had made contact with my mom? He asked me if I wanted to talk to the current owner of the house first, or to the person who led the investigation. I said I wanted to talk to Julie, since I figured if there was a cuckoo person in this whole scenario, it was probably the ghost hunters." She swallowed again, heat rising in her cheeks. "Sorry."

"Eh," Nina said, waving the comment away. "If only cuckoo was the worst I've been called."

Amy laughed involuntarily at that, given how fast she cut the laugh off and how much redder her cheeks grew because of it. "Julie said you guys were really great, though, so I figured it was safe to meet you."

Riley and Nina had already briefly discussed the fact that they'd need to keep the gorier details of what had happened to Iris out of the conversation. Amy would have already known her mother had suffered from a fatal fall down the stairs—there was no need to go into the fact that Riley had witnessed every bone-crunching horror of said fall.

"We were called in because of the activity in the house," Nina said. "It was clear once we got there that the spirit wanted to relay a message. We believe the message is for you."

Amy's eyes welled, but the tears didn't fall. She sniffed hard.

"I know this is a delicate subject, and if this gets too uncomfortable for you, we can stop at any time, okay?" Nina asked.

Amy nodded.

In her soft, gentle way, Nina said, "We know that your mother's death was deemed a suicide. Do you know the details of why it's considered a suicide and not an accident?"

"Mom was allergic to Tylenol," Amy said. "Like, deathly allergic. She had a scare when she was ten or so. She was home sick from school and had a really bad headache. Her dad was home with her, but he'd been on the phone so she got into the medicine cabinet on her own and took two tabs of Tylenol. She started acting really weird and broke out in hives. Her dad realized she was having an allergic reaction, so he took her to the hospital. On the way there, she went into anaphylactic shock. Grandad liked to tell the story of how he drove to the hospital so fast that day, he almost broke the sound barrier." She smiled sadly to herself. "Anyway, he got her to the hospital in time to get a dose of epinephrine. Ever since then, she was really good about making sure not to take the stuff. I don't understand how she could die from something she didn't even keep in the house.

"They did an autopsy and found that she had taken at least three tabs of Tylenol. For someone as allergic as she is, that would easily kill her if she didn't get an EpiPen in time. There were EpiPens all over that house, too. None of them were used. So the theory is that the Tylenol would have killed her if the fall down the stairs hadn't done it first. They tried to tell me that maybe she kept some on hand to take if things ever got really bad for her. As if she were a spy who kept cyanide pills hidden in a pocket in case she was ever arrested for war crimes or something. Ridiculous."

Riley frowned.

"I know she didn't kill herself," Amy said, wiping away an escaped tear. "I know it in my gut. Maybe that's just me being in denial or something, I don't know. She'd just gone through a bad breakup with her boyfriend a month or so before that. Maybe she was more heartbroken about that than I thought?"

Riley had started shaking her head halfway through Amy's musings.

Amy cocked her head at her. "No? Did her message have something to do with the way she died?"

Riley cast a quick glance at Nina, who nodded, letting her know it was okay to answer. "I can…see things. Spirits. Pieces of the past. Stuff like that. Your mom showed me that she actually had fallen twice that day. The first time, she'd fallen off a ladder—"

Amy let out a sound that was somewhere between a laugh and a sob. "Oh my god. I can't tell you how many times I yelled at her for that! My parents divorced about five years ago. He's off in Florida with a new wife and kid already. Anyway, ever since then, she's tried to do all the handiwork herself. She was probably cleaning out the gutters." She shook her head, amused while fighting back tears at the same time.

"We think the fall off the ladder gave her a concussion, which caused confusion," Riley said. "A young guy in the neighborhood either saw the fall or found her lying in front of the house and helped her inside. He gave her something for her headache, and because of her confused state due to the concussion, we believe she took Tylenol by accident. It's possible he had it on him and gave it to her not knowing she was allergic."

Amy's bottom lip quivered.

Nina said, "One of the symptoms of anaphylactic shock is also confusion. We believe her concussion compounded that, which would explain why she didn't get to her EpiPen in time. It's possible she forgot where the pens were."

"She was very disoriented," Riley said, recalling how often Iris had walked into her bedroom from the bathroom, forgotten what she'd been doing, and then had gone back into the bathroom—how she'd brushed her teeth multiple times.

"So you … saw her? Did she talk to you?" Amy lightly pressed a hand to her forehead. "God, I don't even know if I believe in ghosts, you know? I don't know if I'm accepting all this because I need confirmation that she didn't die on purpose. I need closure, I guess, since it was so sudden. Not that I think you two are scam artists or something." Her cheeks heated again, and she buried her face in her hands for a moment.

"Would you like proof?" Nina asked after a moment.

Riley and Amy both turned to her, brows raised.

"What kind of proof?" Amy asked.

Nina explained what EVPs were, and that she had four she could listen to. "You can let me know if it sounds like your mother's voice."

Amy chewed on a thumbnail for a few long seconds before she nodded.

Nina cued up the EVPs on her phone, apparently having anticipated that she might need to share them.

Laying her phone on the table, she turned up the volume. "There are four here. They'll play back-to-back. Riley and I were unsure of the second two. Maybe you'll have more insights than we did." She hit play on the file.

Amy visibly swallowed.

Olivia asked, "Is your name Amy Velasco?"

Iris replied with, "*Daughter.*"

Amy sucked in a breath, hands pressed to her mouth.

Nina's voice asked, "Why are you still here?"

When Iris replied, Nina hit pause on the file.

It still sounded like "painted" to Riley. Nina thought Iris had said "placement."

"Holy crap," Amy said. "Can you play that again?"

Nina obliged, then hit pause once more. "What does it sound like to you?"

"Payment," Amy said slowly. "Gosh, of course *this* would be the thing she harped on, even after she died. Okay, so, when my dad left and made it clear he had no intention of coming back, my mom got a life insurance policy for herself. She'd been more reliant on my dad financially than she liked—we almost lost the house at one point after he bailed on us. One of the things she always talked about was that a woman needs to take care of herself and not be tied to a man because of money. So me being taken care of financially was always a huge thing for her. The life insurance was part of that. But there's a stipulation in the policy that says it can't be paid out if the cause of death is suicide."

"Oh, so you weren't able to claim that money…" Riley said.

Amy wiped away another tear, nodding. "You said there are more?"

Nina hit play again.

Riley's voice asked, "What happened to you?"

She had originally thought the reply had been "down the hall," while Nina had thought it sounded like "I had it all."

But upon this second listen, they all heard what Iris had actually said.

"Tylenol," Riley repeated.

Riley's recorded voice asked, "Are you here intentionally?"

Iris replied with a crystal clear, "*Help Amy.*"

Amy choked back a sob, one hand pressed to her chest. Nina and Riley sat quietly as they waited for Amy to compose herself.

Nina eventually reached out to reclaim her phone, but Amy placed a hand on top of it.

"Can you send those to me?" Amy managed.

"Of course," Nina said.

Amy wiped her eyes and blew her nose on a napkin. "Mom wants me to get this payment, but how am I supposed to do that? It's not even that I need the money. I sold the house, obviously. I couldn't live in that place by myself, especially not after Mom died there. But if Mom is sticking around because she wants me to get her cause of death changed, I feel like I need to at least try. I doubt EVPs are considered viable evidence, though."

Riley managed a laugh. "What we need is to find that kid who helped her. He can confirm your mom fell off the ladder and that he gave her the pills."

Amy perked up at that. "Did she tell you his name or anything?"

Shaking her head, Riley said, "I saw his face, but I don't know his name. I don't know how to find him."

When Amy deflated again, Nina chimed in with, "But we're going to keep searching for answers, I promise. I can't guarantee we'll find all the information you need, but we're going to do what we can."

"What is Julie paying you? I'll match it. This is so much more work beyond a ghost hunt," Amy said.

Nina waved this away. "We're happy to do it. We'll be in touch, okay?"

Amy checked her phone and winced slightly. "I've got to head back to the office."

None of them had touched their sandwiches.

Collecting their food and belongings, they hugged each other goodbye, Amy thanked them profusely, and then she hurried out of the shop, her wrapped sandwich stuffed into her purse.

Nina and Riley walked out onto the sidewalk.

"How you feeling?" Nina asked.

Riley glanced past Nina, where Amy was quickly walking away, clearly trying to get back to work in time. She wondered how far she'd walked to get here. Maybe she'd needed the fresh air to prepare herself for a meeting with two psychics who claimed to have made contact with her dead mother.

"Pretty good, actually," Riley asked. "Any ideas on how to find the kid who helped Iris?"

"Not yet. But we can brainstorm. Beyond that, I have a friend who's a cop. He knows all about me and my abilities. I told him that there's a chance that evidence of Iris's fall is in that front yard. Blood residue isn't the easiest to remove. There could still be some on those bricks around Iris's front planter, and Julie said they haven't done anything to the landscaping out front since they moved in. He might be able to pull some strings if we can track down our good Samaritan and present a good case that will convince my friend's superiors to let him search the yard."

"That sounds promising," Riley said.

"What's going on with your other investigation, by the way?" Nina asked. "You haven't brought up the cameras again. Did you solve the mystery already?"

Her smile faded. "Not yet. It's gotten a little more complicated since then." She gave Nina a quick rundown of everything. "Now that I know Emery possibly was killed across state lines, I'm even more at a loss about what to do."

"Have you been to the site where Brynn and Shawna were found?" Nina asked casually, as if visiting body dump sites was a common outing.

"No. I hadn't even thought of that."

"If you want to take a road trip one of these days, just let me know," Nina said. "Olivia could be a good asset, too. These women are reaching out to you the best they can, just like Iris has. Iris's messages will always be strongest in that house, where the events took place—she likely wouldn't be able to manifest anywhere else. You might be able to tap into something in that recreation area since that's where their bodies were found."

Riley didn't reply.

"Just think about it," Nina said as she started to walk backward down the sidewalk. "Have a good shift."

Right. She had to be getting to work soon, too. Waving, she headed to her own car, scarfing down her slightly soggy sandwich on the drive home.

Throughout her shift, she kept going back to Nina's suggestion. Riley loved a road trip, but when the destination was to a location where women's nude, sexually assaulted, bathed postmortem bodies had been dumped, the "fun" part of it left the equation.

Riley also knew that having something of importance to a victim made it more likely that she'd form a connection that allowed communication. She had yet to make contact with either Brynn or Shawna aside from a few dreams. Being not only in the town where they lived, but in the location where they'd been abandoned to the elements could be her way to forge a stronger bond with their spirits.

At the end of her shift, as she walked out to her car, she pulled out her phone, checking her messages. She had the usual handful from her friends and from Michael, but there was one from her mom, too.

> Talked to Norma. She says Rodney lives in Shawna's old neighborhood. He moved back there when he got out of prison. He served 15 of his 20 years due to good behavior. I'll send you her number.

Riley knew Rodney hadn't killed Shawna and knew from her mom that most of the locals hadn't thought Rodney had been the killer either. Still, how had neighbors felt about a convicted felon moving back into their neighborhood? She wondered how the Rodney Elgin from eighteen years ago had changed after fifteen years in prison.

Hoping she wouldn't wake Nina, as it was after 11 PM, she sent her a text that said:

> I'm game for this road trip if you are. Sunday?

By the time Riley had turned her car on and cranked up the heat to warm her aching feet, she had a reply.

> **NINA:** Sunday is perfect.

Lying in bed that night, Riley spoke out loud to Emery, the spirit she currently had the strongest connection to. She didn't feel Emery's presence in her apartment then, but she hoped she could still hear her somehow.

"I'm going to find you, Emery. If there are others, I'll find them, too," she said, feeling a little foolish.

She curled up on her side and closed her eyes. Just as she dozed off, she thought she felt a hand squeeze hers—a gentle acknowledgement that Emery had heard Riley's promise.

CHAPTER 18

On Sunday morning, Riley crept around her bedroom getting ready while Michael and Baxter slept in her bed. She had just pulled on a sweatshirt when Michael shifted, then woke abruptly with a quick intake of breath, confused when he realized she wasn't beside him. He scanned the room, then sagged a little when he found her in the doorway of the bathroom.

"Hey," he said sleepily, settling back against the pillows.

She rounded the bed to sit next to him, brushing a too-long lock off his forehead. He'd reached a rugged mountain man stage, thanks to his lack of shaving, which she was still digging. But he was in desperate need of a haircut. The morning bedhead had reached new heights.

"You nervous?" he asked.

Baxter mewed softly, then rolled onto his back, taking up much of Riley's vacated spot.

"A little. Nina and Olivia know what they're doing. And I trust them …"

"You're just worried you're going to open a portal to hell by accident and unleash a horde of demons on Earth."

She kissed him. "See, you get me."

He laughed. "You'll be great. Call me and let me know how it goes."

"I will," she said, getting up. She kissed him goodbye, gave Baxter's fluffy white belly a scratch, and then headed for the door. "Go back to sleep."

But Michael was already snoring softly.

On the way to Nina's, Riley called Carter Quincy, realizing that she still hadn't told him that she'd identified Emery. She hadn't informed Detective Howard of this either. She wanted to wait until she had more to give him. Besides, Texas was out of his jurisdiction.

"Hey, Riley," Carter said. "No tips on our mystery woman yet."

"I know her name."

She could picture his dark brows lifting in the silence.

"Her name is Emery Dawson and she's originally from Socorro, Texas. That's probably why no one has been able to ID her in Taos—she wasn't from New Mexico. The reason her spirit is here is because of the camera and her loose connection to it."

"If you're right about this, that makes this story so much bigger. A killer crossing state lines . . ."

"Do you have any contacts in Texas? Cops, other reporters?" Riley asked.

"Not off the top of my head, but my editor might," Carter said. "I'll be in touch."

Olivia was already at Nina's by the time Riley arrived. The pair sat in Nina's Adirondack chairs on the porch, each nursing a cup of coffee. Any hints of Olivia's pinup girl attire were gone today, save the red lipstick. She was outfitted like a nature tour guide—khaki cargo pants; a forest green T-shirt over a long-sleeved black one, which were both tucked into her pants; heavy hiking boots; and a safari hat. Riley stood at the base of Nina's short staircase and looked down at herself—jeans, T-shirt, a light jacket, and ratty tennis shoes. For an October morning, it was a tad warm, but she wondered now if she hadn't dressed warmly enough.

"Hey, Riley," Nina said, waving.

Riley cautiously ascended the steps. "Hey."

Olivia cocked her head, eyeing Riley over the rim of her mug. "Is the anxious energy due to your outfit or the whole communing with ghosts in the wilderness thing?"

"Why does it have to be an either/or situation?" Riley asked.

Olivia laughed. "Fair enough. I overdress when it's going to be over seventy degrees and I'm going to be outside for longer than ten minutes. I swear I could get a sunburn from a too-bright lightbulb. I went hiking out in that area once and stepped on a prickly pear patch that went straight through the sole of my shoes. I almost passed out from the pain."

Riley winced, glancing down at her old tennis shoes again.

Nina laughed now, too. "We'll stay on designated paths. Don't worry."

"Do you know exactly where these spots are? I've never been to the recreation area," Riley said. "Brynn was found on a boat ramp by a bridge and Shawna was in the Rio Bravo campground. But I don't know much beyond that."

Standing, Nina said, "I haven't been out there either, actually. Olivia has volunteered to be our guide."

After Nina grabbed a jacket from inside, they all piled into Nina's Subaru parked at the curb. It would take three hours to get to Taos, and then another half hour or so to reach the Orilla Verde Recreational Area in Pilar, a little village outside the town. Olivia requested to sit in the passenger seat because she got mildly motion sick when she sat in the back. Riley stared out the window as they left Albuquerque and cruised down I-25 N toward Santa Fe.

She let Nina and Olivia's conversation about people she didn't know fill the car as she watched the stretches of low-lying scrubby bushes go by, rocky cliff sides a backdrop against a bright blue sky painted with wispy white clouds.

Riley hadn't been to Taos in years, and as Nina wound her way through the town, she thought she should come back one day with Michael. She was sure she would appreciate the downtown area more now than when she was a kid. The two-lane street they were on was flanked on both sides by squat adobe buildings, all the color of warm sand. The architecture was classic Southwest, which she loved. Many of the buildings' roofs were lined with a row of short wooden beams. When she was a kid wandering around a similar area in Old Town Albuquerque with her parents, she'd asked why so many of the buildings had bird perches protruding from the walls. Her father had explained that they were vigas, which were beams that held up the roof. Adult Riley still preferred the idea that Southwestern architecture was exceedingly bird friendly.

People milled about the shops and restaurants, many arms laden with shopping bags. Riley assumed most were tourists. A building on the right had a giant colorful mural painted on its brown wall, depicting a Native American woman in tribal gear, holding the hand of her young daughter outfitted in a similar manner. The accents on the adobe buildings, benches ringing courtyards, and stair railings were often painted a bright red, orange, or turquoise, the contrast a beautiful pop of color against the sea of similarly designed brown buildings.

As much as Riley would have liked to stop and take a stroll, they continued on toward the small town of Pilar, where they'd find the recreation area. Houses and apartments, many of them in the adobe style, replaced the shops and restaurants. Trees were plentiful, their rich green leaves arching over fences and sidewalks.

NM 570 eventually brought them to a large wooden sign and Visitors Center. Dread filled Riley at the sight. Brynn and Shawna's killer had looked at this same sign and Visitors Center eighteen years ago. How many times had it taken before he thought, "Ah, this would be a great place to leave a body"?

"We'll hit the water in about a mile or so," Nina said, interrupting Riley's dark thoughts, as she continued along NM 570. "First stop is the Rio Bravo campground."

Olivia said, "It's the nicest one out here. There are six or seven campgrounds and Rio Bravo is the Ritz."

"So you've camped out here?" Riley asked, a little surprised, as Olivia didn't strike her as the camping type.

"Only once. I was dating this guy who was super into nature, and he was appalled—that's the word he used—when I said I'd never been camping out here. The guy was crazy hot, so I agreed to a weekend. He didn't want to stay at the Rio Bravo site, though. He said it was one very small step above glamping, so we ended up at one of the more quote-unquote primitive sites. The toilet was basically a glorified hole in the ground. I got eaten alive by mosquitos and burned to a crisp. Utter nightmare."

Riley stifled a laugh. "Did you break up on the spot, or…?"

"I think he wanted to," she said. "That was also the time I stepped on the prickly pears. I was such a mess after that weekend, they practically had to airlift me out of there. He broke things off a day after we got back. I was in so much pain, I started crying on the phone when he told me. He said, 'I'm sorry! I know you did all this for me and that's really sweet.

Maybe we can take things slow' and I shouted, 'No! I want to break up! I'm just so relieved!'"

Nina and Riley cracked up.

"I was still crying while I said it," Olivia said, shaking her head. "He called me a bitch and hung up."

"Dodged a bullet," Riley singsonged.

"Hundred percent," Olivia agreed.

The campground didn't immediately scream "the Ritz" to Riley, but then again, she wasn't much of a camper either. Not even glamping sounded that appealing. The dirt and gravel road Nina slowly cruised down had a smattering of cars and RVs parked at the various campsites. Each site was marked off by semicircles of large rocks, and boasted amenities like water spigots, camping grills, and covered picnic tables. There were also restrooms and coin-operated showers available to the site at large, which Riley supposed was ritzy as hell when you spent all night sleeping in a piece of tented fabric that likely didn't keep bugs out, let alone mountain lions.

"I don't know…" Nina said slowly. "This place looks kind of great."

Olivia shuddered. "Did I mention I also got attacked by fire ants?"

Nina snorted. "This sounds like a montage from a terrible romantic comedy."

"Oh, let me assure you, there was nothing romantic about that weekend," Olivia said.

As they drove, Riley noted that on the covered picnic table of each site, a white "RB" was painted horizontally on one of the poles, followed by a number. Knowing she was about to kill the brief amount of levity that had filled the car, she asked, "Do we know which site Shawna was found in?"

The pair in front grew quiet.

"I believe it was at the end of the campground, but I don't know what the site number was," Nina said.

"Me either," said Olivia, subdued.

Most of the sites toward the end of the campground appeared to be occupied, so Nina circled back and found a parking spot. Riley wondered if anyone would get fussy about them being here when they clearly didn't have a reservation. The sound of rushing water was ever-present as she climbed out of the car. She headed in the direction of it, her messenger bag bouncing lightly against her hip as she went, and walked between two unoccupied campsites. Though the water was close, she couldn't immediately see it, due to the wall of trees and bushes growing near the shore. On the opposite side of the river were rocky hillsides dotted liberally with large chunks of lava rocks and short, scrubby bushes. A large bush with long, spindly branches swayed nearby in the light breeze, the stems topped with mustard-yellow flowers that looked like massive, smashed makeup brushes. Up at the top of the hillside, along the ridge line, she thought she could make out the form of a sheep—possibly a bighorn sheep, given its stark-white backside.

"Hi there!" she heard someone call out behind her, and she turned to find a man dressed in attire similar to Olivia's walking toward the pair. "Can I help you ladies?"

Riley noted that Olivia was holding a large bouquet of flowers. Brows furrowed, Riley walked over to join the group.

"Hi, my name is Nina Galvan," Nina said, hand outstretched to the middle-aged man.

He wore a sand-colored hat with a loose chin strap—the bead at the end of it resting against his chest—and held a clipboard at his side. Shaking Nina's hand, he said, "I'm Paul, the camp host. Did you have a reservation?"

"No. You actually might be able to help us, though," Nina said.

"How so?" he asked, clipboard held to his chest now.

"Do you know anything about Shawna Mack?" Nina asked.

The man gave them all an assessing scan. "You reporters?"

"No," Olivia said. "But we're friends of the Mack family. We were already in the area, so we thought we might have a look around."

The man still looked skeptical. "She was found by RB14. I can tell you that much. They found her laid out in the area between the covered picnic table and the shore."

"Was her body covered?" Riley asked.

"Not that I know of," he said.

"Do you know who found her?" she asked. "The camp host?"

Offering a little sigh, he said, "Yeah. Shook him up really bad. Mostly because he'd left late that night—not all the camp hosts stay overnight—so he didn't see who had come and gone. Someone had reserved RB14 for that night, but never showed."

The killer likely had known the host didn't stay the night here, reserved the spot at the very end of the campsite so no one else could claim it, and then had crept in during the dead of night to leave the body for someone to find in the morning.

"We worked really hard after that to make sure someone was always on-site. It's such a peaceful area. Never expect something like that to happen out here."

"I noticed that there's someone staying at RB14 right now," Nina said. "Would it be okay if we just stopped by the picnic area to leave these?" She motioned to the flowers Olivia held. Mixed among the pink, white, and purple wildflowers were a few wide heads of bright yellow sunflowers. "We just wanted to pay our respects. Her would-be 45th birthday passed last week. Then we'll be out of here."

He thought about that for a moment, then said, "Let me go talk to the campers and ask them if it's okay, hm?" Without waiting for an answer, he sidestepped their little group and marched off.

Riley turned to them. "Where'd the flowers come from?"

"I was overcome with the weirdest compulsion last night that I needed them," Nina said, "so I went out and bought some. I stuck them in the trunk this morning just before you got there. Almost forgot all about them, honestly. Then that feeling hit me again when we parked."

"You claircognizant weirdo," Olivia said, grinning at her, then gave the flowers a sniff.

A minute later, Paul the camp host was enthusiastically waving his clipboard in the air. Riley saw him before the others did.

"Looks like we've been approved," she said.

They walked over to Paul, who stood near RB14 with an older woman. The door to the RV parked at the site swung open and out came an older man and a black lab. The lab bounded straight for Riley, his tail wagging so hard, it spun in a circle like a propeller. She bent down to pet the excited dog, who slid down her legs and onto his back so he could get his belly rubbed. A fine layer of black fur dotted her pant legs and shoes.

"Oh, Shadow!" the woman called out. "You leave that nice lady alone!"

Shadow hopped to his feet at the sound of her voice and bounded away.

When the trio reached the others, Nina said, "Thank you so much for this."

"Not a problem," the older man said. "I remember hearing about the young woman who was found here. I didn't quite remember that it was this campsite, though. We just got here. I hope we don't get visited by any ghosts tonight!" He laughed in that wheezy, hearty way of jolly old men.

Riley, Nina, and Olivia only managed awkward laughter in response.

"You take as long as you need, ladies. We're here for a week, so we'll keep an eye on those flowers. I'm sure the young lady would appreciate you paying your respects," the older woman said.

With that, the couple went back to their RV, Shadow trotting along with them. Paul the camp host wished them a good afternoon, but he said it in a way that implied he wanted them out of there in twenty minutes or less.

Once they were alone, the trio huddled up.

"I think you should take the flowers, Riley," Olivia said, holding them out.

She did so.

"Shut out your other senses here, just as you did while you were in that hallway at Julie's," Nina said. "Focus your energy on these flowers, why you're here, and call out to Shawna."

"Tune out all the extra noise. I mean that both externally and internally. Focus on Shawna, and on this place—nothing else," Olivia added.

Riley tucked the bouquet under her arm and then rooted around in her messenger bag, producing the single picture she had of Shawna. "I brought this, too."

"Perfect," Nina said.

The covered picnic table had nothing on it, nor did the cement slab beneath the green metal awning. The bright white

"RB14" painted on the pole loomed in her peripheral vision as she stepped under the awning and made her way to the dark green picnic table. She placed the flowers and the photo of Shawna on the surface, then sat.

Nina and Olivia were on the back side of the picnic area, standing near the shore and gazing out at the beautiful landscape, as Riley had done when they first arrived. Blowing out a relaxing breath, Riley picked up the photo of Shawna and Malcolm, holding it in both hands.

Are you here, Shawna? We brought you flowers.

Riley glanced to her left, to the general area where Paul said Shawna had been laid out.

What had happened to her during that week she'd been missing? Had she been killed right away, or had she been kept alive for a while? She'd been washed, just as Brynn had been. How soon after death had he done that—*why* had he done it?

Riley returned her attention to the picture, then closed her eyes. She listened—to the soft hush of Nina and Olivia's voices, a faint bark from Shadow inside the RV, the constant rush of the Rio Grande to her left, the faint crinkle of the cellophane that wrapped the flowers.

She felt it then—a presence beside her.

"Don't be scared," she heard, and it took a moment for her to realize it was Olivia's voice.

Riley's eyes opened, but instead of looking ahead to where she knew Olivia stood, she turned to her right, where Shawna, clear as day, sat beside her. The crinkle of the cellophane was from Shawna attempting to touch the flowers.

Shawna wore the same outfit from the photograph and appeared to be the same age, but the difference was the wide black-and-purple bruise that ringed her neck. A wound so violently administered that it was evident even with her dark skin. Riley clenched her teeth. Who had done this to her?

Swallowing, unnerved more by that ring around her neck than the apparition herself, Riley turned on the bench seat, taking in the details of Shawna's profile. Shawna was still fixated on the flowers, her head cocked in confusion or concentration as she tried to touch them.

"Can you tell me who hurt you?" Riley asked.

Shawna's attention swiveled to her. Her eyes were a startling light brown, almost golden. She slowly shook her head.

"You don't know his name?" Riley asked.

Another shake of the head.

"She's … confused," Olivia said, her focus aimed toward Shawna, but not *at* her, so Riley guessed the apparition had only appeared for her. "Not just about what's happening now, but in general. It feels a little like what Iris felt, but the confusion is more acute. My head is … fuzzy."

Nina had joined them now, too. "She was drugged."

Shawna nodded at that.

"You don't remember who took you or how you ended up here?" Riley asked.

Shawna looked around, taking in the scenery, with her brows pulled together. When she refocused on Riley again, she shook her head.

Riley clenched a fist, frustrated not with Shawna, but the man who killed her—and Brynn, Emery, and who knew who else. Was this why Emery was always so damn sad? Her life was taken from her and she'd been so heavily drugged by this monster that she couldn't even remember what had happened to her? Could she not speak because of the damage done to her throat?

An image pushed its way into Riley's mind then, crowding out the thoughts of wanting to strangle the bastard the way he'd strangled these women. It was just a flash of an image, but it was so bright and detailed, it was like a neon sign flaring to life against a dark sky.

"Whoa," Nina said, stumbling and shaking her head as she pressed a hand to her temple. She yanked her keys out of her pocket and held them out. "Uh … Olivia. Can you get me a pen and something to draw on?"

Olivia snatched the keys and ran off, returning what felt like seconds later. Riley watched as Nina sat at the table, closed her eyes, and said, "Again, Shawna."

Then, like Nina had done during the séance when she'd channeled Orin, her pen started to fly across the page as if guided by someone other than herself. The pen moved with such speed, Riley couldn't process how this was happening without Nina looking at what she was doing. What was stranger still, was that the more Nina drew, the more Riley knew it was the same image that had popped into her head. It was a large circle with a smaller one inside it. In the center of both was an intricately rendered tree—reminiscent of the Tree of Life. In front of the tree was the silhouette of a big rig.

"Is that a … logo?" Olivia asked, watching over Nina's shoulder as the drawing came to life.

Riley glanced at Shawna, who still sat silently beside her. "Was he a trucker? The man who took you?"

Another image—this of gray metal siding. Metal was below her, too. A pair of bare, dark legs stuck out in front of her, bare feet dirty. The dark pink polish was chipped on most of the toes.

The image ended.

"Scared," Olivia said, standing to full height again. "Hungry. Thirsty. Confused. So … confused. She wants to know if Malcolm is okay—I just can't tell if she's asking that now, or if she was wondering that then."

"He's okay," Riley told Shawna, staring at her face and doing her best to ignore the ligature marks on her neck. "He's married and just had twin girls."

Tears filled Shawna's almost-golden eyes.

The door to the RV flew open then and Shadow charged out, barking furiously. His hackles were up, but he stopped shy of stepping onto the cement slab the awning stretched over. It wasn't an aggressive bark so much as a fearful one.

The woman came running toward them, calling the dog back. "Shadow! What on earth has gotten into you?"

Shawna vanished.

The barking stopped immediately and Shadow came wiggling under the table, whimpering.

Riley tipped onto her side to address him. "You silly dog! Shawna isn't scary."

Shadow licked her face.

She laughed, sitting back up.

"Shadow!" He wiggled back out and ran to the older woman, who grabbed the dog by the collar. "I'm so sorry, ladies. He must have seen a squirrel."

Olivia was seated beside Nina now.

When Riley took in the detailed drawing of the trucking logo again, she said, "He had her in the back of a big rig. If Emery was from Texas … I don't know, maybe that's how he found women—through his job as a trucker? Or at least how he found places to leave them."

Nina nodded. "We need to figure out what company this logo is for."

"But first we have to see if we can get Brynn to talk to us," Olivia said.

They gathered their things and called a goodbye to the couple who now had Shadow tied up near the RV. The man was attempting to start a fire in the cooking pit.

The picture of Shawna went back into Riley's bag, but the flowers she left on the table. Riley had just stepped off the cement slab when she heard the rustle of cellophane. She turned and eyed the picnic area but didn't see Shawna. The flowers shifted an inch or so to one side.

"Happy birthday, Shawna," she said, then followed after Nina and Olivia.

CHAPTER 19

Nina left the Rio Bravo campground and continued on NM 570 toward their next destination: the Taos Junction Bridge. Brynn's body had been found at the end of the boat ramp nearby.

The road there had several gentle switchbacks, the sides of the two-lane road flanked by dry desert brush. The landscape was dominated by sage-green and interspersed with bright yellows and dull oranges. The most vibrant color out here was the double yellow line painted in the middle of the road. A few mesas dotted the horizon.

The bridge eventually appeared in the distance. It was a small boxy metal structure that no more than one car could drive on at a time. A sign for the boat ramp on the side of the road was placed just before the turn to get on the bridge, so instead of crossing it, Nina turned left and pulled into the small parking area near the top of the ramp.

When they got out of the car, Riley took in a 360-degree view. To their backs were the impressive canyon walls layered in those huge chunks of dark lava rock. Turning back around, the bridge loomed in the distance off to her right, and to the left was the easily accessible boat ramp. A pair of guys in shorts and T-shirts were on their way down the ramp now, each with a kayak hoisted above his head—one red, one yellow. Riley, Nina, and Olivia followed.

The ramp was a wide, cement slope with an incline that could be navigated with little trouble on foot, leading to the calm water below. A family of four was at the bottom of the ramp, and a father and young daughter strapped into bright yellow life jackets had just cast off in a kayak. The mother was trying to get her son's life jacket cinched tight, but he was twisting this way and that in the small boat, loudly asking his mother if she'd seen the beaver that had just slipped under the water on the opposite side of the shore. Riley and her friends waited halfway down the ramp for all the kayakers to make their way into the water and down the Rio Grande.

"I'm surprised the water is so calm," Riley said. "Don't people usually come up this way for white water rafting?"

Olivia said, "Yeah, but this part of the Rio Grande is really mellow. There's about a six mile stretch from this bridge to Pilar that's both very wide and very tranquil. Popular destination for float trips and such. It's a Class II at most around here."

When Riley had first read the reports about where Brynn and Shawna had been found, she assumed the locations had been rather secluded since they were way out in the wilderness. But now after seeing the Rio Bravo campsite and this spot, it struck her that even if the killer had left them in a seemingly remote location, he also had chosen spots where the bodies would be found quickly. The killer could have easily chosen a different area along the river, or in the river itself, where they would have been taken down the higher-class rapids, battered along the rocks and possibly carried hundreds of miles away from their original dump site. Instead, Brynn's body had been left at the bottom of this ramp, frequented by families and people wanting to spend a relaxing day in the calm waters of the river.

"Dumped" no longer felt like the right word. She'd been *placed* here. Washing her body might have had less to do with removing evidence of his identity, and more to do with showing a twisted kind of care for the woman he'd kidnapped, raped, and then murdered. Riley suppressed a shiver, despite the warm afternoon sun on her back.

To their right, and under the bridge, was a little swatch of beach, which Riley was sure was a popular destination for kids and families. The area was relatively empty now, but she suspected that during the summer, cars would fill that lot and people would be entering the water with their kayaks and inner tubes with great frequency.

Once the kayakers were out of sight, and for the moment no new ones were making their way down the ramp, they walked the rest of the way to the water's edge. Riley stood dead center, the toes of her ratty shoes just out of reach of the gently lapping water. The mirror image of the trees and shrubs that lined the river was reflected on the surface of the brown-tinted water, only cut through by the rippling Vs made by the retreating kayaks. The occasional small fish darted among the river rocks. Other than the little boy once more shouting about the sighting of a beaver, Riley was overcome by how peaceful it was here—soothing water, flitting insects, and a faint breeze rustling leaves.

She imagined the scream that might have torn out of an unsuspecting person's throat upon the discovery of a strangled young woman laid out right where Riley stood now. A sound that could shatter the quiet in a place like this, startling birds into flight. Pictures of the bodies hadn't been released to the public. Now that Riley had seen the bruises on Shawna's neck, she could understand why. How much more pronounced had those looked on Brynn's fair skin? Riley was grateful that she'd been able to admire the beauty of Shawna's almost-golden eyes, and hadn't seen the burst blood vessels.

Riley didn't have a physical photo of Brynn readily available, so she took out her phone and pulled one up. She sat on the end of the ramp, stared at the picture a few moments, and then closed her eyes, hoping to make contact with her the same way she'd made contact with Shawna. She idly wondered if Nina had a second bouquet of flowers handy. Riley tried to relax her body and open her mind, just as she'd done earlier. She pictured the light under her name on the Great Beyond switchboard flashing green. *Come talk to me, Brynn. I'm here.*

Riley was distantly aware of Nina somewhere behind her, uttering a prayer to the Goddess as she had before the séance. Olivia wasn't currently speaking, but the faint crunch of sand underfoot to Riley's left told her Olivia was moving around, using her own methods to make a connection to the plane beyond this one.

As strange as the trio probably looked to an outsider, Riley felt deeply appreciative in that moment to have found people who were not only like her, but who were just as invested in finding answers to this mystery as she was.

Their time here wasn't as relaxed as it had been at the Rio Bravo site though, because within twenty minutes, a school bus arrived. It was only a matter of minutes before scores of kids layered in sunscreen and full of pent-up energy went running down the ramp, a harried-looking woman chasing after them.

It was all the same to Riley; she couldn't feel Brynn's presence here the way she'd felt Shawna's. As Riley stood from her spot at the end of the ramp, she brushed off her jeans and turned to find Nina and Olivia walking her way.

"We can wait them out and see if they move on in a bit…" Nina said, but Riley could read her tone well enough to know she'd rather not.

"I don't feel anything," Olivia said. "Well, actually, I might feel too much here. The kids' living energy is fritzing out my connection to any other energy that might be lingering." She shrugged causally enough, but she'd gone a little pale. "Sometimes crowds can be hard for me."

"I'm game for grabbing lunch somewhere and then heading back," Riley said.

"Ohh, yes. I know of a really great Mexican restaurant nearby," Olivia said.

They headed back up the ramp. Riley hoped Brynn truly wasn't here, and not that she was hiding among the brush, watching them walk away.

After lunch—spent eating excellent food and having conversations about anything other than ghosts and murdered women—they piled back in Nina's car to make the three-hour trek back to Albuquerque. Olivia almost immediately fell asleep. Nina put on a pop station, which she softly hummed along to. Riley, unable to keep her curiosity in check any longer, got out her phone and started searching for that trucking logo. It didn't take long to find it. Though there weren't words in the image Shawna had shared even more vividly with Nina than she had with Riley, the images popping up in her search all had a name below the Tree of Life image: Amity Trucking.

Riley searched that next, learning that Amity Trucking was headquartered in Florida. Well, it had been—the company folded in 2011. If the killer had used his trucking routes to find women, places to dispose of them, or both, had the company closing in 2011 derailed his plans? Or had he just found another job with another company?

Dejected, Riley turned off her screen and reported what she'd found to Nina.

"It's still more information than what we had this morning," Nina said. "This guy has gotten away with at least three murders. There's a reason for that. Even with our abilities to communicate with the victims, it doesn't mean that the answers will just be handed to us. Persistence is the most important. Now we just need to move onto the next idea."

Sighing, Riley nodded and settled back against the seat, staring out the window at the passing landscape. *I'm going to find you,* she thought. And this time, she didn't mean Emery, but the man who had killed her.

October, 2021

I stared at the pair of bolt cutters on the counter as I sipped my coffee. I had spent the better part of the week in Carlsbad, tracking the movements of a man's business partner. My client was sure his partner was siphoning money from the business but wasn't sure what he was doing with it. The answer? Gambling at Zia Park Casino out in Hobbs, some five hours away from Albuquerque. He dabbled in table games, but mostly preferred to bet on the horses. He rarely won.

On my way home, I'd purchased the bolt cutters for the padlock on the mystery footlocker under my bed. I had been exhausted when I got home, so I left the tool on my counter. Large chunks of my memory had returned, though the details of my assault in the alley were still lost to me. Could the answers be in that box?

My computer chimed with an email notification. A very specific chime that made me choke on my coffee. A chime from the deep recess of my memory that tore that black curtain even further. I coughed, thumping a fist against my chest.

Dramatically throwing myself into my computer chair, my hands shaking, I pulled up the private email and got visual confirmation of what I already knew. The Client had messaged me.

Had he heard my silent prayers?

The subject line of his message, though, gave me pause.

What the hell did you do?

There was no way he had seen my grainy images on the news, had he? The Nob Hill Prowler—what a horrible name—was a local story at most. He wasn't, and had never been, in-state, so there was little chance he'd seen it.

Right?

Opening the email, I found a paragraph of text replete with exclamation points and the occasional word in all caps, as well as a link to an article from the *Taos Daily Journal*. I jumped directly to the article, as I had no desire to get yelled at through email this early on a Sunday morning.

The story was about Shawna Mack, who would have been 45 had she not been snuffed out by The Client in 2003. The author of the article made a veiled claim that Shawna Mack and Brynn Bodwell had the same killer, but that theory wasn't new—at least not among the armchair detectives holed up in their mommies' basements.

The article was almost a week old. Why were his panties in a twist about it now? I also didn't immediately understand what had him so worried, or how in the hell this article by Carter Quincy had anything to do with me, but at the bottom of the piece was a picture that made my heart stutter.

It was a photograph *I* had taken. Where in the hell had this Carter Quincy gotten *my* photo of Emery?

I quickly got out of my chair, stalked to the kitchen counter, grabbed the bolt cutters, and practically sprinted for my bedroom. I yanked the footlocker out of its hiding place and stared at it. Idle thoughts about Pandora's Box came to mind before I went after the padlock with the bolt cutters. It took a few minutes, and was harder to accomplish than I anticipated, but the steel finally gave way with a satisfying *snap*. Heart racing, I removed the broken lock and lifted the three-foot-long lid. Inside were packages of photographs, negatives in protective plastic sleeves, and rolls of film—some spent, some not. There were folders upon folders of printouts from conversations between The Client and myself. There were scribbled-in notebooks, newspaper cutouts, and paper maps. All the work I'd done with The Client over the years. Oddly, on top, was a framed photograph of my father and me on the deck of a fishing boat. I was five or so in the picture, my mouth open wide and head thrown back as I laughed. The look of adoration on my father's face as he gazed at me caused my chest to constrict so painfully, I slammed the lid of the footlocker closed. My mother had been behind the camera, no doubt. How had she managed to capture such raw emotion from us both?

I shook my head. None of that mattered. Father was dead and Mother wasn't worth thinking about now. Not when I just realized something truly alarming: my father's three cameras, the ones I took with me from California, weren't here.

Letting out a roar of frustration, I punched at the side of my bed, my fist connecting with the side of the mattress. I did it again and again and again. Where the fuck were they? How did Carter Quincy have *my* photograph?

I scrambled to my feet, pacing the small space of my bedroom. Smacking the side of my head with an open palm, I willed myself to remember, to tear down the rest of that black curtain.

Think, dammit! Think. Think!

I tore my apartment apart again, searching for their hiding places. How could I have misplaced three of them? I ripped everything out of my closet, cabinets, and drawers. I shoved my mattress off the box spring, searching for holes cut in the material, for little cavities I might have created to hide my most cherished possessions.

I paused at that revelation, standing among the destruction I'd wrought on my bedroom. I *had* cherished them. Had I taken them out of the locker for their monthly maintenance? It was a task my father had instilled in me so fully that I'd kept it up even after I'd absconded with them.

I closed my eyes, working my way through the routine. Taking the cameras out, clearing off the dining room table, grabbing the cleaning kit from the bookshelf in the living room—a knock sounded on the front door.

My eyes sprang open. It wasn't a present-day knock, but a phantom one. I cautiously walked toward the door, hoping I would remember who had shown up and interrupted my routine. When I was mere inches from the door, hand outstretched toward the knob, I remembered.

Tracy.

Memories sometimes come back all at once, Dr. Singh had said.

This was one of those times.

I had taken three of the cameras to my storage unit in Clovis after I'd caught Tracy snooping around under my bed and the footlocker. After dating for three weeks, she'd thought she'd earned access to my things. Served me right, thinking a long-term relationship was a good idea. I had pulled the cameras from the top shelf of my closet for their monthly maintenance, just as I thought, but had grown distracted by Tracy's unexpected arrival. Keeping the cameras better hidden had been a low priority since no one had been to my place in ages. Tracy had been an anomaly, a bar pickup that had unexpectedly evolved past a one-night stand in a motel. Her presence in my life had made me sloppy.

She'd shown up with takeout and the promise of sex, and because she'd worn down my defenses, I'd let her in. When the afterglow had faded and I woke up needing to piss, I'd found her ass up with her face under my bed.

"What's this?" she asked, giggling, pulling the locker free.

"Put that back." My blood was boiling by the time she playfully tugged on the padlock. I climbed off the bed, hovering over her. She hadn't moved; she just stared up at me laughing, like this was some joke. "Get your hands off my shit."

"What you got in here?" she asked, as she gave the locker and her bare tits another shake. "Is it your porn stash?"

I'd shoved her then, blind rage taking over. "Don't. Touch. My. Shit."

Tracy had toppled over and whacked her head on my nightstand, jostling one of the cameras perched on top. I dove forward to catch it before it fell, grabbing it by the strap before it collided with the ground. Tracy had let out a scream when I lunged for the camera, then she cowered on the ground in the fetal position.

A quick glance around the room told me she'd pawed at the other cameras I'd carelessly left out. She'd even taken the film out of one of them and had left it on top of the dresser. What the hell was wrong with her? I left the film in the cameras as a memento and Tracy had soiled everything because I'd let my dick do all the thinking that day.

"Did you take anything?" I snapped at her.

"W-what?"

"W-what?" I echoed, sneering. "Are you hard of hearing? Did you *take* anything? Why were you putting your grubby little fingers all over my stuff? Who takes film out of someone's camera?"

"I was just looking!" she whined from the floor, still cowering against the nightstand. "I'd never seen a film camera before so I was just poking around. I didn't mean to take it out. I couldn't figure out how to get it back in there so I put it on the dresser. I didn't take anything. Jesus. You don't fucking tell me anything, so I was looking at your stuff to see if I could get to know you better. But all your interesting shit is locked up like Fort Knox—just like you."

I glared at her.

In an attempt to bring some levity back into the situation, she laughed softly, and took on what she thought was a sexy tone. She purred her favorite descriptor for me, "Secretive motherfucker."

Normally it would have made me laugh, too. But the charm, what little there was, had worn off. "Get the fuck out of my apartment and don't come back."

Tracy sniffed hard, startled. "Wait, what? I'm sorry, baby. I was just joking, you know? It's our thing. I didn't mean—"

"There is no 'our thing' anymore. Out," I repeated, walking around the room to pick up her discarded clothes on my floor. I threw them at her one by one—shirt, panties, bra, jeans. "Get. The. Fuck. Out."

By the time her jeans had collided with her face, she was well and truly pissed and had snatched up her clothes, stood, and was hastily pulling them on. "You're a fucking asshole, you know that? My mom was right when she said you sound like a piece of shit."

"You're not exactly a fucking catch either," I said, clutching the camera to my chest as I watched her struggle to pull her pants back on. "Lose my phone number, yeah?"

"Already done," she said, and stalked for the door. I followed after her. She wrenched it open, glowered at me over her shoulder, and said, "Good fucking riddance" before slamming the door.

After locking up after her, I had stormed back to my bedroom to take stock. All three rolls of film were accounted for. It was a foundation-rattling wake-up call that I needed to be more careful. I took the cartridge Tracy had removed from the camera and slipped it into a canister.

The memory fading, I walked to the side of my bed and wedged my fingers behind the headboard. My fingertips met the smooth surface of a film canister, still where I'd taped it that day.

I remembered that I took a roll out of one more camera and put that in the stuffed-to-the-gills footlocker. I had left the third one in the camera, put all three cameras in their respective bags, and taken them to the storage unit the following day, where they'd be safe.

I had planned to bring the cameras back to my place once I was sure Tracy was gone for good, but what I hadn't planned for was getting the shit kicked out of me in an alley as if I were a clueless tourist getting mugged.

I prepaid for the storage unit in three-month blocks, the most the company would allow. Before my attack, I'd still had part of a month left. Which meant I had lost the storage unit due to missed payments and the goddamn facility had auctioned off its contents.

Someone had bought Dad's—*my*—cameras. They had pawed at them just like Tracy had and had taken *my* film. Not only had they developed film that didn't belong to them, they'd shared the photos with the media? I felt violated, sick to my stomach. Who had the audacity to do such a thing?

As I paced, my indignation started to give way to something else as puzzle pieces started to click into place. The Client's anger, the fact that this picture appeared in an article about Shawna—someone had made the connection between Emery and Shawna. Which meant…

Had a picture from Shawna's surveillance been on the roll along with Emery's? I'd used a different camera for Brynn because The Client had specifically requested 36 prints, and there had been an already-started roll of 24, so I'd switched to the Minolta. "*Shit.*"

I was torn between being furious at myself for thinking the roll would be safe in the camera, at the storage unit management for selling off my items while I was laid up in a hospital bed, and at the snooping bastard who had developed these photographs without permission.

I went back to The Client's message, bracing myself for the rage.

I need you to explain to me how in the FUCK this picture is not only being published but is featured in an article about Shawna. We cut ties ten fucking years ago! Why is any of this surfacing NOW? Are you having a crisis of conscience? I told you I'd keep your secrets if you kept mine—if you try to take me down, you're going with me. I have just as much dirt on you, asshole! Rethink your strategy. Be smarter.

I bristled at the last sentence, as it was one I had used with him after he'd stupidly gone after Brynn even when I told him it was a bad idea. He hadn't listened; he'd wanted her too badly. He paid me too much for me to argue with him. What he did with the information I provided him wasn't any of my business anyway. But the media circus that had sprung up across the whole goddamn country was proof enough that I had been right.

When he'd gone back to more sensible targets, we both went back under the radar where we were happiest. Emery had been a smart choice. But now Emery's beautiful fucking face was in the newspaper—thanks to one of my photographs.

How had he even seen the article in this tiny newspaper? I wasn't even sure what state he lived in. Did he have notification alerts set up for their names?

I read his message again. He had just as much dirt on me? I laughed long and loud. He was even more out of his mind than I thought if he believed that. If my hands were stained with blood, it was only indirectly—his were soaked.

I wrote back.

> I have no idea what's going on, but I'll figure it out soon.

Almost immediately, he wrote back.

> I need better than soon.

My computer chimed with another familiar sound—the sound of a payment notification.

Another message followed soon after.

> I'll double that if you make this go away.

Relief threatened to choke me. I hadn't realized until that moment how truly dire my financial situation had become. How worried I'd been. This little influx of cash would cover rent and groceries. Suddenly I felt grounded. Centered. I had a purpose, direction. The Client had given me security all those years ago. God, I'd missed it. I would do this for him, get back on my feet, and then I'd figure out my next move.

I'm on it, I told him.

The other two rolls of film were safe, but if this person had already made the connection between Shawna, Brynn, and Emery, there was a chance they could find the others. Time wasn't on my side.

I grabbed one of my digital cameras, a couple zoom lenses, a notebook, and my keys, then headed for the door. Despite the fact that this was a goddamn shitshow, a little trill of excitement bolstered me.

The Collector was back in business.

CHAPTER 20

Michael had left by the time she returned from her excursion into Taos. She immediately threw herself onto the couch for a much-needed nap, but her dreams had been a jumble. Brynn tumbled down stairs. Shawna lay at the bottom of the boat ramp. Emery ran through a campsite, glancing over her shoulder in terror as someone chased her in the dark. Iris's unconscious body was tossed into the back of a big rig. Then a scene replayed. It was the one Iris had shown her—of her own confusion before her fall, and the young man who had both helped her and expressed concern that she needed to get to a hospital.

Help Amy, a voice said as Iris staggered forward, her shoulder colliding with the doorway that led out into the hall.

Riley woke with a start to the sound of the credenza slamming into the ground. When she opened her eyes, she half expected to be asleep on the hallway floor of Julie's house, but she was on her couch, her body too warm. She kicked off her blanket and sat up. Her mind was filled with images of Iris and her disheveled appearance at the top of the staircase just before she fell.

It occurred to her then that these jumbled dreams might actually be Iris's attempt to contact her. The credenza hitting the floor the first day Riley had been in Julie's house hadn't been to scare Riley, but to get her attention. She wanted Riley to witness her fall. Was she responsible for the sound waking her up now? Riley cast a quick glance around her apartment but didn't see anyone—she didn't sense anyone either.

She remembered something Nina had said, *Iris's messages will always be strongest in that house, where the events took place—she likely wouldn't be able to manifest anywhere else.* Renee Palmer and Pete had used dreams to relay messages to Riley when manifesting wasn't possible. Even Brynn and Emery had made contact through dreams.

Riley sat up straighter on the couch and replayed that scene. This memory was important to Iris. There was something in it Riley clearly had missed if Iris was showing it to her again. Initially, Riley had thought Iris was showing her information solely to help prove she hadn't died by suicide, but that she'd been accidentally poisoned by a well-meaning good Samaritan who hadn't known Iris was allergic to Tylenol.

Yet, after speaking to Amy, Riley realized how important the young man was, too. He was the only other person who knew what happened that day, and since he was the only one still alive, he could help provide the necessary details to the insurance company about the truth of Iris's death. But Riley didn't know the kid's name—hell, she didn't even know if he was a kid. From the way they had spoken to each other—he'd only called Iris "lady"—it was clear they hadn't known each other before that day. Which meant he probably wasn't a neighborhood kid. So why had he been there?

Riley closed her eyes, working her way through the memory. She could see the kid's face, his shaggy black hair, and that he wore a backpack. Most adults didn't wear backpacks, so she guessed he was fairly young. Maybe he'd ditched school that day and had been wandering around aimlessly when he should have been in class. Riley supposed she could search for schools in the area, but did schools keep track of kids' absences from a year ago? And, even more relevant to Riley, would that be the kind of information they handed out to random people off the street with no connection to the kids attending the school? Riley thought not.

He'd been holding a skateboard by his side, but then he'd swung it around to grip it with two hands in front of his lap. Her mind's eye scanned the young man's form. Was he wearing a school uniform? Was there a logo on his shirt, his backpack, his … skateboard? She squeezed her eyes closed even tighter, willing herself to remember what had been on the bottom of that board. An anarchy sticker. A black logo made up of two circles—the inner circle whole, while the outer one was broken in five places—and a stick-figure-style tree in the middle. That one she recognized; it was the logo for Element, a famous skateboarding brand. A red circle with the word "Mongo" crossed out, reminiscent of the anti-smoking logo. And to the right of one of his hands, his fingernails painted black, she could make out another logo that was also vaguely familiar. It was of a skater mid-trick, hand grabbing the board, and the word "Kirky" written below the wheels of his board in a U-shape. The layout of the logo made the board's wheels look like eyes, with "Kirky" shaped like a smiling mouth.

Riley's eyes popped open and she scrambled for her computer. She typed in "Kirky skateboarding" and immediately got an address for a local skate shop.

"Oh!" she said out loud to no one.

According to the hours posted on the website, they were open until 8. If she hauled ass, she might be able to get there before closing. She called Nina.

"Hey, Ry. Long time no talk," she said, laughing. "What's up?"

"I think I have a lead on the kid who helped Iris," she said, a little breathless. "If we hurry, we can get there in time."

"I'm free in twenty. Send me the address and I'll meet you there."

After doing that, Riley brushed her teeth, wrangled her hair into some semblance of a bun, grabbed her purse and keys and was out the door in a few minutes.

Kirky Skate was only twenty minutes away. More notably, it was only a few blocks away from Julie's house.

She waited in the small back parking lot, leaning against her car's driver side door, for Nina to arrive. The shopping area was tiny, and in addition to the skate shop, it had a pizza restaurant and an aquarium store. The lot she was in now couldn't have accommodated more than fifteen cars at a time, and the street parking out front was mostly gone, thanks to the grocery store and chain restaurants on the opposite side of the road that were bustling with people this evening.

Nina pulled into the spot next to Riley's a few minutes later. She walked over, a brow cocked. "So what's the lead?"

"The kid had a sticker from Kirky Skate on the bottom of his skateboard. I thought if he frequents the place enough to put a sticker on his board, someone here might know him."

"Nice," Nina said, nodding.

They walked across the small lot, between the back of the skate and pizza place, and then turned right onto the sidewalk, where the single glass door of the skate shop stood propped open. It was sweltering inside, and Riley immediately wanted to walk back out. It smelled vaguely of sweat and rubber, which was made even more pungent with the heat. When she stepped inside, her foot landed on a thick black mat just inside the door and triggered a chime, letting the worker in the back of the shop know someone had come in.

The right side of the room had a wooden counter with a cash register on it; the front of the counter was so covered in stickers that the wood was hardly visible beneath it. On the wall behind the counter were rows of mounted helmets. To the left, the wall was covered in mounted boards, sans their wheels. The middle of the space was taken up by several turnstiles of graphic tees, while the back wall was devoted to shoes.

"Hey, ladies!" a male voice called from the back. "Sorry for the heat. The air conditioner is trippin' and we can't seem to get it to stop blowing hot air. I also apologize for the fact that it smells like a foot. Several feet."

Nina laughed as the guy reached them, but Riley had frozen. It was him. The same kid who had helped Iris. He was a year older now, and given the patchy mustache and beard he was trying to grow, he was at least past puberty. He still had a very young face, though.

"Hey, uhh …" he said, taking a few more steps toward Riley with his brows raised. "You all right? It's too soon to get heat stroke, I think. Do you need water or something?"

"We're here for a slightly bizarre reason," Nina said. "Maybe we could step outside, though, so she doesn't pass out."

"Uhh …" he said, casting a glance behind him, to where a boss or coworker likely was; the place was devoid of customers this near to closing time. "Yeah, sure."

The bell chimed again as they walked back outside. Riley took in a pull of fresh air. She'd been so excited about her idea, thinking said idea would lead her to another clue on where to find the kid. Not lead her directly *to* the kid.

"So, uhh…what's this about?" he asked, arms crossed as his dark gaze flitted between Riley and Nina.

"Does the name Iris Velasco mean anything to you?" Nina asked.

The young man cocked his head. "No. Should it?"

Finally finding her voice, Riley asked, "Do you remember where you were on March 15th last year?"

The guy visibly swallowed, then licked his lips nervously. "Oh, man," he said, uncrossing his arms. "I did my community service for the tagging already. I…I was told that wasn't going to be on my record since I was a minor." He glanced behind him. "You guys undercover cops or something? Are you here to tell my boss about that? I can't lose this job. I'm so close to being able to afford wheels."

She figured he meant a car, and not skateboard wheels. "We're not cops. Is the tagging why you were on Gimar Court that day?"

She saw it then, the way the words hit their mark. Not to mention how his eyes had grown to comical size.

"Dude. Is this about that lady? The one who fell off the ladder in her front yard?"

"Yes," Nina said. "What were you doing on Gimar Court when you found her?"

He swallowed again. "You swear you're not cops?"

"Swear it," Riley said.

"Well, I skipped school that day and I was bored. If you cut between the two houses at the end of Gimar Court, it lets out into this field. I don't know what used to be there, but there's an area near the back that's really smooth concrete. I think it was the leftover foundation of a demolished building or something. Anyway, when I cut school, I headed over there a lot 'cause there are usually guys skating. But when I was going down the street, I saw that lady fall off her ladder. She whacked her head pretty good 'cause when I got to her, she wasn't conscious. I legit thought she was dead at first, but when I poked her, she kinda squirmed."

"You helped her inside?" Nina asked.

"Yeah. I got her some pills for her headache. I always have Tylenol or something in my bag since I'm good at getting pretty banged up when I'm skating. I broke both my wrists when I was thirteen." He rolled his wrists in demonstration, which cracked faintly like microwave popcorn. "She was really out of it and kept saying it felt like her brain was soup. Soup, man. What the hell? Kinda freaked me out. I tried to get her to go to the hospital but she said she was okay. I left after that and came here, actually. One of my buddies used to work here before I got the job. I got caught tagging a wall on my walk home." He chewed his bottom lip. "Can I ask why? Are you her friends or something? She all right?"

Riley and Nina shared a glance, trying to have a silent conversation about how to break this news.

"She … uhh … passed away the day of her fall," Nina said softly.

"Aw, shit," he whispered. "Was it because of the concussion?" He went from grief-stricken to panicked in a matter of seconds. Hands pressed to either side of his head, he asked, "Am I like an accessory to murder or something because I didn't make her see a doctor?"

Riley held out her hands, placating. "Nothing like that. Would you be willing to talk to Iris's daughter? She's got some legal stuff to work out, and I think your account of things might help."

The guy swallowed hard, then lowered his hands. "Uhh … yeah. I could talk to her. I've felt bad about that day for a year and a half. I've been down the street a couple times since then and a new family lives there. I just kept hoping the lady was okay and moved. This sucks so bad. She was really nice." He swallowed, and straightened his shoulders, some kind of resolve coming over his lanky frame. "I'll talk to her daughter. No problem."

"You're a good kid," Riley said, feeling strange saying such a thing to someone not that much younger than herself, but knowing it would hit home with him because it was one of the last things Iris had said to him that day.

He ducked his head, just as he had with Iris.

Nina had her phone out. "What's your name?"

"Uhh … Randy. Well, Randall. Randall Hale."

As Randy rattled off his phone number to Nina, she typed it into her phone. When she pocketed it, she said, "Her name is Amy."

"Cool," he said, bobbing his head. "Okay."

Riley shook his hand.

Nina did the same but she didn't let go right away. She cocked her head. "Get the green car with the white stripe. The black one is a lemon."

Randy's mouth dropped open as they walked away, Riley barely suppressing a smile. She supposed being claircognizant had its benefits.

They stopped behind Riley's car once they made it back to the parking lot.

"Thank you for your help on this," Nina said. "You're far better at the sleuthing part of it than I am. It's not always needed on the jobs I do, but sometimes it is. If you ever want to join Galvan Investigations as a consulting researcher, I'd love to have you. Just saying." She started to walk away. "Think about it."

Nina told her to "think about it" a lot. Riley had to admit, though, that she didn't totally hate the idea of being Nina's researcher.

On the way home, Riley's mind was filled with the disparate details of the other mystery she was trying to solve. Randy being a witness to the events could be the final piece needed to take care of the main thing keeping Iris's spirit bound to Julie's house. What witnesses were there in Shawna, Brynn, and Emery's lives who could shed light on what had happened in the weeks and months before they'd disappeared? Friends, family, partners. Emery was currently too much of an unknown, especially since she was from a state over. But Brynn and Shawna had been from here.

She recalled the conversation she'd had with her mother about Gigi and the man with the buzz cut. Who else might have seen that man? Had he been prowling around, camera held to his face as he scoped out his next victim? Was it a matter of asking as many people as she could find who were around—eighteen years ago—who might recall a man with that description skulking around?

Rodney Elgin, Shawna's on-again, off-again boyfriend, had been in the same neighborhood as Shawna and Gigi. Her mother had said the guy was out of prison now. Was there a man with a buzz cut in his memory banks somewhere? There could be things he remembered that he either hadn't shared because no one had asked him, or things that had been discounted, just as Gigi's account had been, since the police had been so sure they'd already found their killer.

Riley's mom's friend Norma had a connection to that neighborhood, too. She planned to call her in the morning.

At just after 8, Riley settled on the couch with her laptop and phone. Scrolling through her messages, she opened the thread with her mom and stared at the text with Norma Kling's number in it. Riley dialed her number, hoping it wasn't too early.

"Hello?" a woman answered after a couple of rings, her breath labored. Riley thought she heard the sound of birdsong in the background.

"Uhh … hi. Norma? This is Riley Thomas, Sabine's daughter?"

"Oh! Hi, sweetie," Norma said, huffing.

"Are you busy? I can call back … "

"Not at all, not at all," she said. "I'm just getting my daily walk in. Need to keep fit and lean for the fellas. There's a real looker at my Bingo hall and I figure if I tighten up these buns a bit, he won't be able to refuse. I like a mature gentleman."

Riley fought a laugh, wondering how mature this gentleman was if he frequented Bingo halls. "I respect it."

Norma chuckled. "So what can I do for you? Sabine said you might have questions about the Mack family?"

"Yeah," Riley said, not sure how much her mother had disclosed to Norma. "And about your cousin who was almost kidnapped. Your grandma lived in the same neighborhood as Shawna, right?"

"Sure did. My grandma had been friends with Shawna's grandma. Her grandma was why she ended up in that house to begin with. She and her mama fought like dogs all the time. Two headstrong women who didn't like being told what to do. It was her daddy's idea that it would be good for everyone if Shawna stayed with her grandma and took care of her when her health started going downhill. The family figured if the two of them were out of each other's hair for a while, the distance would help their relationship. Shawna was only fourteen or so when she first got to Taos from Texas. She was all alone there. A couple years later, she got involved with Rodney. I think part of why she put up with his abuse for so long was that there wasn't anywhere else for her to go. And then shortly after her grandma died, Shawna found out she was pregnant.

"I saw them together several times over the years—Shawna and Rodney, I mean—and when they were in one of their good patches, it was clear how much those two could love each other. And love that boy of theirs. Gigi and me even went out to that recreation area with them a few times … some big group outing where a bunch of the kids in the neighborhood and their friends all went to the river.

"My grandma told me how rough that neighborhood could be sometimes, but the good outweighed the bad, usually. Until Shawna wound up dead, anyway. And then that man tried to snatch Gigi a month later. The whole neighborhood was scared."

"Were there any other incidents of women or girls being targeted after Gigi?" Riley asked.

"Not that I know of," Norma said. "Grandma had an ear to the ground there as far as gossip went. If something else had happened, she would have told me. For a good month after the incident with Gigi, Grandma wouldn't even let me come visit her because she said it wasn't safe. For months, Gigi's four brothers and several other men in the neighborhood started their own neighborhood watch program. Bunch of guys walking the streets at night with baseball bats and guns. The cops were convinced Rodney had killed Shawna, and they said Gigi must have misinterpreted what happened to her, so the neighborhood took their safety into their own hands. Maybe that's why nothing else happened after Gigi. That guy, whoever he was, saw that he'd have an armed mob to contend with if he struck again, so he moved on."

"Yeah, maybe," Riley said, lost in thought for a moment. "My mom said Rodney is out of prison now?"

"Yep. I was out to lunch with a friend in Taos the other day and saw him walking out of a grocery store. Most locals still don't think he did it, but he *did* do time for fifteen years, so a lot of people give the guy a wide berth. Most of his family is dead or moved away. I don't know why he'd come back to his old neighborhood, given everything, but maybe familiar places full of awful memories look pretty good after being behind bars for a decade and a half. He also has this … energy about him now. Broken down by the world, dead eyes—that kind of thing. Kind of get the feeling that he *wants* to be alone, so he is."

"Do you have any idea if he ever saw the buzz cut guy?" Riley asked.

"That I don't know," Norma said. "The buzz cut guy sort of became the neighborhood boogie man—women were looking over their shoulders, worried they'd run into him, and the men were on high alert, ready to tackle the guy to the ground if they saw him. Seems like he stayed around long enough to cause pain, and then left."

Left to ruin the Bodwells' and the Dawsons' lives, Riley thought. *Who else was in this guy's trail of destruction?*

"Do you have any idea how I could possibly get a hold of Rodney?" Riley asked, wondering if it was true that the man wanted to be left alone, or if that was the unintentional impression he gave off.

It took Norma a moment to reply. "I could ask around," she eventually said, but Riley got the distinct impression Norma thought talking to him was a terrible idea.

"Thanks. I appreciate you talking to me."

"No problem, sweetie," she said. "What's got you so interested in this anyway? You were just a little thing when all this happened."

"I'm deep in a true crime phase," Riley said.

Norma laughed. "You and every other young woman on this planet!" After a pause, she added, "You take care of yourself, all right?"

After thanking Norma again, Riley hung up and sat back on her couch. Her computer was in her lap a second later. Since she knew Rodney was back in Taos, she started searching for anything she could find on him aside from articles about his arrest. There was only one social media profile and all it had on it was a single picture. The photo was professional, his smile small but friendly.

Half an hour of searching got her to an employment service website and Rodney Elgin's profile. A bit more digging told her he worked as a nighttime warehouse worker for a pet supply company.

Clicking back to his social media page, she sent him a quick message, not sure if he'd ever see it. She decided to go the direct route with him; she didn't want to throw the truth of her ability at him in the middle of a conversation like she had with Carter. Ambushing an ex-con with surprising information felt riskier than doing so with a reporter.

> Hi, Rodney. My name is Riley Thomas. I'm not a cop or a reporter. I'm a psychic medium who is looking for answers regarding your ex, based on some information I've received. I would prefer to discuss this over the phone if you're comfortable doing so.

She added her phone number. Assuming he was able to find the message on this maze of a site, she doubted he'd even reply to her vague rambling nonsense. She hit send.

CHAPTER 21

later that evening, after an exhausting Monday Madness Discount Menu Bonanza shift, she was on a video call with Michael. They were attempting to make a meal together over the phone since their Sunday together had been replaced by her road trip into Taos.

"So why did you have to cover Fran's shift this time?" Michael asked while opening a can of tomato sauce. "Is her kid really sick this much, or is she lying to get out of Monday Madness?"

"Apparently the kid has lice now," Riley said, pouring her can of sauce into the pan of sautéed onions and garlic.

"Poor kid. I had to have my head shaved when I got lice."

Riley gave her head a scratch. "Can we stop saying the word lice?"

Tonight they were working their way through a chocolate chili recipe her dad had made dozens of times, but that Riley had never tried before. Michael had a tendency to "get creative" with ingredients when his pantry wasn't properly stocked, as well as not being the best at reading labels when purchasing food.

Once she had complained about this to Jade, who shared similar woes. Jonah wasn't allowed to go shopping on his own for anything too involved. The guy could write code for complicated apps, but the last straw for Jade was the time she'd sent him out to buy a few things, including green onions, and he'd returned with a stalk of celery.

"What am I supposed to do with this?" she asked him.

His response had been, "What? It's green. I couldn't remember which green thing you wanted." Calling her to ask for clarification on *which* "green thing" apparently hadn't crossed his mind.

Riley, similarly, had realized that instead of pouring a small cup of chocolate chips into his pot of simmering chili, Michael was breaking chunks of chocolate into it. She'd only taken her eyes off him for a minute while she'd been adding the chocolate into her own pot.

"Son of a bitch," he grumbled. "Why is this stuff so hard?"

She cocked her head, watching his back. "Uhh … what kind of chocolate did you get?"

He had successfully broken the chocolate into the chili by then and was stirring it. Glancing over his shoulder at her, so he could look at his phone propped up on a surface across from the stove, he said, "I don't know … the regular kind?"

She squinted at him.

Placing his spoon on the counter, he went rummaging in his trash can for the wrapper. He walked over to the phone, read the label, and wrinkled his nose. "Is baker's chocolate the wrong kind?"

Riley hung her head. "I think that stuff is really bitter."

"Dammit. I put in like three bars," he muttered, then picked up the phone so he could hold it closer to his face. "This is what happens when I'm left to my own devices."

"I should send you a picture ingredient list next time, rather than words," she said.

"Yes, you should totally do that."

He was in the midst of telling her what other kinds of pictures he'd like that had nothing to do with cooking and everything to do with her clad in skimpy underwear, when she was interrupted by a call from a number she didn't recognize.

"I promise we'll revisit this topic later," she said, "but can I call you back?"

"Sure. I'm going to see this recipe till the end, but I have a feeling I'll be eating leftover pizza tonight."

She laughed, hung up with him, and answered the incoming call. "Hello?"

"Uhh … hi," a male voice answered. "This is Rodney. Rodney Elgin?"

"Oh! Hi," she said, not sure if she was surprised more by the fact that he'd called her or that he'd done so the same day. "I'm glad you found my message."

"It's the only one I've gotten on there in a long time, so it wasn't hard to find."

A prolonged, awkward silence settled over them. She needed Nina with her to guide the conversation.

"So is this some kind of joke?" he finally asked. "Some prank to fuck with the guy who spent fifteen years in prison?"

Riley swallowed. "No. It's not a prank."

"You said you're a psychic medium?" he asked, tone dripping with sarcasm. "So, what, you're saying to talk to dead people or something?"

"Yes," she said. "I've talked to Shawna."

"Bullshit."

"If you think it's bullshit, why did you call me back?" she asked, her angry tone matching his.

He didn't have an immediate answer. "Prove it."

Her cheeks heated. "It's not like I can pull her out of a hat like a rabbit. It's not a magic trick."

"Convenient," he said. "You people always call me looking for a story. Pretending to be book publishers and TV producers and to offer me money, but it's usually just some young reporter trying to trick an ex-con into confessing. To get some exclusive story to get a career going. 'Cause of course there's no way I'm innocent, right? Somehow I cheated the system by only getting fifteen years for first-degree murder? Gotta say the psychic medium angle is new. You get points for creativity. But I still call bullshit."

Riley clenched her jaw, her own anger mingling with his, shutting down her ability to think. She wanted to punch something, to claw someone's eyes out.

"You come at me with proof and maybe I'll talk to you." He hung up.

Riley groaned. It took a few minutes of pacing while shaking out her hands and rolling her neck like a boxer about to enter the ring before she was able to calm down enough to call Michael back.

"This is a disaster," he said in greeting. "Everything okay?"

"That was Rodney Elgin."

"Why do you sound like that? What happened?"

"He wants me to prove I'm a medium before he'll talk to me," she said, her voice shaking, just like her hands. "He was … pissed. He assumes I'm not who I say I am."

"To be fair, I'm guessing you'd find it hard to trust people after being in prison, too."

"I guess so," she said, blowing out a slow, controlled breath. Now that the anger had ebbed, she was able to think clearly again. "It took Mindy a while to warm up to the idea of psychic mediums. When I called her out of the blue, it made her relive the worst days of her life. I guess the same would be true for Rodney. I just don't know how I'm supposed to prove it to him that I've talked to Shawna."

"You'll think of something," he said. "My god, this chili is *awful.*"

Riley checked on her own chili, stirring it around the pan. In the short time she'd left it unattended, it had taken a turn for the worse. She took a sampling bite and dramatically stuck out her tongue. "I think I screwed mine up somewhere." She flipped off the burner. "Guess it's pizza for me tonight, too."

"I wish you were here making disastrous chili *with* me."

Her cheeks heated again, this time for a different reason. "Same."

"Baxter can hardly sleep all week, you know. He lives for the weekends—whether you're here or we're there."

She smiled ruefully at that. As if that cat—or any cat—ever took a break from napping. But it was easier to put this all on an animal who couldn't speak for himself. She and Michael had danced around the "living together" conversation dozens of times lately. Both of their places were tiny, so moving into an entirely new place would make the most sense. But would they live in Albuquerque closer to her work, or Los Lunas which was closer to his? Should they find somewhere in the middle? Was she ready to cohabitate with someone again?

Michael laughed. "I can practically hear all the questions circling in your head. Don't stress, okay? You don't have to decide anything. I just miss you, that's all."

"I miss you, too."

After a brief pause, he switched back to his usual goofy tone. "All right! Go order your pizza. We'll reconvene once it has arrived and we'll synchronize a movie."

After ordering pizza, she took a quick shower, wondering how in the hell she'd find a way to prove to Rodney that she could speak to ghosts.

She was awoken at 8 the next morning by a phone call from Carter. "Hello?" she croaked.

"Aw, damn. I didn't mean to wake you."

"It's okay," she said, yawning and sitting up. She rubbed the heel of her palm against her eye. "My schedule is all over the place. What's up?"

"I have news for *you* this time. I just got a call from Lola Bodwell."

Riley's brows hiked toward her hairline. "Is that her … mother?"

"Yep. She said she'd like to talk. She apparently found something in Brynn's bedroom and thought it might be of interest to me. Any chance you want to join me? I was planning to meet her around noon in Taos. I'm in Santa Fe now for a couple hours, and was going to head out to meet her there for lunch. She's at a fundraiser of some kind until 11:30."

Riley didn't immediately reply, thrown by the invite.

"I was thinking that your … skills … might prove useful when talking to Brynn's mom," he said after a beat of silence. "Plus, I feel bad about how I reacted when you first told me you're a psychic. I figured if you're really into true crime, meeting the victim's mom might be up your alley."

It was.

"I just need coffee and a shower, and I have to be back by 4."

"That works. If you want to meet me here in Santa Fe

around 10, we can drive over to the café together. Plus, where we're meeting her has the worst parking situation, so one car will limit the headaches."

"Sounds good," she said. "Text me where to meet you."

After Carter drove out of the parking lot of the mall where Riley left her car, he said, "We're heading to the Taos Village Shopping Center. The locals call it Boujee Village."

Riley had donned her dark purple top with the pearl buttons—the nicest shirt she owned—in a fit of self-consciousness. The fact that Brynn's parents had deep pockets had come up numerous times. She pictured Lola Bodwell with elegantly coiffed hair, a pearl necklace that cost more than Riley's monthly rent, and shoes worth more than her car.

It was a chilly October morning, and a light rain had started to fall. They didn't talk much on the drive into Taos, the radio tuned to an old R&B station.

The sign for the Taos Village Shopping Center stood on a corner opposite an expansive, empty field. Shop names were printed on the dark brown wood in a pristine white font. The buildings mimicked the classic adobe-style Southwest architecture, but instead of everything being a warm sandy brown, their façades were white with black accents. The parking lot for the café was packed with BMWs, Lexuses, and gleaming SUVs. Carter's Prius, though outdated, fit in better here than Riley's old Honda would have.

Carter tried searching for a parking spot on the street first, but after driving five blocks away from the massive shopping center and coming up empty, he returned to the parking lot.

Once there, it took twenty minutes of circling the lot before a cherry red sports car glided out of a spot. Carter pulled in between a pair of champagne-colored Audis. He cast a sideways glance at her. "Told you."

Riley laughed, some of the tension leaving her chest. "I feel underdressed. Too bad my café gown is at the cleaners."

"Along with my café tux, I'd imagine," Carter said with a grin. "Lola suggested we get a table outside. Apparently the inside is freezing all year long."

The patio of the café had an awning stretched over the tables, but to help accommodate for the rain, a plastic cover had been stretched down over the awning as well as the sides of the wrought-iron fence that lined it, shielding the many diners from the elements.

Riley was glad she'd brought her heavy peacoat with her. As they walked to the café, she pulled it on. "You haven't eaten here before?"

"Not really my scene. I checked the menu last night. The wedge salad appetizer is like $15."

"That dressing better be laced with gold," Riley muttered.

Carter chuckled as he held the door open for her. As she stepped in, it was instantly noticeable that the bustling café was colder inside than out. Every table inside appeared to be occupied, though, and the place was loud with the chatter of voices and the sounds of the open kitchen behind a curving glass wall. A whoosh of fire rose in her peripheral vision as a chef threw something into a wok of hot oil.

The man behind the maître d' podium smiled at them. "Good evening. Do you have a reservation?"

"I believe Lola Bodwell reserved a table for three?" Carter asked.

The man offered another little smile and checked something on his podium. "Ah, yes. She requested a table on the patio, yes?"

Riley had only been in here for under a minute and already her teeth were on the verge of chattering. "Yes, please."

"Perfect," the man said, and turned to the counter behind him lined with menus. "Right this way."

Riley and Carter followed after the man who cut through the middle of the room and then made a right out onto the plastic-lined patio. A pair of tall space heaters stood vigil by the patio doors, easily heating the contained space.

The man led them to a table that sat perpendicular to the iron fence. Sets of black linen-wrapped utensils waited for them. Carter and Riley took a seat on the same side of the table, and the maître d' laid out three menus for them.

"Zephyr will be your host this afternoon," he said. "He'll be by to take your drink orders shortly."

Riley tentatively picked up the menu—a black-fabric-wrapped board with a neatly typed menu on brown paper affixed to it by way of delicately tied ribbons in two corners. Carter hadn't been lying that the cheapest thing on the menu was the $15 wedge salad appetizer. She quickly gave up on her perusal of it and set it down, folding her hands on top.

"Did Lola tell you specifically what she wanted to talk to you about?" she asked after a couple of minutes.

Carter looked up from the menu. "Just that she had something she wanted to show me. She wasn't shocked to hear the serial killer theory. My guess is, she's been scouring the internet for information just as much as any other true crime junkie. I've seen many parents attempt the armchair detective thing when they feel like the police aren't doing enough, or when they grow frustrated that their child's case has gone cold."

Lola Bodwell arrived a few minutes later. The relation to Brynn was unmistakable—they had the same blonde hair, blue eyes, and high cheekbones. Carter and Riley got to their feet at the same time, but Lola waved a hand at them.

"Sit, sit," she said, taking a chair across from them, unwinding her scarf from her neck and unbuttoning her coat. "I appreciate you making the trip over here."

"No problem. I'm happy we could meet," Carter said.

Lola quickly ran a hand through her shoulder-length hair to shake free the clinging dots of mist.

"Good call on the outside table," Riley said.

"I know, right?" Lola said, picking up a menu. "It's great inside during the summer, but the rest of the year, it's an icebox. Also, order whatever you want. It's on me."

"Oh, you don't have to do that," Carter said.

Lola looked up from the menu, her bright blue eyes scanning Carter, and then settling on Riley. The grief hit Riley in the chest like a freight train. The woman might have had a breezy, polished façade, but she was a wreck underneath, just as any mother would be who had lost her child. "Yes, I do. Please let me."

"Thank you," Riley said, picking up her menu, and Carter reluctantly followed suit.

Riley opted for the Cobb salad, which was nearly $25. When the waiter came by for their drink orders, Riley asked for water as a way to lessen the guilt.

Once their orders had been put in, Lola placed her folded arms on the table. She tucked hair behind one ear, and Riley could see the slight tremble to her hand before she lowered it back to the table's surface.

"Was there something specific on your mind that you wanted to discuss, Lola?" Carter asked. "I assume this is about the article."

"Yes. I don't know much you're able to tell me, but I wanted to find out how you know the woman in that picture is connected to Brynn's death. And Shawna's too, if your theory is correct." Lola sat a little straighter, her smile a little bigger. "Do you have a source in the police department? Are you two working together?"

Riley suppressed a frown at Lola's hopeful tone.

Carter said, "I have an outside source. The information came to me from someone with a unique insight into the case. My source is confident that the young woman in the photo was killed by the same man."

Lola stared at him a beat, then her gaze swung toward Riley. "Did you write the article with him? I only saw one name in the byline."

"She's an intern of sorts," Carter answered for her. "I can't get into the details of who my source is just yet, for confidentiality reasons. Just know that the source is reliable enough that I believe there's little chance these deaths *aren't* connected. You said you had something you wanted to show me?"

"Oh, right," she said, turning to get something out of the purse that hung from the back of her chair. She produced a Prada wallet, and then pulled out a business card. She slid it across the table.

Carter looked it over and then handed it to Riley. She braced herself for a potential psychic reaction, but nothing happened.

John Anderson. Photographer.
www.andersonphotog.net

There was a phone number, too. Riley turned the card over. Blank.

"Brynn's room was eventually turned into storage space, not a guest bedroom or anything like that," Lola said, and Riley didn't need to be a psychic to sense how much guilt was wrapped up in that statement. "We boxed up many of her things and put them in the closet. But neither my husband nor I have been able to throw anything out. Anyway, I guess I was having one of my low days and I was looking through some of her things. I picked up a box and this card slipped out. I'd never seen it before."

"Had Brynn mentioned seeing a photographer?" Carter asked, clearly unsure why this was significant.

"Sort of. Two weeks or so before she went missing, she asked me if I had the contact information for the man who had taken our family photos a few years back. The photographer had since moved, so I couldn't pass anything along to her. She said she wanted to get some pictures taken of her and Liam. I honestly thought there was a secret engagement I hadn't known about—I couldn't imagine why she'd want pictures like that. It just didn't seem like a Brynn thing to do. But she didn't bring it up again after that."

Riley placed the card back on the table between them.

"A week later, I went into her room to ask her something and she was frantically stuffing a Victoria's Secret bag under her bed," Lola said, her cheeks turning a faint pink. "I'm not naïve or a prude … obviously she and Liam were having sex. It can be weird to broach that subject with your mom. I get that. So maybe she was hiding the bag from me out of embarrassment. But between her asking about a photographer, this card, the lingerie, and the fact that Brynn had told Liam she had an anniversary gift for him … I think she set up a secret meeting with a photographer to get boudoir pictures taken. I talked to Liam a few times about it and that's his best guess, too. Brynn apparently asked him a few times how he'd feel if she got sexy pictures taken of herself."

This might have all sounded like a giant leap taken by a grieving mother to Riley, had there not already been a photography connection to the murders. The cameras that had come out of the storage unit had been well maintained by someone who clearly knew a lot about them, and even if the pictures had been paparazzi-like shots of women unaware they were being watched, they were quality photos taken by someone with talent. The picture of Shawna, her arms outstretched as young Malcolm ran toward her, was an achingly sad picture—not just because Riley, as the viewer, knew what fate had befallen Shawna, but because the photographer had managed to capture the love between mother and child in a way that didn't feel like an accident.

All of a sudden, Riley's sixth sense tingled and in the next moment, there was a fourth member at their table. Brynn sat beside her mother now, gazing at her profile. Riley's eyes had involuntarily widened, she knew, but she was unable to move.

A dark hand swiped up and down in front of her face and she snapped out of her trance.

"Are you okay?" Carter asked.

Riley managed a nod. "Sorry. Did you ask me something?"

Lola cocked her head, studying Riley a moment. "I just asked Carter if he thought this John Anderson could be the one who pulled up behind Brynn in the parking lot that night. Maybe she was meeting him to pick up the pictures, or to pay for them—something—and then he forced her into the car?"

Brynn's head shook back and forth in the corner of Riley's eye. Riley looked over, and when they made eye contact, a voice sounded in her head.

Not John.

"Have you mentioned this to the police?" Carter asked.

Ruthie

Brynn stared straight at her.

Ruthie.

The word was in Riley's head, but she hadn't seen Brynn's mouth move. Not that ghosts had vocal chords left anyway. Riley idly sipped at her water, not sure what to do with a ghost in public.

Lola sighed, redirecting Riley's attention. "Yes, I've called them. I've called with so many theories over the years, and called for updates, that I usually get a 'thank you for the information; we'll be in touch' kind of response. I took a photocopy of the card to them, but I'm sure it's just sitting in a file on someone's desk." She tapped the card with a manicured pointer finger, the polish a light pink. "I called the number and went to the website on the card, but neither one works anymore. I was running out of ideas, running out of hope, honestly, until I saw your article, Carter. I even hired a psychic."

Riley choked on her water. Carter gave her a few solid pats on the back while she coughed up a lung. "Did you have any luck with the psychic?"

"Which one?" Lola asked, shaking her head and laughing. "There have been so many over the years. I'm probably just desperate at this point. But I was thinking you have more resources than I do, Carter, and maybe you could research John Anderson? Even if nothing comes of it, it feels like you're doing more to figure out what happened than the police are. I understand they're all busy, and they don't have the manpower to work their current cases and also cold ones, but you could look him up, right? Researching stories and tracking down leads is what you do."

Ruthie.

"I'd be happy to look into it." Carter took a picture of the card, then handed it back to Lola.

Ruthie.

Ugh, fine! she wanted to scream at Brynn.

"Does the name Ruthie mean anything to you?" Riley asked abruptly.

Lola was so startled by the question that she managed to knock over her glass of water. Riley snatched up the business card before it was ruined, and Carter righted the glass, keeping half of the contents inside. While Riley and Carter quickly unwrapped their utensils to use the linen to mop up the water, Riley could feel Lola boring holes into the side of her head.

Not until the water had been wiped up, and the waiter had handed them newly wrapped utensils, did Riley hazard a glance Lola's way.

"Why would you ask me that?" she asked in a whisper.

Shit. She hadn't meant to get into this today, but Brynn had other plans. "Uhhh … well … "

"The source I mentioned earlier," Carter cut in, "is Riley. She's a psychic."

Riley braced herself. Even if Lola had already been in contact with psychics before this, it didn't mean she would appreciate being blindsided with this information.

Lola, however, pressed her hands to her mouth, her wide, watery eyes focused on Riley. A short, surprised sob issued from her. Slowly, she lowered her hands. "Ruthie was our springer spaniel. She passed away a few days ago."

Movement made Riley's attention shift back to Brynn. *Ruthie.* Then Brynn pressed her hand to her chest.

"Ruthie is with Brynn," Riley said.

Lola just stared at her, head cocked. The hope pouring off the woman was almost tangible. But saying the family dog was with her deceased daughter wasn't exactly a groundbreaking claim. It was something any psychic—even a fake psychic—could say with confidence. It was a nice, comforting sentiment, but it wasn't proof.

Help me out, Brynn.

Just as with Shawna at the campsite, an image flashed in Riley's head like a lit-up billboard on the side of a pitch-black highway. "She's … showing me a bouncing balloon? A *pink* balloon. Sorry, I don't know what that means."

Lola's eyes had gone wide. "That was their favorite game. Brynn would toss her a balloon and Ruthie would knock it back to her with her nose. We found out she liked the game during my niece's fifth birthday party—we covered the backyard in pink balloons for her. After that, we always had a package of balloons around. Ruthie wouldn't play with toys for very long, but she'd play with a balloon for hours.

"She and that dog were inseparable. Ruthie was almost a year old when Brynn went missing. That dog had slept with her every night. When she went missing, Ruthie started sleeping by the front door as if she were waiting for Brynn to come home. One night, Ruthie started howling as if she were in horrible pain. My husband and I woke up and ran to the front room, sure someone had broken in and hurt the dog. But Ruthie just lay there, head thrown back, howling at the ceiling. Ten minutes later, the police called us with the news that they'd found Brynn."

Riley's eyes welled. "I can't imagine how hard this has been for you. Especially since they haven't caught the person who did this."

It took Lola a moment to reply, clearly doing her best not to break down in public. "Knowing those two are together … that brings me more comfort than I can possibly tell you." Blowing out a long, slow breath, Lola said, "So how exactly do you fit into all this?"

Riley gave her the condensed version. "I'm just trying to follow the clues they're giving me. Brynn says the person who did this wasn't John, but I do think your photography theory is valid."

Lola nodded, a bit of her composure returning. "Can you ask her something for me?"

"Actually, just say it," Riley said, eyeing the spot where Brynn still sat, now fully turned toward her mother. "She can hear you."

"Was that you on Christmas?" Lola asked.

Riley, though she was sitting, felt arms wrap around her from behind. She should have been completely freaked out, but a deep sense of comfort immediately overrode the panic. Brow furrowed, Riley said, "She hugged you."

Tears slid down Lola's face, and she nodded. Reaching across the table, she held a palm up to Riley. Riley slipped her hand into hers. "Thank you."

Riley could only manage a nod, as Lola's desire to burst into tears and ugly sob in the fetal position had slammed into Riley when their hands touched, so now Riley was resisting the same urge as Lola. Brynn smiled softly, then disappeared.

Carter cleared his throat, like maybe he, too, was working through a strong emotion or two. "We can't guarantee anything, but Riley and I are both looking into this from every angle we can—both on this plane, and the next."

"I'm happy to help however I can," Lola said, letting Riley go.

"For now, we think it's best to keep Riley's involvement in this under wraps," Carter said.

"Your secret is safe with me." After a long pause, Lola said, "I keep thinking about your article, Carter. The idea that other women were victims to the same monster who took Brynn, but that they didn't get the coverage they needed because a connection between the cases wasn't made?" She shook her head. "It makes me sick. As horrific as all this has been, somehow there was a sense of closure when they found her. At least I knew. But the idea of other mothers having no idea what happened to their girls for years … for decades?" She shook her head again. "I know it won't lessen anyone's pain, but if down the road we need more media coverage, I'm ready to throw money in any direction necessary."

"That's a lovely offer," Carter said.

After Riley's $25 Cobb salad, a half hour of idle chitchat, and a long hug goodbye, she and Carter headed for his car. He carried a to-go box of his half-eaten $35 roast beef sandwich.

A few minutes into the drive back to Santa Fe where they'd left her car, Carter asked, "Did you really see Brynn?" His tone was more awestruck than doubtful.

"Yes. She popped into the chair right next to her mom."

"Wow," he said. "You knew her dog's name and that she liked to play with balloons—how random is that? And that Brynn had given Lola a phantom hug on Christmas." He laughed softly to himself. "That was wild."

"Glad you believe me now," she said, but there was no malice in her tone.

When he pulled up next to her car in the mall parking lot, he said, "Oh, I forgot to mention that I'm taking the wife and kid on a little vacation this coming weekend. I'll still have my phone on me so you can get a hold of me if anything comes up, but I won't be in town. I'm not saying that meeting you and having my foundations shaken to their core had anything to do with it, but I've been thinking about how short life is, you know? Anything can happen. I want to be better about making time for the family."

"I'm also glad I could provide you with an existential crisis," she said, laughing. "Have a good trip, if I don't talk to you before then."

She got out of his car and into her own.

On her drive back, she didn't ponder her own mortality or her place in the universe. There was only one very simple thought in her head that carried her home and through her six-hour shift: *Time to find John Anderson.*

CHAPTER 22

That night, after a scalding shower and scarfing down a bag of pork buns, Riley studied the picture of John Anderson's business card Carter had texted her. She knew there had been nothing on the back of it, but she wished she had the card in hand now so she could have the tactile sensation of it under her fingertips. Maybe it would have triggered a psychic reaction if she had more time with it in a quiet location, rather than a busy restaurant. Putting her pointer finger and thumb together on the phone's screen, she drew them away from each other, enlarging the photo. Using her finger, she moved the picture to the left, then the right. Nothing of note popped out at her that she hadn't already seen.

Brynn's mother had said that John Anderson's site was down, but Riley remembered what Jonah had said about nothing on the internet ever truly going away. She poked around online for a while, and then stumbled on a site called the Wayback Machine. It was an internet archive site that had started back in 1996, keeping an archive of the internet in digital form. There were over 475 billion web pages archived. She clicked the "WEB" tab at the top of the screen and then typed John Anderson's website into the search bar. It produced a listing.

http://andersonphotog.net
rangefinderanders 1996 – 2012
97 capture(s) from 2000 to 2016

There were several other numbers listed with the display that Riley didn't remotely understand. To the left of the stats was a small screenshot of a site with a soft gray background, some text, and at least three thumbnails of pictures. When she clicked the site's screenshot, she got an error message. She wasn't sure if that was because the site in question was no longer active and therefore all that remained was this screenshot, or if her lack of a Wayback Machine account limited what she could see. She copied and pasted the link address into a separate search page just to be sure. A bar along the top stated that "http://andersonphotog.net" didn't exist and that the domain might be available for purchase.

While debating on whether it was worth it to cough up a couple of bucks to get full access to the site, she stared at the few lines of text that were provided along with the website address. She conducted a few searches of random keywords. From what she could tell, the line of italicized text that came after a website's URL was often a piece of information about the owner of the website or the company associated with it.

Rangefinderanders. What the hell was that?

Typing that into her search bar, she got a few results of a "rangefinderanders" leaving grumpy, one-star restaurant reviews, mostly about poor service and overpriced food. One of which was Epicurean Subs, where she and Nina had met with Amy Velasco. Her heart rate doubled. Did John Anderson live in Albuquerque? She checked the locations of the other reviews. Two more were local places, and a third was in Santa Fe.

She did a quick search for "rangefinder" and wasn't surprised to learn that it was a type of 35mm film camera.

Scanning the reviews again, she found that they'd all been posted in the last few years, one of them only a month ago. So the guy was still alive—and grouchy as all get out, if the reviews were a reflection of his usual attitude. She recalled the way she'd been kicked and punched after touching the bomber jacket in Marty's Thrift N Save. The blood on the jacket hadn't been the result of his beating from several months ago, since the jacket couldn't have been on him and in the storage unit at the same time. Had his grouchiness gotten him into trouble on multiple occasions? Maybe he'd gotten into an altercation about the ratio of chicken to vegetables on one of his sandwiches, and had sent it back to be remade. Every once in a while, a customer would come into The Laughing Tiger who would send a dish back multiple times if it wasn't made to their specifications.

Riley liked the idea of him complaining about the price of his gourmet sandwich, and getting popped in the mouth because of it.

Wondering if John Anderson used his handle in other places on the internet, she typed "rangefinderanders reddit" into her browser. The results proved the guy was active on the site, so she did a search on Reddit for his profile. Unsurprisingly, he posted and replied to several subreddit threads related to photography and cameras.

After an hour of getting sucked into countless threads, she found a buried post from him that had been put up recently.

Any of you from Albuquerque?
Due to circumstances beyond my control, a small collection
of my cameras got sold off. Any chance someone has seen a

Canon AE-1, Minolta SRT-101, or Samoca 35 LE in a thrift shop or on eBay lately? I'd gladly buy them back. They were my dad's and they're the last things I have left of him.

Someone had replied just two days ago asking:

Any luck, bud?

Rangefinderanders hadn't replied.

Riley fumbled to call Detective Howard, unsurprisingly getting his voicemail, given the hour. "Hi. It's Riley. I think I found something."

She figured the vague message would get him to call her back sooner.

He did so the next morning. "I'm almost scared to ask what you've found."

"Would you have time to talk to me sometime soon? I have a bunch of information about Brynn and Shawna's case that now involves a third woman. Her name is Emery Dawson. If they're really all connected, that means this crosses state lines. I think I found the owner of the camera that had been used to photograph Shawna and Emery."

He was quiet for a beat. "I'm not sure you took a breath during any of that. This sounds like an in-person kind of conversation."

"Preferably," she said. "Before I do something stupid, I'd like the expertise of a very distinguished detective."

She could hear the smile in his voice when he said, "Whoever said flattery won't get you far in life didn't know what he was talking about. Give me a few days, all right? Things are hectic here at the moment. Just remember that I'm technically always on call, so I can't guarantee I won't end up issuing a rain check."

"I'll take what I can get. Thank you. I know you're busy."

"I'll be in touch soon. I'm looking forward to what you've found out, and also feeling deeply apprehensive."

"That tracks."

When she hung up, she eyed her screen where the message from rangefinderanders was still pulled up. An image popped into her mind of rangefinderanders sitting in front of his own computer, staring at a screen filled with Riley's information. Her gaze flicked to a window, then her front door, wondering if he was out there somewhere.

She hoped she'd found him first.

Riley hadn't yet found a way to prove her abilities to Rodney. She'd been able to prove herself to Lola Bodwell, but she'd had help from her daughter. Before going to bed, Riley thought of what Nina had told her while they were at the campground. *"Focus your energy on these flowers, why you're here, and call out to Shawna."*

Riley didn't know if it would work the same way here in her apartment, in a location not connected to Shawna, but she thought of how Iris had gotten in contact with Riley through her dreams. Riley pictured the switchboard in the Great Beyond again, willing that light above her name to flip to green. Perhaps Shawna could see it and would pay her a visit.

She sat on her bed and stared at the picture of Shawna and her son, scouring every detail of the picture, silently asking Shawna to give her something—*anything*—that would be proof she could use to get Rodney to speak to her. She mentally called out to Shawna and kept the woman in her mind as she placed the photo on her nightstand, turned out the light, and settled in to sleep.

Riley dreamt not of Shawna, but an older Black woman standing on the back porch of a house. It was dusk, and a pair of moths busily buzzed around and periodically slammed into a glass-enclosed porch light on the wall. She was a heavyset woman in her sixties or seventies, and had a head of short curly gray hair. She wore a house dress covered in brown and white songbirds.

"Rodney!" she called out. "I'm not going to call you again. Get your butt inside and eat!"

Though her tone had been stern, her wrinkled face brightened when she saw a young Black boy run toward her. The knees of his pants were caked in mud. "Sorry, Grandmama!" he called, deftly squeezing past her and darting into the house.

"Boy! You better not be tracking mud into my house," she said, following after him into the small, homey kitchen. The walls were a butter yellow, and the faded tile floor had flecks of yellow mixed with the cream and brown tones.

"Sorry, Grandmama," the boy called out from somewhere beyond the kitchen. He emerged a moment later, standing in the open doorway of the kitchen with a mason jar held between two dark hands. He thrust the jar up like an offering. A worried-looking frog sat at the bottom.

"Oh!" his grandma yelped, hand to chest. "Don't you have enough of those things already?"

"Can I keep him? Please? That'll make four. Fred, Barney, Bamm-Bamm, and now the Great Gazoo."

"You and that show." She eyed the jar warily, but then offered a small nod. "That's the last one, boy. Now go wash your hands. Food's getting cold."

Rodney ran toward her and managed to hug her tight around her wide middle without dropping his new pet. He peered up at her and the affection in her face as she smiled down at him made even Riley's heart constrict.

His grandma cupped him behind the head and placed a kiss on top of his head. "Go on," she said softly.

Rodney ran off, presumably to the bathroom.

Then the woman turned to Riley, offering a knowing little wink. "Stubborn as hell, that boy."

Riley woke with a gasp.

What the hell was that?

She knew a little about lucid dreaming—was his grandmother someone who could control her dreams? How had she ended up in Riley's dream when she'd been thinking about Shawna?

She waited until ten that morning—after she'd showered and dressed for work—to call Rodney back. It initially rang so many times, she was sure it would go to voicemail.

"Yeah?" he answered.

A flash of the woman's image on the porch flitted through Riley's mind again—the moths buzzing by the light, her halo of curly gray hair, the songbirds on her dress. The dress, for some reason, felt important. Words she hadn't known she was going to say came tumbling out. "You spent a lot of time with your Grandmama Robin when you were younger. You collected frogs you named after *Flintstones* characters. I'm guessing you were eight or nine when you got the Great Gazoo."

Rodney was silent for so long on the other end that she pulled her phone away from her face to check to make sure he hadn't ended the call. He hadn't.

"That proof enough?" she asked.

"She come to you in a dream?" he finally asked, his voice raspy.

"Yes."

Another long pause. "Grandmama had it, too. The sight, I mean. At least she claimed she did. That, or she had literal eyes in the back of her head. That lady put the fear of god in a person like no one I've ever met."

He talked about his grandma in the past tense, she noted. She recalled the way the woman had looked at her in her dream. She'd *seen* Riley. Did a psychic medium's powers extend beyond death?

"I … apologize for how I spoke to you before," Rodney said now. "Even if you were lying to me, I shouldn't have talked to you that way. You caught me on a bad day."

"And I'm sorry I contacted you out of the blue like that about such a sensitive subject," she said. "So … uhh … I wanted to ask you a few things if you have the time. I'm a consultant of sorts on Shawna's cold case. Some information has come to light recently and I'm helping sift through it."

He was silent for a beat. "Did you have anything to do with that article that came out about her recently?"

"I played a part in that, yes. Would you be willing to meet with me in person? I usually work late afternoons into the evening, so anything before noon usually works better for me. I'm in Albuquerque, so it would take me about three hours to get into Taos."

After another long pause, he said, "I can talk to you, sure. And I can meet you halfway. Santa Fe all right? I've got a bad case of claustrophobia since being let out, so a park or something would be better for me, but I can meet you somewhere more public, too. I work nights, so before noon works fine for me. Or anytime on the weekend. I don't do much else."

"Cool. I'll pick a place and email you."

After ending the call, she sent Michael a text.

> **RILEY:** Remember that time we met a murderer in Santa Fe?

Michael replied half an hour later.

> **MICHAEL:** I'm scared to reply to this …
> **RILEY:** How would you feel about meeting an ex-con in a park?

He started and stopped typing a few dozen times.

> **MICHAEL:** Dating you is an adventure, you know that?
> **RILEY:** Is that a yes or … ?
> **MICHAEL:** You know it's a yes. Do you have the deets yet? Can you email the deets to me?
> **RILEY:** Stop saying deets.
> **MICHAEL:** You love me.

She grinned.

> **RILEY:** Yeah, yeah.

Riley scoured the internet for popular parks in Santa Fe. Finding one just off the highway, she sent the deets to both Michael and Rodney, including a meeting time for Saturday at 11 AM.

CHAPTER 23

Baldwin Park was huge and swarmed with people. It had several parking lots, and Michael had chosen the one on the east side. It was walking distance from a large play area that was filled with children and watchful parents alike. Kids climbed jungle gyms, swung on swings, and shakily crossed suspension bridges.

Michael grabbed her hand and they walked across the grass toward the duck pond, where she said she'd meet Rodney. Off to the left, beyond the play area, a large group of men were engaged in a raucous game of soccer. A line of kids rode down a nearby walking path on their bikes, a little boy pedaling as hard as he could to keep up, shouting at someone who was probably his big brother to slow down.

The pond was more like a small lake, and had a short pier at the end of which was a wooden gazebo. A man stood there, fishing pole in hand. Benches ringed the path that snaked around the pond. Only one of the benches to the right of the pond was occupied, possibly because the ones on the left were surrounded by an army of geese busily mowing down the already well-tended grass.

"I think that's him," Riley said, jutting a chin to the lone man sitting at the bench.

"I'll go hang out by the gazebo," Michael said. "If the ex-con gets shifty, just give me a shout."

Riley laughed, kissed him, then let his hand go, heading for Rodney. From her research, she knew he was in his mid-to-late forties, but if she had passed him on the street without knowing anything about him, she would have guessed he was closer to his sixties. Prison wasn't kind to most.

When she was only a few feet away, he glanced over. He offered her a small smile and stood up, hand out. "Riley?"

"Yep," she said, shaking his hand.

It wasn't until this moment that she really wondered about the danger of meeting someone who had spent fifteen years in prison. It wasn't as if she thought he'd suddenly shiv her, but it struck her then that he had lived a life so wildly different from hers.

"I don't bite," he said, letting her hand go and chucking softly.

Her face heated. "Sorry."

He shrugged, sitting back down. "It's a look I get a lot once people find out I did time." There was no bitterness in his tone, but she had to imagine he was exhausted.

They sat there a minute in semi-awkward silence, listening to the lively energy of the park and watching as a pair of little girls threw pieces of bread to a group of ducks in the pond—despite the large sign nearby telling people not to feed the birds.

For reasons she couldn't explain, out of nowhere, she blurted, "I know you didn't kill Shawna."

When she turned to look at him, his eyes were a little glassy, though they were focused on the girls feeding the ducks.

"That means a lot coming from a psychic," he said, smiling to himself. "Even though I got put away for drug offenses, it felt like I got put away for murder. I'm not trying to make any excuses for myself." He looked at her then. "I fucked up. I own that. But I also did my time. And even if people look at me and just see a felon, I'm not a murderer. I got close—once—in prison when I first went in. It's dog eat dog. I needed to protect myself. But even in there, I wasn't about that. I sure as shit wouldn't have killed the mother of my kid."

Riley nodded. "Why did it *feel* like you got put away for murder?"

Rodney sighed, turning a bit so his side was resting against the back of the bench. His hands rested in his lap, his shoulders slumped. "Shawna and I were … not good for each other. Toxic. When things were going good, they were real good. But when they were bad, they were fucking terrible, you know?"

"Yeah."

"We couldn't seem to stay away from each other, though," he said. "Passionate in all the wrong ways. We were young and broke. Home life for us both wasn't the greatest. I drank a lot … was high as shit, too. We were always stressed about money, would get in a fight, I'd put my hands on her, she'd scream and holler, and a neighbor would usually call the cops. Cops got to know me real good back then. My daddy probably rolled over in his grave every time it happened. He taught me never to hit a woman. But Shawna could get me so damn mad." He frowned. "I'm not like that anymore. The fight's gone out of me. I promise I'm not making excuses. I'm just telling you how it was."

Riley gestured for him to continue.

"Every time shit popped off, I'd leave. I couldn't trust myself around her for long. But my point is, I always stopped. When it got too bad, I'd bounce," he said. "As much as I fucked up,

I'd never, *never* go so far as to kill her. I didn't have it in me then and I don't now. We'd fight, break up, and then one of us would come crawling back. Over and over and over. Then the next thing we know, Shawna is twenty-two and pregnant. I was barely a man myself and I was going to be a dad. And I *wanted* to be a dad for him. He made me want to get my shit together—like he was my chance to fix all my fuckups."

"Malcolm, right?" Riley asked, even though she already knew the answer.

"Yeah," he said, a little involuntary smile tugging at his mouth. "Shawna started working three jobs just to keep a roof over our heads. My grandmama, the one I mentioned earlier, she helped take care of Malcolm for us since we were always working. I tried to get a respectable job, but it was hard to get hired for much even before I'd done time. I worked at McDonald's for a while, but you can't raise a family on that. Selling weed paid the bills a lot better. One thing led to another and I made a connection with a guy selling coke. That paid *really* good. It was dangerous, though. I was stressed the fuck out all the time, always looking over my shoulder. Always worried about turf war bullshit with guys out in Albuquerque and that somehow my kid would get caught up in it."

He stared out at the water again. Riley got the feeling he was working some things out. She didn't want to interrupt him.

"When Shawna went missing, I wasn't even in town. I came back because my grandmama called me one day asking me where Shawna was because she wasn't answering her phone. I blew through a stop sign while I was hauling ass back home, not sure what was going on. I got pulled over and then brought in for questioning, in large part because my grandmama kept calling the police. She kept asking them to search for Shawna because she wouldn't ever abandon Malcolm. They told her they'd file the report but that she probably just ran away, or that she was lying low to avoid me—since that happened once before—and that she'd show up eventually."

"And then they found her body," Riley said.

Rodney lowered his head, staring down at his hands in his lap. "When they had me in for questioning, they'd say stuff like, 'We know Shawna was seeing someone else' and that I was jealous about it, and 'How'd you feel when you found out Malcolm wasn't really yours?' and a bunch of other bullshit. None of it was true, but they kept making shit up, giving me likely scenarios that would have made me mad enough to kill her. They'd seen enough 'guys like me' that they assumed they had me pegged. So they kept pissing in the dark hoping they'd hit something." He shook his head. "One guy, I'll never forget it, said, 'You know what I think happened? I think you two were out there at that campground for a romantic evening, you have sex under the stars, but then she starts running her mouth like always—you said that's what happens, right? She starts running her mouth and you gotta knock her around to make her stop? She does that again while you're out there, ruins the moment, and then you shut her up for good.'"

"Shit," Riley muttered.

"Yeah," he said, working his jaw. "Every time my grand-mama called the police, she told them they should check that camping area. The cops thought it was because we went out there as a family a lot, so maybe Shawna was hiding out in a familiar place. Thing is, Grandmama was saying that because she had the sight—she saw it in her dreams that Shawna would be out there—so when they *did* find her out there days later, they were sure it was because I'd confessed to her. They thought that was her way of calling in a tip without ratting me out. They said they knew she was protecting both Shawna and me, since I was her grandson."

Something Detective Howard and Carter had said came back to her. "Your grandma was the supposed secret informant…"

Rodney pursed his lips and nodded. "That's why I thought you were fucking with me when you first contacted me. I thought you'd somehow found out about her connection to it, and that's what you really wanted to talk to me about."

Nodding, Riley asked, "Did she tell the cops about her psychic dreams?"

Rodney sighed. "Eventually, yeah. Especially when it looked like they were going to try to pin the murder on me. But that's why the cops never said who the informant was. They didn't want to admit that their main source was a crazy old Black lady ranting about her dead granddaughter-in-law coming to her in a dream. They had no way to prove I'd done it, but they convinced themselves my grandmama's tip was the smoking gun. Lucky for them, I was deep into drug running, or they wouldn't have anything to arrest me for."

"That's awful," she said.

He managed a shrug. "Is that how Shawna comes to you? In dreams?"

"I actually saw her. Her ghost, I mean, at the campsite."

Rodney's bottom lip trembled slightly. "Did she speak to you?"

"No," she said. "She just showed me an image—a clue about who took her."

"You really think the same guy who killed her also killed that white lady?"

"Brynn."

"Yeah, Brynn. And the other lady in the picture, too?"

"Her name was Emery," Riley said. "But yes. I think he killed all three, and there might even be more."

Rodney's eyes went glassy again. Riley agreed with his self-assessment; the fight had gone out of him. He looked more numb than angry.

"If they hadn't been so sure I'd done it, maybe those other girls wouldn't be dead, too."

"Maybe," Riley said softly. "Do you remember anything odd about the month or weeks before Shawna disappeared? I know you said you weren't in town when she first went missing, but do you remember anything out of the ordinary before that?"

"To be honest, a lot of that time is a black hole in my head. Too much alcohol and drugs. I've come to terms with a lot over the years. Prison gives you a lot of time to think and work through shit. I'm not saying it's a perfect system, or even a good system, because it's not—it's fucking brutal. I've tried to better myself. What happened to Shawna, though, and the tense relationship I have with Malcolm now?" He shook his head. "That will haunt me for the rest of my life. If I'd been in town that day, maybe she'd still be here. My whole life would be different. Shawna might still be alive. I might hear from my kid other than on holidays and birthdays.

"I can't even be mad at him. Even if I was arrested for something else, even if I swear to him on a stack of Bibles, and on my grandmama's grave that I didn't kill his mom, Malcolm is always going to wonder if I did. He's always going to blame me for his mama not being on this earth anymore."

Riley frowned. She hoped that if she figured out who killed Shawna, it would help ease Malcolm's mind about his father—at least about this.

"Sorry," he said, sniffing hard. "I don't get to talk about this kind of stuff that often. But uhh … to answer your question, I can't think of anything that stands out."

"Did your grandma have any other dreams about Shawna?"

Rodney tipped his head back a little and stared up at the sky as he thought. "She told me that she kept seeing a white guy with very light hair cut in military style. But the asshole cop who was so sure he had me all figured out looked like that. Maybe that cop was in her head a lot because of how hell-bent he was on tearing apart the whole family. I can't ask Grandmama, though … she passed while I was in prison."

"I'm sorry to hear that." Riley would have liked to meet her, though in a way, she might have already met her. In the story Riley's mother had told her about Gigi—the young girl who was almost kidnapped—the man she'd described had a buzz cut hairstyle too. It could be a coincidence, but Riley had a feeling it wasn't. Still, it wasn't much for her to go on.

"Not sure if any of this has been helpful. Turned more into a therapy session for me. You remind me a lot of Grandmama. Maybe that's why."

"That's okay. I don't mind listening," she said. "Oh, I have something for you." She rummaged in her bag and took out the picture of Shawna and Malcolm. "This was on Emery's roll of film."

Rodney choked back a sob as he took it from her. With shaking fingers, he touched Shawna's image, then Malcolm's, both of them captured in a moment of pure joy by a man hiding in the shadows, intending to rip that happiness out from under them like a rug.

"The reason why the picture exists is awful," Riley said, peering over at the photograph in Rodney's lightly quaking hands, "but it's still lovely somehow."

A tear slid down Rodney's face, off the end of his nose, and onto a pant leg. He didn't seem to notice. "Maybe if the cops had seen this, they would have seen how much Shawna loved that boy. They might have tried harder to find out what really happened to her. She never would have left that boy for anything."

"You can keep that," she said. "I should probably get going. Thanks for talking to me."

He sniffed and wiped a sleeve across his eyes. "If I think of anything else, I'll let you know."

They stood. Riley resisted the urge to hug the sad, broken man in front of her, not wanting to overstep. Her clairsentience told her Rodney was resistant, but she couldn't pinpoint why. She thought of Norma's assessment of him: *"Kind of get the feeling that he* wants *to be alone, so he is."*

Her gut told her to hold out her arms. Rodney stepped into them and hugged her, letting out a little choked sob as he did. It took him a minute to compose himself, then let her go, sniffing hard and wiping at his eyes.

She wiped at her eyes too, hoping he had someone in his life that would hug him again later.

Looking down at the picture he still held, he said, "I hope you're able to find the bastard who did this."

"Me too. Stay in touch, okay?"

"I will."

She headed across the park to join Michael at the gazebo, where he'd managed to get into a deep conversation with the fisherman about Bitcoin, of all things. She'd stood nearby and listened to them chatter about cryptocurrency for a while before either of them noticed her. First the beard, then the deep dive into cooking and all its facets, and now Bitcoin? She wondered what was next.

"Nice talking to you, man! I'll check out that site," Michael said, then walked across the gazebo. "How'd it go?" he asked her.

"Good," she said, laughing. "I see you made a friend."

"He's such an interesting guy," he said.

"Is he from here?"

"I'm not sure."

"What does he do for a living?"

"No idea."

It never ceased to amaze her how men never covered practical information in conversations. "I didn't know you were interested in Bitcoin," she said, switching tack.

Michael cocked his head at her curiously. "I'm not."

Men were very strange creatures.

As they headed back for the car, Riley looked over her shoulder to wave goodbye to Rodney, but he was back on the bench, all his attention focused on the picture she'd given him. She lowered her hand and continued on, leaving the man alone with his own ghosts.

October, 2021

On Sunday, the day The Client emailed me for the first time in ten years, I drove out to my old storage unit in Clovis. A phone call wouldn't be enough. When I walked into the office, I forced tears into my eyes, telling the man behind the counter that I'd been the victim of a brutal attack and that the delinquency of my account had been no fault of my own.

"The cameras were my father's," I said tearfully. "He was a war veteran—a true hero. He died only last month, while I was laid up in a hospital bed completely unaware that he'd suffered a fatal heart attack. Those cameras are all that I have left of him."

The man behind the counter seemed unmoved. After keying a few things into his computer, he said, "I'm very sorry to hear about your father, but that unit was auctioned off over the summer. I can't disclose who bought the unit, but if I remember correctly, that was the one some lady with a thrift shop in Albuquerque bought. We all thought it was weird she shelled out so much cash for a table but…" He shrugged.

What was I supposed to do with "some lady with a thrift shop in Albuquerque"?

"Look, I'd help you if I could, bud, our facility doesn't even run the auction." He trundled open an unseen drawer and produced a business card that he then slid across the counter to me. "They're who we usually use. They'd have more information about the sale than we do."

I snatched the card off the counter and stalked for the door without another word. *Thanks for nothing*, bud.

"Dick," the guy muttered.

I resisted the urge to root around in the supply bag in my trunk to find something sharp to slash his tires with. Useless prick.

Fuming, I slid into my car and slammed the door. Why had a woman made the trek out to Clovis to buy a desk from a storage unit? No one would have known the cameras were in one of the drawers until the unit had been bought and paid for and then…surprise! Here's three mint-condition film cameras.

I bashed the heel of my palm against the steering wheel.

I tried the auction company next but got the same result: no one would disclose the buyer of my unit. Customer confidentiality or whatever the fuck. I drove home pissed off but undeterred.

On Monday, I took a deep dive into Carter Quincy, scouring the internet for everything I could find on him. By Tuesday morning, I was armed with information and a packed bag. I would hole up in Taos for a while, where this menace of a reporter hailed from. During my three-hour drive, I felt buoyant. After months of missing memories, the familiarity of my task at hand wrapped me in its sweet embrace. I even looked forward to booking a motel for a few nights.

The Client's assignments were why I paid my rent in monthly chunks—it assured I would have a place to come home to when a job ended, but also granted me the freedom to pick up and leave without worry. I hadn't *needed* to pay for rent in six-month blocks for quite some time, but it was an ingrained habit now. It had saved me from losing my apartment while I'd been in the hospital.

It hadn't helped in the case of the storage unit, though. I clenched my jaw.

I would fix this. I had to.

Some part of me had always been holding onto the hope that The Client would come back to me and we could pick up where we'd left off.

I had been right. He needed me again. My hopes were coming to fruition.

I *would* fix this.

That night, I slept better than I had in months—years, maybe. It wasn't as if the slightly sour-smelling motel bed was particularly comfortable, but there was something familiar in being in an unfamiliar place. The constant, distant hum of traffic lulled me to sleep, like the undulating warbling of a womb.

I found Carter Quincy's address before I found the man himself. He lived on a quiet residential street, and when I found the physical house that matched the one on Google's Street View, I parked at the curb a few houses down and waited. He didn't arrive at home until after 8 PM on Tuesday evening. I wondered where he'd been. Chasing down a story or busying himself with a woman who wasn't his wife?

I poked around outside the Quincys' a bit after midnight, once the lights inside those quiet little houses had gone dark, searching for evidence of security cameras or window stickers advertising an alarm company. I found neither. What I did find, however, was that his neighbor to the right had a dog. I heard a distant yipping just before the *whomp-slap* of a plastic doggie door. Once in the fence-enclosed backyard, the little yipping thing really exercised its lungs. I took that as my cue to leave.

I was back in the neighborhood bright and early the next morning. Around 7, as I waited for Carter to start his day, his next-door neighbor, a twenty-something, pear-shaped woman with long brown hair and tortoiseshell glasses, came walking out of the house with the small brown-and-black Yorkie that had barked at me last night. It continued to yip at everything even while on a walk—cars, cats, birds, people, the occasional leaf rolling down the sidewalk. The woman turned left, away from Carter's house and, twenty minutes later, rounded the block, walking past Carter's house before disappearing inside her own.

Carter emerged shortly afterward, getting into his Prius parked on the street and driving off. He waved at the old man who lived on his other side as he went. The old guy had just stepped out in his bathrobe to fetch the paper off his porch.

I slowly pulled out onto the road to follow him.

Though Carter worked at the *Taos Daily Journal*, he rarely seemed to be in the office, always flitting about town like a hummingbird. Nothing in his movements about town struck me as particularly noteworthy. He wasn't meeting with families of The Client's victims or anything troublesome like that. Granted, only two of those families were local. Carter didn't appear to be making any attempts to leave the state either.

For the entirety of the day, I followed him around town during the day, then watched his small house at night. I noted that his pear-shaped neighbor emerged with her dog again around 6 PM, turning left out of her house.

I got out of my car long enough to root around in my stocked supply bag in the trunk. I couldn't remember when I'd started keeping it, but seeing it had unlocked more memories. The contents of the bag had grown into an eclectic assortment of items. Selecting what I needed, I walked at a casual pace up the other side of the block, knowing the woman would be rounding it soon enough, probably taking the same path with her yippy dog every day at 7 AM and 6 PM, varying her route very little.

Sure enough, within fifteen minutes, the pair turned the corner, heading my way. I heard the yippy beast before I saw it. Awful creature.

"Oh!" I said when they were a few feet away. "Hi, little guy!"

The woman beamed, gazing down at the dog with more affection than the thing deserved.

"Can I say hi?" I ventured.

"Sure. He loves everyone, don't you, Ollie?"

Ollie, the little shit, growled at me.

"Ollie!" the woman admonished, punctuating that with a light stomp of her tennis shoe. "That's not nice. That's not how we talk to our friends."

"Does he like treats?" I asked, revealing a small bag of crunchy bone-shaped treats that I'd stuffed in my pocket.

"Oh, he loves treats. Don't you, Ollie?"

I resisted the urge to say it looked like his owner loved treats, too.

Bending down, I tossed one of the little bones toward him. Ollie sniffed the air, then came out from his hiding place behind the woman's legs. The tiny rat-dog crept forward in an army crawl until he reached the treat, turning his head sideways so he could grab it off the ground while still keeping an eye on me.

"Oh, you're so silly, Ollie!" the woman said, laughing. "This nice man isn't going to hurt you."

I tossed another couple of treats to the dog. By the fourth, I had him tentatively grabbing it out of my hand. "Thank you for indulging me," I said as I stood. "I'm new to the area and my dog is staying with my mom until I get settled into my new place and job. I've been taking long walks trying to get to know the neighborhood, and I've been making new dog friends everywhere I go."

"Oh, that's so sweet," she said. "Well, I hope your fur baby can join you here soon. I'm sure Ollie would love to meet him."

Fur baby? Christ. "Yes, I hope so, too." I tossed another treat to Ollie. "Enjoy the rest of your walk. Maybe we'll see each other again."

"That would be nice, wouldn't it, Ollie?" She blushed lightly as she said it, then continued on her way.

On Wednesday, I watched the woman leave her house again at 7 AM. Boring. Carter, at least, was always doing something different. Around noon, instead of grabbing lunch, he went into a big box store. He purchased arm floaties, a pair of child's swim trunks, and a cooler on wheels. After following him around the store, I got into line two people behind him.

As the chatty cashier rang up his items, she said, "Looks like someone is going swimming!"

Carter smiled good-naturedly as he took out his wallet. "We weren't able to get out of town this summer, so we're heading to a resort with a heated pool to help make up for it."

"Oh, that sounds lovely. Can I come too?" The woman let out a hearty laugh at her own joke.

Carter was all smiles as he left with his purchases.

Was he planning to take my cameras with him on this resort trip? If the cameras *were* in Carter's possession, he hadn't used them outside the house since I began watching him. Did he have them in his little house, displayed on a shelf? I hoped he didn't let his grubby-handed kid paw at the cameras the way

Tracy had done. I pictured a lens smeared with grape jelly, and fought down the bile that had inched up my throat.

I followed him back to his house, where he spent most of the afternoon inside with his family. As I watched from down the street, the idea of the cameras being on display somewhere collecting dust made me see red. I needed to know if he had them. He wouldn't take all three of them to the resort, surely. He didn't know how to care for them the way I did. I nearly broke out in hives at the idea of one of them slipping from careless fingers before plunging into over-chlorinated water.

That evening, I "accidentally" bumped into Ollie's owner.

"Oh, hello again!" I said, coming upon her closer to the beginning of her route this time. "Hi, Ollie."

The little dog ran up to me and sat at my feet, tail swishing.

I bent down to give him a few more treats. If only people were as easily manipulated into compliance as dogs were.

On Thursday evening, I was around a corner in the middle of the route. As I took my time tying the shoe I'd untied myself a minute before, a fuzzy black-and-brown head appeared in my line of sight. Ollie got up on his hind legs, his front paws balanced on my knee. He stared up at me expectantly. The little beast left a pair of paw prints on my clean khakis. I swallowed down the urge to fling him across the street, and instead offered the dog a cheerful hello and a vigorous scratch under his chin.

I fed him a few more treats.

When I stood, his owner waited there, and I noted with an equal mix of amusement and horror that she'd dressed up more than usual. Her hair was in loose curls rather than stick-straight. Her walking pants had been swapped for a pair of dark-wash jeans, and she wore pink-tinted gloss.

"Ollie looks for you every day now," she said, smiling at me in a way that was almost demure. "I'm Vickie, by the way."

"Eric," I said, going with the first name that popped into my head. "I look for … him every day, too," I added, softening my tone just so.

A pink tinge that matched her gloss rose in her cheeks. Perhaps humans *were* as easy as dogs. Ollie needed treats. Vickie needed the hope of a meet-cute she could write about in her diary or—god forbid, on her blog.

We chatted a bit, me making up the details of my life on the fly while she was probably unflinchingly honest. I laughed where appropriate and forced myself to seem tongue-tied at times, flustered by our supposed growing attraction.

There's just something about him, she would probably tell her best friend on the phone later.

When we parted ways, I hadn't asked for her number or asked her out. She was too shy to make a move, I knew. She'd probably spent all day debating on what to do with her hair. And, sadly for her, this was the last time we'd be chatting. What I needed was for her dumb dog to like me.

On Friday evening, Carter started loading suitcases into his loathsome Prius around the same time Vickie came sauntering out with Ollie. Carter and Vickie greeted each other. Ollie yipped happily at Carter, and then the pair started off on their usual route while Carter prepared to take off for the resort with his little nuclear family. Vickie's saunter had morphed into a sad shuffle by the time she'd returned home, not once laying eyes on her new crush. Poor Vickie.

An hour after the Quincys finally departed, I was confident they wouldn't be returning prematurely because they'd forgotten something of the kid's. I left long enough to grab dinner at a nearby burger place, as well as a few snacks to tide me over until I made my move later in the evening.

I was back by 9 PM but waited until just after midnight, when Vickie's lights had been out for over an hour. Vickie never went to bed later than 11:30. I wasn't worried about Carter's older-than-dirt neighbors on the other side. I'd said hello to the old woman once and she hadn't reacted until I'd practically shouted in her face. The Quincys didn't lock their side gate, which was partially hidden by a hydrangea bush in need of trimming. One tug on the gate's pull cord and I was in. I eased the gate closed after me.

Ollie, as predicted, started making a ruckus at the sound, flying out of his dog door. *Whomp-snap.*

"Hi, Ollie," I said softly, and the dog quieted immediately, followed by excited whimpering. "That's a good boy. Want some treats?" I tossed a handful over the fence between the Quincys' yard and Vickie's. The dog went in search of the tiny bones. I heard him snuffling like a tiny fuzzy pig as he tried to root them out in the dark.

After pulling on my gloves, I easily picked the lock on the Quincys' backdoor and pushed it open, peering around the corner of what appeared to be a small laundry room. The Quincys had no dogs, but I noticed the smell of cat before I spotted the litter box in the corner across from the dryer. Hopefully it would be so scared by the intrusion that it would hide and stay out of my way.

I gently closed the door behind me and crept into the kitchen. I stood there, listening, waiting for any sign that someone was still there, but the place was empty. I got to work scouring every inch of the tiny house—in every closet and drawer in search of my stolen cameras. I didn't find them. No sign of the camera bags. No lenses or tripods. I got the impression from the décor that Carter wasn't a shutterbug at all.

They had a small detached garage, as well as a shed in the backyard near a lemon tree laden with fruit. I checked them both. Nothing. A second scan of the house revealed much of the same.

I stood in the middle of the living room strewn with toys, and put my hands on my hips, assessing. Did he never have the cameras? Had someone else developed the photos and brought the picture of Emery *to* him? What if I'd been wasting all this time tracking Carter when it was someone else who had my property?

"Dammit," I hissed, kicking at a discarded action figure lying on a rug, sending it skittering under the couch.

I let myself back out of the house, turning the lock on the doorknob as I went. Ollie was still outside, if all the rustling was any indication. He whimpered when he heard me, then gave the wooden fence a few scratches, searching for his new friend.

Slipping out of the gate, I kept the treats in my pocket. That would be the last time Ollie would ever get a treat from me.

My jaw was tight as I made my way back to my car, wondering how best to figure out the identity of Carter's source. It was back to the drawing board for now, but this hiccup wouldn't stop me. I would find the source, figure out what treat they needed to gain compliance, and I would end the problem.

The thought that put a bounce in my step was that if the problem needed to be ended permanently, The Client would probably pay extra.

CHAPTER 24

When Riley's phone rang Saturday afternoon, not long after her meeting with Rodney, she was surprised to see Carter's number pop up on her screen. She and Michael were still on their drive back from Santa Fe.

When all she did was stare at her phone, Michael asked, "What's wrong?"

"I thought he was on vacation," she said, then answered just before the call went to voicemail. "Everything okay?"

"I'm not sure. I just got a strange call from my cat sitter."

Cocking a brow, Riley waited for the rest. When he remained silent for longer than necessary, she said, "And?"

"And it looks like someone has been in my house."

"You were *robbed?*"

Michael swerved slightly, then softly cursed and mouthed an apology.

"She says it doesn't look like anything was taken, but there were enough things moved around that she called asking if I'd come home early," he said.

"That's … weird."

"You don't know anything about this?"

"Are you asking that because I'm a psychic or because you think I'm a burglar on the side?" she asked in a tone harsher than she intended.

"Sorry," he said, heaving out a long breath. "I don't even know why I felt so compelled to call you."

"It's okay. What did your cat sitter say?" Riley asked. "Was she worried enough to call the cops, too?"

"Michele wasn't due to start until today since we made sure Biscuit was set overnight in terms of food. She was in the area for another client yesterday evening after we left and grabbed some lemons from our backyard. She's got a standing invite to grab them whenever she wants. She went out the back door through the laundry room to get to the backyard, then came back in the same way and says she distinctly remembers locking both the deadbolt and the bottom lock.

"When she got to the house the next morning to check on Biscuit, things were shuffled around and Biscuit was completely freaked out. A few drawers were standing open an inch or two. A couple of cabinets were open. We keep the bathroom door closed when we're gone because Biscuit unrolls the toilet paper if given the chance, but the door was open. Michele hadn't used the bathroom last night but remembers the door being closed. On the back door, only the bottom lock was engaged, not the deadbolt."

Riley gave a little shiver.

"After she called me to ask if we circled back home last night—like maybe we forgot something—and I said no, she was really scared so I had her call the police. She explained the situation and they dusted for prints. While Michele was outside, my neighbor Vickie came over to see what the commotion was about. The cops asked her if she'd heard anything in the night, and said she'd been awoken around midnight by her dog Ollie barking in the yard. That dog barks a lot, so that in itself wasn't weird, but she said he stopped barking almost immediately. Usually she has to get up to tell him to come back in.

"She mentioned that there had been a new guy in the neighborhood several days during the week and he gave Ollie treats every time he saw them. The treats are little bones—like maybe half an inch long. Not the kind of thing Vickie gives her dog. When she was outside this morning to throw something in her trash cans on the side of her house, two of those little bones were on top of the cans."

Riley stilled. "Like maybe someone threw them over the fence to shut the dog up?"

"That's what I was thinking, too."

"Did she describe the guy? Did he sound like someone you might know?"

"White guy, sandy blond hair, mid-thirties, blue eyes," Carter said.

It instantly made her think of the Nob Hill Prowler, but Carter didn't live anywhere near Nob Hill.

"So … I didn't mention this before," Carter said slowly, "but ever since that article about Shawna came out, I could swear there's been a guy tailing me. Same description. He's never approached me, but I've seen him all over town in the last week. In Target, at the post office, driving past the park while I'm there with my kid. He's hardly ever looked at me, so up until what Vickie said, I didn't think much of the guy. I figured he was new to the area and I was noticing him all over town because he's new. But maybe he's not …"

"Crap."

"Yeah," Carter said. "The fact that this guy potentially was watching me enough to know when I left town so he could break into my house? I'm hours away and still feel all kinds of violated."

"I would too."

"If this guy is connected to the Shawna and/or Brynn case, my guess is he was either looking for the negatives of that roll of film, the pictures themselves, or the cameras—or hell, all three."

"And/or the name of your source of said pictures," Riley said, her stomach knotting.

"Exactly. Just keep your eyes peeled and be safe, okay? There's no way he can know where the pictures came from. Not even my editor knows your name. The chances of this guy making a connection between me and you is slim. But still. Keep an eye out."

Riley heaved out a shuddering breath. "I'm sorry if this is ruining your trip."

"I haven't even told my wife yet," he said, and she could hear the wince in his voice. "She and Isaiah went for a walk while I took a call she assumed was for work."

"Maybe wait to tell her until you're heading back."

"Her parents live in Santa Fe. I'm very tempted to drop them off there until this blows over. What if this asshole comes back? The idea of someone breaking into my house while my wife and kid are asleep makes me so goddamn angry…"

"Maybe you should stay with family, too," she said. "I'm sure your editor would understand, especially if you think this is tied to the story."

Carter grunted. "Maybe. Oh, hey, I gotta go. They just got back. Stay safe, okay? I mean it."

"I will." She stared out at the passing landscape, trying to imagine what it would feel like to come home only to realize someone had been prowling around her apartment, pawing through her things.

"What happened?" Michael asked.

The longer she talked about it, the angrier she got on Carter's behalf. "There's no way to know for sure someone targeted Carter because of the article. I'm sure reporters piss people off all the time. But it also seems like the reason why Emery hasn't been identified by anyone in Taos yet is because no one in Taos knows who she is. She was from Texas, not here."

"All except the person who took those pictures," Michael said. "That storage unit was here even if the woman in the picture wasn't."

"Right. Instead of there being someone in Taos who's been waiting years for evidence to materialize about Emery, it's possible that Carter's article made the opposite happen. This rangefinderanders guy is local. It's possible that someone in New Mexico knows damn well who Emery Dawson is and is upset Carter might be close to figuring out her identity."

The expression on Michael's face was inscrutable.

"Hey," she said softly. "What are you thinking?"

"I'm thinking that this guy could target you next. What if he followed you and Carter to that shopping center in Taos? He could have seen you two talking to Brynn's mother. You said yourself that Lola looks a lot like Brynn." He looked in his rear-view and side mirrors. "Hell, he could be following us now and knows you just talked to Shawna's ex. What if he figures out you're Carter's source?"

Riley had thought of all that too, of course, but had been trying to ignore the dull buzz of worry in the back of her head. "Think I should call Detective Howard?"

"That would make me feel better, yes."

She called him, marveling at the fact that a detective resided in her recent call log.

"Hi, Riley," he said cautiously. "I'm sorry I haven't called you back yet. It's been hectic over here."

"I think the owner of the camera broke into a reporter's house last night."

He was quiet for a beat. "Dammit. Okay, I technically have the day off tomorrow, so let's meet in the morning. I apologize in advance if I get called away."

"Okay. I'll see you tomorrow."

Next, she called Fran, asking if she could cover her Sunday brunch shift. Thankfully, Fran was so grateful for Riley taking her last few Monday Madness shifts, she agreed immediately.

Riley was already inside the small Santa Fe diner, armed with her collected information, by the time Detective Howard arrived a little after ten the following morning. He was a late-fifties Black man with a classic dad bod, and his short tight curls were shot through with a generous helping of gray. The last few times she'd been around him in person, he'd had his arm in a sling after being shot by Francis Hank Carras. His arm was no longer in a sling, since it had been well over six months, but she detected a stiffness in his shoulder and arm as he walked. None of this surprised her.

What did, was that he had company.

"Hi, Riley," the detective said as he approached the booth.

"Hi," she said with a level of caution that he usually reserved for her.

With his good arm, the detective motioned to the fair-skinned man standing with him. "This is Detective McGregor. He's part of the reason it took so long to get back to you. I wanted him here too. He's the buddy I told you about who worked on Shawna Mack's case back in the day."

Riley involuntarily narrowed her eyes at him, upset on Shawna's behalf that no one seemed to have treated the case as anything but domestic abuse.

Detective Howard held up his hands in a placating gesture. "Easy there, tiger. McGregor believes the same thing that you and I do—that Shawna and Brynn were victims of the same person."

Her hackles lowered a fraction.

"May we?" Howard asked, gesturing to the booth seat across from her.

She nodded, watching as McGregor slid in, and then Howard.

A waitress came by to take their orders.

When she'd left again, Howard said, "I hope you don't mind, Riley, but I told McGregor about your … abilities."

Riley cocked a brow at McGregor. "And you still showed up?"

McGregor laughed. "I've worked with psychics before, though admittedly with mixed results. Howard vouches for you, though, and that's enough for me. We've been friends for two decades. Every detective has unsolved cases during their careers. Some haunt them more than others. The Shawna and Brynn case—because it's essentially the same case to me—is the one that haunts me. Both because of how the department handled everything, and because I've never been able to let go of the feeling that the man who killed Brynn didn't just get away with her homicide, but Shawna's too. I hate the idea that there might be other victims out there we missed."

Riley's hackles lowered completely, her shoulders relaxing.

"So tell us what you've got," Howard said, jutting a chin at the folder sitting at Riley's elbow.

She started to talk, catching McGregor up on how this all started with the purchase of the cameras. She told him about her trip to the Orilla Verde Recreation Area where she'd met Shawna's spirit and the lunch with Lola Bodwell at which Riley met Brynn's ghost and was given John Anderson's business card. Detective Howard perked up when she covered new ground, namely her discovery of "rangefinderanders." She had printouts, pictures, the fingerprint slide, and the video she took of herself lifting the print off the film cartridge. She told them she'd found out that the third victim, the one who had come after Brynn, was named Emery Dawson.

The men looked three kinds of pissed off that their fears had been confirmed—that this killer hadn't stopped after the media circus that followed Brynn's kidnapping and murder, just that the killer had gone further underground.

"I know that all of this," she said, gesturing to the scattered bits of evidence that were placed around and between the plates of breakfast that had arrived during Riley's recounting of her discoveries, "is just circumstantial. And I don't even have this guy's name. Maybe the 'Anders' from his username is part of his real last name of Anderson, but given how this guy has kept off the radar for this long, it's possible that John Anderson and Anders are both aliases.

"And if Carter and his neighbor are right, and the guy who has been seen all over town and in the neighborhood for a week is the same guy, he told the neighbor his name is Eric. So who the hell knows.

"All I know is that Emery isn't in New Mexico. My gut is telling me her body is in Texas. Even though it's been sixteen years, who knows what clues her remains could hold? Finding her body is the only way to make her spirit stop trying to get my attention. Locating her feels like it needs to be my next step. All that said, road tripping into a different state to try to find her doesn't sound like the smartest—or easiest—thing to do alone. Her last known location was that wetland park, but there's no way to know that's where she is. Texas is a big state.

"So that's why I wanted to talk to you, Howard … and now you, too, McGregor," Riley said, crossing her arms on the table in front of her uneaten Country Potato Medley. "I don't want to go traipsing out there and mess up a crime scene, because I have no idea what I'm doing. I'd love to have police backup with me, but I know that once a case crosses state lines, that can put it in FBI hands. So … what are my options?"

The men stared at her for a moment, then shifted their attention back to what she'd brought them.

It was McGregor who spoke first. "I've got an FBI contact. Let me put in a few calls and then we'll go from there, yeah?"

"And what if they shut you down?" Riley asked.

Howard pursed his lips. "I'd be more than happy to give you off-the-record guidance on what to do out there, should you venture there alone and find something. I'm on board with you finding that girl, but I would hate for either myself or McGregor's actions to result in jeopardizing anything. Evidence could get thrown out or discounted if we violate jurisdiction. Technicalities and red tape could get us all in a lot of trouble here."

"Agreed," McGregor said. "We'll go through the proper channels first, then we'll reevaluate. If the guy who broke into Carter's house really is this Anderson guy, and I'm not saying he is—this is all speculation and hearsay at the moment—he feels threatened. Depending on how long Anderson has been snooping around, it's possible he's already connected you to Carter. If he hasn't, we can't rule out his ability to track you down. So if anything—and I mean *anything*—happens where you feel like your safety is in jeopardy in any way, you call either one of us."

Howard nodded.

A bit shell-shocked that they were so willing to help her, Riley said, "Okay. Thanks." She picked up her fork and idly poked at a cold potato. She wasn't hungry.

Detective Howard said, "Can I request that you—no, beg you—not to pursue any of this on your own? Please don't be a plucky heroine in a novel who goes toe to toe with a criminal. This guy is dangerous. And need I remind you, the last time you went up against a guy like this, *I'm* the one who got shot. Let's avoid that this time, hm?"

Riley winced. "I still feel really bad about that."

Detective Howard waved her off good-naturedly.

"I have to say," McGregor said, picking up the sheet of paper with the drawing of Amity Trucking's logo on it, "even if this all *is* circumstantial, I'm impressed with the work you've put into it."

Her face flushed. "Thanks."

"I'll also admit that as skeptical as I am about psychics—because I've met some real looney tunes in my day..." McGregor started.

Howard chuckled knowingly.

"I know the Renee Palmer case was one of *those* cases for Howard. I may have gotten a little excited to meet you when he told me you were the last piece of the puzzle that helped get that case off the books." He rubbed the back of his neck as he stared at her. She got the impression he was debating how much he was willing to divulge to her when they'd only just met. He dropped his hand. "I've been in contact with Malcolm Elgin a few times over the years. He was only five or six when his mother was killed, so it's unlikely he'd remember much, but I started checking in with him periodically as he got older, both to see if any memories resurfaced, and to assure him that there was still someone looking into what happened. That folder is always on my desk. It would be incredible if I could tell Malcolm definitively what happened to his mother before my career is over. At this point, that's all either of us wants. We just want it solved. Shawna deserves that much." He smiled at her a little wistfully. "No pressure."

Despite the knot of tension that had grown as he talked, she laughed then. "Eh, the Renee Palmer case was over three decades old and I helped solve that one, didn't I? This one should be a piece of cake at less than two. The whole serial-killer-on-the-loose-plus-crossing-state-lines thing is child's play."

The men chuckled.

"Ah, so psychics have a dark sense of humor, too?" McGregor asked.

"It's that or I curl up in a fetal position and never get up again."

Howard grinned at her. "Same."

After they ate, and their plates had been cleared away, McGregor said, "If you're okay with it, I'll take your evidence with me. That way, if my contact gives me the green light, I can get it to him quickly."

Riley nodded, but there was a pit in her stomach as she stuffed all her papers into a folder and shoved that and the fingerprint slide toward him. She'd email the video of her fingerprint collecting to him later.

McGregor folded his hands on top of the folder. "My contact's name is Special Agent Samson. I'll make it very clear that your safety is in jeopardy the longer this guy is allowed to creep around—hopefully that'll light a fire under their asses. If this request *does* clear, things will likely move quickly. I'm willing to bet that the feds already have a file on Emery, since there was speculation for a while that she might have crossed into Mexico. They'll have some insights into where to start searching, and with you alongside them, hopefully we can find her."

Riley swallowed nervously. This was actually happening.

They all walked out together and she thanked them for taking the time to talk to her.

"Stay safe, Riley," Howard said as he headed for his car.

"It was great meeting you," McGregor said. "Remember, if you see a blue-eyed white guy wandering around your neighborhood, call one of us. Profile the shit out of everyone you see."

Laughing softly, she promised she would.

As Riley drove back to Albuquerque, something occurred to her. If Anderson was the man responsible for all this, he'd been described as a younger man—maybe thirties—with sandy blond hair and blue eyes. The description Gigi had given of the man who tried to kidnap her eighteen years ago had been of someone in his late forties, early fifties with white hair styled into a buzz cut. If Anderson had been prowling around eighteen years ago, how could he have looked forty then with white hair, and thirties now with sandy blond hair? Had he started dyeing it? Did he have a really good moisturizer regimen that gave him a youthful glow?

Or had Gigi been wrong after all?

When Lola Bodwell had asked Brynn if John Anderson was the man who had kidnapped her, she'd said *Not John.* But it wasn't clear if that meant the man's name wasn't John, or if John *had* interacted with Brynn, but he hadn't been the one who'd killed her.

An awful thought flitted through Riley's head: *What if there's not only more victims, but more than one killer?*

A few agonizing days later, Riley got a call from a private number just as she was heading out to work. Her heart lurched into her throat.

"Hello?"

"Is this Riley Thomas?" the man asked.

She swallowed. "Yes?"

"Hi. This is Special Agent Samson," he said. "Have you gained any ... insights on the location of Emery Dawson since you were in contact with Detective McGregor?"

Her palms were suddenly so clammy, she was convinced her phone was going to slip out of her hands.

"Hello? Ms. Thomas?"

"Sorry!" she said a little too loudly. *Ugh. Keep it together! This is the freaking FBI calling you!* "No, no new insights."

"All right. Based on current information, we believe the Rio Bosque Wetland Park just outside of Socorro, Texas is the best place to start. We've done sweeps of the place in the past but found nothing. Still, that was Miss Dawson's last known location, as that's where her car was found. Your colleagues, Nina Galvan and Olivia Carlisle, have confirmed that you're all better able to ... make contact in a location tied to the victim. If nothing else, that parking lot may give you some insights."

"Do you think it's possible she's in Mexico?" Riley asked.

"It's possible. Her phone last pinged there. But starting the search in Texas is preferable, as getting you ladies across the border would be more complicated. Our information suggests that the killer disposes of the victim's cell phone in locations far from the body in an attempt to throw off authorities. We believe it's likely he did the same with Miss Dawson's cell phone, and that while it ended up in Mexico, she did not."

Her mouth was suddenly so parched, it was a wonder her tongue hadn't turned to ash. "Okay. Umm … I would just need to get the time off work."

"Make whatever arrangements you can. Ideally, this would happen within the week," he said. "We've done a deep dive into this rangefinderanders person and we've found much more than a few snarky restaurant reviews. This man is dangerous, and if he's escalating, we need to get moving quickly."

"I'm heading to work now," she said, voice shaking. "I'll talk to my boss."

"Excellent. I'll be in touch."

Within forty-eight hours, Riley found herself wedged between Nina and Olivia in the back seat of Special Agent Samson's SUV. When McGregor and Samson had said things would move quickly, they hadn't been lying. Special Agent Lee was in the passenger seat, typing away on what looked like a government-issue Blackberry. Riley had no idea those things still existed.

Their arrival at the parking lot for Rio Bosque Wetland Park was thankfully uneventful, just like their arrival at the El

Paso International Airport had been yesterday evening. The FBI was all about being discreet, so she didn't know why she feared mobs of camera crews everywhere she went, but it was a constant worry nevertheless.

There were no other cars parked in the gravel lot, but she supposed that was due to the fact that it was six in the morning. She scanned the area, wondering where exactly Emery's abandoned car had been found sixteen years ago. When Riley couldn't sleep last night in the hotel room she shared with the ladies, she'd looked up the wetland area again, hoping that going over the same information she'd already read half a dozen times would calm her down. The park was located on the United States-Mexico border, and a short walk into the park would put you at the border wall itself. The park was in El Paso, but was only ten or so minutes from Socorro, where Emery had been from.

Riley peered out the window, eyeing the wide, open lot ringed by thick wooden posts strung together with braided steel. Beyond the makeshift boundary circling the lot was a smattering of trees with a wealth of green leaves. The Orilla Verde Recreation Area had been in desert territory just as much as this park was, yet this location felt more spread out. The big sky of Texas was a clichéd expression, but it felt very true here. The fact that a body had been dumped in this open, expansive area somehow unsettled her even more.

Once Samson had parked, he turned in his seat and looked back at them. He was in his forties and bald but had a well-trimmed dark brown beard and mustache. He had an easy air about him, yet he could also pin a person in place with just his intense stare when the mood struck him. "Remember that the border wall wasn't here when the victim's body was dumped. The area you'll see now is vastly different than it would have been fifteen, sixteen years ago. The wetlands were fully established here by 2007, two years after Miss Dawson went missing. Then the border wall cut off the Rio Grande from the wetland area altogether, which changed the landscape even more. All of this is to say that the changes to the landscape here might have affected where Emery's body was buried, assuming it's here at all."

Riley tried to imagine what the place looked like a decade and a half ago. Had Emery come here to take casual strolls, since the park was so close to her hometown of Socorro? Maybe she had been here dozens of times before she'd been left here permanently.

"We're here as your support," Samson continued, "but otherwise we're going to stand back and let you ladies do your thing. If you think you've found something of note, don't touch whatever it is and have one of us come over to assess. If the victim herself is found, we'll call in forensic backup. They're on standby. Got it?"

Riley, Nina, and Olivia nodded in unison like choreographed bobbleheads.

"Let's go," he said, and got out, then opened the door next to Nina.

Lee, off the phone now, opened the door on Olivia's side. Riley wondered if the men were being chivalrous or if the doors didn't open from the inside. The vehicle's windows were so tinted, she figured that the car was often used on assignments that would require passersby being unable to see who was inside. Which very well could include criminals—criminals whose behaviors had flagged the attention of the FBI. *Who had ridden in the back of this thing?*

As Riley slid across the bench seat after Nina, she hoped they were successful today if only so she wasn't responsible for taking these highly trained men away from important security matters. She wondered how McGregor had become close friends with Special Agent Samson.

Once Olivia was out of the car, Lee circled around to the back of the SUV and opened the trunk. Samson joined him. The ladies stood in silence by the car while the men did lord-knew-what. When the door to the back finally slammed shut, Riley flinched.

The men rounded the side of the SUV, large packs strapped to their backs. Lee looked to be in his thirties and was of Chinese descent, she guessed. He'd had the same easy air about him as Samson did, but now that they were here, he was all business. Riley wondered if he had a military background. Both men had donned sunglasses and were armed with giant shovels, their spades slick and black. Even their shovels looked intimidating.

"If she is here," Samson said, when he noticed she eyed his shovel wearily, "she's under the ground."

Riley's stomach churned. If someone would have asked her a week ago if she would like to be caught up in a case involving federal agents, her true-crime-loving self would have screamed, "Hell yes!" Now she just felt a little lightheaded.

Shit had gotten very real, very quickly.

"Take as long as you need out here," Lee said. "The area looks and feels much bigger than it is—it's only about three hundred and seventy acres."

That sounded massive to Riley, but she also wasn't going to win a mathlete trophy anytime soon.

Special Agent Samson had just said, "Why don't we start here? This is where Miss Dawson's car had been found," when

Riley's attention snagged on something ahead. Without saying anything to the others, and without taking her focus off the walking path on the other end of the parking lot, she stepped sideways to get a better view.

The mouth of the path was straight ahead from where she stood. To the right of the path, just beyond a few of the wooden stakes dotted along the edge of the lot, stood a tall wooden sign welcoming them to the wetland area. And just to the left of that stood a woman in a yellow dress. Her red-painted lips turned up a little on either side when she was sure Riley was looking, then she turned and walked to the left, disappearing behind a low, bushy tree covered in tiny pink flowers.

"Emery," Riley whispered.

The agents whirled at that, scanning the area around them with the intensity of eagles who had just heard their next meal scrabbling in the brush. When no immediate threat presented itself, attention shifted back to Riley.

"After you," Samson said, gesturing toward the path with his free hand.

Riley hesitated.

"We're right behind you, Riley," Nina said. "Trust those instincts. Emery wants to be found as much as you want to find her. Let her show you the way."

Blowing out a steadying breath, Riley started for the path. The sign announced this as the Wetland Trailhead.

The wide sandy road they walked along crunched underfoot. It felt too loud even with the continuous chatter of birds at this early hour. The air was chilly, and Riley zipped up her light jacket to her neck, shoving her hands into her pockets. Trees lined the road on either side, spaced at even intervals. Riley didn't know much about trees, but one type dominated this stretch of road. They were a riot of green in an otherwise brown landscape, and the branches were lined with rows of small oval-shaped leaves, a bit reminiscent of a fern. What was odd about them were the little bundles of curly inch-long fruit… seed pods? She veered toward one, examining what looked like a handful of caterpillars that had all been fused together by their middles.

"Screwbean mesquite," a voice said behind her.

She turned to find Lee eyeing the tree, too.

"They've got them in New Mexico too, you know," he said.

Riley shrugged, stepping back onto the path. "I'm not really a nature girl, I guess. I mean this is beautiful, don't get me wrong. I'm just either working or Netflixing."

He gave her a quick, assessing head-to-toe scan. "And now you're working alongside the FBI trying to solve a cold case."

"My life took a turn for the *very* weird several months ago."

Lee managed a small smile, but it was more fueled by politeness than amusement. Even if McGregor had been impressed with all the information Riley had gathered—information she'd since handed over to authorities—Lee didn't seem to share the sentiment. She wondered if he thought this whole thing was a fool's errand he'd been roped into.

McGregor must have called in one hell of a favor though to get something like this approved so fast. It made Riley all the more determined to be successful today. They walked alongside each other in silence, Lee keeping a firm grip on the shovel.

C'mon, Emery, Riley silently pleaded. *Where are you?*

Nina stopped walking a minute later. Relieved to have an excuse to leave Lee's intensely quiet side, Riley offered him a nod, and then sped up to join Nina.

"What's up?" Riley asked, noting that the agents stood several paces back.

"I think we're far enough in now that we can attempt to make contact," Nina said.

"Did you have to stop *here*?" Olivia asked, pointing at a sign that warned them to beware of snakes.

As Riley grabbed her package of pictures out of her bag, she frowned at the fact that in addition to ghosts, she had to watch for venomous reptiles. She hoped Michael didn't add camping to his growing list of new interests. She handed Nina and Olivia each a picture of Emery from her collection, took one for herself, and then slipped the package back into her bag.

In Riley's picture, Emery sat at a park bench with her untouched lunch laid out on the table, all her attention focused on a book. She held the paperback in one hand, while the other was at her mouth so she could chew at a thumbnail. While it was upsetting that Anderson had been able to watch her long enough to take this picture without her knowing, Riley related to how easy it was to get lost in a book—not only did you forget to eat, but the rest of the world fell away. Anderson had managed to capture Emery's book nerd personality with such clarity, it infuriated Riley all over again that someone as talented as he was had used his skill to destroy young women's lives.

Her mission today was to find Emery. She would worry about Anderson later.

Just as Emery had focused completely on her book, Riley focused entirely on Emery. From the beginning, Riley's gut—intuition, psychic inklings—had told her that Emery had chosen Riley in part because of their similar introverted personalities. Kindred spirits in a way that was a bit too literal in Emery's case.

Riley shut her eyes. Her dominant clair was sight, so she tried to lean into that. She pictured Emery on the path with her, as if the two women were out on a stroll together. She pictured her red lipstick, her flowing yellow dress, and her shy smile.

"She's here," Nina said, cutting into Riley's thoughts.

Opening her eyes, she saw Emery several feet ahead on the path, the light breeze tousling her yellow dress around her calves. Her lips turned up slightly again—such a welcome sight when compared to the overwhelming sadness that had poured off her in the beginning. Was that a hopeful smile? Did it mean they were close? Emery turned left, following the curving path. She walked out of sight beyond the droopy, leafy branches of a mesquite tree.

The three women started forward as one, each drawn forward by the same thing, but in different ways. The agents followed silently behind.

Though there were a decent number of trees here, often there were long stretches of low scrubby vegetation, the view of the expansive sky broken only by swarms of black birds or wispy clouds just now losing their pink and orange hue from the sunrise. It was somehow both desolate and beautiful. An agitated crow or raven squawked incessantly in the distance.

They walked along crunchy gravel paths, uneven sandy stretches, and a well-maintained trail of reddish sand. They crossed a small metal footbridge, paused when a startled jackrabbit loped down the path and into a bank of tall brush, and kept their senses peeled for signs from the woman who had been lost out here for well over a decade.

Off one of the trails, a wide sandy area suddenly opened up to their left. An unexplainable sensation caused Riley to veer off the man-made trail and onto the soft soil interspersed with little tufts of grasses. Beyond the soil stood a wall of vegetation—a combination of spindly brush, swaying cattails, and the occasional screwbean tree. In front of one such tree stood Emery. Her yellow dress was such a bright spot of color amongst all the green and brown, it was mind-boggling that no one could see her but Riley.

She only got halfway to Emery when she stopped in her tracks. Emery's red-painted lips weren't turned up in a smile anymore.

Olivia let out a gust of breath just behind her, placing a hand on Riley's shoulder to steady herself. Then she placed her other hand on her own chest. "God. She's ... so damn ... miserable. Sorrowful. Dejected."

Riley nodded, swallowing down the lump in her throat. Even Carol at the thrift shop, who wasn't a sensitive by her own admission, had sensed Emery's sadness. Riley had seen it etched on Emery's face when she'd stood forlornly at the foot of Riley's bed. That had all been a fraction of what poured off Emery now.

"This is the spot," Nina said, who stood beside Riley, her gaze sweeping the area but always skirting over the exact spot where Emery stood. Nina glanced behind them to where the pair of agents stood on the path, watching them silently. She pointed in Emery's general direction. "She's here."

Samson's expression was unreadable as he said, "Get as close as you can without disturbing anything."

Nina eyed Riley. "You'll be able to find the spot better than we can. I'll stay with Olivia."

Olivia still had a hand on Riley's shoulder. "If we get bitten by snakes, I'm going to be so angry."

Gently stepping away from Olivia, her hand falling away, Riley glanced back at her. Though her tone was light, Olivia had paled. Nina took Riley's spot beside her and wrapped an arm around Olivia's middle, giving her support.

"I've got her," Nina said.

With a nod, Riley walked toward Emery. She hadn't moved from her spot on the edge of the vegetation line, the branches of the screwbean tree her backdrop. When she reached her, Riley asked, "Can you show me the exact spot?"

Emery stepped forward, her bare feet on the sandy ground, though they stayed clean. One step, two, three. She stopped and looked down at the chipped white polish on her own toes, a few tufts of grass poking between them. The spot was covered in moss, grasses, and rocks. Nothing about it stood out as a sixteen-year-old graveside.

"I've got it!" she called out but didn't take her eyes off Emery, who slowly backed up to where she'd been before, partially obscured by the foliage. She leveled her curious gaze at the approaching men. Riley put her own feet squarely on the spot Emery had indicated.

"And this is the exact spot?" Lee asked, his tone dubious.

Emery gave her a confirming nod.

"Yep," said Riley.

The men placed their shovels on the ground, then removed their packs and plopped them into the sand. They squatted and unzipped the bags. Both strapped on gloves. Samson pulled out a device that Riley supposed could be anything from a metal detector to ground-penetrating radar.

Lee moved his bag off to the side and eyed Riley, picking up his shovel as he did so. "We've got it for now. We'll just need some space."

Nodding to them both, and to Emery, Riley walked back to Nina and Olivia. Olivia sat on the path, her legs crossed. Her head was in her hands, and elbows on her knees.

Nina squatted in front of her.

"You okay?" Riley asked.

When Olivia finally lifted her head, her eyes were red, tears threatening to fall. "My grandpa was one of my best friends. He died unexpectedly in a car accident when I was twelve. Drunk driver. It was my first experience with grief. But I was also experiencing the grief of my family. Everyone was devastated. The emotions coming off Emery aren't as bad as what happened when I was twelve, but it's the worst I've felt since then."

Even if Riley had clairsentience to some degree like Olivia did, she was selfishly glad in that moment that it wasn't her dominant clair. Experiencing her own emotions was hard enough, thanks.

"Are you getting anything from her other than sadness?" Nina asked.

Olivia sniffed and tried to sit up straight, doing her best to concentrate amidst the onslaught of emotions. She closed her watery eyes. "It's … she's not just sad. It's … betrayal. She blames herself for what happened. She blames him too, obviously. But she feels guilty that she ended up here."

"Stay put until you feel steady," Nina told her. "Breathe. Don't rush it."

Olivia nodded, sniffing hard again.

Riley and Nina stood, facing the men. The shovels slid into the earth, the sound of the spades slicing into the moist earth somehow comforting. It meant something was happening, that Emery was only a few shovelfuls of dirt away. The men stood six feet from each other, Emery directly between them in the distance. They settled into a rhythm, Samson's spade sliding into the earth while Lee dumped his shovelful to the left of the growing hole. Back and forth—shovel, dump, shovel, dump.

Riley's anticipation of what they would find, the hope she felt with this new bit of progress, warred with the tangle of emotion—sadness, guilt, self-loathing, devastation—coming off Emery. The more they dug, the stronger her emotions grew. Emery was undoubtedly stronger here than she'd ever been in Riley's apartment, Jade's garage, or Carol's thrift shop. But just like in the grocery store with the pissed-off poltergeist, the mounting wave of energy from the spirit was causing Riley's own to rise up to meet Emery's. The closer the men got with their shovels, the more Riley was unable to tell where her emotions ended and Emery's began.

You're okay, she told herself. *You're okay.*

But she didn't feel okay.

She felt like she was being suffocated. It *was* grief, she realized. Just like Olivia had said. But it was Emery's grief over the loss of herself. Over the life she could have lived if she'd made different decisions. Her chest and throat were tight.

Riley wanted to tell Emery that the fault lay entirely at the feet of the man who had robbed her of that life. That no matter what had put her in that man's path, it wasn't her fault that she trusted another human being to be decent. Yet Riley couldn't project that thought any more than she could speak the words. All she wanted to do was curl up in a ball and sob. She couldn't pull enough air into her lungs.

Olivia let out an agonized groan, got to her feet, and stalked down the path, unable to take it. Maybe Olivia could have handled Emery's emotions, but with Riley's heightened as well, Olivia had to flee. Riley wanted to apologize, but she couldn't get that out either.

Nina grabbed hold of Riley's upper arms and gave her a quick bodily shake.

Riley's watery gaze locked on Nina's. It was like the time in the cellar all over again. Emery was nothing but a smear of yellow in the distance now. When Riley blinked, tears slid down her face.

"Focus," Nina said firmly. "Don't let her emotions crowd out your own. Find the *root* of those emotions. She's been waiting for this for sixteen years. Center yourself and listen to her."

Riley nodded, the rest of the tears immediately chased away by the shock of Nina's sharp words. Nina was always a soothing presence, but Riley suspected that Nina's claircognizance told her that what Riley needed was a verbal slap to the face.

Focus. Listen.

"Trust yourself and Emery both," Nina said, her usual, softer tone resurfacing. "I've gotta go make sure Olivia didn't get eaten by snakes."

When Nina let go and walked away, it was like having a warm blanket ripped off her. She glanced over her shoulder, watching Nina go, wanting to follow.

Her sixth sense tingled and she faced forward again, finding Emery standing a mere foot from her. Emery's jaw clenched, her hands balled into fists by her sides. Riley's fight-or-flight instinct was still leaning toward flight, like it had in the store when she'd been cornered by the angry ghost stalking her through the aisles like a predator. Who had snuck up on her. Who had seemed pissed *at* her.

In this case, Riley knew without a doubt that she wasn't the target of Emery's fury. *Find the root of those emotions. She's been waiting for this for sixteen years. Center yourself and listen to her.*

Relaxing the tension in her shoulders, Riley blew out a long shaky breath. "Can you tell me what happened? Was it John Anderson?"

Emery cocked her head, clearly confused.

Did she just not know the name?

Riley fumbled to get her purse open with her quaking hands. It felt like the time she'd downed an energy drink before a job interview and had the shakes so badly, they'd probably thought she partook in recreational drugs. She took out the picture of Emery and held it up for the woman to see. "That's you. Did John Anderson take this picture? Is that who did this to you?"

Beyond Emery, the agents were still busily digging. If they noticed Riley having a conversation with a ghost, they didn't acknowledge it.

Emery's forehead creased. Her image flickered for a moment, like a glitching picture on a TV screen. Riley had a flashback of little Pete in her living room when he'd tried so desperately to manifest using his quickly dwindling energy. The last time Emery had tried to speak to Riley, it had been in Jade's garage. Even Jade had felt the drop in temperature as Emery attempted to pull in energy, yet she'd only managed a single word before the effort had caused her to wink out of existence—at least visually.

"Show me," Riley said quickly, concerned that if Emery kept trying to use speech to communicate, she'd burn out her ghostly battery. "Think in pictures. If it wasn't Anderson who did this to you, show me who did."

Emery thought about that a moment, then nodded and closed her eyes.

Almost instantly, images popped into Riley's head.

Emery sat on top of what appeared to be a boulder. A quick scan of her person revealed that the dress she wore was forest green, not yellow. Looking down from her perch, a handsome man in his forties peered up at her with an expression of longing so deep, even Riley's breath hitched. Though, while Emery's stomach had flipped at the sight of the man, Riley's had flopped.

If Riley hadn't already known that Emery was a modern woman who had lived only sixteen years ago, this man would have made her think this memory was from the '70s. He wore a short-sleeved white shirt tucked into high-waisted tidy brown slacks. The pants were held up by a white belt, and on his feet were brown tassel loafers. The only thing out of place with the ensemble was his very light blond hair, which had been styled into a neat buzz cut.

He held out a hand and helped Emery off the boulder. He smiled warmly at her. Emery had no doubt been attracted to him—and something akin to hope was flitting about as well, but Riley's instinct was to recoil from his touch. He was too close, held onto her hand for too long, and peered down the front of her dress with a little gleam in his brown eyes.

They spoke, the words slipping past Riley like sand through her fingers. Perhaps after this long, the memories of what he'd said had been lost to Emery, too.

The man handed Emery a business card. She took it, the white polish on her nails matching the crisp white of the card.

Bruce Trager

BT Photoworks

Headshots ~ Graduations ~ Weddings

A voice rang out in her head then. A male voice. *"Oh, and if we do end up working together, might I suggest that you wear yellow?"*

Riley stumbled back, breaking the memory. She tried to organize her thoughts, remembering her first dream of Emery. Of her preparing to get ready to meet Bruce who had texted her, the pair excited about their meeting. They'd planned to meet in a parking lot first. He'd asked what she was wearing, and she'd said yellow, just as he requested.

"Were you coming out here for a photoshoot?" Riley finally asked.

Emery nodded, then closed her eyes again.

The images that filled Riley's mind were of Emery arriving in the same parking lot the agents' SUV sat in. It was late—or possibly early—when she arrived. Faint hints of color dotted the horizon. Now that Riley knew what it looked like here in the early morning, her guess was that Emery had arrived in early evening. The parking lot was empty except for one other car. She got out of her own and locked the door, dropping her keys inside her purse. Glancing into her back seat, she spotted her laptop bag. In her haste to get home from work, shower, and then to the park to meet Bruce, she'd forgotten to bring it back inside. No matter. She'd get it later. She pulled out her phone at the sound of a chime.

BRUCE: I'm in the blue sedan.

Emery looked up, noting the car on the other side of the lot. Her phone beeped again.

BRUCE: I brought a bunch of gear with me. Could you help me carry some of it? I might have gone overboard. I guess I want to make up for the idiot who thought he had the chops to photograph a beauty of your caliber.

Emery had flushed at the compliment. Riley's heart was in her throat.

The sound of the trunk popping open pulled Emery's attention away from her phone one last time. Stuffing her phone back into her purse, she walked across the lot to the car. She wore delicate yellow flats.

The man, Bruce, hadn't gotten out of the car yet, so Emery made her way to the trunk to grab a few items. She noted with some curiosity that the license plate had been removed. Looking inside the trunk, she found it empty. Not even an umbrella lay inside. Now Emery's dread matched Riley's.

The heat of someone behind her. A finger pressed into a sensitive pressure point. Vision tunneling to black. Something pierced Emery's neck and she swayed on her feet. Bruce Trager's charming smile had morphed into a predatory leer. He bodily shoved her into the trunk. Emery's legs were weak, her stomach sick. It had all happened so fast.

It was clear to Riley and Emery both that he'd done this before, and their dread doubled.

Emery's vision came and went in fuzzy waves.

He aggressively snatched her purse from her, making sure her phone and keys were inside. "Can't have you trying to run off now, can I?" He looked away from her for a moment. "Did you leave anything in that car of yours? I'll check it before we head out. We're going to have such a good time together, but I need to make sure we won't get interrupted."

Emery could only groan in pain.

"So beautiful," he said, his tone adoring. He stood at the trunk with both hands on the door, her purse hung from his shoulder. "Anders was right. You were worth every penny."

Emery's vision solidified for long enough that she noted the Amity Trucking logo on his crisp navy blue polo shirt. Then the door slammed shut, throwing her into total darkness. Unconsciousness followed a second later.

Riley gasped and stumbled back so forcibly, her heel caught on the thin line of wood that lined this section of the path and she almost fell. She righted herself, then placed her hands on her knees, taking in deep pulls of air into her nose.

That fucking monster.

She stood, eyes closed, rubbing her own stomach in slow, methodical circles to help calm the churning nausea. She was honestly unsure if her sick stomach was because of her disgust at what had happened to Emery, or the memory of the drug that had been shot into Emery's neck.

When she finally opened her eyes, Emery still stood there, expectant. Her out-of-control emotions had settled a bit now that she'd shared this with someone. Nina and Olivia hadn't returned yet.

As the threat of throwing up passed, Riley's mind went into hyperdrive, trying to piece it all together. The camera, the surveillance pictures, John Anderson, rangefinderanders, Bruce's declaration that Emery had been worth the money.

"There are two of them," Riley said to Emery, since she was currently the only one in earshot. "Anders tails women and collects information on them. He did that with Carter, too. He watched him long enough to figure out when he'd be out of town. Either Anders collects information on women to sell it to whoever wants it, or people like Bruce pay him to collect it. I don't think Anders is the killer. He's the collector. Bruce is the one who does the dirty work."

She started to pace on the path, the reddish sand crunching under her tennis shoes. Emery still stood in her peripheral vision.

"Anders must have seen that picture of you in the paper and figured Carter either had access to his recently lost cameras, or at least the film that had come out of one of them," Riley said. "Since both you and Shawna were on the roll, he must have realized that the person who had the film developed potentially has incriminating evidence that could be used against him. Not only for himself, since at least two women he took surveillance photos of ended up dead or missing, but for the person who either hired him for the specific task of stalking women, or who had purchased the information Anders had collected for the sake of selling it."

The idea that someone like Anders had been in Carter's house made her stomach churn all over again. There was no way to know if Anders himself was as violent as Bruce, but he at the very least was morally corrupt.

"We got something!"

She whirled toward the agents. Emery had materialized across the sandy expanse again, hidden amongst the foliage.

Riley started running before she realized she'd made the decision. The pounding of footsteps told her Nina and Olivia were on their way, too.

Samson was torso-deep in a hole, bent over—Riley could only see his back.

Lee had that government-issue Blackberry pressed to his ear. "Confirmed. Send a team now."

A gust of breath whooshed out of Riley at the sight of a steel drum lying on its side in the hole. Emery's folded-up body was in there. Riley knew it without a doubt. Her bottom lip trembled as she looked up at Emery, whose frown matched Riley's.

"I'm sorry," Riley said, eyes welling with tears.

Me too, echoed in her head, and then Emery was gone.

CHAPTER 26

Nina, Riley, and Olivia stood back and watched as a forensic team arrived. Riley told the other two her theories about who had killed Emery, and who had aided in her capture. Otherwise, they quietly watched the professionals at work. Once the steel drum was out of the ground, a few members of the team collected things like soil and flora samples, while someone else was given the task of getting the drum open. It didn't take long to confirm that a body was inside. She knew the police, FBI, and forensic specialists would be tasked with using things like DNA and dental records to make a positive identification, but when a piece of yellow fabric was extracted from the drum and placed in an evidence bag, Riley had all the confirmation she needed.

The local police were called, and Nina, Riley, and Olivia all were asked to give statements. While Riley spoke to someone, Special Agent Samson sidled up next to her.

Addressing the officer, he said, "Because of the sensitive nature of this case, we ask that you do all you can to make sure the names of these three women don't get passed along to the media. We'll need their expertise as we work through the case, and their anonymity will be crucial."

The officer nodded. "Understood."

Samson, covered in a fine layer of dirt, nodded at them both and walked back to the crime scene.

It felt like hours later when they finally headed back to the entrance of the wetland park. Riley knew Emery was safe with these people, and that they'd all work tirelessly to identify her. She still whispered a goodbye to her anyway, unsure if Emery was gone for good, now that her body had been found.

This time, when they reached the parking lot, it was packed with cars—a news van among them. Lee cursed under his breath and ushered Riley, Nina, and Olivia into the SUV before the news hounds had a chance to make their way over.

A small crowd of fifteen or so looky-loos had materialized, too, all huddled together in the middle of the lot. Riley wondered if some of them had arrived intending to take a walk in the wetlands, only to be told by the police standing at the mouth of the hiking trail that the area was closed. Would others hear the news of a body found in the park, and try to take other paths into the area? Had someone posted about it on social media?

Lee was on his phone again by the time they were all inside the SUV. "The media caught wind of it already. We need more officers down here to help maintain the integrity of the site."

Samson pulled out of the parking spot and eased back the way they'd come hours ago. As Riley stared out the window— Nina seated in the middle this time—her attention snagged on a man. There was nothing outwardly interesting or standout about him, but she found herself unable to look away. Instead of focusing on the anchorwoman who was just emerging from the news van as the others around him were doing, the man glared daggers at the passing SUV—perhaps upset that he couldn't see who was inside.

He lifted a camera to his face and snapped a picture of the retreating vehicle. Nina and Olivia didn't react, though they were deep in conversation.

He was in his thirties, but the hood had been pulled up over his head, masking his hair color. Had his eyes been blue?

Hours later, Riley, bone-weary, walked out the doors of the Albuquerque International Sunport, her duffel bag hung from her shoulder. Nina and Olivia were driving back together and had already made their way to the parking garage. Riley knew she could have hitched a ride with them, but she needed a bit of distance.

Riley's smile was so wide it hurt when Jade's car pulled up at the curb. Jade darted out of her car, her head of curly brown hair flapping as she ran, and tackled Riley in a hug so fierce, it almost knocked them over.

Riley laughed, hugging her back.

"It's all over the news, girl!" Jade said, pulling away. In her best news anchor voice, she said, *"Today, thanks to an anonymous tip, the body of a young woman who went missing in 2005 was found in the Rio Bosque Wetland Park."*

Riley wondered how long the "anonymous tip" thing would hold. She knew the request had come from the FBI, but how much more sensational would this story become if it was revealed that the "anonymous tip" had come from a trio of psychics?

Jade said, "There aren't any real details yet. Tell me everything on the way to Michael's."

"Michael's?" Riley asked.

"We played rock, paper, scissors on a video call to decide who got to pick you up," Jade said, looping her arm through Riley's and dragging her toward her car. An airport attendant had already grown incredibly irate that Jade had left her car idling at the curb. "He was so bummed about losing that I told him I'd deposit you on his doorstep in exchange for hearing the story first on the way."

Riley burst into tears.

"Oh, babe," Jade said, stopping abruptly to stand in front of her. She cupped Riley's face in her hands.

The attendant blew his whistle. "You have ten seconds to move your vehicle or it's getting towed!"

Jade shot a glare over her shoulder at him. "My best friend is going through some shit!"

"Find someone who cares, lady!" the guy yelled back. "Five seconds!"

Jade groaned very loudly, which made Riley laugh, only for that to dissolve back into tears. "Okay, let's go. You're all right. You want a cheeseburger or something?"

Riley sniffed, letting Jade pull her the rest of the way to the car. "Can I have onion rings, too?"

"You can have whatever you want. I'm not the one who has to make out with you later," Jade said, pulling open the passenger side door. Riley slid in, eyeing the back seat that was positively jam-packed with wedding supplies. When Jade got in on the driver's side, she strapped in, flipped off the guy on the corner—who blew his whistle at her in reply—and pulled out onto the road.

They grabbed burgers, fries, and onion rings from a drive-through and then hopped on the highway toward Los Lunas. It wasn't until Riley had tearfully inhaled all her onion rings that she started to talk, telling Jade about Bruce Trager, how Emery had been lured out to the park under false pretenses, and how the asshole had not only murdered Emery, but had stuffed her body in a steel drum and then buried it in the middle of the park.

"God, this is so awful," Jade finally said, her voice catching. "And you think that's how this guy got Brynn and Shawna, too?"

"Yeah. I don't know who came to who with the stalking idea, but Bruce had been paying Anders for information on these women. They were both photographers."

"What are the odds?" Jade asked, shaking her head.

Riley's Cheesy Deluxe had been halfway to her mouth. She lowered the burger. "Slim to none ... I bet that's how they met. They could have made a connection through their love of photography first, and then later found out that their stalking and homicide hobbies intertwined."

"Match made in hell," Jade muttered.

Riley took a bite of her burger, chewing slowly. A few tears tracked down her face again. "I don't think he stopped at Emery. I think he got better. And I think Anders kept helping him. Anders is in New Mexico but I don't know where Bruce is, assuming he's still alive. Anders wants those cameras back because he doesn't want any of this tied back to him."

"Too bad there was only film in the one camera," Jade said. "I wonder if there was anything hidden in that storage unit that people missed somehow. It's just so weird that the cameras and desk were the only things in there. Maybe he used that space to write up his dossier on whatever woman he was stalking."

"There was the bomber jacket, the mug of coffee, and the lantern, too," Riley said.

"And that hideous camera bag," Jade said.

Riley had completely forgotten about that. "Did you ever look in that thing?"

"Nope," Jade said, glancing over her shoulder for a second. "This car is a mess. I honestly don't think I've touched much back here in weeks. The bag is probably still in here. Maybe under your seat?"

When they arrived at Michael's half an hour later, Jade pulling into the long driveway of his duplex, Riley practically threw herself out of the car before Jade had parked it.

"Hey, ladies," Michael said, stepping out onto his porch.

"Hi. Love you. Nice to see you," Riley said, yanking open the back passenger side door and squatting so she could see into the abyss of Jade's back seat. She moved a cardboard box full of what looked like kid-size gold laurel leaf tiaras. What in the hell was she going to do with those? Clearly, Riley had fallen off her "Keep Jade in line" maid of honor duties in the midst of trying to solve another cold case.

Riley shoved an arm under the passenger seat, blindly flailing around until her fingers brushed coarse fabric. She pulled the bag free. Hurrying around to the trunk, Riley plopped the bag on the closed door.

Michael came over and Riley angled her face up for a kiss even while only having eyes for the camera bag. It reminded her of a fabric lunch container. The bag was square with a lid that flipped back, and a clip in the front. Inside, the bag was divided into sections. On the right, in the biggest compartment, two smaller bags had been wedged into the hole. The other slots, she imagined, were for things like extra lenses and canisters of film.

She checked the smaller bags first, which were basic carrying cases. She checked zippered outer pockets, inner Velcroed ones, and dug fingers into small mesh-covered spaces. Nothing.

"What's she doing?" Michael whisper-asked Jade.

"Looking for clues?" Jade ventured.

Riley got to work rummaging around in the bigger bag. Nothing in any of the side or inner pockets. There was a zippered pouch in the lid of the case. Empty. The partitions in the bag were made of a squishy slate gray foam. She pulled all of those out, revealing a flat rectangular base, which allowed the bag to keep its form. It was Velcroed down and she needed more force than she would have expected to pull it free. She discarded the rectangular piece on the trunk, sure she'd find something lying on the bottom of the bag. More nothing. *Dammit.*

"Oh shit," Michael said, and picked up the rectangular bottom Riley had tossed away. He flipped it over, revealing a white envelope that had been affixed with several layers of packing tape.

"Oh shit," Jade echoed.

Handing the square back to Riley—which was about the size of a mortarboard—Michael said, "I'll go get a box cutter" before hurrying into his house. Baxter gave a yowl from behind the screen door.

"What do you think is in there?" Jade asked, holding fast to her own elbows.

Riley absently shook her head.

When Michael returned, Riley watched as he carefully made a cut along the edge of the envelope where it had been fastened to the square. Once he'd freed the envelope, he handed it to Riley.

The moment she took it, an image slammed into her. A desk sat in front of her—not the industrial one from the storage unit, but a standard office desk. One of the cameras from the unit, the Minolta, Riley thought, sat on the desk to the left of a man's arm. She recognized the blue and white logos running along the neck strap. A computer screen took up most of her view. The man's hands were on the keyboard, and Riley watched as he typed out a message in a white box.

> I don't care what you do with the information I give you, but Brynn was a mistake. Choose the ones who don't have parents with fat checkbooks and you'll succeed for a lot longer. And the longer you succeed, the longer I get paid. Win-win. Be smarter.

The flash of memory ended and Riley placed a hand on the trunk of Jade's car to steady herself.

Michael placed a hand on her elbow. "Okay?"

She nodded. "Uhh … do you have gloves by any chance?"

Michael took off again, returning with a box of latex gloves. Riley cocked a brow at him.

"What? Sometimes I change my own oil."

Pulling out a pair, Riley strapped them on, then used the box cutter to carefully cut one side of the envelope open. She figured if Anders had licked the envelope to seal it, his DNA might still be on the flap, so she wanted to leave it as intact as she could. Inside the envelope were negatives that had been cut every fourth frame. Lifting one, using the light from Michael's porch light, she peered at one of the squares.

She instantly recognized Brynn Bodwell. Anders had photographed her getting into her car at the parking lot of a school; tying her shoe as she sat on a bench, clad in running gear; and as she walked her beloved dog Ruthie. There were more negatives of Shawna in this batch, too.

Riley felt sick to her stomach again. "I think Detective Howard was right."

"About what?" Jade asked softly, arms folded tight across her chest. Given how pale Michael had grown, they'd been able to see what was on the negatives, too. They had put it together that the bag sitting on Jade's trunk belonged to a man who played a role in the death of at least three women.

"When Shawna was killed, the police were so convinced that Rodney Elgin was the murderer, they had tunnel vision," Riley said, slipping the negative back into the envelope. "They never really considered anyone else. After Brynn's murder became national news, Anders told Bruce that Brynn had been a mistake. She was too high profile, from a too-rich family. He told him to go after targets people would care about less."

"So he went back to Black women," Jade said, tone hollow.

"Black women with fewer family ties. They usually get labeled as runaways, or women who've made 'poor life choices' so they're lower priority. Same with sex workers. Like they brought it on themselves. It wouldn't be the first time someone targeted people they thought wouldn't be missed. The Green River Killer chose sex workers and runaways, murdering at least forty-eight women before he was caught. Samuel Little killed ninety-three people over thirty-five years, specifically targeting sex workers, runaways, and Black women because he believed they mattered less, so no one would come looking for them."

"I don't even know what to say to any of this," Michael said.

"Not much to say other than this Anders guy is as much of a piece of shit as Bruce is even if Anders didn't kill them," Jade said, heat darkening her light brown skin.

"He gave him the tools to find them," Michael agreed.

Riley clearly looked shell-shocked, so Michael grabbed Riley's belongings out of the car while Jade hugged Riley goodbye and told her to call her in the morning. After Riley put the envelope of negatives in a zippered bag from Michael's kitchen, she took a long hot shower and then curled up on the couch with him and Baxter. He put on a movie, but she was so exhausted, she fell asleep almost immediately.

Though her sleep was restful and dreamless, when sunlight poured in through the blinds in Michael's living room, she'd awoken with one thought on her mind: she was going to do whatever she could to take Anders down. Because where they found Anders, they'd find Bruce Trager.

November, 2021

The day the news broke that a body was found in the Rio Bosque Wetland Park, I was sitting in my car at a park where Carter Quincy played with his kid. Emery's name hadn't been revealed yet, but it would be coming soon. I hadn't contacted The Client, hoping he wouldn't hear about it wherever he was in the country, until I had made more progress.

An email from him came in shortly after a breaking news alert from one of the national channels popped up on my phone.

> YOU SAID YOU WERE HANDLING THIS! How the fuck did anyone find her? Who is this anonymous tip? What the hell am I paying you for if this has gotten worse since you started, rather than better? Do something, Anders, or I will DESTROY you. If I go down, you're going down with me.

I didn't know what he expected me to do! Carter did nothing of note, met no one of note. If anything, his behaviors had grown even less interesting since his trip. The man was already dreadfully boring to begin with. My leads had dried up. I was doing the best I could.

They haven't identified her yet. That will take some time. Don't
worry. I won't let you down.

I needed to talk to Carter alone, away from witnesses, away
from his family. He needed to tell me who his source was so I
could fix this. I left the park and went to Carter's office at the
Taos Daily Journal.

I strolled up to the receptionist's desk, placed my hands on
the faux wood and said, "I would like to speak to Carter Quincy."

The lady at the desk was on the phone and held up a finger. I
stood to full height and peered through the glass wall to my left,
behind which sat several people in cubicles. People didn't move
about, waving papers above their heads announcing they'd just
gotten a lead on their newest story. They looked like zombies.

"I'm sorry," the receptionist said, redirecting my attention.
"Mr. Quincy isn't in the office today."

"Where can I find him?"

She was in her mid-thirties, and attractive enough if one
liked mousy brown hair, pencil-thin lips, and sweater sets. I did
not. When she eyed me warily, she became even less appealing.
"Who did you say you were again? Did you have a scheduled
appointment?"

"Yes. We were supposed to meet here this afternoon but,
as you can see, I've been stood up. If you could give me his
personal cell phone number, I'll get out of your hair." A personal number would allow me direct, discreet access. It would
make it easier to lure Carter away, to get him to meet me in a
secluded location so we could chat.

"You can find his contact information on our website. It's
t-a-o-s—"

"I'm quite aware of what your website is," I said evenly, knocking my knuckles on the surface of the desk. The mousy thing flinched. "I need his personal number. Why would I need his office number when you've already established that he's not here, hmmm?"

Somehow her thin lips thinned even further. "I'm not authorized to give out personal information."

"This is a matter of life and death."

"I'm sorry. If you give me your name and number, I can leave a message for him and he'll see it first thing in the morning."

"The morning? I must speak with him *now*. I wouldn't be here if it weren't urgent." I placed my hands on the desk and leaned toward her. She leaned back, her cheap office chair creaking beneath her. "You don't understand how important it is that I speak with him."

"I'm going to have to ask you to back up," she said, though her voice quavered.

I pressed a hand to my temple, fighting off a sudden blinding headache. *Minimize stressful situations*, the doc had said. *Well, doc, I don't have the luxury of minimizing stress when I have people like this woman to contend with now, do I? She couldn't see that I wasn't some nutcase off the street? My livelihood is hanging in the balance and she doesn't have a shred of sympathy for me!*

A hand wrapped around my forearm and I yelped. When I whipped my throbbing skull to the right, I found a burly security guard beside me. The receptionist was on her feet now, peering at me around the fake leaves of the Ficus tree beside her desk. What a coward!

"All right, buddy," the guard said. "Why don't you go walk this off?"

"Walk this off?" I asked, then snatched my arm from his loose grip. I straightened my shirt. "I'm not intoxicated."

I just have a headache so acute, I'm mildly nauseated.

Even though the guard didn't touch me again, I was escorted out of the building like a common street thug all the same. My frustration was so overwhelming that, for an hour, I stalked around the neighborhood the newspaper office was nestled in.

I eventually drove back to Carter's neighborhood, watching his house in my rear-view. I spotted Vickie walking Ollie around her usual path. I could see her searching for me, coming around the corner with anticipation lighting up her features, only to have that hope slough away when I was nowhere to be found. Desperation was so unbecoming.

Perhaps an ambush was in order. If I threatened Carter in front of his family, he'd be so fearful for the life of his wife and child that he'd tell me what I needed to know out of a sense of self-preservation.

I liked this idea.

My phone pinged, breaking my concentration. I tore my gaze away from Carter's house. My throat tightened, worried The Client had sent another rage-filled message. He had yet to reply to my last one. I hoped that meant he was mollified for now.

I had very few notification alerts set up on my phone, one of which was for any responses I received from my Reddit post about the missing cameras.

So far, all I'd received was an asinine "Any luck, bud?" from FoToS4LyFe. No. No luck, bud.

The alert that had just come through was from that very post. I sat up a little straighter. Someone named Clair4U had replied.

Hi! I think my aunt bought your storage unit! She owns a thrift shop in Albuquerque. One of the cameras was bought by someone already—sorry!—but we have the other two. I'm so glad I found this post. I was searching for more information on the Canon AE-1 and found your post instead. Kismet, eh? She would love to give them back to you since they're heirlooms. Plus no one in the family knows how to use film cameras! Would you like to meet up?

Kismet, indeed.

A picture was attached, showing the two remaining cameras. My heart lurched at the sight of them. My attention shifted to the third item in the photo—the camera bag I'd forgotten all about. A cold sweat poured over me. Son of a bitch! The bag looked intact. The thrift store owner hopefully hadn't found the Velcroed bottom. I should have superglued the thing down.

No matter. I would meet this person and the guilt she felt about selling off the other camera would loosen her lips, and she'd cough up the information I needed to track down the buyer who threatened to unravel the life The Client and I had woven for ourselves.

I started up my car and pulled out onto the road. Carter was a dead end anyway. As I looked in the rear-view mirror, I spotted Vickie standing on the corner a block away, head cocked in a manner as curious as her little dog. There was no way she'd recognized my car, was there? Just before I turned right at the next stop sign, I glanced into the mirror again. Vickie had moved on.

Within a few days, Clair4U and I had set up a meeting in Epicurean Subs. It was one of the more detestable locations Albuquerque had to offer, but if it meant I could get my cameras and bag back, I would stomach walking into the place. When I stepped inside the shop, which smelled too heavily of spices and vinegar, another recovered memory surfaced. I had ducked into this very shop during one of the days I had been trailing Kendra on her way to work. I wondered if silly little Digby had ever gotten over her.

Kendra. Kendra's overgrown oaf of a new boyfriend who I had nicknamed Axel/Gage. *That* was who had done this to me! He was the reason I was here now, attempting to reclaim my cameras from a stranger.

I found a young Black woman sitting at one of the tables. My camera bag sat on the booth seat beside her. She smiled at me when I entered.

"Are you rangefinderanders?" she asked, standing with her hand out.

"And you must be Clair4U." I shook her offered palm.

She flinched so violently when our hands met that I wondered if she'd gotten an electric shock from the contact.

"Sorry," she said, laughing lightly. "That's me. Clair4U, I mean." She returned to her seat.

I inwardly groaned. She wasn't just going to give me the cameras and let me go on my merry way. I reluctantly slid into the chair across from her.

"I'm sorry we only have two of the three. Were you very close to your father?"

"Thick as thieves," I said. "Do you happen to know who bought the other one? I would be more than willing to pay double what they bought it for. I don't know how much you know about cameras, but the one that sold was a rangefinder."

"Oh, like your handle!" she said.

Yes, you simpleton. "Exactly. It was my father's favorite."

She reached for her purse and took out her phone. "I asked my aunt that very thing just before I left to come here," she explained as she swiped at her phone screen. "Let's see if she answered me yet. She doesn't take down customers' information or anything when they make a purchase, but she has a very popular email list she encourages people to sign up for. She thought he might have signed up."

She absently placed the camera bag on the table as she continued to scroll through her phone. I quickly fumbled to open it, checking that the cameras hadn't been damaged.

"Those are yours, correct?" she asked.

I heaved a sigh of relief. "Yes. I was holed up in the hospital for nearly four months. When I got out and found out my unit had been sold, I was devastated, thinking I'd lost this piece of my father."

"I'm glad we could get them back to you," she said, still fiddling with her phone. "Oh! My aunt replied. It looks like he signed up for her email list after all. Would his email address be helpful?"

She looked up at me with her innocent brown eyes. The Client would have liked this one.

"An email would be incredibly helpful," I said, resisting the urge to rip everything out of the camera bag to assure myself that the negatives of Brynn and Shawna were still there. "Thank you."

A chair suddenly pulled up next to me. My head whipped left, and my gaze settled on an older Black guy in jeans and a tucked-in black shirt. Was this Clair's dad or something? My lizard-brain instincts kicked in a second later. There was something about cops that stood out like a sore thumb. This guy had cop written all over him even as he casually rested an elbow on the table a foot away from mine. My attention shifted to Clair. Her arms were crossed and she was leaned against the plushy booth. The wide-eyed innocent expression was gone. In its place was one that very clearly said she wanted to claw my face off.

"Are you Anders Pedersen?" the cop asked.

My palms itched. I looked from him to the woman and back again. A lump formed in my throat. I didn't know what to do.

"He seems confused," the lady said. "You're also known by another name, right? The Nob Hill Prowler?"

Oh shit.

"Sorry," I said, standing up so quickly, I almost knocked my chair over. I held my hands up in innocence. I was so unnerved, I'd forgotten my cameras on the table. "I'm not sure what's going on here, but I think there's been some kind of misunderstanding. I'm not who you think I am. I just wanted my father's cameras back."

I bumped into the unforgiving body of someone behind me and whirled to find a guy who looked even more like a cop than the one at the table. At least it wasn't Axel/Gage ready to pummel my face again. "Sorry, bud. I was just leaving."

Someone grabbed hold of my wrist and pulled it up behind my back. "Anders Pedersen, you're under arrest for your involvement in the murders of Shawna Mack, Brynn Bodwell, and Emery Dawson."

The cop said other things, but there was a horrible ringing in my ears. I didn't resist as he handcuffed me, mostly because my knees had gone wobbly. And the ringing—like an alarm bell only I could hear—rattled my brain around my skull. I was escorted out the door and down the sidewalk. The ringing persisted. The men spoke to me. I know they did. But I couldn't hear it. I peered in at "Clair4U" as the cops led me away. She offered me a little finger wave.

My lip twitched.

She was Carter Quincy's source. She had bought *my* cameras, developed *my* film, and had ruined *my* life.

The ringing stopped abruptly, the absence of it nearly deafening.

There were myriad things I should have been thinking then, but as I was put in the back of a sleek black vehicle and driven away, only one word filled the silence in my head, repeating like a mantra, like a heartbeat: *How?*

CHAPTER 27

Anders Pedersen had been arrested nearly a week ago and Riley had yet to hear anything. She had started staying at Michael's place, making the long drive to The Laughing Tiger from his house most afternoons. Even though she knew Anders was in custody, her anxiety told her he was lurking around, watching her just as Hank had. Anders, though, made Hank's antics look like amateur hour in comparison. Anders had turned stalking into a business.

Riley and Michael were curled up on his couch Saturday afternoon watching a movie when her phone on the coffee table started to ring. "Detective Howard" scrolled across the screen. She fumbled for the phone so quickly, it startled Baxter off the couch.

"Hi!"

"We have a bit of a situation."

Her stomach flopped. "What kind of situation?"

"Anders has stipulations for giving up information, and part of those stipulations are that you tell him how you figured out who he was." When she didn't immediately reply, Howard said, "The self-importance wafting off this guy is enough to choke a person. He thinks he's smarter than everyone in the room, but it really seems to piss him off that you're the one who got him in hot water."

"Me?" she asked, incredulous.

"He said he'll give up the name of Mack's, Bodwell's, and Dawson's killer," he said slowly, "if *you* tell *him* how you figured him out."

Riley blinked in rapid succession. Clearly the cops hadn't divulged the fact that they already knew the killer's name—Bruce Trager—and that law enforcement of several stripes were working to track the guy down.

"Hello?" Howard asked after several beats of silence.

"Sorry. I had to pick my jaw up off the floor."

Howard chuckled darkly. "You absolutely do not have to talk to the guy if you're not comfortable doing so. We can negotiate for something else." He cleared his throat awkwardly. "He also has implied that there are others out there that Bruce murdered, but that we'll never find them without his help."

Riley already had confirmation that there were others. When she'd shaken Anders's hand in Epicurean Subs, a snapshot of memory had slammed into her. She'd seen Anders taking a picture of another Black woman—one other than Shawna and Emery. As much as the guy creeped her out, Riley was in this for the long haul. "I'll talk to him."

His little exhale of breath, however slight, told her he was relieved she'd agreed. "Now, let me state that as much as anything he says can be used against him in a court of law, anything *you* say can potentially be used as well in his defense. One thing that's on our side right now is that Anders isn't a wealthy man. His lawyer is court-appointed and likely has a full docket. That said, this case is largely circumstantial and we're still waiting on a warrant to search his apartment and computer. His lawyer might try a defense of 'They have nothing on my client, and their key witness thinks she can talk to dead people' and the case could potentially get thrown out."

Riley's stomach flipped. She hadn't even thought of that as a possibility.

This meant, if she went through with this, she'd need to get a solid confession out of the guy. If he thought he was the smartest person in the room, he also thought he was smarter than *her*. Maybe he hoped she would divulge all her sleuthing secrets, allowing him to assess how much she truly knew. If her intel wasn't damning enough in his eyes, what would stop him from pleading the Fifth when it was his turn to talk?

Something Detective McGregor had said came back to her. *It would be incredible if I could tell Malcolm definitively what happened to his mother before my career is over. At this point, that's all either of us wants. We just want it solved. Shawna deserves that much.*

"I'll do it," she said again, more confident this time.

"Okay," Howard said. "I'll arrange a meeting and get back to you."

Three days later, Riley walked into an Albuquerque police station with Michael and a lawyer friend of Rochelle's that she'd met only two days ago. Wendy had passed the bar recently but hadn't established herself as a practicing lawyer yet. Riley's parents, Michael, and Riley's friends all figured it was the best—and least expensive—option on such short notice. Riley hoped that if they showed up in smart clothes, that it would do half of the work for them.

The lobby of the station was all sleek lines and marble. It was quiet inside aside from the phones that rang every few minutes. The wide space had a few benches taking up the area between the glass front doors and the long counter that bisected the room. A handful of front desk clerks were busy with phone calls and paperwork. Riley wasn't sure what she expected—maybe a small holding cell off to the side filled with hostile criminals.

Riley's mind was so abuzz with wildly bouncing thoughts that she didn't even see Detective Howard approach her until he was right there beside her.

He cocked a brow at her. "You all right?"

Riley swallowed hard. "I think I need water or something?"

Howard nodded once and then made his way across the lobby to a water cooler.

"I'll get us checked in," Wendy said before marching across the tile floor to a bank of receptionists' desks.

Michael stood in front of Riley and cupped her face in his hands, making her look at him. "You got this. Do you know how proud I am that you got under a psychopath's skin? I mean, that's no easy task, babe."

She managed a faint smile. "That's because he's also a raging narcissist."

"True." He kissed her, making her forget for a moment where she was and who she was about to go meet. "I'm still proud of you."

Detective Howard cleared his throat.

Michael let her go and took a step back. Riley, face on fire, took the small offered cup of water from the detective. She knocked it back, but her mouth was still parched.

"Remember that this guy requested this meeting because his ego has been bruised," Howard said. "I don't think there's an altruistic bone in his body. He's going to try to get you to do all the talking. Any of those talking points we went over a couple days ago are still game, but if any of us watching get the sense that things are going sideways, we'll pull you out."

"She's not going to be alone with him, is she?" Michael asked.

"Nope. Both lawyers and myself will be in there with her, and Anders will be handcuffed to the table."

Michael nodded calmly at that, as if anything about this wasn't batshit.

"Ready?" Howard asked.

Riley considered bolting out the glass doors, screaming the whole way. "Yep."

After kissing Riley goodbye, Michael settled down on one of the benches with a book. Riley followed after Wendy and Detective Howard, thankful that at least one of them knew the way, because her mind was a panicked buzz again.

Detective Howard stopped at an interrogation room in the middle of a sterile hallway, the lights above them too bright and harsh. He offered her an encouraging nod, then swung the door open.

It was a room not unlike the ones she'd seen on her many true crime shows. Plain walls—one of which was taken up by a dark two-way mirror—and a large table surrounded by five chairs. Two of them were occupied. Riley swallowed as she stared at Anders Pedersen. She'd seen him almost two weeks ago in Epicurean Subs, and while that setting had been more dangerous, she somehow felt even more anxious seeing him here. Detective Howard placed a gentle hand on her arm and she flinched.

"Go ahead and have a seat, Riley," he said.

As she did so, Anders's eyes never left her. She and Wendy sat across from Anders and his lawyer, while Detective Howard took a seat at the head of the table across from the door. She was glad he was there, but even gladder to see that Anders's hands were in fact handcuffed to the table. Giving the room a quick scan from her new vantage point, she spotted a broad-shouldered man by the door with sandy blond hair, a scar above his right eye, and a no-nonsense expression. Riley was glad he was there too, serving as muscle in case Anders tried anything fishy.

The two-way mirror was behind her, and she wondered if Special Agents Lee and Samson were back there. To say Riley was nervous as hell that she'd screw this up was an understatement. She didn't want to say or do anything that could affect Shawna's, Brynn's, or Emery's cases. She didn't want to disappoint the detectives or special agents who had put so much faith in her abilities.

While the lawyers discussed a few things across the table, Anders still only had eyes for Riley. He was an unremarkable-looking man. Not attractive or unattractive. Average height and build. There were dark rings under his dull blue eyes; she suspected he hadn't been sleeping well. She liked the idea that she was the reason for his tormented rest.

There was a slight curve of his nose that had no doubt been broken, and a faint scar lined his chin. His beating had been extensive if he'd been out of commission for four months. Howard had said that Anders had a court-appointed lawyer because he couldn't afford one of his own. Was that because his medical expenses had eaten up what little money he had, or was he unable to pay that either? She had to imagine a bill for four months of care would be astronomical without a stellar health care plan.

It was then that Riley realized the talking had quieted, as had her frantic nerves. Something like calm had settled over her now that she sat here in front of Anders. Had someone asked her something?

"The floor is yours, Anders," his lawyer said.

Anders adjusted himself in his chair, the chains on his handcuffs clanging on the table. His lip curled at the sound. "How did you come to be in possession of my cameras?"

Riley's posture was relaxed, her back pressed firmly against the backrest. With her legs crossed, she placed her folded hands in her lap. "My friend bought them from a thrift store. There was film inside one of the cameras, so we sent it off to get developed. One of those found-footage stories you hear about on the news, you know? We thought there might be something of historical significance on the film."

Anders clenched his jaw. "How did the picture end up in the possession of the reporter?"

"I brought it to him," she said, knowing the matter-of-fact tone would annoy him even more. "When I saw Shawna on the roll of film, I knew Emery must have been one of your victims, too."

"Not mine," Anders said. "I was paid to do a job and I did it. That's all. Doing your job isn't a crime."

"What he did with the information wasn't any business of yours, I know," she said, keeping her tone just shy of bored. "You told him Brynn was a mistake, though. You knew what he was doing and offered advice on what to do better next time, didn't you?"

Anders bristled.

"You don't have to answer that," his lawyer said.

Riley said, "You told him that victims like Shawna were better targets. Women the media cared less about. Women who didn't have parents with fat checkbooks. If he chose better targets, it meant he had women to kidnap, rape, and kill, and you had money flowing into your account. Who cares what happened to these women as long as you got paid, right? You might not have killed them with your bare hands, but you gave him advice on how to be smarter. Win-win for you both."

Anders lurched forward, the table's edge pressing into his chest. His lawyer leaned over, attempting to offer counsel, but Anders ignored him. Riley willed herself not to flinch away from Anders. Up until now, he'd been as mild-mannered as his appearance. Now real hints of a temper, of a personality, were poking through. His blue eyes darted wildly, as if he looked at every inch of her face, he'd figure out where he'd gone wrong. All his building rage spilled out in one desperate word: *"How?"*

She offered him nothing but a smug little smile.

His face grew so flushed, it was nearly purple. It occurred to her as she sat here, reveling in the knowledge that she'd figured out how to push this stranger's buttons, that something similar had happened the first time she'd met Francis Hank Carras. She'd slipped into a flirtatious persona as a means to get information out of him. She'd chalked up the transformation to Jade's assessment that Riley was an incorrigible flirt—at least she had been back in college. Now, with Anders, she was smug and nonchalant.

She realized that this was part of her psychic gift, too. Her clairsentience allowed her to sense emotions, not just of the dead, but the living. Not as strongly as Olivia could, but what Riley had always thought of as an ability to figure out how people tick was more an ability to feel their emotions and shift her behaviors based on them. Hank responded to flirting. Anders responded to what he perceived as a slight to his intellect.

"How what?" she asked, having taken an excessively long time to reply, solely to rankle him further.

"How. Did. You. *Find me*?" he snapped, slamming his fists on the table, making both lawyers and the chains of his cuffs jump.

"Easy," Detective Howard said.

Riley cocked her head at Anders. "What, because you were so careful?" She chuckled softly.

"Yes," he said through gritted teeth. "I've been called a ghost. No one can see me. Except you did. I want to know how." He cocked his head too, mirroring her. "Where did you get your name?"

"Excuse me?"

"Clair4U," he said. "Your name is Riley, not Clair. So where did you get it?"

"I made it up."

"Liar," he said. "You know, there's a rumor that the anonymous source who led police to Emery is a psychic. A *clairvoyant*. I mean, it seems fairly outlandish that after sixteen years, someone walking in the area with a metal detector looking for loose change happens upon a metal drum buried five feet underground."

"Oh, I get it. You're bent out of shape because a twenty-five-year-old waitress found your secrets and you're trying to find a way to soothe your ego? The only way anyone would ever outwit the brilliant Anders Pedersen is if the supernatural is involved. How could you possibly compete with that, right?"

He glared at her.

Riley told him about the John Anderson business card Brynn's mother had found, the Wayback Machine, the handle he used as both his registrar and on review sites to complain about overpriced sandwiches. She told him about the negatives she found hidden in his camera bag. None of that had been supernatural.

As she spoke, he went from purple to ashen gray.

"I have a question for *you*," she said. "Does the name Gunner Lowry mean anything to you?"

"Should it?"

"Probably. He called in a tip to the police that the guy who tried to snatch Brooke Winters off the street is the same guy he caught spying on his girlfriend Kendra."

Anders worked his jaw. "I guess Axel or Gage wasn't that far off," he muttered, more to himself it seemed than to her.

"Your composite sketch was all over the news. It was a pretty good likeness, too. Turns out that after Gunner knocked you around, he went through your wallet and found your ID. He committed your name to memory, just in case."

Anders swallowed.

"He saw your picture on the news and realized it was the same man whose face he smashed in some four months ago," she said. "You said you were a ghost? Gunner saw you long before I did."

"I was fine until he *assaulted* me," Anders snapped. "Has *he* been arrested? He almost killed me. Aggravated assault is still a crime in this country, the last I heard. What he did was worse than anything I've done."

"Why were you watching Kendra?" Riley asked.

"Because I was paid to," Anders said, the words slipping out without thought.

His lawyer winced beside him and tried to whisper counsel again, only to have Anders wave him off.

"That's just what you do then? Watch people for money?"

"It's not as crude as you make it sound," Anders grumbled.

She cocked a brow at him.

"There's not much difference between what I do and what a private investigator does. A man was heartbroken over his breakup with Kendra, so he paid me to find her when she stopped answering his calls," Anders said, indignant. "I help husbands find wives who have run off with their kids. I catch cheaters in the act."

"And help serial killers find their next victim."

"All I do is find the information I'm paid to find. I can't be held responsible for what my clients do with it."

"Intent has to count for something," Riley said, leaning forward. "You're not a dumb guy, Anders. You knew. You *knew* what he was doing and you kept helping him. You sentenced each one of those women to death because you cared more about the number in your bank account than you did about the fact that those women were people. They had families and friends and lives and you gave this guy a road map on how to end all of that."

Anders stared at her for a long beat, then sat back. "I'm done talking."

The man standing vigil by the door took a few steps forward. Riley's attention swiveled toward him.

"Ask him about tomorrow's storm."

"What?" she hissed, realizing too late that she'd just spoken to a ghost while in the company of several people, including a psychopath.

"Tomorrow's storm," the man said, standing at the end of the table opposite Howard. "Ask him."

Riley inwardly groaned. Anders wasn't exactly the kind of

person she wanted to share this secret with. Why did this man want to talk about the weather of all things?

Tomorrow's storm.

Tomorrow's storm.

Tomorrow's storm.

Ugh! He was even more persistent than Brynn had been.

"What do you know about tomorrow's storm?" Riley asked.

Her lawyer leaned over to say there wasn't a storm on the horizon, but Anders cut her off. "Why would you ask me that?"

An image flashed in her head of a boat floating among chunks of ice.

"It was the name of a boat." Riley glanced at the man beside the table and recognized the similarities now. They would have had the same nose had Anders' not been broken recently. Her gaze returned to Anders's pale face. "Your father's boat, to be exact."

His dull blue eyes scanned every inch of her, his mind no doubt working overtime. "I'm done talking," he finally repeated, but she noted sweat dotting his brow.

She tried a few other tactics to get him to talk, but he'd fully shut down on her.

"I think my client is done," Anders's lawyer finally said.

She pushed out of her chair, disgusted with him. Even now, there wasn't a shred of remorse in him. The whole time she talked to him, he was looking for an out, a way to convince whoever was listening that he was innocent, and that all the blame was on Bruce.

Anders's father lingered by the door again. When she looked at him, a word popped into her head. She turned back to Anders.

"Was your father's name Magnus?"

Anders's gaze scanned the area behind Riley. The raw hope on his face shone through for only a moment before he shielded it. "My father's name wouldn't have been hard to find."

She knew then that *he* knew what was happening here. Her sixth sense tingled. Magnus was beside her now. In her ear, he whispered something, then vanished. The message made absolutely no sense to her, but she repeated it anyway. "Your father says you're standing with your beard in the mailbox."

Both lawyers in the room looked at her as if she'd spoken in tongues. Anders's mouth, however, had dropped open.

He quickly turned in his chair, looking left and right, but was limited by his cuffs. "Is he here?"

"Not anymore," Riley said. "You were right about the clair thing. All I can tell you is that they don't show up for just anyone, and they don't show up without a reason. I suggest you listen."

CHAPTER 28

Over the course of the next few weeks, Riley got updates about the case. Detective Howard, Detective McGregor, and Carter Quincy called, emailed, or texted her on what felt like a rotating basis. She didn't hear directly from Special Agents Samson and Lee again.

A couple of days after Riley's chat with Anders, he decided he was ready to talk. The message she had relayed to him, she learned later, was the translation of a common Norwegian saying that had been used often by his late father. It was a saying about getting caught up in other people's problems and getting trapped because of it. Anders told Detective Howard that he'd had a tumultuous relationship with his father, and yet it had been his father's words from beyond the grave that had finally swayed the man to fess up to what he'd done.

"I don't think the guy suddenly had a change of heart or anything," Howard told her. "He doesn't seem to have much of a conscience. But I do think Anders believes in the afterlife and the idea of not confessing to his role in the murders made him twitchy. I think Anders is nervous about the idea of running into pissed-off dear ol' dad when takes his final dirt nap."

"Always covering his own ass," Riley said.

"Basically. He's rolling over on Bruce now. Anders is under the impression that if he gives us everything we need, it will lessen his sentence. He's on the books for Brooke's attack, as well as being the Nob Hill Prowler. Not only did Gunner Lowry call in a tip about him, but so did a Tracy Kirk. Apparently she used to date the guy and recognized him from the composite sketch. And—my personal favorite—is a teenager who works at Epicurean Subs called in saying the composite sketch looked like a guy who screamed at her for two solid minutes about his sandwich being made with the wrong cheese."

Ha! She knew it.

She wondered what Tracy Kirk was like. The idea of dating Anders Pedersen was nothing short of horrifying. "Any idea where Bruce is?"

"The FBI is working on that with us," Howard said. "Last I heard, a team of cybercrime guys were scouring both Anders's computer and the dark corners of the web chasing down every place rangefinderanders has been. They'll find the guy eventually."

"Did you find the other cartridge of film?" Riley asked, knowing that yesterday, Nina had gotten a vision about a cartridge taped to the back of Anders's headboard.

"Yep. All this may all still be circumstantial, but the amount of it piling up is going to make it nearly impossible to say Anders didn't actively stalk women for Bruce knowing full well that the women would end up dead. How all of this will hold up in a court? I don't know. That'll be up to a jury to decide."

Carol and Marty both got their fifteen minutes of fame, too, when the FBI and police both dropped by their shops to question them about the storage unit purchased in Clovis. Marty had called Riley after the FBI had left, telling her how she'd handed the bomber jacket with the blood on the cuff to Special Agent Lee.

"This was the most exciting day of my life!" Marty had told her.

Carol, in contrast, had cried when Riley talked to her, relieved that the woman in the yellow dress who had briefly graced her store had found some semblance of peace.

Two weeks later, Bruce Trager was found living in suburbia outside of Denver, Colorado. He'd been a long-haul truck driver for two decades and had grown up as a military brat. He spent most of his childhood moving from place to place, and once he was an adult, he got a job that allowed him to keep moving. As an avid outdoorsman, he knew his way around recreational areas, wildlife reserves, and parks.

Riley had worried that it would take months for the FBI to compile enough evidence of Bruce's travels from nearly two decades ago, including getting hold of dispatch logs from a trucking company that had shuttered its doors. But when authorities pulled him over for a routine traffic stop, and then asked if he'd be willing to talk to them because he matched the description of someone they were looking for in connection to a homicide case, he'd confessed within a matter of days. Apparently once he started talking, no one could shut the guy up.

Once he'd been caught, Bruce, a sixty-five-year-old man who got around with the use of a cane, had rolled over on Anders almost immediately, also assuming that if he gave the police all the information they wanted, including everything Anders had done for him, it might lessen his sentence.

"I have a quote here that's pretty incredible," Carter said one day. "Detective McGregor told me, and I quote, 'We were talking to the guy about a series of terrible murders he committed. He'd confessed to six at that point. Six women in nine years. He stalked them, raped them over the course of several days, strangled them to death, and then disposed of their bodies. I mean, the last four were found in steel drums he'd buried in remote areas. Heinous. And yet the thing he can't stop talking about is how he couldn't have done any of those things without Anders's help. Bruce said he would have been too sloppy on his own. He tried to kidnap a girl on his own once, a Black teenager, in the months after Shawna. The girl got away. Slipped right through his fingers, he said. He needed Anders. Those women would all be alive, he said, if Anders hadn't given him the tools he needed to be successful.'"

Goosebumps had risen on Riley's arms at that. Not just because of what Carter had told her, but also from the confirmation that Gigi hadn't been lying about the man who had tried to snatch her. Bruce had been brazen enough to drive around looking for another victim in the same neighborhood as Shawna's. If Gigi had been taken more seriously, if the police had even entertained the idea that Bruce had been the same man who had killed Shawna, if they had been on the lookout for a guy like Bruce and had plastered his face all over the news, that might have saved Brynn. It might have saved Emery, as well as the other women they found—Rose, Zoe, and Mia.

Bruce had been left floundering for a job after Amity Trucking went belly-up in 2011, the same year he'd kidnapped eighteen-year-old Mia. Mia had walked home from her best friend's house in her rural town in Georgia one evening, and no one ever saw her again. Mia had lived with her mother, who had been out of town with her new boyfriend for the weekend. Bruce knew that because Anders had known it. Mia had walked that path home in the dark countless times. She'd grown up there. It was only a ten-minute walk and it was a safe, quiet neighborhood.

The town had been in shock that a young woman could vanish without a trace.

"I went out there," Carter told her a couple of days later. "To Georgia, I mean, to talk to Mia's mother. When I got there, Mia's best friend and brother were already there. No one had come around or called since 2011 to even follow up on the case."

"Did you tell them there was a chance Mia was the last victim of a serial killer?" Riley had asked, wondering how one broached such a subject.

"I tried to keep it vague. I told them I was working on a story about missing and murdered Black women, which isn't untrue. They told me that the brother of Mia's best friend, Daniel, was the prime suspect. He'd been in jail for a nonviolent drug offense and had gotten out a week before Mia's disappearance. He also left town the day after she went missing. Rumors had spread that Daniel had made advances on Mia—which Daniel denies, even now—and that she'd been so disgusted with him, that she'd fled in the middle of the night to get away from him. When the cops interrogated him, they presented him with a scenario. They suggested Daniel had followed her to her house, enraged that she turned him down. In that ten-minute walk in the dark, they'd fought, Mia wound up dead, and Daniel had panicked since he'd just gotten out of jail. He disposed of her body and fled town for a while.

"While it was true that Daniel had left the day after Mia's disappearance, it was because he'd gone to visit friends in Florida since he was finally out of jail. It was an alibi that could easily have been confirmed, yet the police still saw the timing as suspicious.

Given his history, they called him back to Georgia. They shredded the guy's reputation. Social media campaigns were created both for and against him. He'd been the kind of kid who had always gotten in trouble—mouthy in class, dabbled in selling weed, a couple of fistfights in bars. It was a small town and he got labeled a troublemaker from a young age. So when Mia, a quiet, bookish, straight-A student went missing, who happened to be best friends with the sister of the town menace…well, I don't think anyone even considered an outsider like Bruce.

"The crazy thing is, a couple people had called in a tip that a blue sedan they hadn't seen before had been parked outside Mia's house the next morning. One caller even said they thought they saw Mia get into the passenger side willingly. The car didn't have license plates."

In the snapshot Emery had shown her, Bruce's blue car hadn't had license plates either. Had Bruce used the photographer ploy on Mia, too? Riley wondered if Bruce had that same unexplainable charismatic pull that Francis Hank Carras had. It was an energy that sucked people in, as if they gave off a pheromone that reorganized your brain chemistry. Cult leaders had it, too. It was easy to stand back and say that you yourself would never be duped, tricked, and lured into a false sense of security by pretty words coming out of a pretty face. Anders might have given Bruce the tools to more easily insert himself in these women's lives; but Bruce had figured out what to say to them to get them to trust him, a trust he then shattered at the first opportunity. The two men had complemented each other in the worst way.

The next time she heard from Carter was two weeks later, and all he'd sent was a text. *The story is hitting national news tonight. Lola Bodwell got it a premium spot.*

So, that evening at 6 PM, Riley, Michael, Jade, Jonah, Rochelle, Nina, and Olivia piled in front of the TV at Riley's parents' house. Her dad had foregone one of his large, fancy meals and had ordered three kinds of pizza. Riley was too nervous to eat. Everyone else was so nervous, they devoured most of the pizzas in under ten minutes of their arrival.

The TV blared.

"We're coming to you tonight with a breaking news story that's still unfolding. In 2003, a woman named Shawna Mack was found strangled to death at the Rio Bravo campground in Taos, New Mexico. Six months later, a second woman, Brynn Bodwell, was found in the same recreation area, also strangled. The two cases weren't connected then, and both went cold. In October of this year, there was an unexpected discovery in a case that up until that point, no one knew existed. The body of Emery Dawson was found by a visitor to the Rio Bosque Wetland Park in El Paso, Texas who was out with his high-powered metal detector looking for hidden treasure. He never would have guessed that he would find the body of a Socorro, Texas woman who had been missing since 2005.

"There are now two men in custody. Anders Pedersen, a Norwegian-American man from Albuquerque, New Mexico, who has made a living stalking women for a fee. Bruce Trager, Pedersen's most lucrative client, split his time between running a photography business and being a long-haul trucker. Trager paid hefty sums to Anders for dossiers on these women, giving him a blueprint on how best to snatch his next victim—everything from daily schedules, to food preferences, to summaries of information compiled from social media, often based on pictures and posts the women themselves had unknowingly supplied.

"Since the men's arrest, the bodies of Rose Williams, Zoe Davis, and Mia Robinson have all been found. Like Emery Dawson, Rose, Zoe, and Mia had been stuffed into steel drums that Bruce was able to easily obtain during his work as a long-haul truck driver. In the dead of night, he would choose a remote recreational area which he would then frequent several times a week. He made several trips to his location of choice to dig a hole he would then cover up with plant debris. If the spot hadn't been disturbed overnight, he would return to dig the hole a little deeper, as well as cart out any excess dirt that would be displaced by the steel drum he'd lower into it later, using dollies he had on hand thanks to his job. Once the woman was buried, he would move on to the next town and select the next woman, then wait for his dossier—his blueprint for kidnap and murder—from Anders Pedersen.

"It's believed that Trager, the operator of the now-defunct BT Photoworks, used his very real credentials as a professional photographer to lure young, beautiful women into his web of lies with the promise of a break as a model. He claimed to have connections in the film, TV, and fashion industry, and that he was on the brink of exciting change in his career, eager to bring fresh new modeling talent with him on his path to success. In reality, he lured them away for his dark purposes.

"Trager stopped his murder spree in 2011 in part because the trucking company he worked for, Amity Trucking, went out of business. In the interim, Trager took a job in construction and suffered a severe injury in a forklift accident. It has been reported that Trager took that accident as a sign from the universe. Signs are what guide his life, he claims, and when he not only suffered a horrible accident, but survived it, he took that as a sign that it was time to change his ways."

The screen changed. Now, lined up in two neat rows, were the smiling faces of six women. Shawna, Brynn, Emery, Rose, Zoe, and Mia.

Without cutting away from the images, the news anchor's voice supplied a voice-over. "In a statement from Emery Dawson's mother, Leslie, she says, 'I've spent sixteen years waiting for the day I got a phone call about what happened to my baby girl. I knew in my heart that she hadn't been a runaway, but no one would listen to us. There is no pleasure in saying "I told you so" now. I would have much rather been wrong.'"

Tears tracked down Riley's face. She knew that none of these six families would ever truly heal from a loss this terrible, but she hoped this would give them some sense of closure.

"Zoe Davis's little sister," the news anchor said, the screen still filled with the faces of the women, "says that Zoe had always been a free spirit. 'She was the kind of girl who never met a stranger. She loved trying new things, meeting new people, and experiencing what life had to offer. The idea that someone saw that bright light in her and snuffed it out breaks my heart. I want her to be remembered as someone who loved life with her whole heart. Not a day goes by that I don't miss her.'

"From Rose's cousin, we received a message that says, 'Rose's dream was to break into Hollywood. She was so beautiful, so talented. She had the voice of an angel. She used to post her original songs on Myspace, hoping someone would discover her. The wrong person found her and destroyed our family. I hope people never forget her name—I can't.'"

The screen returned to the grim expression of the woman behind the desk. "Both Anders Pedersen's and Bruce Trager's cases are expected to go to trial."

Riley could only marvel at the coverage of the story—one that focused on the victims, not the murderer. Bruce Trager's photo hadn't even been shown. He didn't matter. The documentaries and deep dives into his psyche would come eventually, but at least for tonight, it was these women who got the spotlight.

Her mother muted the TV. There was only a brief stint of stunned silence before everyone erupted into chatter. Michael hugged Riley close to his side and kissed her temple. She was glad they were all so invested, but she felt wrung out.

Her phone started to ring and she pulled it out of her hoodie pocket to find Rodney Elgin's name on the screen. "Oh shit. Guys, it's Rodney."

Everyone quieted immediately.

"Hey, Rodney," Riley said, leaning into Michael's side as she pressed the phone to her ear. His arm tightened around her.

"My boy called me tonight," Rodney managed before he broke down.

Riley choked out a sob, but tried to hold it in, mostly because so many eyes were on her. "Yeah?"

"We both cried like damn babies," Rodney said. "He said he was sorry that things turned out like this. I told him I got a lot to make up for. We're going to start real slow, but I think we're gonna arrange something so I can meet my grandbabies for the first time. Isn't that wild? I'm a grandddad."

"That's great, Rodney," Riley said. "Really."

"I know you were nervous meeting me, and I can't say I blame you," Rodney said. "But thank you from the bottom of my heart for that picture, and for giving me the benefit of the doubt. Thanks for letting me talk and tell it my way. I don't get a lot of that these days."

"I hope you and Malcolm get to know each other again," Riley said.

"Me too," he said. "Me too. I'm real glad I met you. It's so good to know there are more people like my grandmama out in the world."

"Thanks. Take care."

After disconnecting the call, she sniffed and wiped the sleeve of her sweatshirt across her eyes. She was just about to tell everyone what Rodney had told her when Nina and Olivia both sucked in a breath.

Riley froze.

The six women who had been on screen minutes ago were now in her mother's living room. Riley could only guess that they'd been able to manifest here because there were three mediums in one place, all of them thinking about the women at the same time. Riley's, Nina's, and Olivia's energy had pulled the women to them, allowing them to show themselves. Even the non-mediums in the room had an energy that the ghost women could feed off of.

They stood in a line, Shawna on one end, and Mia Robinson, who looked closer to an innocent-faced sixteen-year-old than an eighteen-year-old, stood on the other. All at once, they placed a hand over their chests and slightly bowed their heads. It was the same gesture Emery had used when Riley vowed to find out what had happened to her.

Thank you, they all said.

One by one, they disappeared. Emery lingered the longest, beautiful in her bright yellow dress. And then she was gone, too.

CHAPTER 29

It had been several weeks since the news broke about the women who had been murdered and left across the country by Bruce Trager. She'd taken a week off work, unable to focus on much of anything. When Riley had confessed to her boss that not only was she a psychic medium, but that she'd played a role in helping solve the cold case that was all over the news lately, her boss had enthusiastically given her the time off as long as Riley promised to provide full details later.

Riley and Rochelle had started a nightly re-watch of *Tiana's Circle,* live texting each other into the wee hours. Though Riley had resumed staying in her own apartment, Michael had started to openly float the idea that maybe it was time they looked into finding a place to live in together. When the adrenaline rush of the last few months wore off, she was sure she would be all over the idea, but for now, she needed to decompress.

She was an introvert through and through. If Emery were still here, Riley knew she'd understand.

Today would have been Riley's day off had she been working. Yet, she wasn't in her apartment. She was in her parked car, already second-guessing her decision. The task at hand paled in comparison to the ordeal she'd gone through in recent months, but still.

MICHAEL: You can do it, babe!

JADE: You'll be great!

ROCHELLE: Kick butt and take names!

Riley stared at the group text, trying to let their encouraging words bolster her. The bolstering was interrupted by a phone call from Nina.

"Hey," Riley said. "What's up?"

"When you get a chance, can you swing by my house?"

Riley cocked her head. "Uhh … sure. Is everything okay?"

"Everything is great. I just have a check for you."

"A check?"

"Yep. Amy Velasco got the life insurance situation straightened out. Between Randy our skater friend and the police doing a thorough search of that front yard—they found Iris's blood on the bricks on the front planter—the insurance company had enough proof that Iris didn't die by suicide. As a thank-you, Amy sent me a check for our detective work. You were just as much a part of this as I was, so I'm splitting the cash with you. It's not going to buy you a villa in Italy, but it'll buy you groceries for a couple months at the very least."

Riley was tempted to argue.

"You can't refuse it. I won't allow it," Nina said. "Plus, I'm hoping that the excitement of extra money will nudge you in the direction of accepting that consulting position I offered you at Galvan Investigations."

"Ah, this is bribery," Riley said, smiling.

"Damn straight. The check is waiting for you when you're ready."

"Thanks," Riley said, and disconnected the call.

Riley wondered if Nina's claircognizance had been the reason for that call at this moment. Either way, it had been enough to convince Riley to get out of her car.

She hiked her purse higher up on her shoulder, heaved out a breath through her nose, and marched forward. In through the sliding glass doors, across the chipped linoleum flooring, and straight into the toothpaste aisle. It was currently deserted.

The pissed-off ghost energy slammed into her almost immediately and she whirled around.

He stood in front of her, fists clenched, jaw set. Her own fists clenched involuntarily. She recalled Nina's words that had helped her so many times lately, and tweaked them to fit the situation and the ghost she faced now.

Don't let his emotions crowd out your own. Find the root of those emotions.

She unfurled her hands, letting her fingers hang by her sides. She slowed her breathing and closed her eyes.

He's been waiting for who knows how long. Center yourself and listen to him.

She opened her eyes. She wasn't afraid. She'd faced down the likes of Francis Hank Carras and Anders Pedersen—flesh and blood monsters. She'd freed Pete from his decades of being trapped at Jordanville Ranch, had helped Amy learn the truth of what had happened to her mother, and found Emery's body.

This guy couldn't hurt her.

"Hi," she said, looking the pissed-off ghost in the eye. His off-the-charts fury wavered for a moment. "Tell me what happened to you. I'm here to help."

If you enjoyed *The Forgotten Child* and want to be one of the first to learn about upcoming sequels, join my mailing list at: melissajacksonbooks.com

As a welcome gift, you'll receive a free e-copy of *3:12*, a short story that takes place a few months before the events of *The Forgotten Child.*

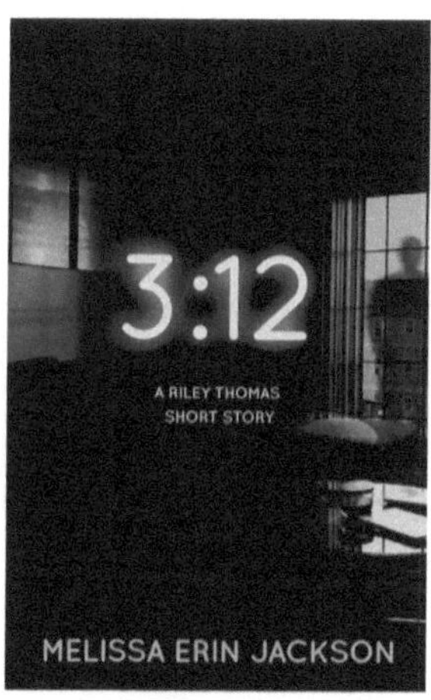

Please consider leaving a review if you enjoyed your time with Riley. Reviews are an author's lifeblood. More reviews mean more sales, and more sales mean I get to keep writing stories.

Melissa has had a love of stories for as long as she can remember, but only started penning her own during her freshman year of college. She majored in Wildlife, Fish, and Conservation Biology at UC Davis. Yet, while she was neck-deep in organic chemistry and physics, she kept finding herself writing stories in the back of the classroom about fairies and trolls and magic. She finished her degree, but it never captured her heart the way writing did.

Now she owns her own dog walking business (that's sort of wildlife related, right?) by day…and afternoon and night… and writes whenever she gets a spare moment. The Microsoft Word app is a gift from the gods!

She alternates mostly between fantasy and mystery (often with a paranormal twist). All her books have some element of "other" to them…witches, ghosts, UFOs. There's no better way to escape the real world than getting lost in a fictional one.

She lives in Northern California with her boyfriend and way too many pets.

You can find out more about her books and join her newsletter at: https://melissajacksonbooks.com

ACKNOWLEDGEMENTS

I'm lucky to have a wonderful group of supportive readers and critique partners. Thank you to Jennifer Laam, Garrett Lemons, and my mom for being there for me every time I have a writing meltdown (which, let's face it, is often). You always know how to pull me back to the surface.

Beta readers are my favorite people. I appreciate all of you who took time to get to know Riley and offer me your feedback.

Thank you Krista Hall (Sorry for the nightmares!), Brittany Gray, Lindsey Duga, Christiane Loeffler, Susanna Woods, Sylvia Shipp, Rose Erickson, Sheralan Marrott, Dawn Klemish, Kayla Henley, Cathie Bucci, Caren White, Tessa Osbourne, Heather Nelson, Saundra Norton, Molly Sardella, Nikkie Witbrod, and Cathy McMahen.

Thank you to Margarita Martinez for not only being a great copy editor, but for being one of the most fangirly cheerleaders I've ever met. Benedict and David don't know what they're missing!

Thank you to Maggie Hall for the gorgeous cover (And the swag! And the map!) and Michelle Raymond for the beautiful interior design.

Thank you, Mom, for being one of my first readers, and for the great drawing of Orin's house. I still find it terribly rude I didn't inherit any of your skills.

Thank you to Victoria Villarreal and David Clifford Turner for bringing the audiobook to life. I'm going to have to include creepy dudes in every book now so can keep you around, David!

And, finally, thank you to Sam for simply being you. You're more supportive than you know, you're my favorite person on the planet, and I heart your face.